CARA CRESCENT

DEDICATION

To mom
Miss you.

ACKNOWLEDGEMENTS

A huge thank you to my family and friends editors, Jean
and Yelena, my critique group partners Aedyn Brooks
and Marissa John, my editors,
& the wonderful women at Killion Group, Inc.
I'd be lost without the lot of you.
Lastly, I entered this book into several RWA sponsored
contests under a different title. Sometimes it won,
sometimes it lost, but I always received an abundance of
constructive criticism and encouragement from the
volunteer judges that make those contests possible.
I can't express how valuable you've all been to me.
Thanks.

When the Original is no longer cursed,
She'll come to thee as three.
All as humans first,
Then as daemons, are set free:
The beacon burning bright,
The shadow hidden from sight,
The blighted, damned knight.

-The Black Book of Daemonology

CHAPTER 1

Twenty years ago

When human, James had lived by sword and cross. He'd dedicated his pathetic life to the words within one old book. He'd lived by that book. He'd killed by that book. Back then, he'd been little more than a monster cloaked in human skin and bolstered by a mortal soul.

Now he was just a monster.

He'd retained his human form, but his soul had died long ago and he no longer lived by the ideals in that fucking book. He'd ignored them for ages, deciding that the only purpose for the paradoxes of religion was to drive men insane. A red herring of sorts to hold him immobile as life and death, good deeds and evil, continued to unfold around him.

So why then did his damnable mind keep returning to that book?

Because things were changing. Times were changing.

He felt the end drawing near. And while he knew that book bore nothing but hatred and disdain for his kind, his mind kept insisting that if he found a way to understand the beginning . . . perhaps he'd discover a means of escaping the end. Or at least rediscover his humanity and redeem himself before Armageddon. Mostly, he concentrated on Genesis, because, as all daemons knew, that's when everything went to shit.

His mark came into view just ahead: A slender

woman wrapped in a fine, calf-length coat. She had shapely legs. Her companion seemed to think so, too. The blond-haired male kept making a show of sneaking peeks, teasing giggles from her despite the cold and the rain.

James snorted. She wouldn't be laughing for long.

He couldn't carry out the assassination here. Downtown Seattle buzzed with activity even at this late hour. Humans raced about in their cars, eager to get to the next entertainment of the night and hurried along the sidewalk with their hoods raised to avoid mussed hair and makeup from the weather. Such weighty concerns they had, these favored mortals.

The rain didn't bother him, not enough to even don a jacket, though the drips of water did make seeing through his shades in the darkness a challenge.

As he stalked his prey, his thoughts returned to that book. It kept his mind off the fact he would soon kill the woman. It prevented him from wondering why this job hadn't come from his usual source. Why Julius Crowley and the Council felt the need to break protocol by ordering this hit.

He knew he wouldn't like the answers. *So, don't think about it.*

How did the story go? Reciting the damn book from memory failed him. Now, he only remembered the gist. In the beginning, there had been nothing. No stars scattered throughout the void. No void, actually, because there was nothing. Which was a paradox of sorts, because there was God. There must have been a god.

The couple stopped at a crosswalk, waiting for the light to change. The woman placed her hand on the blond man's chest, rose to her tiptoes, and kissed him. She pressed her mouth to his right there in the rain with humans all around.

James paused, too, hiding in the shadows of a dark alleyway. He'd existed almost a millennium now and had yet to see a miracle. Never met God. Instead of finding peace in the rhythmic cycles of the world, he found chaos and pain. And yet, even after all this time, he couldn't say He *didn't* exist.

He tugged off his sunglasses long enough to drag his hand down his shaved head and face, pushing away the rivulets of rain cascading down his features.

God was an asshole—He'd abandoned him in his darkest hour and every day since—but He was out there. Somewhere. God in His infinite, yet questionable, wisdom had created angels called the Watchers—the two hundred angels who had eventually fallen from grace. Giant creatures filled with emotion, insight, and power, yet no free will.

The traffic light changed and his mark crossed the street. James followed with a shake of his head.

The Watchers were God's first mistake. After a time, God made other angels. He created a vast universe with stars and planets and granted these angels dominion over the world of Raquia. He made humans and gave them the Earth and gifted them with free will. Another mistake. Or maybe just a very bad decision, because man fucked up everything.

The blond male slipped his hand down the woman's back and patted her ass. She spun around, walking backward for a moment to shake her finger at him, though a welcoming smile curved her lips.

The Watchers, the sons of God, lusted after the daughters of men. They set themselves up as gods on Earth. They fathered the Nephilim—corrupted, maniacal progeny that devoured all they came in contact with—with humans. And God, the all-seeing Almighty, sent a flood to destroy the Nephilim nearly wiping out humans in the process. He banished the Watchers to Machon, stripping them of their flesh after forcing them to watch their kin die.

His mark turned down an alleyway between two towering office buildings. The scattered street lights illuminated the alley a dull, colicky yellow. The thrumming music from a nearby club drowned out the sounds of human chatter from the main road. The rain muted the report of the woman's heels on the asphalt.

The Watchers remained on Machon to this day, watching Earth from their prison cells, and directing the Guardian—protectors chosen from the last remaining kin of the Watchers—to assassinate those who threatened the balance. Because, hell, no one wanted another Armageddon. But He'd allowed daemon-kind—who were vampires like him—and other daemons who were either cursed or blessed by the Watcher's Magic—to remain among humans. Now the only thing standing between humans and Armageddon were the very creatures humans feared and loathed: Daemon vampires.

James drew his Guardian dagger, a hollow silver blade with designs cut down the center to reveal a strip of wood caught between the two halves. The silver made quick work of most daemons, the wood took care of the rest. Either, if stabbed in the right spot, would eliminate a human.

Leaving daemons here was another mistake. A fatal one, really. God never should have left the monsters amid the humans. It was like leaving a child to guard a stash of candy. And yet, this mistake fascinated him most. There was a lesson there. Somewhere. Just beyond his reach. Maybe even the answer to his dilemma. Did daemons have free will? The angels didn't, but humans did. Daemons were a little of both.

Did it matter? None of the choices he made seemed to lead anywhere good. He'd failed as a priest, as a man, and he wasn't faring much better as a daemon.

Come on, now. Focus. James put aside his inner debate and picked up his pace, closing in on the woman and her date. He lifted his blade.

Pain sliced though his skull, halting him in his tracks. For an instant, he thought someone had hit him, but he searched the shadows, finding no one.

His mark strolled along the alley, her arm looped with her mate's. She tipped her head to the side, resting her cheek on his shoulder as they walked, blissfully unaware how closely death stalked her.

James started after them again. A tugging sensation gripped his mind, pulling his attention from the woman. The compulsion to turn away grew demanding, becoming tangible. He stopped mid-stride. His body jerked around to face the other direction. Tendrils of fear closed in as a burst of adrenaline washed through his veins.

What was happening?

He'd be damned if he left an assignment unfinished—his one claim to success. Maybe this hit had been ordered by the Vampiric Council—the Guardian overseers—instead of the Watchers, but that didn't mean he could let himself fail.

James fought against his body, pushing away the unnatural need to abandon his prey. With renewed determination, he turned back toward his mark and picked up his pace, avoiding the puddles scattered across the asphalt. Again, he closed in on the woman.

The compulsion in his mind metastasized, becoming irresistible.

He stopped shy of the couple as pain burst into his head like fireworks. He doubled over, gripping his head in his hands, knocking his shades to the pavement and dropping his blade. Shit! His gaze shot up.

His mark glanced back, her eyes glowing in the dim light, widening as understanding dawned. Her features twisted in fear and revulsion.

James grabbed his blade, dragging himself up to stand on wobbly legs. He wiped his eyes with the back of his forearm, trying to clear away the blur caused by the pain in his head. "Augustina Saar, Historian." Jesus, his voice shook. He cleared the thickness from his throat. "You were accused and tried for blatant disregard for our Discovery Laws and—"

"Liar." She braced her legs apart, facing him.

"You deny the charge?" James motioned to the male by her side. "And yet I see proof." He pressed the heel of his hand to his head as if a bit of pressure might stop the pulsing ache behind his eyes.

"I've mated a human, not broadcasted the truth of daemon-kind to the masses."

His stomach roiled. *What the hell was wrong?* Daemons didn't get sick and yet his head spun, filling him with a disconnected sensation, making him sway on his feet. *Jesus, pull it together.*

The blond male tried to pull her behind him. "Kill me. If I'm gone, no rules have been broken."

James gave the male his attention. He didn't expect a human to be so honorable, nor to understand their laws. Damn. The male would have to die. "He knows too much."

"No." Augustina's skin split as she began to transform, preparing to fight. The flesh didn't tear, there was no blood, her skin simply came apart at hidden seams along her limbs, torso, and face. A knotty black substance spilled out, expanding and lifting the remaining strips of her flesh until they were smooth, cream-colored battle scars on the creature. Its oblong, amoeba-like body resembled a corrupted, twisted brain with several limbs bursting out at odd angles. Those limbs were clawed, the ridges and strands of muscles and ligaments enhanced by the creature's too-tight flesh as opposed to covered by it. Three eyes of different sizes and colors appeared in the front of the pulsing mass, the only impressions of any type of face.

Well, shit. He'd expected a vampire like him, but she was a baldander, a protean daemon. No wonder Crowley had bestowed this dubious honor on him; this was a fucking suicide mission. Augustina wouldn't even break a sweat as she crushed him to dust. James' gaze fell to the Historian's mate. The blond male stepped back. Not in fear. Not in shock. He seemed to want to give her more room. The male knew far too much.

Meeting James' gaze, he grinned. "You're in some shit now, Guardian."

Christ, he needed to salvage this. If he took the human hostage and forced—

"Don't you look at him." The ground trembled as she put herself in front of her mate.

Perhaps he'd leave the human alone for now. His gaze jerked back to the baldander. "You've been found guilty."

"By who?" Her voice vibrated through the air. "Not the Watchers, I'd wager. Julius Crowley sent you, didn't he?"

James paused. How did she know? "You broke—" He blinked away the blur in his vision, cleared the growing tightness from his throat. "You broke the Discovery Law."

"He's using you. He's furious I won't tell him what he wishes to know." She swiped at him with one of her massive claws. "Leave now, Guardian. I don't want to hurt you."

James jumped to the side, but she clipped the building with her claw. Brick rained down, pelting his body. Christ, much more and they'd draw an audience. He needed to put a stop to this quickly or he, too, would be guilty of breaking the Discovery Laws. He leaned back on the wall. "I'll use my talent, Historian." Vampires all had special abilities. Gifts handed down to them from the Watchers they descended from. He hadn't used his since he was a neophyte—it was too damn dangerous, but she'd left him little choice tonight. "You're a seer. Tell me how tonight ends if I use my talent."

The baldander folded in on itself, diminishing in size until the whole protean mass fit back within her human form. "Don't. You'll kill everyone."

He opened his mouth to tell her to prepare for her destruction and pushed himself away from the wall.

Pain exploded in his head again. A thick pressure crammed his throat. He clutched at his neck. "Leave her. Obey us." His whole frame jerked in response as the first alien voices left his mouth. Abyss-deep and guttural, his vocal cords strained to accommodate them. "You must—" He clenched his jaw, refusing to let the voices speak. What the hell had Crowley gotten him into tonight?

The Historian came closer and her mate drew her back out of reach. She was almost near enough for him to stab her, or for her to ash him. "The Great Ones speak through you."

The Watchers chose now to use him as a fucking puppet? He struggled to take another step toward Augustina, but the pain shooting through his head forced him to bow low, tearing a shout from his throat. He fell to his knees, the icy puddle beneath him seeping into his jeans.

The Historian pushed away her mate's protective embrace and approached. She cupped his face in her hands. "I know what you seek, Guardian." The Historian leaned close, her eyes swirling with liquid fire. "The Watchers will lead you to what you desire. Heed them."

As if he had a choice. The pressure in his head built. He couldn't speak. The Watchers held his body immobile, leaving his existence to hang by the Historian's mercy.

"Surrender, Guardian. Quit the fight."

What was she doing? She could destroy him now, take him out with his own blade and he'd not be able to protect himself. Instead she seemed to be trying to . . . soothe him.

"Be at ease. She needs you."

Who? He didn't have any current attachments.

He stopped struggling, allowing the tension to ease from his muscles, and closed his eyes. The low buzz of traffic and the noise of the city faded, leaving behind the whine of an airplane passing under cloudy skies.

James opened his eyes. If able, he would've cursed. The alley, the Historian and her mate, were gone.

"The house." The Watchers wrung the words from his vocal chords. "She is in the house. Save her."

CHAPTER 2

Jesus. He imagined the monstrosity of Victorian revival might have swallowed her—whoever she was—whole. The two-story house glared down with dead eyes. Sneered wickedly with its jagged, broken porch. The faded-blue station wagon parked in the drive and plethora of dolls and brightly colored hoops littering the unkempt lawn were the only signs of human life—those and the green haze of the shield blocking his entrance.

How the hell did they expect him to get past the door shield? The barrier protected the inhabitants from his kind and, if he dared cross the threshold without permission, he wasn't sure if he'd survive the resulting shock. Something uncomfortable—something he didn't want to name—slithered up his spine. Never, not once in the millennia he'd worked as the Watchers' personal assassin, had they asked him to save someone. It went against his job description.

A warning pain speared through his head. "Hurry."

He stood up, pivoted in a slow circle, and checked out his surroundings. The forest beyond the yard sat quiet except for a choir of frogs. Noting the abundance of cedars and firs, he figured he was still in Washington, somewhere west of the Cascades.

He strode up the porch steps, the old wood groaning under his weight, as he searched the darkness for potential threats. At last, the headache and the stifling pressure in his throat disappeared. He banged on the wall near the door, avoiding the shields on the windows and door. Seconds later, the door swung open. His eyes picked up fragments of light from the dark interior. Like a feline at night, he made out the sparsely decorated entryway.

A young Latina girl stood there, eight or nine years old, her face dirty and tear-streaked. Her wide, terrified eyes overpowered the rest of her features.

You have got to be fucking kidding me. He had no experience with kids. He started to walk away but a warning pain flared behind his eyes. He let out a low growl and turned back to the child. He imagined he looked to her innocent gaze like an ordinary man rather than a monster, though his eyes surely glowed in this lighting. Humans couldn't see door shields, so as far as she knew, nothing held him back.

She squeaked.

An unfamiliar restless energy crawled under his skin, urging him to action, demanding he get inside. "Speak up."

The girl flinched at his demand.

Come on, get in the game. What would a human do? He scrubbed his hand over his shaved head and knelt on one knee. "What's your name?"

"Trina."

"What's the problem, Trina?"

"It's my fault." She spoke to his knee, unable or unwilling to look at his face. "Are you a policeman? Can you help my friend?" A fat tear ambled down her cheek, leaving a clean trail in its wake.

"Yeah, sure." He leaned as close as he dared, the warning buzz of the door shield filling his ears. "You have to invite me in."

She chewed her lip for a moment in indecision. "'Kay, but don't tell Nan. You promise?"

A howl in the distance lifted the hair at his nape. He wheeled around, scouring the darkness beyond the porch. "Yeah. You have my word."

"Please, come in." She backed away to give him room.

The door shield dematerialized, allowing him to cross the threshold.

Nearly a dozen girls peeked out at him from behind the rundown furniture in the living room and kitchen. A door with another shield stood in front of him beneath a sprawling split staircase. "Where?"

Trina pointed upstairs. "I think Nan's gonna kill her."

He took the stairs two at a time. Only one heart beat as he neared the room. He didn't stop when he reached the door. He kicked it in. Blood and sweat scented the air. An old woman wielded a whip over her head, the metallic barbs punctuating each leather thread glimmered in the light. Her heart throbbed fast and hard. Her face contorted with rage.

The focus of her ire was a young girl, close in age to those downstairs, bound at the wrists with a rope suspended from the ceiling. She didn't move, her legs dangled, her arms bore her entire weight. Shredded and bloody, her nightgown stuck to the oozing welts crisscrossing her back.

The scene dragged him back to another time. One he didn't want to remember. Was this who he needed to rescue? Were the Watchers giving him a chance to right the wrong he'd done so many centuries ago? Shaking himself out of his stupor, he edged closer to the small human. Compared to the old woman's, her heart whispered its rhythm, but the beat remained steady.

"Get out!" The old woman wiped the sweat from her eyes before swinging her weapon in a wide arc, her fat arm jiggling. Her heart thrummed loud, competing with her shriek. "Get out of my house!"

He wanted nothing more than to wrap his fingers around her neck, to choke the life out of her. He wanted to beat her the same way she'd beaten the girl and more, until she never got up. He wanted justice for this girl and justice for the girl in his past.

He couldn't do any of those things. The Council forbade Guardians from killing humans. Despite what the Watchers wanted, the Council would deem the old woman an innocent since her actions didn't affect their kind. The laws demanded they keep their interference with humans to a minimum. . . . Then again, her heart was working too hard. Skipping a beat here and there. He flipped off the lights, closed the door and rounded on the woman, knowing his eyes glowed.

"You." She gasped, breathless. "I know what you are." She swung the whip, missing him in the darkness.

He advanced.

"I knew you'd come. I had a vision." This time the threads burned over his cheek. "I curse your black heart."

"I'm already damned." He didn't bother to brush aside the leather threads as they struck his face.

Her heart pounded faster. Harder. "She deserved punishment." Her free hand rubbed over her breastbone.

He glanced at the girl. No child deserve such a beating. They said the other girl, Lilith, had deserved her fate. He'd failed to protect her and his fuck-up resulted in his cursed existence. Turning back to the woman, he cocked his head to one side. He wouldn't fail this time.

"You want her." Her swings were growing weaker, erratic.

"She's a child." His tone dismissed her statement.

"Still, someday. . . ." She paused, breathing hard. "I've seen her future. Yours, too." She clutched at her arm. "It's an abomination, what will come, and I curse you. Before you get what you truly want, I curse you to destruction." She ended on an asthmatic wheeze, swaying on her feet.

He edged closer with slow, measured steps.

The old hag stopped speaking.

He grabbed her wrist, lifting her arm so the whip hovered between them.

Her heart raced. Harder, it beat.

He pried the whip from her knotted fingers.

Faster it beat.

He lifted the whip and her eyes grew wide.

Harder it beat.

She shook her head, gasping, trying to tell him no.

He nodded. Stepped forward until her back rammed up against the wall.

Faster. Harder.

The old woman clutched her chest, eyes bulging. Grasping a fistful of his shirt, she tried to steady herself, seeking support from the daemon she loathed. Her knotted fingers clawed her skin and a malodor filled the room as she lost control of her bodily functions.

James closed his eyes, taking solace in the delicate whisper of her heart tearing. Her body slid to the floor as her grip slackened. Her heart beat a couple more times, and fell silent as the chambers emptied. A ragged, fathomless sigh escaped and the light left her eyes.

He dropped the whip in the old woman's lap, slipped his blade from his thigh-sheath and returned to the injured girl. She seemed terribly pale and still. He lifted her with one arm and cut the rope.

The sweet scent of lavender, mixed with the metallic smell of her blood, hung heavy around him. Sitting with her in his lap, trying not to cause her any more discomfort, he cut the bindings and put away the blade. If he hadn't fought the Watchers, he would have arrived sooner. He might have prevented this.

She was a cute kid. Dark hair framed her pale oval face. Freckles dotted her nose and cheeks.

Someday . . .

He glared at the old woman. She didn't know anything. Her rant had been nothing more than a feeble attempt to scare him. Bullshit, all of it.

The girl's brow furrowed and she snuggled closer. Hell, she didn't need to wake here with that woman's body only feet away. He stood, cradling her in his arms, and strode out of the room. A sea of young faces watched from their various hiding places, but the Latina girl, Trina, waited alone at the base of the stairs.

She gave his charge a worried glance. "She okay?"

"She'll live. Where's her bed?"

"Downstairs. I'll show you." She waited for him to descend and led him through a dirty kitchen, and down into the basement. The dank walls lay barren, with no windows or decoration. Light came from dim fluorescent bulbs. Thirteen drab, uncomfortable-looking cots decorated the room. He figured the house for a foster home but the decor suited convicts more than children.

Trina stopped at the head of a cot. "This one is Lilith's."

He nearly tripped over his own feet. She had the same name as the girl he'd failed to protect? He shouldn't be surprised—déjà vu had assailed him as soon as he'd walked in on the scene upstairs. Did this Lilith have the same haunting eyes as the other?

Laying her on the cot, he kept her on her side, getting her into what looked like a comfortable position. Was this it, then? Now that he'd saved her, had his penance been paid? Would he become human again and earn his reward? Hell, he didn't feel any different. He rose to leave.

Lilith's hand shot out, gripping the collar of his shirt. She tugged until he sat on the floor, his face level with hers. Yes. She possessed those same ancient eyes, much too old for her age. Her gaze held him captive. Why had the Watchers concerned themselves with this small human's fate? Why had their lives crossed paths twice during his long existence?

Worry creased her brow. "You're hurt." Her voice sounded hoarse, she must have screamed for some time. She reached out and touched his cheek, the tips of her fingers butterfly-soft under his left eye.

No one ever dared to touch him.

Trina scooted around to look. "I got this stuff once, Nan didn't know, and it was like black and gooey and sticky, and I squeezed the goo in my hands, then I clapped hard like this"—she showed him a big clap—"and the stuff went everywhere, and the goo looked like that." She paused to point to his face and take a much needed breath. "And—"

He covered her mouth with his hand. How could someone so small say so much about nothing? The whip must have left a gash on his face—one that must look black as void, instead of red with blood since he hadn't fed in a while. "Enough." He frowned. "I'm fine."

Trina leaned over and whispered into Lilith's ear, "I think the ground shakes when he talks."

Lilith nodded, the movement causing her to grimace. Her pain-filled gaze met his. "Are you a giant?"

He shook his head.

"You saved me. Are you an angel, then?"

"Farthest thing from it." He didn't want anyone's praise. Didn't need it. What he wanted was his humanity. His reward. "I was late." Too late. That must be why he wasn't changing.

"I think you got here right on time." Tears welled in Lilith's eyes, her smile a tad wobbly.

Trina plopped down on the cot, grinning outright.

What now? Why weren't they terror-stricken like the small humans hiding upstairs. . . . Jesus, she was human. And he'd treated her like a wounded daemon. She needed a goddamn doctor, not bed rest. "We need to get you to a hospital."

Lilith shook her head.

Nobody told him no. He gave Trina his full attention. "Call nine-one—" He stopped speaking when she, too, shook her head. He didn't have patience for such impertinence. "Why not?"

Trina shrugged. "I don't want to get in trouble with Nan."

Nan? She must mean the old woman upstairs. With a

finger under her chin, he forced Trina to meet his glare. "Would you rather get in trouble with me?"

They both nodded, appearing unperturbed by the threat of his wrath.

Refusing to be humbled, he tried using the truth to scare them. "She can't hurt you. I killed her." He should've kept his goddamn mouth shut. Now, they both watched him with wonder in their eyes.

James scrubbed his hand across his head. Men feared him. Daemons cowered in his presence. But these two insignificant human girls acted as if he were no bigger threat than a goddamned puppy. "Shouldn't you be scared? I thought little girls feared monsters."

They shared a confused glance, but it was Lilith who spoke. "You said you killed her."

CHAPTER 3

Present day.

Everyone carried emotional baggage around—regrets and karmic debt accumulated through life. Lilith Caldwell's baggage just happened to manifest into an entity—a gossamer vision of a sickly little girl who had made its first appearance during a hospital stay when Lilith was ten and recovering from a brutal whipping. She'd named it Aimee, hoping to make friends. There was nothing sweet and innocent about the entity, though. She discovered quickly enough that Aimee could change from little girl to hideous monster in the blink of an eye. Never again did she make the mistake of thinking it friendly or benevolent.

Lilith's gut tightened into a sickening knot as she guided her car down the main drag of Carnation, Washington. The pentacle she'd hung from the rearview mirror swayed softly. She kept to the twenty-five mile an hour speed limit and still drove from the cemetery at one end of downtown to the high school on the other in under a minute.

She'd avoided this place for close to twenty years. Everyone here knew her. Pitied her. She'd gone from the girl who'd lost her mother to the girl who'd seen her grandmother killed, to the girl who'd been beaten, to the girl who saw imaginary things.

Little had changed since her childhood: The

modernized buildings housed the same old shops; street signs and storefronts still argued over the true name of the town—some read Tolt, others Carnation.

The future lies in the past.

Gods, she sure as hell hoped so, because with each mile closer to home, Aimee seemed to become more corporal, as if returning to the place she'd originally manifested gave her more power. She'd swear she had heard Aimee breathing. Lilith reached over and turned down the heat, trying to determine if she'd imagined the sounds. There. Faint, wheezy breaths. She grasped the steering wheel tighter as she stopped at a light, cutting her eyes to the side. In her peripheral vision, the entity stood on the backseat, staring out the window. Aimee seemed . . . solid. Little clouds fogged the window with each rattling breath.

A shiver danced over Lilith's skin.

Making the hour drive back to the airport and catching the next plane out might be a good idea. Didn't matter much where she went—as long as she got away from here. As long as Aimee returned to her vaporous form.

No. The note said: *The future lies in the past. Go home. It is time.*

And she wanted a future.

She'd received handwritten notes at every stop on her itinerary. Her job, procuring products for the Grigori coven's webstore, sent her on an almost constant loop around the globe.

She'd ignored the first note when it arrived: "Your future lies in your past."

The second one, too: "The truth lies in the past."

But the notes kept coming with just those two messages. For months. The unsigned messages waited for her at the front desks of the hostel in Brazil, the hotel in Hong Kong, the Bed and Breakfast in Kuwait and the hotel in Mombasa. No one knew her itinerary, not even the coven of witches she purchased goods for.

Still the notes found her, arriving before she had. When the last one she received came, telling her to go home, she'd had the first stirrings of hope that if she did as the note instructed she might find what she'd lost so many years ago. She might regain her Magic.

She had no idea who sent the cryptic notes. Someone must have followed her in the past, stalked her to know where she went next. And perhaps the author of those notes wasn't some benevolent godmother come to make her world better. They might have known Aimee would become corporal. Maybe this wasn't a chance at a fresh start, but the beginning of the end. Her end. She dropped her head to the steering wheel. "I don't know why I'm here."

Behind her, someone honked.

She jerked upright and stepped on the gas, giving the driver an apologetic wave. Desperation, that's why she'd come home.

She'd lived in a nightmare for nearly twenty years. Not some nameless, faceless imagining, but a terror shadowing her every waking step. As time wore on, she'd learned the new rules of her life with Aimee and abided by them. She'd isolated herself to protect everyone else. She'd learned to turn inward to find peace, to find any happiness. And somehow, she managed to keep others from thinking her insane. Somehow, she'd managed to move through each day one dogged step at a time. Never looking back; never bothering to look forward.

Now, she had hope. Like a glutton at Thanksgiving, she'd begun stuffing herself with impossible dreams. Dreams of Aimee fading away. Dreams of being whole again and having her Magic restored. And, gods help her, hope could be a terrible thing.

She turned off the main road and headed down the last stretch to her past.

Aimee moved across the backseat, the cushion making popping sounds as her nails punctured the cloth. Her asthmatic breathing drew closer. Louder.

Lilith shook her head. No, the noises must be her imagination run awry.

The entity leaned forward over the passenger seat, and on the next breath Lilith inhaled a rotten, decaying odor. Something fell on her shirt. She glanced down in time to see a chunk of graying flesh turn to ash on her shirt. With a shout, she brushed the ash away, pressing harder on the accelerator.

Aimee started trying to crawl into the front seat, her skin sloughing off in strips with every movement, leaving raw flesh behind. What little hair the toddler-sized entity still had stuck up in haphazard clumps. Her face had changed, too, looking closer to a snubbed-nosed reptile than a child.

"L-Li—" Saliva dripped from Aimee's sharpened baby teeth as she tried to speak her first word.

Lilith's heart pounded, trying to bash its way right out of her chest. She tightened her hold on the wheel with icy fingers and blinked to clear the tears from her vision.

This is what you get, child. This is what happens when you overreach. Nan's voice echoed in her mind.

"Li—"

Okay, all I need is a plan. A plan. A plan is all I need. The mantra ended in a Lennon-like tune and she had a sudden, overwhelming need to giggle. She must have lost her ever-loving mind. Maybe if she left town, Aimee would stop manifesting. Aimee could go back to haunting her and she could return to the life she knew. Except that life wasn't much of a life at all.

The road ended up ahead. The overgrown path to her childhood home came into sight and for the first time in her life, Haven House seemed a safe haven. Now that she'd arrived at the one place she'd avoided for most her life, she discovered she *wanted* to go inside. She pressed harder on the accelerator.

Aimee reached out and touched Lilith—her skinless

flesh wet and sticky on her cheek. Lilith shuddered.

They hit the overgrown, dirt path at fifty miles an hour and Aimee bounced away. Lilith struggled to control the car over the dips and hills of a road that hadn't been used in decades. Branches from overgrown trees raked down the side panels of the car, screeching in protest.

Finally, the weathered sign came into view: HAVEN HOUSE: A HOME FOR LOST SOULS

Aimee regained her footing and lunged into the front seat. For a heartbeat, she did nothing more than cling to the dash with her claws and stare out the windshield as the house came into view. Then, quite distinctly for a being who'd never spoken before today, she said, "No."

Lilith floored the gas pedal.

This time, Aimee held fast, bracing her small, mis-shaped legs on the seat. Her attention shifted and she launched herself at Lilith, making her lose her grip on the steering wheel. Claws sank into her arms. A fresh burst of adrenaline raged through her. She slammed on the brakes as the car started to spin, grabbing for the steering wheel and beating Aimee back with her purse. The entity hissed and tried to wrench the makeshift weapon from her hands, then she disappeared amid the sounds of twisting metal and shattering glass.

Something hit Lilith across her face and chest with enough force to stun her. For a heartbeat, she sat there, trying to get her bearings. Her face stung. Her arms hurt. White dust coated the air, her clothes. The airbag hung lifeless from the steering wheel.

Aimee screeched and writhed from where she'd gotten trapped half-in, half-out of the windshield. Blood surrounded the hole, soaking into the spider web of shattered glass.

Lilith fumbled with her seatbelt, her hands shaking so hard it took several tries before she unclasped the belt. She needed to get into the house.

The cracks on the glass spread wider, deeper, as

Aimee struggled to free herself.

Lilith grabbed her purse, let herself out of the car, took one step on unsteady legs and tumbled to the ground. *Get up, get up. Run.* The crackle of glass grew louder. The whole vehicle swayed. Lilith took off for the front door, feeling around in her bag for the keys to the place as she went. Glass shattered. She looked back, caught sight of Aimee, and tripped on the steps leading to the porch.

Aimee shook the glass from her body, glancing around until she spotted Lilith.

Oh, gods. Oh, gods. Lilith turned and darted up the rest of the steps. With the key in hand, she got the door unlocked on the first try and pushed into the house as Aimee's claws clicked and scratched up the porch steps. Lilith slammed the door, locking it.

Aimee hit the other side with enough force to make her jump.

Oh, gods. Okay. I'm okay. Clasping a hand to her chest, she gasped for breath.

Now what? She was stuck. This old place wouldn't have food or water. No heat. She'd left her clothes and the few supplies she'd retrieved from storage outside in the car. Dear gods, she didn't even know if the house remained secure after all this time.

Shuffling and panting noises came through the door. Nails scraped along the seam. The handle jiggled. Aimee wanted in.

Lilith wandered around the foyer, her ears still ringing from taking the airbag in the face, peeking into the darkened rooms to either side. White sheets covered the furniture and boards blocked the windows.

The kitchen lay to the right of the foyer, the living room to the left. The old home didn't have any hallways on the ground floor, each room leading into the next through archways. If she walked through the living room, she'd end up in a study, which led to a family room, which led to a dining room, which led right back to the kitchen on her right. The sole door leading to the ritual room sat across from the front door, dead center in the house, under the sprawling split staircase. Once upon a time, that's where she'd received lessons in Magic with the rest of the Grigori coven

Back when she'd been a witch. Long ago when she'd possessed Magic.

Just as she reached for the door handle, the pipes shuddered in the walls and the buzzing in her head stopped. Not buzzing, running water. Slowly, she lifted her gaze above her, as if she could see through plaster and walls to whoever hid in the bathroom upstairs.

The future lies in the past.

Either she turned tail and fled right back to the very angry, very corporal entity waiting outside or she faced whatever might be upstairs.

"Choices, choices."

Gods, she missed her Magic.

Lilith backed away from the staircase, and reached for her purse. In lieu of Magic, a weapon would have suffused, but she didn't have one of those, either. She improvised, grabbing her keys. Her attention returned to the split staircase. If she remembered right, several steps on the left staircase creaked. She headed for the steps to her right. Trying to make as little noise as possible, she inched up the stairs, fisting her key chain and adjusting the keys to poke through her fingers, the way her self-defense instructor had taught her.

She'd have been better off returning to the airport instead of coming here.

You're always overreaching. Always looking for more than you have. More than you deserve. Nan's words echoed in her mind. Muffled noises came from the bathroom at the end of the hall.

On the second floor, she stopped on the landing overlooking the foyer and contemplated the dark hallway before her. There were three bedrooms and a bath up here. Thin lines of light bordered the closed bathroom door at the end of the hall. She gripped the keys tighter and headed down the hall, glancing into the first doorway on her right, the punishment room. Darkness obstructed the details of the space, but that didn't stop the memories from flooding back. For a heartbeat she swayed, shaken.

The scent of blood and sweat filled the air and her skin blazed as if flames licked her flesh instead of the barbed tails of Nan's whip. Her arms ached from holding her weight, but her feet refused to stay under her.

Lilith shook her head and pushed away the memory. She started forward again, after taking a deep breath. She gave the darkened room a wide berth, pausing only briefly to peek into the two bedrooms on her left as she passed. Both appeared uninhabited. Ahead, a shadow moved under the bathroom door.

It's a squatter. A human being. Just take down whoever it is and ask questions later.

She reached the end of the hall and lifted her hand to twist the doorknob. The door swung open. Fear overrode everything else for a heartbeat. A big shape came toward her, blocking out the lights in the bathroom. She cocked her arm back and launched herself at the trespasser.

"Oh, hell no." His deep voice vibrated through her even as he knocked the keys from her hand and spun her around. "Will you—"

Eyes. Nose. Throat. Groin. Knees. She threw a punch, aiming for his throat.

He blocked her, palming her fist and re-directing her momentum away from him. The move forced her to step forward. Left her vulnerable to attack.

"Who the hell—"

She caught her balance and rammed her elbow back into his gut. Except his stomach seemed to be made of steel and her whole arm went numb, as if she'd slammed her funny bone onto a table top.

He grabbed her arm and swung her around.

Lilith turned within his grasp and kicked his knee out from under him.

"Shit!" He tried to brace his weight against her to catch his balance, but she hadn't gotten both feet under her yet.

She fell flat on her back and he came down on top of her. She shoved against him, gasping, and punched him in the face even as she brought her knee up.

He blocked her with his thigh, moving his weight higher up her body to straddle her hips. "Hey." He gathered both her hands into one of his and held them to the floor over her head.

She tried to buck him off. *Oh gods, he's going to beat the shit out of me.*

"Damn it, *stop.*" He lifted her a little, shook her. "I'm not going to hurt you. You attacked *me.*" He shook her again. "Why?"

Finally, her brain kicked back into gear. He hadn't hurt her, not really. Restrained her, yes, but as big as he was he could've incapacitated her in seconds had he wanted to. She couldn't see much, her hair blocked her view and he sprawled over her, holding himself at arm's length, leaving nothing above his six-pack visible. His legs straddled hers, his jeans stretched tight over thick thighs. Right above where their bodies met, her attention zeroed in on his belly button. He had an outie. A man with an outie couldn't be all *that* bad.

"Let me up."

"Are you gonna stop?" His voice sounded abnormally deep, as if he'd injured his throat at some point. "Can I get your hair out of your face now, so I can see who the hell you are?"

She nodded. She didn't have much of a choice with his weight pinning her down.

"I'm gonna let your hands go, but I'm warning you, lady . . . you hit me again and I'll hit back. Got it?"

"Yeah."

He released her wrists and his weight shifted as he

pushed the hair from her face.

Eyes, black as obsidian stared back at her, and gods help her, he had a rugged, intimidating aura even if he hadn't been lying on top of her. He looked mean as hell. His straight, broad nose, angled cheeks and strong jaw line could've been chiseled in stone. He didn't have any hair, both his jaw and head were shaved clean.

He shifted slightly and the light from the bathroom caught on the silver pendant he wore. A small dragon's eye in the center of a larger sideways eight. A fresh burst of adrenaline pumped through her. The dragon's eye, a triangle with an upside down Y in the center, symbolized danger. The sideways eight represented infinity. Together, they translated to infinite danger.

Last time she'd laid eyes on that symbol was when she'd summoned her mate to rescue her from Nan. *Her mate.*

CHAPTER 4

The future lies in the past. She searched his face, her gaze zeroing in on two thin scars below his left eye. *Holy shit.* "You." She lifted her hand to touch the whip marks.

"Lilith Caldwell?" Those dark eyes widened.

She nodded, surprised he remembered, that he recognized her. She certainly didn't look the same after twenty years. But he did. Disturbingly so.

"What the hell are you doing here?"

"Presently, I'm getting crushed into the hardwoods."

"Sorry."

His deep baritone vibrated through her, making her all the more aware of his weight. Of the places where his body pressed tight to hers and the fact that he'd grown aroused. Her gaze dropped from his as heat suffused her cheeks. "I, uh . . . maybe—"

"Yeah." He grimaced and pushed away from her. When he stood, he gave her his back and her breath caught at the sight of two barely healed wounds above his shoulder blades.

Great, so she'd attacked a wounded man who was her mate and also happened to have saved her life. *Way to go, Lil.* "Look, I'm sorry. Are you all right?"

"Fine."

And as surly as ever. As a child she'd been very impressed with him for saving her from Nan, but then he'd disappeared into the night, breaking her heart. A wistful smile tugged at her lips. At ten years old, she'd fully expected her hero to come equipped with a white stallion and willing to carry her off into the sunrise to marry her. Little girls had funny dreams.

But here he stood.

She got to her feet, still breathing hard, still shaking from the adrenaline rush. How was this possible? After all these years, her mate looked as hard and strong as she remembered. It had to be a trick of the lighting. "Did you—" She wet her lips, and sucked in a steadying breath. "Did you send me the note?"

"What note?" He strode down the hall, not even sparing her a once over.

She followed. "The one telling me to come home."

"Seriously?" He headed into the punishment room and flipped on the light. "You think of this place as home?"

Okay, so he hadn't called for her. And she hadn't summoned him. So why was he here?

She hesitated at the threshold, but the room looked nothing like the chamber she remembered from childhood. The windows had been boarded over and he'd made the space his own. He had a bookshelf and dresser pushed up against one wall and a bed against another. A sleepy, orange-striped feline lifted his head from the mussed sheets.

Lilith stepped into the room.

Her mate whirled on her. "What are you doing?"

"There's no sense in shouting from the hallway."

He motioned around the room. "My room isn't that big."

She shrugged, walked to the bed and picked up the cat. "He yours?"

"No." He dragged his hand over his head and braced his hands on his hips. "I don't know where George lives, but he hangs out here on occasion. What are—?"

"George?"

"As in the mad king. The damned feline acts crazy as

hell most days."

She pulled her gaze from the lump of fur purring in her arms and her mouth went dry. Her mate's jeans rode low on his hips, showing off the muscular V dipping down below his waistband. Her gaze stroked over the ridges and planes of his abs, chest, and shoulders. Gods help her, he had an amazing build. Too bad he didn't seem half as interested in her as she was of him.

Parts of her body, too long ignored, tingled to life. Scars crisscrossed his chest, marked his shoulders, his neck. Her gaze caught on one, an oval of webbed tissue at the base of his throat and her heated blood turned to ice in her veins.

Gods help them both. He was a daemon.

Not all were terrible. Daemons descended, through biology or Magic, from the Watchers—the two hundred fallen angels. Even as she stared at the webbed oval scar at the base of his throat, she denied what she knew him to be: Vampire. She couldn't possibly be mated to a vampire. They fed off blood and they all had special . . . talents. Abilities handed down to them from the Watcher whose blood they carried. And yet, she didn't fear him. She feared *for* him. His being here put him in danger, more so than he had any way of knowing.

Lilith dragged in a deep breath. "I suppose you'll be leaving now."

Slowly, he shook his head.

She wet her lips. "You can't think . . . ." She paused as her voice cracked, and started over. "You can't think to stay here."

"Why not?"

He pinned her with those black eyes and her mind went blank. "What?"

"Why. Not."

She huffed. Contrary male. The amusement lighting his eyes irritated her. She squared her shoulders and tipped up her chin. "I know what you are." Even as the words left her mouth, a pit seemed to open in her belly.

He dropped his gaze and backed up a step.

That hadn't been fair. As a witch, she knew the power of words. They could create or destroy and hers had done the latter. Damn it. Whatever his race, he'd also saved her life and he was her mate. Karma would bite her in the ass if she repaid him with cruelty. She cleared her throat, hoping he didn't catch the slight strain in her voice. "You were my hero."

His gaze shot back to hers, but his eyes narrowed as if he didn't trust her sincerity. By the look of him, she doubted he trusted anyone. He seemed . . . feral.

She stomped down the urge she had to hug him. He might be her mate, but she couldn't keep him. If she wanted him to continue to breathe, she had to send him away. "I am truly grateful to you, but you can't stay here."

When the coven found out she'd come back, they'd come looking for her. And if they discovered him, they'd destroy him.

Nan had been right after all.

Life-mates were not for witches.

Not even Magic-less witches.

She still smelled of lavender.

Lilith. She was still irrational and unpredictable, two qualities he didn't find appealing. And she still didn't fear him. Something had scared her, probably whatever made her bleed, but it sure as hell wasn't him.

She seemed unaware of her wounds—the knot forming on her forehead and the blood blooming on her sweater at both shoulders. Part of him wanted to ask what happened, but the last thing he needed was an entanglement with a human. Especially this one. He was already too interested in her.

She'd grown tall and slender, with just enough curve to her lithe body to turn a man's head. Dark hair framed her delicate features. Those big, soulful brown eyes held him captive, though—always those eyes. Her pink sweater enhanced their chocolaty color, and brought out the rich hue of her cheeks and lips. Her denim jeans fit like a second skin and those boots . . . . Man, he'd love to see this woman in nothing but those leather boots.

Focus.

The way she'd stared at him a moment ago gave him a partial hard on all over again and he needed to get rid of her before he did something about it. Christ, what was he thinking? He couldn't touch her. He was far too old for her and a vampire to boot—the worst sort of daemon. She, on the other hand, looked like a goddamn angel. A young one.

Like the old woman said, being with her would be an abomination. He'd never redeem himself in God's eyes if he soiled her with his hands. And that's what he wanted—redemption and an end to his endless existence.

So, focus. Get her out of here. He turned away and retrieved a gray t-shirt. "Where'd you learn to fight?"

"I took classes."

"You paid someone to teach you that?" He waved his hand to where they'd grappled in the hallway.

She propped one hand on her hip. "I dropped you."

"Luck." He snorted, jerking the shirt over his head. "I wasn't trying to hurt you. If I had, we wouldn't be having this conversation."

She blinked, clearly not intimidated. "Well, then, I thank you for not wanting to kill me or whatever you're insinuating." Her toe tapped against the hardwoods. "Regardless, we can't live here together."

"Exactly." Where the hell were his boots? "You remember where the door is?"

She gasped. "This is my house."

He paused. "You bought this place?"

"Well, no." Finally, her gaze slid away. "Not exactly. I inherited it."

He harrumphed. He spied his boots, grabbed them

and sat on the edge of the bed. "Yeah, well, living here can't be good for you." He shoved his boot on.

"But what? It's good for you living in this mess?"

He jerked his other boot on. "I don't have time to play Suzie-homemaker and I don't like guests."

She made a noise suspiciously like a snort. He turned to glare and she stared back with those big, innocent eyes. "Well, you'll probably be feeling crowded pretty soon."

"Oh? Me, alone, in all this space. I doubt it."

"Trina will be joining me."

He froze. That name should mean something. . . . "The little Latina upstart who got you into that mess with the old woman?"

Her jaw dropped. "It wasn't her fault."

"That's not what she said."

"She was nine," she sputtered. She set George down on the bed and folded her arms over her chest. "It wasn't her fault."

Whatever. As he tied his boots, his nape tingled. She must be scowling daggers at his back.

She sighed. "Why are you here, anyway?"

That was a damned good question. One he couldn't answer. He glanced around the room as if his surroundings might provide an answer. He'd set up this place as a bolt-hole years ago, but rarely used it. And while he remembered crashing here due to an injury a day or two ago, he didn't remember any of that time. When she'd attacked him out in the hall, he'd felt like he'd just woken from a nightmare. Hell, it didn't make any sense. Someone must be fucking with him.

He stood, facing her and found the sight of her almost painful. She was beautiful, vibrant, alive. And him, hell, he was so fucking ancient, he couldn't even recall his exact age. He felt like dust in human form. *Get out of here. She'll be gone by the time you get back.*

He grabbed his keys and backpack, and strode out of the room. George raced past and flew down the stairs, ready for a night of prowling.

James paused at the top of the stairs and turned to her. "Look, I gotta go to work. Leave my stuff alone. If you want to take a shower and clean off the blood—"

She jerked to attention, looking at her sweater where he'd pointed.

"—go ahead, but I expect you to be gone when I get back."

He descended the stairs at a quick clip.

"I'm not leaving." A note of desperation entered her voice. "I have to be here."

"Why?"

Lilith snapped her mouth shut, remaining silent.

To hell with her, then. James opened the door.

"Don't!"

The way she shouted at him, he half expected to be attacked when he opened the door. No ambush waited on the porch, but the sight in the yard stopped him dead. His lips parted.

What in the hell?

She'd driven her little blue Toyota Camry head-first into the old cottonwood on the other side of the dirt drive. She'd left the car on and with the driver's door open the car pinged urgently.

He leaned back against the doorjamb. This he wanted to hear. "You, uh, left your car running."

She sat on the stairs and covered her face with her hands. "Oh? I didn't notice."

Like hell. He thrust his thumb over his shoulder. "You going to go take care of it?"

Her gaze shifted to the side and her heart-rate increased. "I'm, uh, afraid of'—she looked up, as if searching for divine intervention—"being outside. It's a phobia." She made a little waving motion with her hand. "You know, I'm agroa, argoa—"

"Agoraphobic." Christ, she didn't even know how to pronounce the condition.

"I can't go out there." Her gaze darted from him to the

open door and her heart increased tempo again, turning a little erratic. "Please, don't leave the front door open."

Liar. She expected him to believe she was agoraphobic and still drove herself here? But something out there scared her half to death. Shit. He'd walk away from anyone else. But not her. He cursed. "Are you going to tell me what the hell you're doing here?"

Her eyes narrowed. "Are you?"

A burst of ill-placed humor erupted from his chest. His rusty amusement sounded so foreign, he clamped his mouth shut. He needed to get out of there. He let the door slam shut behind him, but instead of walking around the side of the house to where he'd parked his bike, he headed toward her car. The hair on his arms lifted and he slowed as he approached. Something had been out here with her. Some kind of lesser daemon. The air still held a current of electricity from the creature's manifestation. He glanced back toward the house. Is that why she refused to say anything? If she thought him human, she might worry he'd think her crazy.

No. She'd seen his scars and those lovely eyes had filled with wariness when they'd settled on the one at the base of his neck. She knew what he was, which made him wonder . . . what was she?

At first glance, Lilith appeared human with a beating heart, and warm and rosy skin. Her eyes didn't have the shine of a nocturnal predator. She didn't have any of the trademarks of a lycan or vampire. Still, that left a slew of other daemon races, some of which were impossible to detect without a thorough examination.

He walked around to the driver's side, peering in the windows and the open door. Whatever had attacked her had left. He pulled the seat back, tucked the airbag out of his way and sat behind the wheel. He turned off the ignition, silencing the infernal pinging. Aside from the front-end damage and the deployed airbag, the windshield needed to be replaced. She'd have a hell of a time getting the job done without risking attention from the police. Not with that bloody hole in the center of the glass.

That's why she'd hit the tree, to throw her attacker into the windshield. A slow smile spread on his face. Good girl. She had mettle and Christ, did he like that.

A pentacle hung from the rearview mirror. He touched the pagan symbol, sending it spinning on its chain. They'd killed anyone in possession of such a mark back in his time as a human. Nowadays, they were a fucking fad.

His gaze dropped to the dash. Long, narrow marks scarred the surface. The passenger seat upholstery sported similar damage. That explained the blood seeping through the arms of her sweater. She'd faced a daemon with claws.

Neither vampire nor lycan did this, but something smaller. Odd. At one time, as many daemons as humans walked the earth, but since the portals to the daemon realm closed, he'd seen fewer and fewer. He'd honestly thought the only daemons left on this side were vampires and lycans. So where'd she find this one?

James turned the engine on, backed the car away from the tree and parked at the end of the drive. He'd make arrangements for the repairs. Fixing the car wasn't a problem.

She was the problem.

He got out and leaned his forearms on the roof. All these years, he thought he'd somehow failed the night he'd rescued her from the old woman. The Historian said he'd find his humanity and reward at this house if he obeyed the Watchers. He'd assumed he'd rescued the wrong person or fucked up the job in some way because he'd never found his humanity. This house held no portal to paradise. But now he wondered. . . .

Maybe his assignment with her wasn't finished.

Was that why he'd woken in the house this morning with no memory of the last few days? Had the Watchers done something to ensure he'd be here when she arrived?

He eyed the house over the top of the car.

Who the hell was she?

CHAPTER 5

Lilith wanted to disappear.

Her mate must think her a complete basket case. She hadn't even thought to turn off the car. Granted she happened to be running away from Aimee at the time, but she couldn't tell him that. He'd want her to explain how she became so familiar with his world and she could never tell him about the coven.

The door opened and he shouldered his way in with her bags.

She shot to her feet. "I didn't expect— Thank you." She dropped to her knees next to him and flipped open her suitcases and unzipped her bags, checking to make sure Aimee hadn't hitched a ride inside in one of them. Once satisfied no evil entity lurked beneath her underwear, she stood. "I, uh . . . ." She folded her arms in front of her. "I'm sorry for earlier."

"Seems you've had an eventful day." He shrugged. "I'll make allowances."

She bit her cheek to keep from asking for his excuse for his rudeness, not wanting to start another argument. He'd just dig his heels in again. "I appreciate you seeing things my way and I am glad I got to see you again."

He leaned back against the door, and smirked. "I think you've mistaken my intentions."

He'd brought in her bags, obviously she would be staying and . . . . "You are leaving, right?"

"Yeah. I gotta go to work."

She didn't like the amusement lighting his eyes. "And . . ."

"What would you like me to bring home for supper, honey?"

Lilith closed her eyes and counted to ten. "You. Can't. Stay. Here."

"I'll pick up whatever looks good." He opened the door and headed out.

What exactly might a freaking vampire decide to bring home for dinner? "Wait." She lunged forward, wedging her foot between the door and the jamb. "I prefer veggies. Yogurt. Cheese. Crackers. Fruit."

He leaned against the other side of the door jamb, his face inches from hers.

"Bottled water. Soda. Chocolate. Oh, gods, I'm going to need chocolate."

He chuckled. "Listen. The house . . . it makes a lot of noise around twilight. Change in the temperature or something." He met her gaze, the intensity there belying his casual tone. "Don't get spooked."

"Twilight?"

"Mm." He nodded. "Astronomical twilight, too, but I should be back by then."

Ghosts appeared at twilight and dawn. "You're trying to scare me."

"No, I'm giving you a heads up so you don't kill yourself running away from a bunch of harmless noise."

She looked up to the sky. Dark clouds made the evening appear further along that it was, surely the only reason he could be out there, but twilight wasn't far off.

"You'll be fine." He pushed away from the door. "My assistant, Lou, will be out with a crew to fix your car later."

"No. You don't have to do that." She already owed him for his help twenty years ago.

"It's already done. Leave them alone to do their work. Don't pester them."

The repairs would eat a huge chunk of her savings.

"I'll pay for whatever—"

"They won't charge for the work."

She sighed. Of course not.

He slipped on a pair of sunglasses and disappeared around the side of the house.

Lilith closed and locked the door. Great. Now she owed him twice.

A moment later, the rumble of a motorcycle raced passed. She grinned, shaking her head. He seemed the type to ride a bike.

Gods, what had she gotten herself into? She'd come with the hopes of finding a way to get rid of Aimee. Now Aimee lurked somewhere outside this house, a ghost haunted the inside of the house, and she'd gotten herself more indebted to the mate she couldn't keep because he happened to be a vampire. "I am so screwed."

The house swallowed up her words, the place too quiet now with her mate gone. White sheets covered the furniture. Boards blocked the window, leaving thin tentacles of light streaming through.

Damn it. He'd gotten to her. She was officially spooked.

He probably expected her to be long gone by the time he came back. Not a chance. She owned this house and she fully intended to make this her home.

A bit of light and a good cleansing would keep this old place from being so creepy. She knelt down and pulled out the small box that contained her smudge sticks from her suitcase. As a child with Magic, she'd been able to not only cleanse the negative energy from a space by smudging, but also any dust or grime. In her hands as an adult with no Magic, they'd only chase away negativity. She stood with the items and turned toward the kitchen, only to stop dead in her tracks.

The lights were on. All of them.

She glanced up the split staircase and sure enough even the hall at the top glowed with warm light. Did the ghost turn on the lights? She pulled her phone out of her pocket and searched for the time of twilight in Carnation. No. She still had plenty of time before twilight.

Magic?

Hope unfurled in her belly. Lilith closed her eyes, envisioning the darkened house. Imagined slowing the currents of electricity flowing through the walls until it stopped.

She opened her eyes.

The house was dark.

With all the excitement this evening, she hadn't noticed the subtle change. But now, standing still, she couldn't miss the old power thrumming through her veins. Not anywhere near as strong as in her youth, but her Magic had *returned.*

Once again, she pictured the house lit with soft glowing lights and they flickered back to life. With a whoop, she danced a little jig in the front entry, shaking her bootie and shimmying her shoulders until peals of joyous laughter overtook her. "Thank you, gods. Thank you. Thank you."

She needed to call Trina. She started to take her phone out, but paused. No. First she needed to make sure it wasn't a fluke. Her grip tightened on the box of smudge sticks. *What was the spell?* With Magic, she could give this house a proper cleansing. She'd need to be careful not to overdo. She wasn't as strong as before. But the cleansing spell was simple, and one she'd done often as a child. *What are the words?*

She removed one bundle and lit the white herbs with a match, blowing on the end of the stick. The flame died and as the sage continued to smolder; thick white smoke billowed up from the end of the wand. The pungent, earthy smell replaced the musty odor permeating the house, helping to calm her.

The words.

"With smoke so pure, positivity is ensured. And a scent so clean, to make every surface gleam. For this I ask, or something more. With respect and love, I do implore."

She waved the wand over the round table standing in the middle of the entryway and the grime evaporated, leaving polished wood in its wake.

Lilith grinned. The words weren't quite right, but they'd do.

She walked toward the living room, leaving behind gleaming hardwoods with each step. Holding an abalone shell under the smudge stick to collect the ashes, she wandered the lower rooms, waving the smoking wand toward each shelf, chair, and window.

If only she could do the same for—damn. She'd failed to get her mate's name again. Both times she'd met him he'd appeared so serious. Did the man ever smile? Oh, he smirked several times, but did he smile? At one point this afternoon, when he'd started to laugh, he'd seemed to startle himself with the burst of humor, but the lines in the corners of his eyes indicated at one time he had smiled often.

What the heck was she supposed to do with him? If he stayed, the coven would eventually discover him, but as his mate, she didn't like the idea of kicking him out if he had nowhere else to go. Maybe she should give him a little time to find another place. Heck, she'd help him. And if he did end up staying here a day or two, she'd make sure he learned to smile again. That's the least she could do in return for his help.

Gods, what was she thinking? She must have lost her mind.

Lilith pulled her phone out and dialed Trina.

"What's up?"

Lilith answered in a sing-song voice. "Guess who has her Magic back?" Silence. "Trina?"

"I'm speechless. Are you serious?"

Lilith grinned. "Sure am. Right now, I'm doing a cleansing spell at Haven House, making everything shiny and bright."

"What about Aimee?"

"Um, well, she's . . . gone." Lilith cringed a bit at the half-truth. Technically, Aimee wasn't here and she saw no reason to worry Trina by telling her the entity might be lurking outside somewhere waiting for her.

"Did you tell the coven?"

Lilith sighed. "No. There's no reason to. They didn't want me and I have no intention of running over and asking to be reinstated."

Trina scoffed. "Their loss. You and me, we'll have our own coven—the Outcast coven." As kids they'd bonded quickly, ostracized by the other girls. The orphans feared she'd tattle on them to her grandmother. They'd feared Trina for different reasons. Trina possessed chaos Magic, and was both empath and telepath. Her ability fascinated Lilith, and years ago she'd allowed Trina to open a link connecting their minds and enabling them to chat without being overheard. Unfortunately, their link only worked when they occupied the same space.

"Sounds good to me." She glanced over the freshly cleaned lower rooms. Beautiful. She returned to the foyer, tucked the phone between her ear and shoulder and opened the door underneath the split staircase. If Haven House possessed a heart, the ritual room contained it. "Listen I, uh, I need some advice."

On the floor in the center of the room was the sacred circle, which encompassed a pentacle, its points stretching out to touch the walls. Cobwebs hung from the rafters, a buildup of residual Magic, which lingered long after the witches left.

"Advice. From me?" Trina asked.

"Yeah, well, you have more experience with men and—"

"Men? Hold on." She heard a flurry of movement on the other end of the line. "Okay. I'm comfortable. Who is he?"

Lilith's lips twisted into a wry smile. "Um, well—"

"Gods, Lil, you got your Magic back, Aimee left, *and*

you met a guy. You've had a hell of a week."

More like a hell of a day.

"Please tell me you didn't pick another spineless little twerp."

"Ah, no. He's—"

"Good grief, dish already."

"Quit interrupting. I hate it when you do that." Lilith took a deep breath. "He's my mate."

"What?"

"My. Mate. My mate. Mate. I damn well know you know what I'm talking about. Don't make me say it again."

"Okay. Okay. I'm just having a mild heart attack over here. Are you serious? Lilith, we've talked about this. He was like forty when we were kids. If he's your mate, you're not going to be able to have a serious relationship with him until the next lifetime."

She drew in a calming breath, nodding. "Yeah, except he . . . ."

"He what?"

"Okay, don't freak out."

"I'm already freaking out. You sound like you're hyperventilating. What did he do to you? Wait, he's like what . . . sixty now, what *could he possibly* have done to you?"

Lilith laughed, the sound a little shrill. "Oh, I'm thinking he's older. Except he doesn't show his age much. He looks . . . ."

"What?"

"The same." Lilith grimaced.

Trina didn't speak.

Lilith continued to cleanse the ritual room while waiting.

"Tell me he's gone through major plastic surgery."

"I can't."

"Goddess bless you, you can't keep him."

CHAPTER 6

I've told myself that. I tried to kick him out, but he saved my life and now he's fixing my car and he's coming back tonight bringing me groceries and I need food. I didn't eat on the plane. And he really doesn't seem interested in moving out. And holy gods, he's hot as hell."

"Yeah, literally. He's a fucking daemon, Lilith." Another flurry of movement came from the other end. Trina must have gotten up to pace. She always paced when working out a problem. "Okay, maybe we're making more of this than needed. What do you think he is? A djinn? Gallu? Some sort of shifter?"

As if she'd ever been so lucky. "How long have you known me?"

"A vampire. Right. Because everything has to be difficult with you."

"I know what I should do, but I've got this weird urge to see him happy even though he's annoyingly bossy. Cantankerous, even." She nodded to herself. Grouchy. "For the half hour we talked I spent most of the time annoyed, but I couldn't stop staring. I kept wanting to give him a hug, like some crazed, lonely purple dinosaur with daddy issues. What do I do?"

"TMI." Trina blew out a deep sigh. "Gods, Lil, part of me wants to scream at you to throw him the fuck out. If the coven finds out—"

"Yeah, Rowena wouldn't hesitate to sic the coven on

him even if he is my mate."

The coven preferred to keep their identity and abilities a secret. In the past, when less careful, humans feared them, making survival a challenge. And daemons . . . for many ages witches and daemons worked together in peace. All the way up until the Clearances. Legend said the vampire race turned on the coven. Ever since, each generation of the Grigori coven hid from both humans and daemons.

"Exactly, but the other part of me knows how lonely you've been. You deserve a little happiness."

Lilith nodded. She did, damn it.

"But don't put too much into this. You don't know for sure if this is the life you'll find happiness with him."

"I know."

"And you know how harsh life-mates can be on each other before they finally come together."

"I know."

"He's really hot?"

Lilith laughed. "He's got that thing."

"What thing?"

Finished cleansing the ritual room, she closed the door and headed upstairs. "When a man has really tight abs and they form that v."

"Okay, you have to at least mess around with him a little. A quick one night stand before you send him away."

Didn't that sound heavenly? Except she'd never been much of an enticement to men and he was way out of her league. "He's kind of intense. I doubt quick is in his vocabulary. And . . . I'm not so sure he sees me in that way."

"What do you mean?" Trina made a rude sound. "Good gods, Lil. He's your mate. Look, I know you. Don't get all 'he'll never like me' and 'I'm not pretty enough.' You're gorgeous. He's your mate. Flirt with him."

Lilith rolled her eyes. She stood too tall, with the curves of a two-by-four, the breasts of a pre-pubescent girl, and when she tried to flirt she ended up acting like a clown—but arguing with Trina would be an exercise in frustration. "'Kay."

"Come on. You read those dirty books, right?"

Her cheeks heated. Gods, she never should have told Trina about her little addiction. "Erotica. It's called romantic erotica."

"You must have picked up a few moves."

Yeah, in her fantasies. "Okay, I'll flirt. I'll let him stay a few days and see what happens."

"Maybe it'll be nice to have him around for a little while. You won't be alone in that house and if he gets out of hand, you've got your Magic. Use it. Just keep him away from the coven." Trina paused. "What's it like?"

"Haven House?" She walked into Nan's old bedroom and a shiver raced up her spine. "Creepy as hell. All the old furniture is still here, covered with sheets. He hinted the place is haunted, though I'm not sure I believe him." Nan's belongings were gone, except for the bed and an old scarred bookshelf. The window had been boarded over.

"He told you that? I thought they weren't allowed to speak of anything to do with daemon-kind to humans?"

"Well, no. He said the house makes a lot of settling noises." Lilith began smudging the room.

"And you got 'ghost' from settling noises."

"He said the noises happen at twilight and dawn."

"Oh. Go out for a bit."

"Yeah, maybe." Lilith hedged, not wanting to tell her about Aimee.

"Maybe what? Only one person has died at Haven House."

"But the place has been empty for two decades, squatters might have been here, or kids coming around to explore or—"

"You're reaching."

Yeah, she was. She opened the closet and froze. A pile

of dolls and stuffed animals sat in the middle of the closet floor. "I should go. I'll call you later." They said their goodbyes and she hung up the phone, slipping it into her back pocket. She recognized them as toys she and the other girls of the Grigori coven had played with as children. She spied her doll amid the others and picked it up, straightening the lavender dress and placing the doll on the bookshelf.

In a rare moment of kindness, Nan took them to visit a woman who made the toys and allowed each of them to pick out one to take home.

That last night, Nan had taken the toys in an effort to encourage the girls to admit they were wrong.

Lilith closed the door, pushing away the memory. She went to the window and pulled the slats down. Her mate probably put them up to keep out the sunlight and while she'd leave the rest of the windows covered for him, she fully intended to enjoy the view of the foothills from her room.

She entered her mate's room across the hall. Since he made arrangements for her car to get fixed, she'd tidy his space. She made the bed and discovered a knife under his pillow. Gripping the handle, she eased the blade out of the worn leather and admired the abstract designs cut down the center of the silver blade that revealed what appeared to be a strip of wood underneath. She'd seen pictures of similar daggers in her mother's Grimoire. Only one group a vampires carried them, some kind of daenomic police force that had once helped the Grigori coven maintain the balance by ensuring daemon-kind didn't abuse their power and overwhelm the humans.

Returning the dagger to its hiding place, she finished straightening the bed.

So why had the vampires tried to kill off the coven during the Clearances? Now the two groups shared no trust between them.

Daemons are dangerous creatures, they'd sooner kill

us all than work with us. When she'd been a child, she'd argued fiercely with Nan over such claims.

As she cleaned, she browsed his books, surprised to find all classics. One had been placed backward. She extricated it from between the others. It was an old worn copy of the Bible. The book shook in her hand as she slid it back into place and a wave a weariness washed over her. Gods, she was overreaching with her Magic. She snuffed out the remains of the smudge stick and ended the cleansing spell.

No more Magic until she'd had time to recharge.

She went back downstairs and, in the living room, she packed up her remaining smudge stick and closed up her suitcases.

Upstairs, a door creaked open.

She caught her breath and strained to hear. After several moments of silence, she allowed herself to breathe again and shook her head. Noise, as her mate said. Still, the way he'd said it made it sound like so much more. They needed to have a talk about his scare tactics. If he insisted on staying here, she refused to put up with any more rubbish.

She lined her belongings up at the bottom of the stairs and returned to the living room to remove the sheets from the furniture.

Footsteps ran across the floor above her. She clasped her hand to her chest, as if to prevent her thundering heart from escaping. Her gaze followed the disembodied sounds into her mate's room and then back into the hallway upstairs. The noise stopped.

Something was up there. Was a ghost making all that racket?

Or had Aimee found a way in? Her gaze slanted toward the front door. She could go out to dinner and come back well after nightfall, but what if she ran into Aimee out there?

Something banged in Nan's old room and made her jump. The noise repeated, over and over until she covered her ears. She forced herself to sit, clutching the sheets to her chest. Her whole body trembled. The temperature dropped, making her erratic breath visible in puffy white steam clouds.

A ghost, then. Not Aimee.

She pulled out her phone and returned to the same website as before to find out how long twilight lasted. Twenty-three minutes. Twilight lasted *twenty-three minutes.*

Something bounced down the stairs. Thuds echoed in the empty house as the object hit each step, counting out its progression.

Lilith stood as the noise neared, her hand covering her mouth to keep her from screaming and drawing attention to herself. She stepped closer to the entryway as a small object hit the bottom step and rolled across the hardwoods. A puff of blond hair kept it from rolling far. It rocked for a heartbeat, spun a bit, and settled facing her.

A doll's head.

Her doll's head.

The purple ribbon she'd stolen from Nan's sewing box decades ago still held the blond hair in place. Innocent blue eyes stared back, the face frozen in a sedate smile.

The eyes blinked.

Did the ghost sense her presence? Or was it fishing, looking for someone to torment?

Gods, she wanted her mate to come home. She'd sell her own soul to have him here. She'd let him stay. Just for the week. She'd keep his presence hidden from the coven and that would give her time to figure out what to do about Aimee.

And the ghost.

And her mate.

CHAPTER 7

James parked his motorcycle, glancing again at the text: Juanita Beach, 2am, 2v + hhbl. The translation: Assassinate two vampires exchanging human hostages at 2:00AM at Juanita Beach. The bl stood for blind. For one reason or another, he wouldn't need to worry about the human hostages witnessing his altercation with the other daemons.

He strode across northeast Juanita Drive toward the beach. Between the late hour and the windstorm battering the area, the streets were deserted.

The Watchers, the beings who provided him and the other Guardians information on their marks, weren't infallible. They didn't predict the future, though at times the accuracy of their measured guesses appeared to be more like precognition. They saw and heard everything and everyone. Everywhere. With information gleaned in their vision, they calculated probable outcomes. However, they didn't read thoughts and so they couldn't predict all potential factors. Sometimes the smallest detail changed their expectations and complicated matters.

The lights flickered off. Aside from the wind-whipped trees and the waves splashing against the boardwalk, silence reigned.

The park didn't have a wide selection of vantage points. He chose a wide, low-hanging branch in an oak which provided a good view of the parking lot, grounds, and lake. Whichever way his marks arrived, he'd see them coming. Only one structure lay on the grounds—a building with lavatories on one side and storage sheds on the other.

He removed his backpack, stripped off his helmet, gloves, and jacket, and placed them on a crook in the branch. Leaning back against the trunk, he unzipped his backpack and took out a PVC bag filled with blood. Using the built-in tube as a straw, he drank his fill while he waited for his prey, his thoughts turning to Lilith.

He must have lost his fucking mind.

The Vampiric Council would be appalled by his actions this afternoon. The Watchers would keep their keen sight focused on his every move—they'd demanded he protect her, not live with her.

I've just got to keep my hands off and protect her.

Lilith had become a bit of an enigma over the years. She'd changed him the first time they met, centuries ago when he'd still been human. He had no doubt it was her, albeit in a previous life—one he'd ended. She'd affected him the second time they met, when he'd killed Nan. He'd tried to remain detached when he'd rescued her, when he'd tried to redeem himself. But she'd been so brave, showed such strength and compassion. She'd forced him to rethink his views of humans, even his view of himself. And now, as a full-grown woman, she disturbed him in a much more profound way.

His skin prickled in warning. He scanned the area, a shadow in the distance drawing his focus. The shape of a man stumbled out of the shadows, his eyes glowing, giving him away as a daemon.

Julius Crowley. Wonderful.

Crowley strolled closer with his hands shoved into khaki pants, his long-sleeved, white dress shirt plastering to his chest, first one way, then another as the wind whipped around him. Usually, he wore his blond curls slicked tight to his scalp, but in this weather they blew in a riot around his head, giving him an even more youthful mien.

They'd been friends once, but somewhere along the way Crowley had changed, and not for the better. He worked for the Council now, ensuring the Guardian did whatever the Watchers demanded.

James carefully kept his gaze from meeting Crowley's. The son of a bitch was a mesmerist and James had no desire to become Crowley's puppet. "Jules."

"James." Crowley leaned against the base of the tree and looked up. "Long time."

"Yeah. What, about twenty years now, eh?" Last time he'd seen Crowley had been the night he'd helped Lilith. Jesus, it was a goddamn reunion, the only one yet to show up was the Historian. "What brings you back to Seattle?"

"Heard you've been on the missing for the last three weeks."

James just kept himself from reacting. *Three weeks?* How in the hell had he lost three whole weeks? Thinking he'd lost a couple days had been disturbing, but this . . . . "I—" *Shit.* James cleared his throat. "I needed to nurse an injury. Forgot to call it in, that's all."

Crowley held his hand out. "You know the rules."

James dug his phone out of his pocket and handed it over. Jesus H. Christ. All his muscles tensed in preparation for battle. If truly injured, the Watchers wouldn't have sent him any jobs. But he hadn't been injured. Not enough to account for three weeks' lost time. He must have three weeks' worth of unfinished kill orders on there.

"Anything new going on with you?" Julius asked, scrolling through the phone log.

"New?" What, like losing three weeks of his life? Like taking in a gorgeous human woman as a new roommate? "Nah, man. You?"

"No."

Jesus, what was taking so long?

Julius lifted his gaze and stared at him for a long moment, saying nothing.

James didn't move. Didn't dare lift his gaze to meet that of the other vampire.

Julius handed his phone back.

He took the device, requiring every ounce of will power not to check his history.

A branch broke free in the wind and Crowley swatted it away. "What's your assignment?"

James shifted his weight on the branch. "Trafficking."

"Ah."

"You?"

"They got me looking for a woman."

"The Watchers?" *Shit.* He'd been so surprised, he almost looked into the bastard's eyes to see if he was pulling his leg.

"She's about thirty. Has a birthmark of a crescent moon."

His gut bottomed out. He'd once known a woman with such a mark, and he'd left her reincarnated form back at Haven House. "Hope to hell it's on her forehead, otherwise you're pretty much fucked. This time of year, everybody's wearing coats."

"If you see her, anyone you think might be her, call me." Crowley started to walk away.

Smug bastard. He damn well knew the Watchers hadn't assigned Crowley to Lilith. They had sent *him* to protect her. James folded his arms over his chest. "What I don't get, is if this is so damned important, why the Watchers didn't notify all of us. Seems a little . . . off."

Crowley leapt onto the branch, putting himself eye level with James.

Jesus, he hated this fuck. Hated not being able to look him in the eyes. Lowering his gaze made him feel like he was giving way to the bastard. Bowing to him.

"The Watchers protect humans. They maintain the balance through us," Crowley stated.

"You didn't answer my question. Why is she so important?"

"She's dangerous."

"To who?" Obviously not the humans since the Watchers didn't want her dead.

"To us." Crowley tipped his face, trying to crawl into James' line of sight. "Who will help the Watchers maintain the balance if there are no vampires?"

James turned away. "I'll let you know if I see anyone suspicious."

"Do that." Crowley leapt down and swaggered off toward Juanita Drive.

James swiped his thumb across his phone, checking for missed calls and texts. Lou had called last week and the one before, Ghost and Walker had both texted a couple times, but nothing from the Watchers.

He hadn't taken a job in three weeks and he had no memory of the time. Had he been injured worse than he'd thought? His gaze went to where Crowley crossed the street. Or was someone screwing with him? He hated Crowley, but the bastard was a good mesmerist. He only needed a half-second of eye contact to get into someone's mind.

And he wanted Lilith.

Hell, maybe he was overreacting. He didn't know Lilith to have a birthmark in this reincarnation. But his gut said she did. His gut screamed that Julius Crowley and the Vampiric Council must be the threat he needed to protect her from.

Which would be a problem, because while the Watchers directed him to who he needed to assassinate, the Council managed the Guardians. If he ended up going up against Julius Crowley, ultimately he would lose. He might kill Crowley, but others would come for him. They would hunt him through eternity. For now, he'd be best off doing nothing. To wait. Watch. And if his gut turned out to be correct . . . then he'd have to somehow destroy Crowley without anyone knowing he'd done the deed. James sighed. That would be impossible: The Watchers saw everything and God only knew if they were all on his side.

James checked his watch again, eager to get this job over with so he could return to Haven House.

A black Honda Civic with a neon-green racing stripe whipped into the parking lot, its glass muffler rumbling, and backed into a space near the waterfront. The driver shut off both lights and engine. Minutes later, a second car zoomed in, an old red Camaro. The vehicle may have seen better days in the 'eighties. The Camaro drove in next to the Civic so the drivers' windows were side-by-side.

The guy in the Camaro thrust his hand out the window, flashing a small wad of cash. The Civic driver reached out, snatched the money, and dropped a small bag in the other's hand in one seamless movement.

This wasn't what he was here for. James rested back against the tree.

The Camaro drove away. The Civic stayed.

Just his luck—one minor detail changed. The morning just got more complicated. He checked his watch: 1:53 AM. With a little luck Mr. Civic just wanted to count his money before he left.

But at 2:00 AM, he still sat in his car.

A small moving van lumbered into the lot, U-Haul printed across the side in front of a picture of the State of Arizona and images of the desert.

This must be his mark.

A Hispanic male got out of the driver's seat of the U-Haul, locking the door behind him. He checked out the Civic, his eyes glowing in the darkness. Appearing unconcerned with the trespasser, the vampire headed for the sole building on the grounds. A gust of wind kicked up, blowing hard across the beach. The vampire's long coat lifted up behind him, the solidness of his body turning vaporous. As the wind died down, his body obtained its original form.

James scoured his hand over his head. Great. A phantom talent. The ability allowed the vampire to turn to mist at will, which made them difficult as hell to fight. All vampires possessed various talents and they used them often, which made his job that much harder. He couldn't use his, it was too damn unpredictable in a densely populated area such as this.

Another male approached on foot from the other side of the park and once he entered the building, James leapt down from the tree. He went to grab his blade and realized he'd forgotten to strap on his sheaths—he'd been too distracted by Lilith.

He inspected the area and found a sapling supported by two stakes. He pulled his gloves on and yanked the stake out of the ground, tucked it between his belt and jeans, and walked around to the side of the building. Steeling himself for the confrontation, he swung open the door labeled Men and strode inside. The scents of urine and bleach assailed him. Three stalls lined the wall to his right. Dead ahead, plastic mirrors hung over three sinks. The vampires huddled in the far corner near the urinals, an attaché case laid out on the last sink.

"You've been tried and found guilty of trafficking humans. Surrender or die."

Both vampires shared a glance before the Hispanic's eyes dropped to James' throat. No doubt he was searching for the Guardian pendant James wore. He handed his cohort a ring of keys. "Take these, Luis." He shut the attaché case and picked it up. His gaze darted around, marking the small rectangular windows above each stall.

They were all shut tonight. The bastard meant to run, and he only needed a small opening, just enough to get the attaché case through and to keep from impaling himself should his body solidify partway through.

James shook his head. "I wouldn't try it."

They acted like cornered animals—frightened and

desperate. He blocked the one easy exit, and the Vampiric survival instinct wouldn't allow surrender.

The door swung open behind James. Mr. Civic strode into the middle of the tension wielding a small pistol. "Dude, I don't know what's going on. This is my territory—"

Oh, for Christ's sake. One minor detail changed and the whole damn night went to hell. James kicked the gun out of his hand, grabbed him under an arm and a leg, and hefted him up and over, throwing him toward the two vampires.

The Hispanic shoved Luis toward James and scrambled into a stall. Mr. Civic crashed into the wall where they had stood seconds ago and dropped in a heap on the dirty floor.

"Damn it, Carlos," Luis turned ghostlike and staggered right through James.

James whirled around, his fist shooting out, connecting with Luis' back and slamming him into the wall head first. Stunned, Luis slid to the ground and stayed there.

Two down.

James strode toward the stall where Carlos fumbled with a window latch, frantic. He kicked the door in. It connected with Carlos, who grunted as he flew face first into the wall. James grabbed him by the back of his shirt and jerked him away from the window. He hauled his fist back, aiming for Carlos' face. Carlos shifted to mist and James' fist rammed into the tile wall behind him, the ceramic exploding under the force. The phantom dove under the stall door to retrieve the attaché case.

James grabbed his foot and started pulling him out of the stalls.

Carlos faded again. James' hand grasped nothing. "Goddamn it."

The hair on James' neck prickled. He twisted around. Luis' fist slammed into his temple, the keys he clutched slashing into his skin. The force threw James off balance, pushing him back onto Carlos. James kicked his leg out, connecting with Luis' calves. Luis' feet came out from under him and he fell, cracking his skull against the sink as he went down.

James turned back to Carlos, struggling with his inconsistent form. Every time his grip tightened, Carlos turned into an apparition, slipping through his fingers. James grabbed the stake from his belt. He waited for Carlos' spectral form to take on substance, then drove the stake down hard into Carlos' chest. Carlos exploded into a shower of dark, sooty ash.

James stood and stretched, his gaze landing on Luis. The vampire struggled to stand. His hands shook so hard he couldn't get a grasp on the sink to pull himself up and his legs didn't look like they were much better off. A deep black gash slanted over his brow where the skin split. His body kept blinking in and out of focus. Teeth chattering, Luis' eyes widened and he took another weak swipe at James with the keys.

James kicked him in the head. Hard. "You're no good at this, Luis. You don't seem to be able to control your talent." He squatted in front of the vampire, cocking his head to the side, narrowing his eyes. "You must be a neophyte."

"Why are y-you d-doing this?" He sank back, trying to take shelter under the sink. "Who the hell are you?"

Questioning Luis would be useless—he was too new. He wouldn't know anything of value about the daemons who hired him. Hell, the neophyte didn't even know of the Guardians. "Good luck in the Eidolon Wastes." James brought down the stake, ending Luis in a spray of ash.

He dumped the weapons in the garbage, grabbed the attaché case, and left.

Now he just needed to free the humans, pick up some groceries and go sort out his situation with Lilith. By now, she'd experienced a taste of life at Haven House.

With a little luck, she'd be ready to talk.
   From here on out, everything would be simple.

CHAPTER 8

Why the hell had he thought this would be simple?

Lilith must have unpacked and started making Haven House into her home and she must be very human.

The door shield was back.

James stood in the yard, staring at the green haze preventing him from entering the house. What if she didn't let him in? An anxiety he didn't want to acknowledge slithered under his flesh.

He strode up the porch steps, shifted the grocery bag to his other arm, and rapped his fist on the wall next to the door. When no one answered, he banged again. Harder.

The door swung open. "Gods, you scared the crap out of me."

Something in him eased at seeing Lilith whole and healthy. Her damp hair suggested she'd just bathed, and she wore the most hideous, antacid-pink robe he'd ever seen. He had no doubt she wore nothing underneath, and she'd tied the belt in such a way he could remove the paltry barrier with a quick tug with one finger.

A brief vision flashed in his mind of advancing on her, hooking his finger in the belt, and spreading the homely garment to gaze at the beauty beneath. Burying himself in . . . . He mentally shook himself, raking his hand over his scalp as if he could reach in and rip such thoughts from his mind.

Focus. "What the hell are you doing answering the door at this hour like that? I could've been someone dangerous."

Her expression suggested he'd lost his mind. Hell, he must have. If he kept on this track, she'd never invite him in.

"If you didn't want me to answer, you shouldn't have knocked."

He sighed. "What's wrong? You looked scared when you opened the door."

"You have the knock of a SWAT team. Of course I looked scared. Are you gonna yell at me every time I see you?"

"Probably."

She harrumphed. "Well, at least you're honest. Did you forget your key?"

"Yeah."

"Well, come on. I don't like keeping the door open."

Right. Now what? That sure as hell didn't sound like an invitation. The door seal certainly hadn't accepted it as one. Christ.

James shifted the grocery bag to his other arm. "Look, we got off to a bad start earlier. I, uh . . . ." Jesus, this sucked. "I don't have any place else to go. I need to stay here. I'll, uh, pay you rent or whatever."

A speculative glint entered her eyes. She folded her arms over her chest and her gaze shifted from him, to the door.

Fuck.

"You know, I realized after you left that we've met twice now." Her gaze followed the entire outline of the doorway as if searching for the barrier. "You've saved my life and fixed my car. We're going to be living together . . . And I have no idea what to call you."

"James."

She gave him her full attention. "Your whole name."

He let out a rueful chuckle. Someone who knew about

daemons could do a lot with a name. Summon them. Trap and torture them. Who the hell was she, some sort of daemon hunter? "I've got chocolate out here." He put on his best smile. "And ice cream. It's probably starting to melt."

She shrugged. "It's cool tonight. It'll keep."

Ah, Christ. She was good. He felt certain she knew exactly his race and the rules of his existence. But the way she worded everything, the innocence in her expression . . . hell, she may have very human reasons for her questions. "Why do you need my full name?"

Her grin spread. "Why, that way, if you turn out to be a thief, I'll know who to report to the authorities."

Yeah, she was good. He could walk away. He could . . . . . No. He couldn't. His chance at humanity lay within those walls. His shot at redemption, the opportunity to find paradise was somehow linked to her. "Samael James Pasquino." The name, not spoken in almost a thousand years, felt strange and awkward on his tongue. "I go by James."

Her eyes widened and her jaw went slack. She cleared her throat. "Please come in, James. My home is your home."

The door seal dematerialized.

"Jesus." He stared at her for a long time, trying to determine if she understood what she'd done. She'd not only given him free access to this house, but any other she ever chose to inhabit.

"Hurry up, I want to close the door." Her focus shifted past him to scrutinize the night.

His gaze raked over her as he entered and shut the door, a sense of possessive pride filling him to near bursting. She may as well have claimed him as her own.

She backed up a step for each he advanced until her back pressed against the wooden banister. He caught himself reaching for her and lowered his hand. "Why'd you do that?"

"Do what?" She inhaled a shaky breath, but her gaze

met his with a steady defiance he admired.

She had no idea what she'd done. It hadn't meant anything to her.

He forced himself to back up a step, to look away from her.

The floors shined, prompting him to glance around. Everything looked fresh and clean. She must have spent the entire night scrubbing the place down. "You've been busy."

"I see you have, too."

He arched his brow.

"Do you always come home looking like this?"

Lord, she sounded vexed. Home. He rolled the foreign sounding word around in his mind. He'd never thought of this place as home. But she'd offered him that. *My home is your home.* She'd claimed him. *And you can't touch her. Period.*

Remembering her question, he glanced down at himself. He still wore the same clothes from earlier—jeans, a sleeveless tee and a jacket. "Yeah. Pretty much."

"I meant your face."

Shit. He'd fed earlier tonight before taking on those two phantoms. He must have bruised.

"Come with me." She towed him into the kitchen and waved him to a seat at the table.

"Anyone ever tell you you're kind of bossy?" He set the bag of groceries on the table and sat.

She snorted, pulling a clean towel out of a drawer and filling it with ice. She returned with her makeshift ice pack and held it out to him.

He folded his arms across his chest. "What do you think you're going to do with that?"

"Humor me." When he didn't move, she placed the ice pack on his forehead and his hand over the pack to hold it in place. She went back to the counter. "Is this a fluke, or a regular occurrence?"

He ignored her question. "You don't need to make a fuss." He set the ice pack on the table. No one ever fussed over him before, and he liked being left alone, damn it. Still, he lounged there and watched her.

"You look like hell." She opened another drawer and removed a couple of tiny brown bottles.

"Where'd you get all that stuff from?" He reclined back in the chair, stretching his legs out in front of him.

"My bags." She opened two bottles. "I'm a purchaser for an online store. They sell all-natural supplies, herbs, essential oils, that kind of thing." Taking a measure of clear gel, she mixed it with a couple of drops of dark liquid while muttering under her breath.

A bitter, astringent odor filled the kitchen and he pulled a face. "It reeks."

"It's the arnica." She walked back to where he sat, her gaze dropping to the discarded ice. She shot him a disgusted look. "You could be more helpful."

"I told you, this isn't necessary." His paltry wounds would heal by tomorrow with or without her fussing.

"Hold still."

After watching her angle for a comfortable position in which to treat him, he took hold of her waist and tugged her down onto his lap to keep her from leaning forward and unintentionally give him a view down the front of her robe.

She didn't look like she remembered what she meant to do.

He pointed to his head.

"Right." She cleared her throat and began prodding at his temple with a gentle touch. "You're lucky. There doesn't seem to be any hidden injury under the cut, but I don't like the look of this lump." She cupped his cheek with one warm, silken hand to hold him still while she applied her stinky gel.

He couldn't concentrate on the rest of what she said. Her full mouth, inches from his, shaped out each word, her pink tongue darting out to moisten her lips. How would she taste? Would her lips feel as soft as they appeared?

Finished with her task, Lilith moved her gaze to his. She still cupped his stubble-roughened jaw in her hand. He had fixed his stare on her mouth, making her skin tingle. Making her aware of her nakedness under her robe.

She had no idea why she'd given him free access to the house, to her. When she realized he needed her invitation to enter, she'd had the perfect opportunity to send him away. She asked for his name expecting him to tell her to go to hell. But for a moment, while he stood there coming up with excuses for why he needed to stay, he appeared lonely. A little lost. And when he'd given her his name, his trust, she refused to allow his risk to go unrewarded.

And now, for the first time, she started to wonder how his presence here might endanger *her.* Oh, she didn't fear he'd attack her . . . but she did fear her reaction to his presence.

She forced herself to say something. Anything that might break the tension. "You never answered my question. If this is going to be a regular event, I'll keep some salve prepared."

He shook his head, his gaze never leaving her mouth.

Restless energy stirred in her belly.

He brought his face closer to hers until each burst of cool air he exhaled caressed her face. His lips parted.

Oh, gods, he meant to kiss her. She needed to tell him no.

But the tremor shimmying through her laid waste to all the shoulds and woulds racing through her head. It had been years since her last kiss. She'd forgotten the feel of a man's touch and she wanted to know the feel of her mate.

Abruptly, he slouched back against the chair, his lips pressing into a thin line. His gaze darted around, landing on everything but her. "I—" He stopped, took a deep breath and let it go. "You didn't need to do any of this, but thanks."

Damn him. He'd given her the perfect out. She should stand up and go clean up the counter. She should go to bed and forget about this.

But now she wanted to kiss him.

She leaned forward and pressed her lips to his. He tightened his grip on her waist, his fingers sinking into her flesh and dragging her closer.

She let her hands wander up the bulge of his chest, over his shoulders, up to his neck. She parted her lips, catching a hint of his taste, just enough to want more.

He made a sound—half groan, half growl—and his hands circled her wrists like manacles. He thrust her back. "This can't happen."

No, it couldn't. She released a shuddering breath. What the heck had she been thinking? She stood and turned away. She'd kissed a vampire. A freaking vampire. Gods knew what else he'd done with that mouth of his. She should be disgusted. Except he tasted . . . nice.

Maybe she just needed to hear him admit to being a vampire to make it real. She turned and leaned against the counter. "Why?"

He dragged his hand over his head. "What do you mean, why?"

Did he not plan on telling her? Her gaze narrowed. "Are you gay?"

"No."

"Married?"

"No."

He didn't plan on telling her. Her temper sparked. "Impotent?"

"Jesus, Lilith."

She put on her most innocent expression. "What?"

"Of course I'm not impotent." He turned to face her, holding his arms out to his sides. "Do I look impotent?"

She bit her lip to keep from laughing in the face of his

outrage. Her gaze slid down from his broad shoulders to his narrow waist and lit on the impressive evidence of his arousal. Her humor vanished. "No." He looked fit. Healthy. Lickable.

Furious. "No more questions."

Eventually, he'd change his mind and want to talk. And when that time came, she'd make him suffer. "Fine. If that's what you want." They wouldn't talk. But she had every intention of flirting. Now that she'd had a taste, she wanted more.

Christ, he needed to talk about something else. He needed to move around to wear off some of the restless energy he had. "Everything okay tonight? Any problems?"

Her right brow arched. "What happened to no more questions?"

Right. He grabbed the bag of groceries and started putting things away.

She snatched a yogurt out of his hand with a murmured thank you, retrieved a spoon and sat on the counter top. "There's a pile of toys upstairs in the closet—"

"Best to leave those alone."

"Oh?"

"They're a good distraction for the—" . . . *ghost.* This was insane. The Discovery Laws forbade him from telling her anything about their world she didn't already know. And he couldn't quite tell how much she knew. He straightened and closed the fridge. "How long are we going to dance?"

"Dance?" She leaned back, one hand propped on the edge of the sink and gave him a sassy grin. "You know, I missed both my proms, and I've always loved to dance." Just as one of her sooty lashes lowered in a wink, her hand slipped into the sink. Arms and legs splayed for a heartbeat as she fought to regain her balance, showing him way too much.

And not nearly enough.

She straightened and set down the yogurt cup. Clearing her throat, she swiped at her cheeks as if trying to brush away the fiery stains of her blush.

James coughed to cover his grin. She was fucking adorable.

Focus. "Come on, what are you?"

"A female." She shrugged. "What are you?"

He let out a frustrated laugh, propping his hand on his hip before meeting her gaze. "A male."

"Well, I suppose that's all we really need to know, isn't it?"

"Lil." He walked to her, bracing his arms on the counter at either side of her legs and met her gaze.

She had eyes like fire agate. Though dark, chocolaty brown, they seemed to have bits of green and amber in this light.

What the hell had he wanted to say? He needed to stop letting her distract him. "No more games. Why'd you come back?"

She inhaled a shaky breath. "I, uh, I guess I'm just trying to find myself."

Jesus. He shouldn't have gotten so close. Her heat seemed to sink into his flesh. The scent of peaches chased each throaty word she spoke.

Focus.

"Most people go to the big city for that. Or travel. Why'd you come here?"

"Well, when you lose something, they always tell you to go back to where you last remember having it."

"It's been that bad, huh?" Before thinking better of it, he stroked his finger down her cheek. "Talk to me, Lil. Tell me what's going on. How much trouble are you in?"

For the barest moment he thought she'd give in. Her eyes misted and she swayed toward him. She seemed to want someone to confide in. But then she blinked and cleared her throat, pasting on a smile. "No more than usual."

His whole body tensed. Usual, as far as he knew, involved being chained up and beaten nearly to death. His gazed dropped to her mouth.

Come on, focus.

Oh, he was focused. Focused on trying to remember what peaches tasted like. On trying to imagine the sweet fruit infused with Lilith's unique flavor. "What can I do?"

Her breath, shallow and quick, fluttered against his skin. "Kiss me."

If he didn't know better, he'd assume she was a succubus, sent here to test his will. He refused to budge an inch.

She lowered her gaze. "You still haven't said why this can't happen."

"We're too different. It'd never work out." She put her warm palms flat on his chest. He mentally shook himself, forced himself to say what needed to be said. "I'm too old for you. Christ, you and I, we're not even in the same orbit. You—"

She shoved him. "No more."

Gods, she was a stupid woman. Why had she thought he might be interested? Just because fate dictated them to be mates didn't mean he'd want her in this lifetime. Or the next. It meant eventually, in one of their lifetimes, they'd find happiness together. That's all.

He was gorgeous.

And she was clumsy. Too tall. Too skinny. Useless. Nothing.

Nan's voice rose from the grave to taunt her within the confines of her mind.

You'll never be anything.

You're mother thought you were special, but you're not. You're nothing.

You have no mate. Who would want you?

James backed up a step. "No more what?"

"Words." She glared. "I don't like what I'm hearing."

"What, you don't like the truth?"

The truth lies in the past.

Was that the truth she'd traveled all this way to discover? More proof that she was nothing. Nobody. Not even good enough for her predestined mate.

He folded his arms over his chest. "We don't even know each other."

And she didn't even fly in the same orbit. She gave him her back, stiffening her spine when she sensed him approach.

James cursed. "I'm going to bed."

Bed? Now? It couldn't be later than three AM. It was still dark outside. She shook her head. He wasn't going to bed, he was avoiding her and right now, that suited her. "Fine."

"Fine."

"Good."

He growled as he stalked passed. A moment later the front door opened and she heard him calling for the cat. Kissing noises floated into the kitchen and she glared in the general direction of the door.

"Damn cat." The door shut and his booted feet thumped up the stairs.

She'd found her mate and he didn't even want her. Gods, she'd been so worried about him wanting to stick around and getting caught by the coven.

And all he wanted was a place to sleep.

Lilith slouched against the counter and pressed her hands to her eyes.

She would not cry.

Would. Not.

There was no reason to. He was a fricking daemon. She couldn't be his mate. She knew that. So why the hell did his rejection hurt so damn bad?

She knew she didn't inspire romance. Or lust. She didn't even inspire mild liking in balding, overweight tax adjusters.

Male or female.

Ugh. She didn't want to think about it. She went to the entryway and grabbed her book out of her purse. She'd read tonight, like she did every night and fall asleep to someone else's romance, someone else's passion.

She returned to the kitchen and sat at the table.

Over the years, fictional characters had filled the void in her life where intimate relationships should have been. It kept the loneliness from becoming overwhelming. She didn't have to risk heart, mind, or body for her fictional boyfriends. And, well, books were like drugs to her. Eventually, even that wasn't quite enough. She needed more. So she'd started reading romantic erotica.

And gods help her, she couldn't get enough.

That's what inspired this madness tonight. But, life didn't work at all like a book. At least hers didn't.

"Lilith!"

Good gods, he'd better not be this moody all the time.

"You owe him." She took a deep breath. "He saved your ass." She snatched her book off the table. "It would be rude to kill him."

She switched off the lights and meandered out to the foyer, hoping the wait annoyed him as much as he irritated her.

He glared down at her from the top of the split staircase. "I told you to stay out of my stuff."

As if instructing a small child, she said, "Why can't you say, 'Thanks for cleaning my mess.'"

"I liked it that way." He strode back into his room and slammed the door.

She went upstairs. As she passed his door, she heard the click of his lock.

That was the last straw.

"Oh, get over yourself. I'm not going to sneak in there and attack you while you sleep."

She heard him snort in response, just before she slammed her own door.

CHAPTER 9

Rowena rearranged her gifts on the altar one last time, putting bowls filled with apples and pomegranates in the center so they'd be surrounded by the tiny censors of incense. She'd already called the corners and cast the protective circle around her ritual space.

The girls had built the circle of standing stones complete with an altar all within the privacy of her backyard years ago. And it was private, even without a fence. The Snoqualmie River backed her property, drawing a line between her and the steep incline of the Cascade foothills. On her right was state protected wetlands and forest and on her left, a campground she'd charmed so that no one ever thought to use it. And while the wind and rain whipped the vegetation around her, and the river swelled from the excess water, everything within her ritual space remained dry, protected from harm by her spell.

Rowena lifted the blood-red Legacy stone and let it hang from its long, silver chain. She'd been trying for years to unlock its secrets. "Great Hekate, goddess of shadows, shine your torches on this stone and reveal to me what is hidden within." She placed the chain around her throat and let the stone drop to rest between her breasts.

And nothing happened. Again.

She almost cursed out loud. There were visions locked

within the stone. Knowledge that would tell her how to wage her war against daemon-kind. The stone held the proof she needed to convince the rest of the coven to help her gain revenge on behalf of the Grigori coven's ancestors.

She also suspected the stone would reveal the true identity of the Original. She glanced down at her Grimore and read the poem again.

When the Original is no longer cursed, she'll come to thee as three.

All as human first, then as daemons are set free.
The beacon burning bright,
The shadow hidden from sight,
The blighted, damned knight.

She had one aspect of the Original, the beacon. She just needed to find the other two. With their combined power, the coven could decimate daemon-kind.

Someone clucked their tongue three times and Rowena whirled around. A male stood in the shadows, his outline barely visible amid the wind-whipped trees, his eyes glowing silver, reflecting the light from her candles.

"Seems you're having some trouble communing with the gods, Madam High Priestess."

Him.

She hadn't seen this male for almost twenty years. Well, he never came close enough for her to *see* him, but he was the only daemon stupid enough to approach her. "I'm doing fine."

"Are you?" He waved a hand toward her offerings. Offerings which still filled the bowls to bursting. "And yet Hekate can't be bothered to accept any of your gifts. Perhaps you've fallen out of favor."

Her brows drew together. Valid point. Why hadn't the goddess at least acknowledged her? Why hadn't she accepted the offerings? *Don't let him see you rattled.* She propped her hand on her hip. "What do you want, Daemon?"

"I want to know what you did to Lilith."

This wasn't the first time they'd had this discussion, but it was the first time in two decades. Why now? Part of her wanted to know, but the bigger, more sensible part of herself wanted him gone. "Go to hell."

"Been there, done that."

She folded her arms over her chest. "Show yourself."

"Tell me what I wish to know."

She shook her head. "Seems we are at an impasse."

He inhaled deeply, releasing a long-suffering sigh. "I felt her today. Just for a few moments. Where. Is. She?"

Rowena froze. The demented daemon couldn't have *felt* Lilith. She'd cursed the child when it had become apparent she was a danger to not only herself, but to others. Her only regret was that she hadn't bound the dybbuk to her sooner.

Then again, Nan wouldn't have allowed it. The old woman feared Lilith and was always ranting about her committing some abomination and starting Armageddon. Rowena scoffed. Was Lilith dangerous? Yes. Was she now? No. It was simple arithmetic. Lilith plus one dybbuk equals no Magic. No Magic equals no daemons. Problem. Solved. "You, Daemon, are wrong. She's gone. And she has no Magic."

"And you, Madam, are a fucking liar." His voice notched up with each word.

"Temper, temper." Rowena threw her head back and laughed. "What are you going to do about it, eh? Nothing, that's what."

"Perhaps I'll stand out here all night. What do you think?"

Her smile faded. The bastard thought he could trap her in her ritual space? She grabbed her Grimore, spun with a swirl of her cape and transported herself into the safety of her home. Outside, those silver eyes glared at the swirl of smoke she'd left behind. He walked into her ritual space and picked up an apple, the protective shield having disappeared when she crossed its boundaries.

She lifted the window. "Go back to hell, Daemon, and do not set foot on my property again." She slammed the window with a resounding thud.

As she walked into the living room, she flicked her wrist and the television turned on. She glanced at the screen and groaned. Revelations Industries. Again. All anyone had talked about over the last week was how RI lost their bioweapon to the enemy who had, in turn, used it on American soldiers.

Cowens. Non-Magical humans always screwed up everything. The picture showed rows of men strapped down to beds in a medical facility. They were covered in tubes for IVs, breathing, food. Rowena shook her head. If she thought for two seconds the cowen would allow their help she'd send Kat down there. Her daughter could heal almost anything. Rowena turned up the volume.

"Dr. Edwin Moss, the new director of RI, is working around the clock to find a cure for the infected soldiers. Until that time, the men will stay quarantined within RI's facility."

"What a waste." Rowena flicked off the television. "Good strong boys, every one of them. And they'll all die."

What a shame.

CHAPTER 10

Lilith couldn't catch her breath.

Wispy remnants of dreams clung to her mind like sticky cotton candy, trying to draw her back to their sweetness. But she couldn't breathe. She was burning up. And something weighed down her arms and chest. Lilith went rigid, lying motionless while she tried to figure out what was happening. Her skin prickled in awareness as something neared her face. Puffs of hot, sour breath brushed over her lips.

Aimee. How the hell had she gotten in?

Lilith squeezed her eyes shut tighter, as if by not seeing the monster, it wouldn't see her. But in the blackness behind her eyelids she had no anchor to reality, just her imagination, which only amplified her fear.

Aimee wheezed, snuffling as if trying to breathe through a crushed nose.

Lilith ran through the few spells she remembered, settling on a simple binding spell. She visualized the blankets separating them, and wrapping around Aimee to protect her.

Blankets tighten with all your might. Blankets protect me from harm this night.

The blankets squeezed around Lilith's body, pinning her arms to her sides.

What the hell? *Specific, you dolt. Be specific.*

Pretending to still sleep, she tried rolling to her side.

Sharp nails bit into her arms and she yelped. Damn. Damn. Damn. She needed to get her arms free. Then she could leap up, throw the cover over Aimee and run.

Run where?

James. He'd help her.

Aimee's claws grazed over her cheek, and then those spongy fingers prodded her mouth, trying to wedge between her lips.

Lilith turned her face first one way and then another.

Industrious in her cause, Aimee continued to try to force Lilith to open her mouth.

She refused, sensing the malevolent intent behind her desire. She tightened her lips against Aimee's prying fingers, clenching her teeth and holding back a reflexive gag. She tried a new spell. *Blankets loosen, blankets lite. Let me free, don't be so tight.*

The material loosened and Lilith pulled one arm free of the comforter and punched Aimee.

The entity screeched, slashing out, her claws catching Lilith under the chin.

Lilith screamed, lunged up, pushed Aimee away, thrashing against the blankets and anything else that touched her.

The door swung open, revealing two silvery orbs floating near the top of the opening.

She launched her pillow at the open doorway.

"Hey!"

The lights flipped on.

James entered the room, glancing around. "What the hell is going on in here?"

From the corner of her eyes, she caught movement. George slunk out of the room, glancing back at her with a hostile glare.

How had the cat gotten in here?

Gods, had she dreamed the whole thing? Her cheeks heated. Did she just have a major meltdown because the cat tried to curl up and sleep with her?

James took in the room all at once, searching for the intruder. He could smell the son of a bitch. That same scent of fresh ozone he'd experienced in the car. He crouched down to look under the bed, but saw nothing. Not even dust bunnies. The closet, too, stood empty aside from the pile of dolls he'd left for the ghost.

The window was wide open, allowing bursts of cool, fall air to whip around the room. A few wet leaves plastered themselves to the sill and across the floor leading to her bed. Someone had crawled in through the window.

Why the hell had she taken down the boards?

So you can't sneak in here during the day, dumb-ass.

And then what, they jumped back out? He'd been sitting in bed reading when she screamed and it had taken seconds for him to get to her room. So where was the intruder?

He strode over to the window and scanned the dark yard. Nothing moved. If someone left via the window and down the trellis, they'd already found cover in the forest. The pouring rain would obscure any evidence her attacker might have left behind. He closed the window and yanked the curtains shut. This wouldn't have happened if she'd left the boards up.

Christ. If he hadn't been avoiding her, he'd have been with her, able to protect her when the attack happened. He never fell asleep until well after sunrise when the rest of daemon-kind also slept.

He faced her. She sat in the middle of the bed, one knee drawn up to her chest, the other leg folded in front of her. Pale and drawn, her face framed wide eyes. Three thin red lines cut along her jaw, and her chest was a bright, angry red around the edges of her tank top. Her left shoulder bled. These were fresh, not from the scabbed-over wounds from earlier. A thin trickle of blood ran right over a birthmark of a crescent moon.

Just like the one Julius Crowley asked about.

Who is she a danger to?

Us.

Hell, maybe she *was* a daemon-hunter.

"What the hell is going on, Lilith?"

"I don't know." She twisted the hem of her pajama pants around her finger.

"Bullshit."

She looked up, but quickly glanced away. She lied, he saw it in her body language, heard it in her heart.

"I can't help if you don't tell me what happened." He tried to keep the impatience out of his voice.

"I . . . I had a nightmare."

"You had a hell of a dream, then." He used his finger to wipe away the blood trickling down her arm and held it in front of her face.

Her eyes widened.

"Talk to me."

For a moment he thought he'd won their stalemate, then she shook her head. "I can handle this. I'm not ten anymore." Her chin rose, but a shudder ran through her, ruining her bravado.

She didn't trust him. Didn't want his help. "Fine. Be stubborn." He strode back to his room, letting the door slam shut in his wake.

Maybe he should leave. Lilith was temptation personified and irritating as hell. According to Crowley she was a danger to vampires and the Watchers hadn't given him any new directions. He'd based all his assumptions about his role in her life on decades-old instructions and the ranting of a Historian he'd been sent to kill.

Fuck.

"What do you want me to do?" He whispered the question to the empty room, but the Watchers heard him. They heard and saw everything. "Tell me, damn you. Say something or I'm out of here."

His phone beeped and he checked the message.

Protect her.

"From who?" He paced the length of the room. "Come on. At least give me that much. Who?"

The phone beeped again.

Everyone.

Lilith hugged her knees, staring at the closed door across the hall. Alone, she didn't feel as brave as she had with James in the room. She refused to turn off the lights and sleep was out of the question.

Her chin stung. She prodded along her jawline at the scratches.

George crept into view in the hallway, at first, nothing but two glowing eyes visible. He skulked closer, pausing in her doorway. The cat held her stare, ears back, mouth open, panting.

The feline didn't look well.

His fur undulated along his side, something pressing against the inside of his flesh like a baby within a womb.

The entity was in the cat.

Lilith sucked in a hard breath and scrambled to slam the door, but George slunk forward, disappearing under the bed.

Crap. Lilith jumped to her feet, standing on the bed. Gods, she felt silly, like the women in those old Tom & Jerry cartoons. But she sure as hell didn't know what else to do. She was a little afraid to use her Magic again. Her gaze lit on the door across the hall and she leapt from the bed, landing with a thud in the empty hallway.

She banged on his door. "James!" She maintained a steady tattoo with her fist, keeping her attention on the bed in her room, making sure nothing tried to sneak up behind her.

The door swung open.

"I don't want to be alone." She gripped the doorjamb with one hand and his arm with the other. "Can I stay with you?" Gods, she sounded shrill.

Sighing, he scrubbed his hand over the top of his head.

Unable to meet his gaze, her attention locked on to the words: Calvin Klein scrawled across the top of his boxers. "I promise I won't try to seduce you."

He cocked one brow, his lips parting.

Ah, gods, why had she said that? "Please, don't leave me out here."

Stepping back, he motioned her in with a jerk of his head.

She slipped into the room.

"You want in, too, George?"

Lilith swung around, a scream burgeoning in her throat.

George hissed, slinking down the hallway.

"Well, fuck you very much, too." He shut the door. Without a word, he strode past, pausing to tug on a pair of faded jeans over his boxers and got back into bed. He lifted the comforter, waiting for her to get in.

She laid down, trying to keep an appropriate amount of space between them so he wouldn't kick her out. If she didn't come up with a plan for getting rid of Aimee, she'd be begging entrance again tomorrow.

Stacking her hands under her cheek, she lay on her side, facing away from him. Part of her wanted to confide in James. To talk through everything that happened since she'd returned. But if she told him about Aimee, he'd want to know how she knew about daemon-kind. She couldn't tell him she was a witch. He'd be horrified and hate her. He might even go after the coven. And even though she wasn't technically part of the Grigori coven, if she revealed even a hint of their existence to a vampire, the coven would see it as the worst kind of betrayal.

Just as much of a betrayal as putting her mate at risk by not telling him an evil entity possessed his cat.

Oh, gods, if Aimee possessed the cat, that meant she

could do the same to them. That must have been what Aimee had been trying to do. To crawl into her mouth and possess her.

A shudder ran through her. She was running out of options. For now, she'd just have to do her best to keep her mate safe until she figured everything out.

James switched off the lamp and waited for Lilith to settle down so he could sleep. Her heart beat as fast as a hummingbird's and she shook violently. He'd never get any sleep with such a racket. "You ready to talk about it?"

"No."

All righty, then. He should've demanded she tell him what the hell happened before allowing her admittance to his room. Yeah, right. He wasn't quite that much of a bastard. Although, when she'd asked to stay in here, his first instinct was to tell her no. Not just no, but hell no. It was one thing to protect her, another entirely to sleep next to her. He didn't need to be this close to her.

But something had been in that room. And she was scared. And dawn would arrive soon. He almost moaned aloud. He'd forgotten about the fucking ghost. Damn it, it'd be best if she'd fall asleep before Nan arrived for her morning terror. The last thing Lilith needed was another scare. "Be still."

"I am being still."

"You're shaking the entire bed." Jesus, she'd never fall asleep at this rate. He rolled to his side, wrapped his arm around her waist and hauled her up against him.

She let out a little squeak of surprise, but didn't fight him. Ha, as if. She made herself right at home, scooting about until her head rested on his bicep, her back against his bare chest and the back of her thighs on the top of his jean-clad legs.

Within moments, she settled down. She quit shaking. Her heart rate slowed to an even pulse. Her body relaxed and her breathing quieted to the uniform rhythm of sleep.

The heady warmth of her body seeped into his, relaxing him and making him feel more human than he had for centuries. The cadence of her heart and her rhythmic breathing lulled him.

Before long, he slept.

When he entered the tent, the lash of the whip snapped, but the prisoner made no noise. She must have passed out.

He removed the white mantle emblazoned with a red cross that covered his chainmail. He didn't want her blood on the garment—Pope Alexander III had blessed it for him when he'd become a Templar. The sounds of battle still raged outside in the distance. The scents of horses, sweat, blood, and manure tinged the air. He should be out there, fighting God's war, not dealing with her. But the sun had just dipped below the horizon and the battle would end soon. Their enemy was in full retreat.

The prisoner hung from her arms, her feet barely touching the ground. Considering the thick webbing of lacerations the whip seared into her back, a grown man would have lost consciousness by now.

"Enough." He spoke in Latin, walking around to stand before the prisoner. "She can't confess if you kill her."

"She doesn't need to. We found the mark of the devil on her. Here." The guard pointed to a birthmark on her shoulder, a crescent moon.

He raked his gaze over the guard, staring until the bastard left.

James stood in front of her, legs braced apart, arms clasped behind his back. He was hard pressed to hide his shock when she lifted her head and met his gaze. She had ancient eyes, bewitching. While the deepest of brown, other colors seemed to swirl within, bits of blues and ambers. The pure scent of lavender coming from her chased all other scents away. Perhaps he'd been too hasty in dismissing the charges. Maybe she was a witch. Witches, though, were said to be ugly, foul, and corrupt. The description didn't fit this young woman.

"What's your name?" When she continued to stare at him in silence he tried another approach. "My name is Father James Pasquino."

The girl rolled her eyes. "Lilith."

She surprised him again. "Your parents named you after a demon?"

"They named me for a goddess." Her belligerent tone beckoned for argument.

"Your parents raised you heathen, then?" He frowned. She could be no more than fifteen summers. Could he fault her for her parents' sins? She didn't have the dark skin common with the Saracens; she must be a camp follower. "Convert to Christianity and I can let you go."

"Otherwise?"

"They'll burn you as a witch. I won't be able to do more than give you extreme unction. Convert."

"I'll not."

"You don't know what you're saying." He dismissed her conviction. "You're too young to die."

Her eyes narrowed. "I won't renounce my beliefs—they're my own."

"So you wish me to believe this is all a misunderstanding?" He folded his arms over his chest, rocking back on his heels. "A disagreement among faiths, with no foul intent?"

"I don't care what you believe. Unlike you, I don't wage war to force people to my beliefs." She spat on the floor. "That's true evil, killing others because they believe differently."

He found himself incredulous. "You consort with the devil and you call me evil?"

"There's no devil in my belief."

"And no God."

"I do believe in your God." She smiled. "As one of many gods and goddesses. Yours is no more powerful than the rest."

"That's blasphemy."

"And killing in your God's name is not?" She sighed. "My arms ache and my flesh burns—let me down if you want to talk of faith and philosophy."

It sounded like an order. "You want to play a witch, get down yourself."

"We all have rules to follow, Father." She spoke the last word with scorn. "Have you no compassion?"

"Say you're not a witch." He had no stomach for the killing of women but she continued to stare at him with a mutinous expression. "Speak the words, woman."

"I am not . . ."

He nodded encouragement to her.

". . . evil." She finished with a grin.

"In your opinion."

"I've never taken a life." Her head cocked to the side. "Can you say the same?"

He reared back as if struck. He killed every day in the name of God. He was tired. He no longer saw the justice of this war. The Crusades would never end. He ran a hand across his head. "You're accused of conjuring fire. I've come to either hear your confession or give you last rites. The choice is yours."

She shook her head. "I need neither."

"Your arrogance will get you killed."

"So mote it be." Her tone indicated her decision final, the words an admission of witchcraft, but her expression held no anger. No fear. She pitied him, he realized.

Unsettled, he made the sign of the cross and started the prayers.

"What if I told you I protected the Templars? That I protected you?" she asked.

He paused. "We have God on our side."

She snorted.

He continued the rite.

"I think you and I will meet again, Father."

He shook his head, pausing long enough to remind her, "You're going to die tonight."

"Still, someday. . . ."

He glanced up, prepared to scold her for the constant interruptions, but he lost his train of thought. Her eyes—eyes as green as a fresh blade of grass—looked straight through him. A shiver darted up his vertebrae, making the hair at his nape stand on end.

"You'll be more open-minded by then. I think I might like you under different circumstances."

This wasn't how a person marked by the devil behaved. Not even his fellow priests would be so kind if in her position. He didn't know what to think, and so he continued his prayer.

"You'll lose your soul tonight, Father." She sounded sad. "They'll be back soon and there is no one left to protect you. My sisters are all dead."

James ignored her.

"May I ask one favor?"

He sighed. "You can ask."

"I don't want to die a coward, screaming in the flames."

A yawning abyss seemed to open within his gut. "I cannot let you go." He wished circumstances were different. He had no desire to see her die as such, either.

"I'm not asking you to betray your duty. I'm asking you to end my life before the flames reach me." Clear and bright with unshed tears, her gaze held no madness. She understood what she asked.

He forgot his prayer. He risked death for his faith every day. But would his conviction be as strong as this slip of a woman's in the face of certain death?

Men came and took her away. He made an effort to plead her case, but three men of good standing swore they saw flames shoot from her hands. They said he'd been fortunate—the fire streaked past him into a stand of trees.

He couldn't argue. He'd seen the same. There was no hope for her.

James strode along the perimeter of the crowd. He'd never been to a burning before. He didn't think, after experiencing battle, anything could shock him.

He was wrong.

The soldiers crowded around, jeering and throwing stones and rotten food at Lilith. Tied to a pyre, she could do little more than endure the humiliation. And she did so with grace. She didn't yell back. She didn't curse. She stared into the crowd in silence. At him. Silently trying to convince him to do what she'd asked.

He'd never killed a woman before, vowed to never commit such a grave sin.

A soldier he didn't recognize walked up to the pyre with a torch and set the straw ablaze.

Though James couldn't hear her voice, he read his name on her lips. "James."

Before he even made the choice consciously, he drew his sword from its sheath. The crowd was too thick for him to get close, at least not in time. He stood on a bale of hay, said a prayer for accuracy, and let his sword fly.

James woke with a gasp, his skin so hot that for a moment he thought flames licked his flesh.

Lilith shifted against his attentive body, grounding him in the present. Her body heat warmed him. Uninhibited in her slumber, she'd draped herself across him, her head tucked under his chin, chest-to-chest, her legs entwined with his. She moaned in her sleep.

What haunted her dreams? Did memories of her attacker intrude? Or did she dream about a past life? Of unbending priests and fire and great swords?

She let out a soft cry and he enfolded her in his arms, holding her close.

Footsteps pattered up the hallway.

Damn, he shouldn't have allowed himself to sleep before sunrise. He rolled to his side, lowering Lilith to the mattress so she lay between him and the wall.

The door opened, hinges creaking. The old bitch was noisy as hell most nights, but harmless.

He pulled the comforter over Lilith, hiding her from the ghost. No need for it to realize there was someone new to terrorize. And better if Lilith didn't see the old woman.

The ghost approached the bed and he clenched his jaw, bracing himself. For what, he didn't know.

And then he remembered.

Pain scored into his back, bringing back the memory of those missing three weeks. Of the dawns and dusks. The bitch was feeding off him, keeping him too weak to leave, too weak to do more than wander the fucking house in a daze.

Until Lilith woke him up.

This morning he didn't have the option to fight. Not if he wanted to keep Nan's attention from Lilith. He didn't even have time to move away from her, so he curled his body around hers, hoping to hell she stayed asleep. Better for Nan to feed from him than her. Nan couldn't fully manifest with his energy. He didn't have a true life force, the darkness keeping him in existence would do little more for her than what it had already done.

But if Nan got hold of Lilith, it'd be a whole different story. Lilith lived. She had a soul, a hot commodity among the dead.

A low moan snuck past his lips. His back hurt like hell. He fixed his gaze on his charge and counted out the minutes until dawn broke, relegating Nan back to wherever she existed between twilights.

CHAPTER 11

Lilith startled awake. Unsure what caused the jolt of adrenaline to flash through her veins, she opened her eyes to find James staring down at her in the darkness, his face a bare inch from hers, his eyes glowing silver. For a heartbeat, she thought he might have something amorous in mind, his body lay half over hers, one arm curled around the top of her head, the other across her body. But his posture was more protective than anything. His whole frame trembled, his lips drawn into a thin line.

He'd tugged the comforter over her, leaving her a small pocket for fresh air. The room had grown cold; their breath showed as little white puffs of steam. The ghost?

A shudder ran through James, and he lifted his hand to lay a finger across her lips. His breath shook out of him. "Shh."

A fresh surge of adrenaline pulsed through her veins and she tried to sit up, to see what caused the lines of strain on his face.

He pushed her back down. They struggled silently. She had no chance of winning their stalemate; he was far stronger. She didn't want to lie here quietly while he hurt. Tears welled in her eyes. Damn him.

He curled the arm he tucked around her head, drawing her face into the crook of his neck. Pressed his lips to her ear. "Be still."

Unable to do anything else, she lifted her hand and cupped his cheek, trying to soothe him. His arm tightened around her. So she pressed her lips to his throat. Quiet moments passed, seeming to bleed together. She was ready to scream in frustration by the time he slumped on top of her, unconscious.

Footsteps pattered across the floor. The door slammed. The house grew quiet. Dawn had arrived.

"James?"

A shiver of apprehension scuttled across her bones. He couldn't be dead. Vampires had already died. When taken from this world, they dissolved to ash, the remnants of their spirits relegated to the Eidolon Wastes to wander as the formless, voiceless. And James still had form.

She reached around his back. Just above his shoulder blade, her fingers skimmed a hole in his flesh. A big one.

"James?" She wriggled out from under his weight, envisioning light flooding the room. The lights flipped on, just as she rolled him onto his stomach.

The ghost had left two oval-shaped wounds, each about an inch around, on his back. The edges of his skin were red and raw, but beyond the layer of muscle tissue she saw nothing but a thick, inky blackness. No blood, no bone. He was empty.

Think.

She read something about vampires leaking energy the way humans bled. They could die, just like a human, from open wounds. She covered both wounds with her hands and closed her eyes. Gods, she wished she had her Grimoire. The few spells she remembered were child's play. Cleaning and turning lights on and off. Nothing that would help him heal. Nothing that would've protected him or herself. Useless, just like Nan had always said. Vampires self-healed; if she kept pressure on him long enough, his body would take care of the rest. Or she could bleed on the wounds.

She didn't need to cut off a limb, she just needed to

bleed on him. Reaching under his pillow, she grabbed the knife she'd examined earlier. She unsheathed it and drew the edge over the side of her hand, gasping at the bite of the blade. She smeared her blood over one of the wounds, then pressed her hand to the other.

Immediately, his skin started to grow. New pink flesh filled the void, making the wound smaller.

Lilith lifted her hand, squeezing the cut until more of her blood welled up and pressed it to the other wound. Within minutes, both disappeared, leaving nothing but scars. She grabbed a towel off his dresser and cleaned the remaining blood away. Then ran downstairs to get a bandage for her hand from the kitchen. When she returned, she crawled back into bed, covered them both with his blanket, and curled herself around her mate.

Three times now, he'd saved her. Blasted man. Her debts were stacking up

He'd been right. She wasn't in the same orbit as him. Not yet.

CHAPTER 12

James found Lou's mobile office parked in a darkened lot in downtown Bellevue. Three bikes were already lined up outside, suggesting half his team were already inside. He parked his bike and walked up to the bloodmobile.

As a phototroph, Lou's Vampiric talent allowed her to thrive in sunlight and like most, she worked two jobs. During the day, she earned her living as a phlebotomist. At night, she ran errands for him and the other Guardian in the area. Lou had added a new sticker to the back bumper: I BRAKE FOR VAMPIRES. In her profession, she could get away with such things. No one would believe the short, round, busty phlebotomist was a vampire anyway.

Walker, Ghost and Shadow all hustled out of the trailer and headed to their bikes. Walker caught sight of James. He paused and pointed to the trailer. "I'd keep your helmet on if you go in there."

Ghost chuckled as he dragged on his helmet. "She's been in a mood ever since you missed your last appointment. You all right?"

James rolled his eyes. "I'm fine."

Shadow shook his head. "Poor Ghost couldn't make payment tonight. She's not pleased."

Great. Lou wouldn't allow him to escape without paying up. Not if Ghost already got a pass. He rapped his knuckles on the door.

It swung out, revealing Lou's surprised face. "Hey, there's my man. Come on in, James."

James stepped into the small mobile home, the whole thing rocking under his weight. "How you been, Lou?"

"Worried." Her tone got stern. "You're two weeks late. How many years have I been doing this and you always keep the same routine. You come like clockwork on the first Thursday of the month. I started to think you were the one they referred to in the e-mail."

James shrugged, not wanting to discuss it. Last night he'd remembered something. Something he was sure accounted for his missing time . . . but the memory had faded by the time he woke. And tonight before he'd left the house, Lilith kept asking about him. How did he feel and was he all right. "Been busy. What happened?"

"I got an e-mail a couple weeks ago saying the west coast is down one Guardian." She shrugged. "That's all the Council ever tells us. We don't know who, unless one of our guys doesn't show up."

"I haven't gotten any messages saying my patrol area got bigger, so I doubt it's any of ours."

"Still, check in more often, will you?" Lou nudged him with a dimpled elbow. "I worry about you. You're my favorite."

"Why?"

"I guess I just like you big, surly guys." She poked him playfully in the chest.

He shook his head, grinning despite himself. "I meant, why the concern?"

"Well, I—" She glanced around as if checking for eavesdroppers.

Rolling his eyes toward the ceiling, he said, "Just us here, Lou."

"You gotta promise to keep this on the down low, a'right?" She waited for James to nod, then explained in a hushed voice, "So some of us, you know, we get bored, and no one tells us nothing. And with the way the Council monitors communication, we can't chat on our phones. So, some of us started keeping in touch on one of those human-vampire chat rooms."

He knew of the sites. A whole subculture existed of HVs—humans who wanted to be vampires—pleading among Internet predators to change them. HVs would do anything, pay anything, for a transformation. Those offering transformation were the worst sort of criminals. Occasionally, HVs just lost their savings—many didn't get away with their lives. "Please tell me you're not encouraging those people."

"No, no, of course not." Lou brushed away his concern. "We ignore the HVs, and everyone there thinks we're just like them. We don't get much attention. But anyway, don't interrupt if you want to hear this."

Crossing his arms over his chest, he gave her a pointed glare.

"'Kay, so here's the scoop: Between all of us, we've counted one hundred-thirteen Guardian destroyed. Most of those just in the last few weeks, mind you."

Her claim was outrageous. "That's not possible." The Guardian were trained warriors. Rarely did one fall, much less so many. Not even in times of war had the Guardians taken such a loss.

"You bet it's true, big guy. And I'll tell you another thing: The Council isn't replacing them."

Now that couldn't possibly be true. "How are all the territories getting coverage?"

"They're not," Lou said. "So Lin Sue over in Sapporo, Japan? They used to have six Guardians. Now she's the only one left in the region."

He couldn't believe the Council would shut down territories. Still, Lou was trustworthy. Her tale must be based in some kind of truth. "All right, I'll look into it. Listen, Lou, I'm sure this is nothing, but I don't want you to tell anyone else what you just told me." If what she said turned out to be true, trouble was brewing, and it came from home base. "Do me a favor, hop online and tell the others the same thing. One of you talks to the wrong person and you could all be in the kind of trouble you don't walk away from."

"Sure, James. A'right." Lou spun her chair toward the computer and relayed the message, her acrylic nails tapping across the keyboard. "It's posted. They'll all see it when they log in."

"Good."

"I got something for you." She spoke in a singsong voice, waggling her eyebrows.

"I hope so. I'd be upset to find out you gave away what's mine."

"We couldn't have that now, could we?" Lou picked up his backpack and started loading in units of blood, giving him tidbits of information on each. "So, now, this here is from Miss Jennings; lovely woman—doesn't drink, doesn't smoke. You'll like this. This here is from Mrs. Oliver. She's a doll, a real health nut. Oh, and guess who came by? Mr. Roberts, so I'm putting a unit of his in here, 'cause I know you prefer vegetarians." She winked at him and finished packing his bag.

"Thanks, Lou." He scrubbed his hand over his head. "Hey, listen, is there any chance I could get a little extra?"

Lou's eyebrows crept up high on her forehead.

Hell, he shouldn't have asked. None of them did. The only reason they needed more than what they got is if they had someone else to feed. "Actually, never mind."

"What's she like?"

He closed his eyes. "An angel." He shook his head. "I'm losing my fucking mind, Lou."

She grinned. "Give me two days. I'll have what you need."

"It's just in case. I probably won't need it."

"You'll have it if you do." She winked.

"Thanks." He got up, ready to leave.

"You ain't going anywhere yet. Ghost didn't have anything for me tonight." Her frown eased and she shot him a wink. "You know what I want."

Moaning, he fell back into a patient recliner. She'd been so distracted with everything else he thought he might escape before she remembered. "I swear, if you ever tell anyone. . . ."

"You know me better." She hugged the backpack to her chest. "This is purely for my own pleasure."

He slumped back in his chair, giving her one last glare before making his ridiculous payment. She started giggling before he'd even gotten halfway through the joke. He never had figured out if she found the bad jokes amusing, or if she found humor in his annoyed monotone but by the time he reached the punch line, Lou's laughter filled the blood mobile, and his payment was complete.

CHAPTER 13

Comfortable, you little bastard?"

Lilith slammed the kennel door shut on George and carried it into the ritual room. She'd searched the entire house twice before finding the damn cat and it was nearing 2:00 AM. James could return any time and she refused to go another night with both Aimee and the ghost to contend with.

She closed her fist around her bandaged palm. The odd thing was, James didn't seem to remember what happened this morning. When he'd woken, she'd asked him how he felt and the blank look he gave her didn't seem to be an act.

She managed to ensure they missed a twilight confrontation that evening by luring James outside so she could marvel over the repairs done on her car. Not only had his friends replaced the windshield, but they'd also repaired the bumper and replaced the airbag. The impossible man refused to let her pay for the damages, insisting she accept it as past rent.

Leave it to her to find the sweetest vampire in existence. As a child, she'd sat through countless daemonology lessons and never had it been even hinted that vampires might be anything other than cold-blooded killers.

James seemed to be anything but.

She eyed the kennel warily. Without access to her family Grimoire, she'd been forced to search online for various expulsions and binding spells. Without knowing exactly what Aimee was, finding the right binding spell proved difficult.

Her training stopped when she was ten years old, being an outcast from the coven, leaving her inexperienced and unpracticed. She didn't have as much knowledge as she would have liked for this undertaking. Banishing Aimee would be a matter of trial and error. She'd spent the evening doing research and practicing spells. She'd captured Aimee. She could do this. She could. No problem.

She dropped the kennel in the middle of a circle of thirteen brown and white candles and started the first ritual. "San Cipriano, I invoke thee." Though she shut all the doors and windows tight, the candles flickered as a breeze blew through the room.

"Lend me your experience and wisdom." She lit several bowls of incense—frankincense, jasper, sage— while speaking the rest of the incantation, and sprinkled turmeric on a bowl of smoldering resin. The smoke blended, letting off a heady, rich odor.

George sneezed.

"You'll be okay, George. Just kick her out." She waited, disappointed when nothing else happened. This wasn't the right ritual.

"So you're not an evil spirit." She flipped the page. "Then you must be some type of daemon."

She grabbed a large gilded mirror from the wall and walked around the room, letting everything reflect into the mirror, including George. She set the mirror against the wall. She held her hands over her head and visualized a bright light shining into the reflective glass. Starting as a small spark, the light grew into a brilliant ball of yellow light.

The kennel started to rattle. At first she thought the spell was pulling Aimee out of George and into the mirror, but the reflection remained the same, just her holding the ball of light and the room as usual. No daemon trapped in the glass.

Still, possessed George threw himself around violently. She edged closer to the kennel and the cat grew frantic. When she let the ball of light fade away, George settled. He reacted again when she created another orb.

Aimee wanted her Magic.

That's why Aimee attached to her. Why hadn't she realized this before? Probably because she'd been told both events were separate parts of her karmic punishment. As a child she'd trusted the high priestess and accepted Rowena's explanation. She'd felt guilty for her part in Nan's death and her expectation of retribution from the universe made her gullible. She hadn't lost her powers for her part in Nan's death, Aimee had been sucking the Magic right out of her.

White-hot rage shot through her veins. "Now I'm pissed." The only question was, had Rowena believed the rubbish she'd told Lilith or had she known what Aimee was?

She shook her head. Rowena was the only mother figure she had, and while strict and somewhat misguided in her beliefs, she didn't think the high priestess would ever intentionally hurt her.

The cage rattled with a vengeance.

Aimee must be some type of Magic-eating daemon and that meant any spell that included holy water should bind her tight. With a decent bestiary, she could pinpoint exactly what Aimee was. Maybe then she could figure out where it had come from. First things first, she had to get Aimee out of George before she killed the feline. She had holy water, so she could at least get Aimee bound into a jar. Now, she just needed a Bible.

Lilith ran upstairs to James' room and grabbed the Bible she'd seen there yesterday. Back in the ritual room, she rummaged through the items on the altar, selecting a bottle of holy water from Notre Dame, salt, and a glass jar with a lid.

Opening the Bible to Psalm 91—the psalm of exorcists—and read the verse out loud. The kennel stopped moving as Aimee listened. "You who dwell in the shelter of the Most High . . . ."

The kennel rattled violently and she raised her voice to be heard. The cage banged against the hardwood floor, knocking over candles.

Gods, she hoped she could do this.

James let himself into the house and glanced around. Lilith had turned on every single light in the place. Her voice came from the room under the stairs, her muffled words vaguely familiar.

When he first arrived he'd been curious about that room—about why a door shield remained intact there, but not on the front door. Whatever was in there, wasn't meant for his kind.

She banged on something behind the door. Her voice grew louder over the racket. He strained to make out her words, the rhythm tugging at his memory. A Bible verse?

There was a loud crash, then silence. He started to walk away.

Lilith screamed.

Swinging around, he eyed the door seal. How the hell was he going to get in there?

The old, rusty kennel gave up the battle, breaking apart.

George crouched, ears back, panting. He retched, as if he needed to cough up a fur ball. The cat dry-heaved a couple of times. His mouth opened in a too-wide feline yawn.

Aimee's three-fingered hands came out first, pulling the rest of her body in their wake, squeezing strangely out of the too-small opening. She shed George's body like a cheap coat, letting him fall in an exhausted heap on the floor. Aimee sprung, desperation making her quick, agile.

Lilith shouted, throwing the only weapon she had, the Bible.

"Lilith, are you okay?" James called through the door.

Damn. "Don't come in here. I'll be out in a minute." She hoped.

She scrambled away from Aimee, bumping into the small altar and sprawling to the floor. The contents of the altar scattered in every direction. Some of the bottles shattered, spilling essential oils and mixing with the burning incense embers. Flames leapt from the floor. For a heartbeat, Lilith froze. She needed to put the fire out, but Aimee—

The small entity jumped through the flames.

Lilith snatched up one of the summoning jars and darted out of reach.

Flames spread across the floor between them, forcing Aimee back. Outraged, she let out a high-pitched keening screech.

Lilith covered her ears.

"What's that noise?" Gods, he sounded worried. He pounded on the wall. "Answer me, Lilith."

She circled back to the upturned altar, keeping her eyes focused on Aimee. She needed the salt and holy water to finish the banishment.

James continued banging. "Answer me."

"I'm fine." Figured he'd decide tonight he wanted to be a Chatty Kathy. "Did you have a nice evening?"

Did I have a nice . . .? "What the hell are you playing at?"

Behind the door, her heart beat a frantic rhythm and a softer, even faster heart beat elsewhere in the room, which he recognized as George. Other displaced noises came from other areas. Something was in there with them and it didn't have a heartbeat. Whatever was in there was daemon. Which meant Lilith was in there fighting for her life and he was . . . unable to do a goddamned thing.

He needed to find a way to help her. He extended one finger, thinking to test the seal. The damn thing sensed his intention. A bolt of green energy leapt out to meet his finger. The charge threw him back. He bounced off the far wall and landed in a heap on the floor. For a moment, he lay still, catching his breath and trying to regain his wits.

An otherworldly shriek came from inside the room. He sprang to his feet and flew to the door. Lilith's screams punctuated each of the previous shrieks. This time she made no sound.

"Lilith? I asked you what that noise was!"

"Uh, just George." She wished he would shut up and let her concentrate. Where had the holy water fallen? "I'm giving him a bath."

Lilith pulled a face. Why'd she say that? He'd never believe it.

She spied the bag of salt in the debris. Bending down, she scooped it up as she passed. She needed the damn holy water. Dodging around the growing flames, she stayed just ahead of Aimee. She opened the jar and poured a handful of salt into it before dropping the bag on the floor and resealing the jar. Where was the holy water? Smoke filled the room, burning her nose and throat. Her eyes watered, making it difficult to see.

Aimee had the advantage now. She stood low to the floor, well under the gathering smoke. Her claws clicked against floor, sometimes skidding across the slippery hardwoods.

Lilith paused, searching the debris for the bottle of holy water and Aimee took advantage, leaping toward her with her claws extended. She darted away from Aimee, going back the way she came. There. The bottle of holy water had gotten wedged underneath the altar.

Flames surrounded the whole thing.

Aimee screeched, rushing her again. Lilith lunged back, but wasn't quick enough. The entity grasped her legs, tripping her. Lilith fell, yelping as Aimee's sharp claws clung to her leg, piercing her skin.

"Lilith, invite me in." James' voice sounded rough with anxiety.

"No." A coughing fit gripped her. She kicked her leg to get Aimee off, but the creature clung tight. Aimee's claws tore at her flesh as she climbed higher.

"There's smoke coming from under the door."

Like she didn't know the damn room was on fire. "I'm busy." Coughs punctuated her words. She rolled onto her belly and crawled to the altar, clutching the summoning jar in one hand. Reaching into the flames, she grabbed for the bottle. She gasped. Oh, gods that hurt.

"Jesus, Lil, please. Invite me in."

It took three more tries before she finally grabbed the bottle of holy water.

Aimee crawled onto her back, her claws digging in, puncturing her skin.

"Just say the damn words and I can help you." James thumped the wall hard.

She rolled to her right, taking Aimee toward the flames. The entity screeched and let go.

Getting to her feet, she opened the summoning jar and set it in front of her. She uncapped the holy water. "Come on. Where'd you go?"

"Damn it, Lilith, will you answer me?"

Aimee rounded the altar, leaping for her face.

Startled into action, Lilith swung the bottle of holy water. The spray splashed across the entity, leaving smoking pustules across her skin.

Aimee shrieked. Her body becoming vaporous as she was sucked down into the summoning jar toward the salt. Lilith slammed the lid back onto the jar and screwed it on tight.

"Ha, got you!" She shook the jar. "Oh gods, I really did it." She laughed. "I can't believe I actually trapped you."

"That's it. I'm coming in."

Lilith's gaze flew to the door, then darted around the wrecked room, the oils, and the altar . . . the fire.

She closed her eyes and visualized a tropical rain falling in the ritual room. The pull of Magic tugged at her aura. Thunder rumbled through the room. Thick clouds gathered across the ceiling.

It began to rain.

James strode into the kitchen, grabbed one of the chairs, and returned to the front hall, holding it in front of him like a battering ram. He hoped to break down the door with the chair before he got zapped by the door shield. If she was trapped, he'd at least give her an exit.

After two strides, Lilith opened the door and he came to an abrupt halt. Smoke billowed out around her.

She smiled, dripping all over the floor, looking like she'd been the one taking a bath. Her hair was wet, her pajamas damp, clinging.

He set the chair on the floor with exaggerated care, and glared. Taking a couple deep, assuaging breaths, he tried to calm down. She was alive.

George meowed. The drenched feline skulked out between Lilith's legs and shot up the stairs like he had demon hounds hard on his tail, leaving a trail of water in his wake.

He stared at Lilith, incredulous. Her expression epitomized innocence. Yeah, there was no way in hell she realized blood bloomed through her pajamas. Between that and the smoke, she had another thing coming if she expected he'd buy the bath story. "You gave my cat a bath?"

"Mm-hm." She held out his Bible. "I'm sorry." She shrugged. "I borrowed your book." He reached out to take it and water gushed out under the force of his grip.

She cringed. "It, ah, got a little damp."

He ignored her confession and let the ruined book fall onto the chair with a wet thwack. "Do we need to call the fire department?" All things considered, he sounded amazingly calm. "Maybe an ambulance?"

"Don't be silly. It was just a little incense run amok." An ill-timed coughing fit gripped her. "Everything is fine." She waved her hand in front of her face. "Was there much smoke out here? You sound choky, too."

He counted the rafters in the ceiling. She was safe, that's all that mattered and despite the blood, she didn't appear too badly hurt. Still, he had an overwhelming desire to paddle her ass. Once in control, he scrutinized her from top to bottom through narrowed eyes. She was a mess—a beautiful mess to be sure, but a mess nonetheless. "I think it's your turn." He motioned her into the kitchen.

"My turn for what?" She closed the door behind her.

"You're bruised." He pointed to her face where her cheek had started to swell. "And bleeding, and what's this?" He lifted her arm. "Oh, burned. As if from fire." He kept hold of her arm and walked toward the kitchen. "Just for future reference, you're supposed to use water for a bath. Not flames."

CHAPTER 14

Her mate had a sarcastic streak.

Lilith let him lead her into the kitchen. She was tired and, of course, as soon as he'd brought attention to her injuries, they started hurting like hell. "Has anyone ever told you, you're grumpy when you get home from work?"

"No. No one's ever tolerated my surly nature long enough to notice." He lifted her up onto the counter like he might do for a child.

She smiled despite her soreness. "I think you might have just made a joke."

He shot her a little half grin. The transformation in his face made her breath catch in her throat. His whole countenance changed when he smiled. A handsome male even when scowling, that little grin made him irresistible.

He handed her a dishtowel. "Dry off."

She patted her face and arms as he searched the drawers. "Where's the smelly stuff you made for me?"

"You told me you wouldn't need any more."

He raised his brow a notch, calling her bluff.

"Fine. Top drawer, next to the sink."

He held a jar up and, when she nodded, he opened it, making a face when the smell assailed him. He stuck his fingers in the goo and proceeded to apply it to her cheek.

"Mm, somehow I had the feeling you wouldn't listen to me."

"Mm, somehow I had the feeling you would need it again," she mocked.

He'd been fighting again. She dipped her finger in the jar and dabbed at his mouth where the skin split on his lower lip. She'd have rather leaned forward and kissed him. Let her tongue slide over his full lower lip and . . . . "Besides," she said to break the silence and force her mind from her imaginings, "I needed it tonight."

His expression darkened. "Don't do that again."

"What?"

"Whatever you—" He seemed to realize he'd been yelling and stopped. He took a deep breath, his gaze meeting hers. "Whatever you were doing in there. I couldn't get to you."

"Were you worried?" No one but Trina ever worried about her. Warmth spread through her limbs. "I thought you didn't even like me." Gods, why did she say that? Of course he didn't like her. He pretty much told her that outright last night.

"What about the burn?"

"Cantharis. In the same drawer there's a tiny brown bottle with a red label." He pointed to a bottle. "Yep. Just mix it with gel from—" He pointed to the bottle of gel she'd used before. "Yeah. See, you're a natural."

"I didn't say that." He smoothed the cantharis over the blisters on her forearm. The gel soothed her inflamed skin as soon as it touched her arm.

"What?"

His head bent down to his task, bringing his face close to hers. "I never said I didn't like you."

"You like me?"

He glanced up, and froze. If either chose to move a fraction of an inch . . . . He straightened. "Don't push your luck."

She grinned at his disgruntled tone, which earned her a glare. She was starting to understand, the surliness and sarcasm were armor, and underneath, well, she couldn't wait to find out what lay underneath.

"What about a bandage?"

"There's gauze in the second drawer." She pulled off the wet bandage around her hand. The cut had stopped bleeding and scabbed over. She didn't need to rewrap it.

"Why do you keep this stuff in the kitchen?" Gently, he wound gauze around her arm.

"Easy access. We tend to be a bit accident prone." Spells didn't always work the way they intended. He didn't need to know specifics, though.

"You and Trina?"

"Yeah." She got the word out before a yawn snuck up on her. "Although I think after tonight George should probably join the ranks." She shrugged, smiling. "You seem a bit accident-prone yourself. You'll fit right in."

He didn't appear to appreciate her comment. "What for the cuts?"

"Arnica."

He eased the loose, damp fabric of her pajamas as high as they would go in search of the wounds causing spots of blood to bloom on her clothing.

Not wanting to see the damage, she kept her gaze on his face.

He grimaced and shook his head as he went to work. Gods, he was handsome. All she wanted to do right now was find out what the scruff on his chin felt like against the sensitive skin of her neck.

"How'd you learn about this stuff?"

"Nan taught me."

"The old woman?"

She nodded. "My grandmother."

His hand stopped moving. His gaze shot up.

She looked away. "I'm not like her." She didn't even like claiming Nan as family.

He lifted her chin until she met his gaze. "I didn't think you were. I'm just surprised. I guess I should have realized when you said you inherited this place."

Her body ached something fierce. The effects of the oils made her drowsy as they seeped into her bloodstream but a surplus of adrenaline still flowed through her. Sleep would be a long time coming.

James pulled down her pant leg, released her leg, and pointed to her stomach. She glanced down to see blood staining the front of her favorite lavender tank. "Oh, damn. I liked this pajama top."

James chuckled as he lifted the bottom edge high enough to treat the scratch on her belly.

"What?"

"I think most women would be falling into hysterics right now."

"You have a low opinion of women."

"I just meant most people freak out about their wounds long before they notice their clothes are ruined." He pulled her shirt down.

She shrugged in response. "I liked the lacy straps."

Angling around, he started to lift the back of her tank. Understanding he intended to inspect her back for injury, she straightened and shoved him away. "I'm fine, you don't need to—"

"Quit being a baby."

"James." She frowned. "It's ugly. Just leave it alone."

CHAPTER 15

*S*hit.

He'd forgotten. Of course she'd have scars from that night. The old woman, her grandmother, beat her until she'd bled and then beat her some more.

James sat the salve on the counter, drew off his shirt and tossed it next to her.

She stared.

He shrugged. "I have more than you."

A rueful grin tugged at her lips. "Scars are kinda hot on guys. Not so much on women."

"You gay?"

Her brows beetled in confusion.

"If you're not into women, then your opinion of what's sexy on a woman is a bit skewed."

She frowned. "I'm too tired to figure out what you just said, but I'm sure you're wrong. I like you with your shirt off, though, so I'll forgive you."

He released a startled laugh. "Jesus, you're a piece of work."

She tried to wink, but she must've been tired as hell, because her lid stuck, as if preferring to stay closed.

He chuckled. Christ, she was cute as hell. "Come on, Aphrodite. You're about to fall off the counter you're so tired. If you're not going to let me take care of those cuts, we're done." He forced her to look at him. "Go get ready for bed."

"And you call me bossy." She leaned forward and kissed his cheek.

Just a quick brush of her lips on his skin, but his face burned where her lips touched.

"Thank you."

He managed a nod.

She slipped off the counter and left the kitchen without another word.

James released a deep breath.

Hell, he wasn't sure he could remain here, in this house, so close to her without touching her. He'd never wanted a woman as much as this one. But giving in would condemn them both.

The Watchers saw everything.

And then there was the problem with Crowley. If, indeed, he did have to terminate the son of a bitch, he'd be on the run for the rest of his existence. At which point, the Watchers would probably assign her a new bodyguard if she still needed one.

Fuck. There was no way to come out the winner in this situation.

Except maybe paradise would be at the other end of his sacrifice. James snorted. Not fucking likely. Not with the lusty thoughts Lilith provoked.

Once James finished cleaning up the kitchen he turned off the light and went into the living room to do the same.

Lilith was curled up in the high-backed arm chair in the corner with her book. She'd changed into some kind of baby-doll night shirt that left way too much of her long, shapely legs uncovered.

He almost went upstairs. Would have, maybe, if his hands had stopped shaking. But not being able to get to her when she'd been in danger still sat too fresh in his mind.

"Not ready to sleep?"

She shook her head and glanced up. "I'm a bit wound up still."

"Me, too." She looked better. The cuts and scrapes seemed smaller now that the bleeding had stopped. She kept the arm he'd bandaged cradled in her lap. "Do you need painkillers or anything?"

"I took some Ibuprofen." She didn't even look up from her book.

He sat in the center of the couch, toed off his boots and propped his feet on the ottoman. He'd never bothered coming in this room before. It had a warm ambiance.

Bullshit. He scoffed. The only warm thing in this entire house was Lilith. He studied her while she read, following the line of her legs down to her pink nail polish. He blew out a breath of frustration.

"You don't have to stay with me."

"Don't think I can sleep, either."

"Oh." She started to lift her book again, then let it fall back to her lap. "Do you want one of your books from upstairs?"

"Nah." He was too damn tired to bother. "What are you reading?" James closed his eyes and let his head rest on the back of the couch. If he didn't stop staring at her he'd have a tent in the front of his jeans.

"Um, well, it's a story about a Marine who gets involved with—"

Military. "Perfect. Read to me."

"Read this? Out loud?"

"Yeah. Why not?" He cracked his eyes open to catch her gaping at him. Hell, had his request been so odd? "Never mind."

"No. I'll read. From the beginning?"

"Whatever page you're on." He didn't care about the plot, he just wanted to hear her voice and calm himself before they went to bed. He closed his eyes again.

"Okay." She drew the one word out on a sigh before clearing her throat. "'She spread her lips wide over Donovan's engorged shaft, tonguing him until he moaned.'"

James' eyes flew open.

"'His fingers tangled in her hair, guiding her into a rhythm that had her growing damp with desire, had her rocking her hips to and fro as if his cock already plunged deep inside her aching c—'"

"What the hell are you reading?"

She lifted her gaze and blinked. Sat there in that pristine white nightgown, with the prim scoop neck, looking as innocent as a choir girl. "It's called 'Coming Home.'"

"I'll bet." More like cuming home. "It's porn."

"It's a romance. There's this Marine who—"

"—shoves his dick down some lady's throat."

Lilith gasped. "No." She set the book aside. "It's . . . well, it's . . . ." Her lips twisted into a rueful grin. "There's a story line. A romance. That lady happens to be his wife, who he's learning to love again after being away at war."

"Fine, it has a storyline. That makes it soft porn."

"It's a beautiful story."

He waved his hand toward the book. "Why are you reading that?"

"Why not?" Her humor disappeared. "Don't you go getting all high and mighty. I read 'this stuff'"—she picked up the book and shook it at him—"because it's filling a need. And because I like these stories."

"What need? You're a beautiful woman. You could have any guy you wanted."

Her gaze narrowed. "I call bullshit."

Warning sirens went off in his head. He sensed a trap, but he'd be damned if he could see what the hell it was. "Have you even tried to meet someone?"

"Why, yes. Yes, I have." She folded her arms over her chest. "And I have met men. Men who I flirted with. Some, I even kissed. And they all shut me down."

Christ, she wasn't talking about men, she was talking about him. "We both know I'm no good for you. I'm too damn old. And I don't do virgins."

"I'm not a virgin."

His mouth went dry. "Now I call bullshit."

"Why?"

"You move like one." They shouldn't be talking about this. "You don't flirt right."

"I don't . . .?" she sputtered, her face turning red.

"Now, don't get upset." He gave a little wave of his hand. "You're cute. Adorable. Not sexy."

"I can do sexy." She stood and walked across the room, sitting primly on the ottoman next to his outstretched legs. She leaned back on one arm, crossing her legs and tossing her hair back. One strap slipped off her shoulder and she quickly put it back where it belonged, wincing from using her injured arm to do so.

He wet his lips. "Like I said, cute."

She slumped. "What am I doing wrong?"

"How the hell am I supposed to know? I'm not a woman, I don't know."

"Well, you obviously know enough to tell me I'm doing it wrong."

And there it sat, the great yawning abyss. He'd walked straight into the trap. Now he either needed to retreat, or explain. And he never retreated. "They"—he made a twirling motion with his hand—"move different."

"How?"

He scowled. "They . . . ." He tilted his hand side to side. "Well, when they walk, they—" Christ, he had no idea how to explain this. "You said you've had sex."

She shrugged. "Once. He was pretty drunk. It certainly wasn't anything like what I read about in—"

"Forget the goddamn book."

Wide-eyed, she stared.

"I shouldn't have yelled. Sorry."

"You don't understand. I mean look at you." She waved a hand toward him. "I can't imagine you've had this problem in your life. Women probably fall all over you. I can't even get a man to look at me."

"Oh, I guarantee they're looking." Looking.

Fantasizing. Masturbating to the memory.

"Then they obviously don't like what they see."

Christ, she was gutting him. "Like hell."

"So what's the problem?"

"You move like a virgin."

She pulled a face. "Seriously? We're back to that?"

"It's a big damn deal." He threw his arm to the side. "It means long-term commitment."

"You don't have to growl at me." She looked away, but not before he caught the glimmer of tears in her eyes. "I'm not looking for long-term anything. I just want to feel wanted. Just once."

Wanted?

She wanted to feel . . . .

Oh, he wanted her.

He dragged his hand over his scalp, then scrubbed at his face. *Shit.* He sat up. "Close your eyes."

She cut him an uncertain glance, but complied.

"Now, be still." He scooted the ottoman closer and, as he inhaled her scent—lavender and woman—his dick took notice. Hell, he was fucked six ways to Sunday. He couldn't take this too far, couldn't take anything for himself. He'd just give her a taste of how it was meant to be. Let her get her confidence back. And then go take a long, cold shower.

He put his hand to the back of her neck, delving his fingers into her hair. Holy Mother of God, she was soft. So fucking warm. All he wanted to do—

"Are you going to kiss me?"

"No."

Focus, you rat bastard.

"I'm going to teach you how to move sexy."

And probably self-combust in the process.

"Relax. Let your head fall back."

She jerked, opening her eyes.

"Keep 'em closed." He couldn't think straight when staring into those deep brown eyes of hers. "Breathe."

A forgotten breath shook out of her lungs.

"Good." He leaned forward, and though he said he wouldn't, he brushed her lips with his, sipping at her sweetness until the full weight of her head rested in his palm. "When a woman entices a man, she's giving him a glimpse of what she'll be like in bed." He ran his hand down her cheek, the curve of her neck. "Each is different, some are coy, some blatant, others almost secretive, but they all move like they do in bed."

Her lips spread in a smile, as if she thought the idea ludicrous. He ran his tongue over her full bottom lip, erasing her humor. "I'm not saying they walk around thrusting their hips and moaning."

She laughed, a low husky sound that shot straight to his gut.

"But when they move, they remind a man of the long, sensual grasp and pull right before orgasm. Have you experienced that?"

She nodded. "By myself."

Already half aroused, the image her admission brought to mind had his cock standing at full attention. He closed his eyes, trying to get himself under control. "It's different during intercourse. There's not that steady, perfect beat taking you straight to the finish line. It's all about the getting there."

"Show me."

Just a taste. Give her a taste and build her confidence. Just a taste so you can get her out of your head.

"Spread your thighs." Christ, his voice sounded like wet gravel.

She uncrossed her legs, parting them, leaving him just enough room to slip her naughty book between her knees had he so desired. Jesus, she was adorable. Sweet. Tempting.

He placed his foot between hers, nudging her legs apart. Bit by bit she widened her stance, his foot chasing hers until she had spread her legs wide, her nightgown stretched tight over the tops of her thighs. "Mm, good.

Now put your good arm behind you and lean back."

The position thrust her small, pert breasts out. God, he was a base bastard. He drew his hands down, over her breasts, stomach, hips, and thighs, her thin nightgown doing little to shield her from his touch. "You're beautiful. Sweet."

"I'm tired of being sweet."

"Nah. You don't want to lose that." He dragged his palm up her silky thigh. "Makes a man think of all the ways he can corrupt you." *Like me. Right now. Trying to think of every way I can get inside you without completely debasing you.* He cupped her heat, barely stifling the low moan wanting to break past his lips. Her panties were damp.

Her lips parted and she pressed into his palm with a sultry roll of her hips.

"Mm. See? There it is."

"What?"

Just a little more.

He slipped his hand under the white scrap of lace, groaning at the damp heat waiting. She must be aroused from that damned book, but for now, he'd let himself imagine her desire belonged to him.

You shouldn't.

He followed the soft seam of her sex, back and forth, sinking deeper with each pass.

"James." She arched, her eyelids squeezing tight as she tried to help him find her entrance. His middle finger pressed past her lips and sank deep.

Her breath came fast and shallow. The pulse at the base of her neck thrummed so hard it fluttered just beneath her skin. He withdrew a bit and added a second finger, pressing the heel of his hand to her clit. "Find your pleasure, Lilith."

She froze, her entire being stilling.

"Breathe, baby." He curled his fingers inside her, pressed his lips to her throat. "Come on. Pretend that's me." A shiver ran through her. "My cock buried deep inside you. What do you do?" He tightened his grip on her hip, guiding her into a slow, easy pace.

She rocked her hips. With each languorous thrust, her breasts rose, their tight peaks teasing him through the thin, white gown. Her head lolled back, all those rich brown locks cascading down her back.

He kissed her bared throat, needing to be closer, skimmed his teeth down the curve of her neck. This was torture. He wanted her naked. He wanted her spread out before him so he could feast on her. He wanted his dick in her. His fingers. His tongue. Teeth. He wanted it all.

I've seen what will come to pass between you and her. It's an abomination.

No. He wouldn't let things go that far. He'd stop. But he wanted more.

You'll never get what you truly want.

"James, please. It's not enough."

Beyond reason, he lifted her, dragged her panties down her legs and hauled her into his lap so she straddled him. He eased her back down onto his hand, this time slipping his thumb into her pussy, his damp fingers pressing against the puckered rosette behind.

Her eyes opened. Not brown eyes. Not now. They burned with jade fire, pinning him in his own skin. She was going to reject him and it would damn well kill him. He'd pushed too hard and she was going to tell him to fuck off.

She took her bottom lip between her teeth and sank down. She gasped as he breached her with his finger, her own slick desire easing his entrance to her virgin hole. Her body clamped down around his digits, fluttering in anxiety over the new intrusion.

And still she held his gaze.

"Easy, Lil. Give yourself a minute." He sure as hell needed a minute. He was about to come in his goddamn pants. He was supposed to be giving her the lesson, not the one being schooled. "You got this, baby." Hell, yeah, she did. He'd never been this turned on by a woman. "Show me sexy."

CHAPTER 16

Oh, she could do that, because for the first time in her life, she felt sexy.

James watched her every move with a hunger she'd never experienced being the recipient of, but had always longed to. The deep rumble of his voice urged her on. His shattered breaths were loud bursts in the silence around them. The scent of his arousal chased hers.

She closed her eyes, squirming down harder on his hand, her whole frame shivering from the slick glide of his fingers. Lilith arched her back, bringing her breasts up and shaking out her hair as she rotated her hips, grinding down on both his hand and the bulge of his erection.

Now she understood. As she chased the pleasure he offered, her body had taken over, knowing how to move. How to entice and seduce. She undulated over him in an erotic lap dance, bringing her hands down over her neck, lowering the scooped neck of nightgown to reveal her breasts.

He jerked her closer. Latched onto one puckered tip. Shock waves rocked through her, making her lose her rhythm. She wrapped her arms around his head and pressed her lips to his smooth scalp.

Cool air teased her damp nipple as he abandoned it in search of the other. He nipped her, stroked his tongue over the bud and drew it into his mouth. He held her tight to his body, urging her to a faster pace.

She tried to draw back, not wanting the moment to end, but he wouldn't let her, holding her fast and curling his fingers inside her. So she moved, seeking pleasure for them both, rocking so she dragged against the engorged length of his arousal confined in his jeans.

He cursed, tensed under her, and lifted his hips up in one long, needful thrust.

Wet heat bloomed under her thigh and she knew he'd come.

She'd made her mate come.

Her inner muscles tightened, and she shouted as she pushed past that invisible boundary, her body pulsing out her euphoria. He withdrew his fingers and pressed his thumb to her clit, drawing out her pleasure.

After, she held tight to him for several minutes as she waited for her heart to slow, for their breath to return to normal.

"Don't move." He set her on the couch and went upstairs. A few moments later he came back in fresh jeans with a washcloth. He kissed her while he tended to her. Slow needy sips and teasing bites.

And then he laid her back on the couch, curling himself around her and whispering the silliest praise.

She tucked her face beneath his chin, hiding her ridiculous smile and tried to ignore the absent heartbeat beneath her ear. Tried to ignore how foolish and dangerous this was.

Who knew a vampire could touch her heart? No. She'd misstated the situation. He hadn't touched her heart.

Her smile faded. He'd stolen it outright.

Lilith woke alone.

He'd left her on the couch with nothing but one of the dust covers to keep her warm.

Bastard.

After he'd taken such sweet care of her, he did this?

She flipped aside the sheet and sat up, rubbing the sleep from her eyes.

He'd been wonderful.

She frowned. Actually, he really had. Leaving her here, alone, was completely out of character.

Something rammed against a wall upstairs so hard the pictures shook in the living room.

She jumped to her feet and, trying to make as little noise as possible, went upstairs.

The closer she got to his room, the faster her heart pumped. The noises coming from the room suggested James struggled with someone in there. She pressed her back to the wall next to his door.

"You're unnatural." The raspy voice, brittle and light as fallen leaves, wasn't familiar.

"Fuck you." James sounded odd. Weak.

A brief struggle followed his curse. The wall shook again.

"I'll stop this abomination. I won't let you destroy everything."

Lilith nudged the door wider, and as they came into view, the air seemed to congeal in her lungs.

That was no ghost.

It must have been feeding off James for quite a while because it had become a skin-walker—nearly corporeal, but it still looked far from human. Reed thin, its brownish-gray skin was pulled tight over thick bones. It had four arms. With two, it held James against the wall, his feet dangling. The other two ended in hooks buried in his chest. The skin-walker stiffened, began to turn.

Lilith pushed her back against the wall, holding her breath. That's why he didn't want her involved. The skin-walker would never become fully corporeal feeding off a vampire. But if the skin-walker did the same to her . . . it could possess her, or take her life force for its own, killing her.

Briefly, she considered attacking it with Magic. She

was stronger after her bout with Aimee, but she still didn't trust herself. She might just as easily hurt James as the skin-walker—and that was only if whatever spell she came up with didn't backfire.

"What's a matter? Losing your appetite already?" His words slurred, as if he could barely stay awake.

He must be trying to pull the skin-walker's attention back to him. Gods, she'd put him into an impossible situation.

"Where are you going?"

Shit.

The other two bedroom doors were both closed. Lilith padded down the hall to the bathroom. She slipped inside just as the skin-walker entered the hall. She didn't dare close the door, instead she stepped into the tub, hiding behind where the shower curtain bunched at one side.

With each footfall, something heavy dragged on the floor in its wake.

James.

She put her hand over her mouth. The sounds of struggle had stopped. Either he'd passed out or was trying to prevent those hooks from tearing his chest wide open.

The skin-walker came closer, opening the doors to both bedrooms, listening. Searching.

How long until dawn? Surely astronomical twilight must be over.

Closer.

Thump, drag.

Her heart skipped in her chest.

Thump, drag.

A vicious tremor shook her so hard, she feared the skin-walker might hear the whisper of her nightgown over her flesh.

Closer.

The skin-walker stood outside the bathroom door. Must be listening to her, listening to it.

She didn't dare peek around the shower curtain. The bit of navy blue cloth was a paltry defense.

Adrenaline ran rampant through her veins, making her skin crawl. Making her itch with the need to run. To scream. To do something.

Minutes passed. She hoped they were minutes, but, gods, she couldn't tell. It felt like hours. Her body grew tired, aching from standing rigid. The adrenaline, having not been expended, made her light-headed. Her belly roiled.

Was the skin-walker waiting? Letting her grow confident it had departed so she'd walk right into its hooks? Or had dawn arrived? If dawn had arrived, that meant James lay unconscious on the floor, leaking the last of his energy while she cowered.

An old prayer her mother taught her came to mind.

Watchers of old, Watchers of night,

Please keep me safe in darkness and light.

She peeked around the edge of the curtain.

Nothing.

Watchers of old . . .

Her mind latched onto the prayer and kept her imagination at bay. Chanting the words in her head kept fear from paralyzing her.

She stepped out of the tub, listening.

Nothing.

Edging towards the door, she paused as each sliver of hallway came into view.

James lay on the floor, unconscious.

Watchers of old . . .

She poked her head out the door and, seeing the empty hall, stepped over him. She needed his blade.

Bit by bit, she crept down the hall, pausing at each room, listening before moving on. With each step she grew more confident. Dawn must have arrived, forcing the skin-walker back to wherever it existed between twilights.

Quickly, she went into James' room and retrieved the

knife from under the pillow.

She whirled around.

There, the skin-walker rose to full height, towering over her. Glowering down at her. Its face drawn tight into an all-too-familiar mask of disapproval.

Nan.

She screamed.

Nan lashed out with all four arms.

And vanished with a howl.

Lilith's breath shuddered out of her, only to hitch again as James lurched into the doorway. He leaned heavily against the jamb. "What happened? You okay?"

"Get in bed, you foolish man." She ducked under his arm, helping him across the room. They barely made it before he passed out, half on, half off the bed. She struggled to get his feet up, and pulled a pillow under his head.

She cut her hand, re-opening the wound from last night and let her blood drip into the wounds on his chest. "You're foolish. Brave. Very dear. But stupid."

He didn't respond. Likely, he wouldn't remember any of this. And the protection he'd provided, was now at an end. Nan had seen her. When twilight arrived, she'd be coming for her.

She'd have to risk going to the coven. At the very least, she needed her mother's Grimoire for a spell that would send Nan back where she belonged.

Good gods, had this been what the notes spoke of?

The truth lies in the past.

The future lies in the past.

So was Nan her future?

Or her truth?

CHAPTER 17

That afternoon, James woke to the sound of the doorbell.

Groggy and feeling as though he hadn't slept a wink, he growled, slitting his eyes.

The door downstairs opened and he heard Lilith's voice. Jesus, what the hell was wrong with him? He felt . . . hung-over. Sick.

What the hell had happened last night? He remembered coming home and not being able to get to Lilith when she'd been in danger. He'd tended her wounds . . . Oh, Christ. He'd tended *her.* Quite thoroughly.

His cock hardened as he recalled her coming apart in his arms, the scent and feel of her wet heat. *Fuck.* So much for not taking anything for himself.

He pulled himself out of bed. He still had his goddamn pants on. He hadn't taken their indiscretion any further, at least. But the last thing he remembered was curling up behind her on the couch downstairs. He must've been half asleep when he'd come up.

He grabbed some clean clothes and headed to the bathroom.

"Good morning."

Lilith's voice brought him to a stop. She stood at the base of the stairs, a beaming smile on her face. The front door stood wide open and a big, burly male shouldered his way in carrying a box. With a wave of her hand, she said, "The rest of my stuff arrived from my storage unit today."

He must have frowned because she started up the stairs. "It's not much."

James held the bundle of clothes in front of his crotch, trying to hide the fact that he still had a raging hard-on. She looked beautiful this morning. Glowing. *Stop looking for signs she enjoyed last night as much as you did. She's not glowing, that's the fucking sunlight lighting up her hair.*

Sunlight. She was allowing sunlight to invade his sanctuary. "How long is this going to take?"

"Not long. By the time you're done with your shower, they'll be gone." Her brows drew together. "Are you all right?"

"Yeah."

She searched his face. "You don't look too well. Maybe you should rest more."

"I'm fine."

"James, about last night . . ." She walked up to the landing.

"It won't happen again."

"Gods, I hope not, I was terrified."

Terrified? Oh, Christ, what had he done? He searched his memory, but she'd never said no. Never hinted she didn't want him to keep going. "Look, I shouldn't have touched you." He looked everywhere but at her. Jesus. He knew to expect her to shut him down, but this must be a record even for him. "You didn't exactly tell me no."

She touched his arm. "I wasn't talking about you touching me. That I liked. That, I'd love to happen again."

His gaze shot to hers. Her eyes were warm, her expression open. *What the hell was he missing?* "Then why say you're terrified of me?"

"Not you. The ghost." She laid her hand on his chest. "What did it do to you?"

He shook his head. "You must've been dreaming."

She frowned, glancing away. "But you feel all right?"

"Yeah. Fine." Christ, she looked entirely too kissable. "I gotta clean up."

He went to the bathroom, stripped down, and took a quick shower. He dried off, wrapped the towel around his waist, and wiped the steam off the mirror. He didn't expect to see his reflection and he didn't. Still, he couldn't help but check now and again.

From the way most reacted to him, he'd always assumed he was hideous, frightening. He glanced down at himself. His body was covered in scars and he'd fed recently, so the bruises from his fights discolored his skin, as well. Not what most would consider attractive. But in Lilith's eyes . . . . Well, he saw himself differently when she looked at him.

He stroked his hand over his bare head and down his face, trying to determine his features. His skin was smooth, two eyebrows just where he would expect them to be, and two eyes below. His nose was straight, his mouth felt like what he thought a normal mouth should. He didn't find any major deformation. Maybe he wasn't so terrible to look at.

He rubbed his hand over the rough stubble along his chin. Every time Lilith dropped one of her feather-light kisses on his face, her skin reddened from his whiskers. James opened the medicine cabinet and found a razor. He lathered some soap, smoothed it over his stubble, and shaved. Jesus, if the Vampiric Council could see him, they'd be disgusted.

But they couldn't possibly understand. Lilith had shaped his whole existence as a daemon. That's why he was fascinated with her. After he'd killed her all those centuries ago, he'd been transformed physically into a daemon. The guilt from his actions, his inability to see past the confines of his human life made him rebel. He'd been bastard for the majority of his existence as a vampire. He'd lived for himself, shunning any morals he'd had in his human life.

Until the Watchers directed him to save Lilith. He'd started coming around then. He'd realized the life he had gave him no pleasure and only added to his guilt. He'd crafted a set of morals to live by, and stuck to them. And now, all he wanted to do was break those morals. He wanted to be a part of her life. He wanted to be a part of her. Christ, he just wanted her. But eventually, she'd hate him.

He shook his head. In his human life, he did his best to ignore women after he'd taken his vows. Then, as a vampire, he'd used them and allowed them to use him to slake lust. Only now, after all this time, did it occur to him what he really wanted.

A mate. And why not? The Historian had taken a mate.

When he finished shaving, he rubbed his hand over the smooth surface of his skin. Better.

He banged the razor on the edge of the sink a couple of times. Hair didn't fall to the sink.

Ash did. It bled into the running water, turning the liquid black.

James closed his eyes. What was he doing? He wasn't human. He didn't have a soul. Couldn't have a mate. She'd run screaming from him if she ever really saw him or the things he did every night. And if the Council found out about her, he'd cease to exist.

Lilith had sexy down pat.

They had spent the afternoon moving boxes and talking amiably. She continued to break down his defenses, and he tried to ignore her smiles, her touches. She was constantly touching him—placing her hand on his, touching his arm, and patting his knee. And if she wasn't touching him, she was reminding him of last night with the soft sway of her hips. He didn't know how much more he could take.

If that wasn't enough, she had changed the house,

too. Transforming Haven House from an occasional sanctuary to something he never expected to have, something he hadn't thought to desire—a home. It was more than the stuff she decorated the place with, more than the cleanliness or the pleasant scents. He had memories here, now. Because of her.

And it was slowly killing him, because he still couldn't figure out what she was or how much about daemon-kind she knew. Knowing those things would determine whether or not he could have her. It would determine whether this was a dream or a nightmare.

So as they unpacked he questioned her, coaxing her to talk about her travels abroad by asking about the various tidbits she'd collected on her trips.

His attention shifted to the kitchen. She'd gone in there to get some dinner and soon he'd get his orders for the night and have to go to work. He needed a better plan, because in the last three hours, he'd discovered everything but what he needed to know. He discovered she had an adventurous streak, flitting from country to country. He discovered he liked her sense of humor. He discovered he enjoyed talking to her.

But he still didn't know if she could be his.

Lilith entered the living room carrying a sandwich on a plate and a glass of soda. She broke into a sly smile as she sat. "You sure you're not hungry? I'll share."

Vixen. He chuckled. He couldn't help it. This was becoming a comedy of errors. He damn well knew she knew what he was and that he couldn't eat. He opened another box, and glanced up. "Dishes."

"Just unwrap them and stack them here. I need to wash them before I put them away." She took a bite and sat back, watching him. "So, you never did tell me why you decided to live here."

He smiled, pulled out a dish and unwrapped it. "Neither did you. Not really."

"I guess you could say I felt drawn back." She brushed her hair back off her forehead in a feminine fashion.

"You?"

He shrugged. "Don't know. Woke up one day and I was here. You know how it is." Her gaze narrowed, so he mimicked her expression. "Did you live here with your grandmother your whole childhood? I mean, until she died?" He paused. "And come to think of it, why were there so many kids here that night?"

She waited until her mouth was empty. "I moved in with Nan when I was nine." Lilith sipped her soda. "I lived with my mom until then. She was an amazing lady." The corner of her mouth lifted in a shadow of a smile. "She had the aneurysm just after my ninth birthday. Then, Trina's mom was killed in a car accident. She didn't have any family, so they asked Nan to take her in, too. Soon after, the others came for similar reasons. Trina and I named the place Haven House." She smiled. "All lost souls welcome. They loved the idea and made the sign."

Seemed odd for so many deaths to happen in such a short span of time. Carnation wasn't a big town.

George hopped up onto the couch and meowed. Lilith broke off some bits of her sandwich and set them down in front of the feline, who lapped them up.

"Who's they?"

She took a large bite of her sandwich and he could almost see the wheels turning in her mind. She dabbed her mouth with a napkin and then held it in front of her mouth. "The community."

Jesus, for someone who told falsehoods as often as she did, she was a horrible liar. Even if he couldn't hear the changes in her pulse, there was no way he could miss her tells. She always touched her face as if she wanted to hide, and her beautiful eyes couldn't meet his. "Oh?"

"Carnation's a small town. Everyone is in everyone else's business." She kept her eyes on her sandwich, picking it apart as she spoke. "All the girls were from local families. If not for Haven House, we'd have been scattered across Washington in foster care." She shrugged. "I guess everyone thought keeping us together would be best."

It sounded like a reasonable answer, but her erratic pulse said her tale wasn't the truth. She made it sound like all the girls had known each other before living here, which made sense, there was only one school, but if all their mother's had died in a short time period . . . where were the dads? "What about your father?"

"Don't know. My mom kept his name to herself." She shrugged, tucking some hair behind her ear. "I doubt he was interested. I never was." She brought her hand to her face again.

"Growing up with no family is tough."

"I had Trina." She picked more crumbs off her sandwich. She didn't mention Nan or the other girls who lived here. So, she didn't think of them as family.

"What about you?" She met his gaze. "Do you have any family?"

"No." He balled up some of the packing paper, hoping the noise would deter her.

"You must have at some point. I refuse to believe you spawned from ether." She grinned. "What were they like?"

He shrugged.

"Come on." She leaned forward, whispering, "Just tell me the safe bits."

He raised a brow, but relented. "My mother died when I was born, my father when I was in my twenties." He shrugged. "Not much to tell."

"Did they live in Washington?"

"Italy."

"Italy?" Her expressive face showed her surprise. "You don't even have an accent. Do you speak Italian?"

Damn, why couldn't he seem to keep his mouth shut around her? He gave her a quick nod.

"Say something."

He murmured several sentences in Italian and her eyes went liquid.

"Beautiful. What did you say?"

He stood and took the empty box to the entryway. "I said 'I'm done with this box and I need to grab another.'"

Her suspicious gaze followed him as he walked away. "Liar."

He motioned up the last of the boxes. "Where does this one go?"

"It's books. I already cleared off the shelves but be careful, that box is heavy."

He rolled his eyes at her nagging and picked the box up, carrying it into the living room. He started removing books and lining them up on the shelves, browsing the titles; the Bible, the Dead Sea Scrolls, The Gnostic Bible, and the Torah. Seemed she had a thing for religion. "So did you pick one yet?"

"Pick one what?" She set her plate aside and took a sip of her drink.

"A religion."

"Oh. I'm not religious, but I find them fascinating."

Of course she wasn't, she had a pentacle dangling from her rearview mirror. Maybe she'd talk about that, though. "You don't believe in God?"

"Yeah, of course I believe in a higher power. But I'm more spiritual than religious. I'm eclectic—I take what rings true and leave the rest."

More diplomatic nowadays, but her statement reminded him of their first conversation centuries ago. "Ah, so you're a heretic."

"I just see things differently. To me, religion is the box people stuff their spirituality into in an effort to understand it better. Each theology has benefits, and each has a dark side. I think, in the Book of Thomas—he wrote, 'If a blind person leads a blind person, both will fall in a hole.' For me, that statement exemplifies religion—the blind leading the blind."

She'd changed quite a bit since they'd had a similar conversation, and she posed intriguing ideas for someone like him, a daemon no religion would want. If he could take the religion out of spirituality, wouldn't he then have the tiniest hope? The small possibility that maybe God still had a use for him. Maybe even still loved him?

"I'm sorry. I kind of went off on a tangent there. I apologize if I offended you. You're Christian, right?"

James shrugged. "Catholic, at one time." He squeezed the Bible in his hand. "A priest, actually." He braced himself for her reaction.

For a long moment, she stared, her lips parted. "I've been lusting after a priest." She covered her face with her hands. "Is that a bad sin?"

He let out a short bark of laughter over her unexpected confession. He wasn't sure what kind of reaction he expected, but that wasn't it. He sat down and scoured a hand over his head. "I have no idea, but I'm not a priest. Not anymore."

"You don't exactly have the, uh, aura of a priest," she said, as if she hadn't heard him.

"I'm. Not. A. Priest. Anymore." That's all he needed, her thinking of him like that. Why the hell had he admitted that to her?

"So how does one become not a priest? I thought the priesthood was a lifelong commitment."

Jesus, he didn't want to talk about this, but he'd only make himself look worse if he avoided the question now. He stood and started putting her books on the shelf. "You can ask to be laicized, you can just walk away, or they can have you excommunicated."

"Which was it for you?"

He grabbed another armful and gave her his back again. Christ, he was a coward. "Excommunication." He lined the books up on the shelf.

"Does that happen a lot?"

He turned to gauge her expression, but found no judgment. "No." *Not unless a mortal sin had been committed.*

Lilith's gaze followed him while he unpacked more

books and he couldn't imagine what she might be thinking. Maybe they hadn't laid all their cards out on the table, but she damn well knew what he was. She knew he was damned. So why had she asked? To rub his nose in his shame?

He thought the conversation done, but after a while she spoke again, whisper soft. "It doesn't matter, you know. It was a man's decision in a religion created by men for men. Men make mistakes."

"They didn't make a mistake. I'm not welcome in their faith nor in their heaven. Now let it go."

"My gods, James." She stood. "Why would you want such a thing? The Creator, She made heaven for humans."

"And hell for . . . ." Shit. He blew out a breath. He couldn't keep up this charade forever. Eventually he'd slip up. And then he'd be guilty of breaking the Discovery Laws.

"She made Machon for . . . Her other creations."

His gaze narrowed. What was she? She seemed human, but no human would give a second thought to any of God's *other* creations. The only human religion he knew of that acknowledged Machon at all was the Jewish tradition.

Her hand settled on her hip. "If you had ever bothered to read any holy book but yours, you might not be so set on heaven."

"Oh?"

"Machon is hell for humans, true. It's dark and hot and a myriad of creatures freely roam the place. For humans, it'd be a frightening, uncomfortable place."

He folded his arms over his chest. "And for . . . the others?" He lowered his gaze. He'd had plenty of chances to see Machon before the portals had closed. He wouldn't do it, though. It'd be like admitting failure. Admitting he belonged in hell.

"Constant darkness with no fear of the sunrise? I'd think that might be pleasant for some. And the heat?

Some might welcome the constant heat. Not having to hide. Having an entire world to explore at their whim." She nodded. "Yeah. I think for some, it might just be heaven."

She must be daemon. Somehow, some kind of daemon he'd never come across before. He wet his lips. "The Watchers were sent there as punishment."

"She stripped the Watchers of their flesh and imprisoned them in towers." Her response was immediate and vehement. "Total isolation from each other and everyone else is the punishment, not Machon. The Watchers cast shadows of blankness so they can't see each other amid everything else."

His grip tightened on the books he held. "How do you know so much about it?"

This time, she looked away. "The Torah, *The Alphabet of ben Sira*. All the Holy Books." She shrugged. "It's all there, for anyone who cares to look, for anyone willing to piece all those books into one story."

Damn her. Why couldn't she give him a straight answer? "So you're proposing that hell isn't punishment?"

"Not for daemons."

His gaze shot up, tangling with hers. He had his confirmation.

"For daemons, I rather think heaven would be hell."

"And I'm not wretched in your Creator's eyes?" He took a step closer.

Her lips parted and her brows drew together. "Why would you think that?"

"I haven't exactly lived the life of a saint."

She scoffed. "I didn't imagine you had." She sighed. "I bet if you told me all your sins, I could forgive you every one."

Christ, that would be a losing bet. "I doubt it."

"I don't. And I'm just a woman." She picked up the stack of dishes he'd unpacked, started to turn and then paused to shake her finger at the ceiling. "She created all things with full knowledge of what would happen over the course of all our lives." With a shake of her head she headed into the kitchen. "You insult Her with such thoughts."

James stared after her for a long moment.

Was it that easy? Had he been twisting himself into knots all this time trying to be something he'd never be? Something he might never be happy being again? Slowly, he followed.

She'd dragged a chair over to the counter and stood on it, with her back toward him, removing her grandmother's dishes from the top shelf. Just going about her business as if she hadn't just changed everything for him by handing him a bit of hope. As if she hadn't just given him the acceptance and compassion he'd been searching for all these centuries. They were tenuous gifts. He knew that. If she ever did find out about his sins, she wouldn't forgive him. He wouldn't expect her to.

His gaze followed each of her actions, trailing down the length of her willowy form. She'd worn jeans today. The denim hugged her slim curves, shaping to her legs.

She wasn't human. She couldn't possibly be, not with so much knowledge of daemon-kind. She'd claimed him by giving him access to any home she chose to live in. And she'd marked him last night with her heat and her scent.

Like a moth to the flame, he went to her. This wouldn't end well. It couldn't. But right now he didn't give a fuck. Right now, he just needed to be near her. He placed his hands on her hips to keep her steady before urging her to turn around.

"James?"

He wrapped his arms around her hips, pressing his face to her belly. God, she smelled good, the light scent of lavender rode in on each breath, easing him.

"James." She spoke his name softer this time, her arms cradling his head against her as if this were the most natural thing for him to do.

Gently, he tugged her down until she sat on the edge of the counter. He pushed the chair away with his foot. Those deep brown eyes followed his every move. She didn't appear concerned by his actions in the least—she never had. Just curious. Always curious.

CHAPTER 18

Butterflies erupted in Lilith's belly as she waited to see what he would do.

He set one hand on the edge of the sink, rubbed the other across his head the way he did whenever frustrated, then set it on the counter on the other side of her.

A warm tingling spread throughout her limbs. She wasn't exactly certain what had brought this on. Didn't understand why he looked at her with such affection. She touched his face. "What?"

He leaned closer, his voice soft and deep, like the rumble of thunder in the distance. "I shouldn't do this." He met her eyes, his gaze a gentle caress. "But despite my best efforts not to, I'm falling i—"

She placed her fingers on his lips, silencing him. She didn't want him to say the words. She wanted it—she wanted him to love her so much, but she couldn't bear to hear the words, not when she still feared telling him who she was. Not when they were both lying to each other.

They needed to have a long talk, but damn it, she couldn't betray the coven.

Her gaze fell to his mouth, mesmerized by her fingers caressing his full, firm lips. She let her hand fall to the corded sinew of his neck and stroked him there. She dragged her eyes away from his mouth and met his penetrating gaze.

He leaned in closer, until his breath danced with hers. He had her in such a state of heightened awareness her skin felt too tight. Every atom clamoring for his touch.

"This isn't a good idea." He stroked his thumb over her cheek, softening his statement. "I know this isn't going to end well, but I can't fight this anymore. You need to tell me to leave this house. Tell me to get out. To go away."

Not a chance in hell. She used her grip on his shirt to pull him closer. The kiss was gentle, lingering, and achingly sweet. She'd just begun learning the feel of him when he pulled away. She couldn't repress the sound of protest that escaped. Her very essence thrust against her flesh, trying to follow.

He searched her face, looking for something. She couldn't say what. Her heart seemed to halt in her chest while she waited for him to make his decision.

Dear gods, don't let him walk away again. "James?"

His mouth slanted over hers again and the universe tilted.

Where his first kiss had been sweet, the second grew demanding, carnal. He held her face in his hands, exerting gentle pressure on her chin with his thumb, until she opened for him. His tongue swept in, sending shivers of desire racing through her. Over and over his tongue thrust, mating with hers until she trembled and clung to his muscular arms, intoxicated by his unique taste. He surrounded her. His strong arms wrapped tight around her, his skin beneath her fingers, his masculine scent infused in each breath.

He pulled her closer, forcing her legs wider to allow his embrace. The long, hard length of his erection pressed intimately against her. Finding the bottom edge of his shirt, she sought out his skin. Traced the edges of the first scar she came across before spreading her fingers wide.

The low growl in the back of his throat encouraged

her. She pressed deeper into his embrace.

He tangled his fingers in her hair, pulling her head back, deepening the kiss. He wrested complete possession of her mouth.

She wanted more. His hands moved over her body, trying to touch her everywhere at once. Her face, back, hips. His knuckles caressed the sides of her breasts and her nipples hardened in response.

His phone vibrated, jerking them out of the moment. They leaned on each other, foreheads touching, their uneven breathing fanning each other. He took the offensive device out of his pocket, silenced the call, and checked the message before setting the phone on the counter.

His gaze swept over her face and his hand followed, touching her brow, her cheek, his thumb rubbing against her tingling lips. "I should go." Regret laced his words.

"If you have to." She searched his face. Did he regret having to leave? Or kissing her?

"I'll see you in the morning." He gave her one last quick kiss and strode out of the room. She let her head fall back against the cabinets as she fought a riot of conflicting emotions.

Then he came back.

"Damn, but you make me feel like a kid," he said before their mouths united again.

In the back of her mind, she hoped he would ignore the call and stay. His hand slipped up the back of her tee and she thought her prayer answered.

The phone he'd dropped on the counter began clattering on the tiles, making them both jump. He silenced it once again, but his attention stayed on her. She cupped his face and drew him back. Their lips barely touched before the house phone started ringing. His cell vibrated again. Her phone rang in the other room. Whoever wanted him to leave, wanted him to do so now.

His hand scraped over his head. "I need to go." Then he gave her a grin that made her heart melt. There was happiness in his smile. Excitement. "I'll hurry, okay?"

She smiled in agreement, and he dashed out the door.

The phones fell silent.

Not trusting her legs to hold her weight, she remained perched on the counter, and worried for James.

She closed her eyes, murmuring a quick chant to elicit his safe return, as she'd started doing every evening. "Watchers of old, Guardians of night, guide him home safe, before morning's light."

Upstairs, a door creaked open. Twilight had arrived. With as little noise as possible, she raced to the front door, grabbed her purse from the end table, and let herself out. She let out a shaky sigh with her back pressed to the door. She'd almost forgotten about the ghost. Something had to be done.

Yeah, she needed to visit Kat and get her mom's Grimoire. Her place wasn't far, maybe she'd just walk. Some fresh air would do her good after being stuck inside Haven House for the last couple days.

James pulled around the side of the house on his bike, stopping by the porch. "You headed out?"

"I'm going to visit a friend."

He nodded, but he didn't look pleased. "Be careful."

"You, too."

CHAPTER 19

Lilith knocked on Katherine O'Hickey's door. The high priestess' daughter had always been Lilith's contact for the coven and, last she heard, Kat had her Grimoire.

The door opened to reveal a curvy woman with a riot of red curls, wearing a coat and scarf. "Can I—"

Lilith saw the exact moment it dawned on Kat who she was.

"Goddess be praised." She popped her head out the doorway, glanced both ways and hurried Lilith inside. "Does Mother know you're back?"

"No. You're the only one." This wasn't exactly the reception she'd expected and she started wondering if Kat had sent her the notes. "What's going on?"

Kat's green eyes shifted to the side. "Oh, you know how Mother can be."

"Not really. She kicked me out of the coven when I was ten years old."

"Right." Kat pulled her into a quick hug. "I'm sorry. She's been acting crazy lately." She shrugged. "Here, sit down." Kat moved some books off a nearby armchair. "Would you like some tea? I just made a pot."

"Sure. If it's no trouble." She motioned to the coat and scarf Kat wore. "Were you heading out?"

Kat's hand stroked down the coat and plucked at the scarf. "I get cold sometimes."

She left room and Lilith took off her jacket. Thick

tomes filled bookshelves lining the walls and more books crowded the end tables and chairs. Polished stones and jars of herbs were scattered across every surface. She'd call the place a mess, but a controlled chaos played out amid the disorder and everything appeared impeccably clean. She pulled up her sleeves. Gods, Kat kept her place warm.

The television was on, showing current coverage of that Revelations Industries, Inc. disaster. She glanced toward the kitchen. It must be tearing Kat up, watching all those men suffer, knowing she could help, but not being allowed to. She shook her head. The coven could do so much good if they weren't so busy hiding all the time.

Kat returned with two cups of tea and after handing one to Lilith, she cleared a spot on the couch and sat. She shut off the television. "What can I do for you?"

Lilith took a deep breath. "I hoped you might still have my mother's Grimoire?"

"I do." Kat stood and opened a cabinet by the window. She took out a large cloth-covered book and handed it to her. "You know the rules. If you can open it, you can have it."

Ah, yes. The rules. Rowena had taken the book from her because she'd lost her Magic and couldn't open it. She'd been inconsolable—losing access to the Grimoire was like losing her mother all over again. She'd felt like such a failure both as a witch and as a daughter.

Lilith pulled the cloth off the Grimoire. Her ancestors had tooled a triquetra into the leather cover and she ran her fingers over the design. Her throat grew tight. Gods, she used to sit by her mother's side for hours, watching her perform spells from this book.

I'm bringing it home with me, Mama. She closed her eyes, envisioning heat radiating from her palm. The latches melted away. A little teary, she shot Kat a victorious smile.

Kat winked. "I'm very happy for you, Lil."

She opened the book and paged through the handwritten parchment pages. Every witch in her line had written spells in this book. Drawings and charts filled some pages, while neat, tight writing scrolled down others. This was her family's legacy. She closed the book and the latches sealed shut.

"It's all yours." Kat grinned. "Everyone will be thrilled to see you."

"Really?" She was sixteen last time she'd seen Rowena. The high priestess had caught her trying to rally the other girls into finding a spell that would rid her of Aimee. Rowena had sent her away and forbade her to visit the coven because she feared that the entity might attach to one of the other girls should they try to remove it. After that, she only saw Trina on an irregular basis and when Rowena found out, she'd signed Trina up for the Navy. Ever since then, the only contact either of them had with the coven was through Kat. It had been Kat's idea to hire her as the coven's purchaser.

"Mother is . . . having second thoughts about sending you away." She met her gaze. "Both you and Trina."

The news floored her. "Really? Last time I saw her, she said I needed to stay away for the good of the coven."

"I know. And while I doubt she would ever apologize, I'd like to. The rest of us want you both back. We have for a long time and I think Mother is finally seeing the wisdom in that."

"Has something happened?"

"No." Kat sipped her tea. "Yes."

Lilith sat back in her chair and held her tongue. Kat had always been a little skittish around others. Always sweet, she was the healer of the group, but for whatever reason, she'd never had much confidence.

"Mother has decided that our purpose as a coven is to destroy daemon-kind."

Lilith's face heated. She forced herself not to react, not wanting to give anything away to the high priestess's daughter. "Oh?"

"Apparently, she's seen a vision of the End Times and says they'll soon be upon us. She says we must take our place as protectors of humans against the daemons or all will be lost."

Lilith glanced at the television. Times were changing. The world grew darker day by day. Still, she couldn't quite believe the world might end. "The End Times?" Lilith shook her head. "Seriously?"

"That part, I believe. You remember Brenda?"

Lilith nodded. As a child Brenda had always been very serious—too serious to want to play.

"She developed prognostic capabilities in her early twenties. She's seen similar visions, though she disagrees with Mother's conclusion that we need to protect the humans."

Lilith paused, her teacup halfway to her mouth. "She thinks we need to protect the daemons?"

"Not exactly. She says it isn't clear, but that Mother's conclusion is drawn from a belief that all humans are good and all daemons are evil, which can't possibly be the case."

No. She knew all too well how evil some humans could be.

"Mother claims the daemons turned on the old coven during the Clearances."

"Well, that's nothing new. She's been telling us that since we were kids."

"She says we're ready to eradicate them. Well, once you and Trina are reinstated, that is."

Interesting. "What do you think?"

Sweat beaded on Kat's forehead. "I think the answer to what happened during the Clearances is in the Legacy Necklace." Kat rubbed her throat, adjusting her scarf. "I think I'm not interested in being part of destroying entire races based on the words of a woman who can't use the necklace."

"That's a strong statement." What she really wanted to know is why she should believe that they'd decided to rebel. Rowena had ruled over the coven with an iron fist since before her mother died. So why now? "I don't remember any of you having problems with Rowena before, what happened?"

The corner of Kat's mouth curved up. "When you're raised to trust everything your high priestess tells you, it can be difficult to come to terms with the fact that she might be lying." Kat shrugged. "Maybe even to herself."

"You think that's her problem?"

"I've never been able to ascertain if Mother truly believes eradicating daemons from Earth would benefit mankind . . . or the coven."

Lilith took a sip of tea. "Without daemons, there would be no one who could challenge the coven."

"Exactly." Kat shook her head. "The goddess took great pains in ensuring balance. Of creating checks and balances in nature. What Mother wants to do would destroy the balance and give the coven . . . give *her*, too much power."

Which would put the coven at odds with the Watchers they drew their power from. No wonder Kat seemed so nervous. "What are you going to do?"

"Not me." Kat met her gaze. "You."

Lilith shook her head. The last thing she needed right now was to get entangled with the coven. "I didn't come back to rejoin the coven. I never even considered the possibility."

"You have Magic, you opened the Grimoire." Kat set aside her tea and leaned forward. "Some of the women remember things from when we were young. Things their mothers used to say about you being the next high priestess."

"No." Lilith set aside her own tea. This was ridiculous. She was mated to a fucking vampire, no way would the coven want anything to do with her when they found that out. She stood, ready to leave. "Nan repeatedly told me I was nothing. That I'd never be anyone special."

"Exactly." Kat stood, blocking her exit. "Why? To keep you down. To prevent you from reaching. She and Mother were tight."

The truth lies in the past.

Not the truth "lay" in the past. The truth lies in the past.

So who was lying? Nan? Kat?

Kat dabbed at her brow with the end of the scarf and Lilith zeroed in on the action. "Are you sick?" It was far too warm in here for a coat and scarf. "Why are you wearing that?"

Kat tried to brush past her and Lilith grabbed her arm.

She hissed, her whole body tensing.

What in the world? Lilith pulled up the sleeve to Kat's coat, revealing swollen bruises beneath. She pulled down the scarf to find more of the same. "Who did this?"

Kat shot her a sidelong glance that spoke volumes.

Good gods, all this time she'd thought Kat the luckiest of them all because her mother still lived. She thought Kat lucky, so she chalked the woman's skittishness up to shyness. She'd ignored Rowena's high-handedness, thinking her simply over-protective. "Can't you . . .?" She motioned to the bruises.

"Heal myself?" Kat shook her head, her face flushing with color. "We all have limits."

"Gods, Kat. What the hell is going on?" She started unbuttoning the coat. "You need this off before you melt."

Kat lifted her chin, allowing Lilith to unwind the scarf. "She's demanding we capture daemons to sacrifice on Samhain." She gasped as Lilith pulled off her coat. "I stood up to Mother, that's all."

She set the coat and scarf aside and stared at Kat. More was going on than what she'd admitted so far. Something must have happened to instigate their rebellion. "Why?"

Kat's eyes filled with tears. "I get lonely." Her cheeks colored and she looked up at the ceiling, blinking hard. "I mean, we all do, right? The others, they have their daughters, at least."

Loneliness Lilith understood. "I know. Me, too."

"So, I asked the goddess to help me find my mate." Kat swiped at her eyes with her sleeve.

Lilith sucked in a deep breath. "You didn't."

She nodded.

"Rowena found out?"

"No." A burst of ill-humor burst from her. "Gods, no. It's just when she started in with all this crap about capturing daemons for sacrifices . . . ."

Lilith closed her eyes. "Who's your mate?"

"He doesn't want me to say his name out loud."

"Dear gods." Her mate must be daemon.

"I've only met him on the astral a few times. But now I know he's out there. Now I'm worried. I mean, what if the coven does start hunting daemons and he's sacrificed?"

Lilith took her hand.

"I remembered what you did when we were kids, you know. And your mate, he showed up. And I thought, what if my mate is out there? What if I didn't have to be so lonely and . . . ." She shrugged helplessly.

And now she needed a champion. Someone who would stand with her. "Okay." She pulled Kat into her arms and gave her a gentle hung. "Okay, I'm on your side. I'll help with over-throwing Rowena, but that's all I can promise right now. What about the rest of the coven?"

"We need thirteen to overthrow Mother."

"So if we count you, you just need me?"

"No, we need Trina, too." She sighed. "It's complicated. Sit down." They both resumed their seats. "When a coven accepts a high priestess, each witch gives her a token of her power to make her stronger. Therefore, each of the witches in our coven must take back that which they gave."

"And you gave nothing, because Rowena is still alive. You don't officially become a part of the coven until she dies."

"Correct."

Lilith shook her head. "But technically none of us gave Rowena anything, our mother's did."

"They are your family's powers. You can reclaim them."

That sounded far too easy. "Why am I sensing there's more to this?"

"The purpose of each witch giving the high priestess a token of her power is so that there can't be a small part of the coven who disagrees with the rest and overthrows her. You all have to agree to this. You all need to confront her and take back your powers. Together."

Together. And what if one witch decided to have second thoughts? It sounded like suicide. If they didn't succeed, Rowena would kill them. The thought startled her. Would Rowena kill them? Maybe. Though years had passed since she'd seen the high priestess, she remembered her as a fierce, passionate woman and seeing what she'd done to her own daughter... "Rowena will fight."

Kat slumped back on the couch, wincing. "You have no idea."

"And what about the Legacy Necklace? What's that?"

"The legend says that the high priestess of the coven who died during the Clearances recorded the events in a memory stone. Rowena has the Legacy Necklace, but it doesn't work for any of us. That leaves you and Trina. One of you will be able to unlock the visions inside. One of you will be our next high priestess."

That would be a positive thing for Trina. She'd always been one of those people who seemed most at home when she felt useful and needed. And a week ago, even she would have welcomed such a thing. To be not only welcomed back by her mother's coven but promoted to their high priestess. It would've been an honor. Now, it sounded like a curse. If the coven chose her, she couldn't be with James, not with the hostilities between the coven and the Vampiric Council. Lilith lifted her hand to massage her temples. Did she want to be with James? It would mean giving up any rights to be with the coven. If Trina became their high priestess it might cool their friendship. No, Trina wouldn't allow that; she'd remained her friend through everything.

"A high priestess can abdicate, correct?"

"Yes." Kat looked away. "If she finds her coven unacceptable."

"Wait a minute. If you know that either Trina or I could unlock this stone, what makes you think Rowena hasn't figured it out?"

"She knows." Kat bit her lip. "That's why she's having second thoughts, I'm sure. She knows she needs you to unlock the stone, but I don't see her giving up her position gracefully. Mother will expect that you and Trina are ignorant of all this and I'm sure she'll have a plan of her own to keep her position."

"Great." Lilith slumped back in her seat.

Kat nodded toward her Grimoire. "What do you need the Grimoire for?"

"I have a ghost. Well, actually more of a skin-walker. One that I need to talk to while keeping myself safe."

"I can make a potion for you. You'll just need to sprinkle it around the room you're in and the spirit won't be able to cross." Kat's brows drew together. "Are you all right? You don't have ghost sickness do you?"

Lilith tipped her head to the side. "What's that?"

"When a spirit feeds off the living, the victim can experience memory loss, exhaustion, depression."

"No, not me." But James experienced similar symptoms. "What's the cure?"

Kat stood and opened a book. "From what I remember, most of the cures are worse than the cause. Let's see, in cases of possession all cures require destroying the ghost by having it enter a body and then killing the host. Well, unless you can exorcise the spirit and trap it, but that doesn't destroy the spirit."

"But what about ghost-sickness. That's not the same as possession, is it?"

"No, no. Sorry, I'm just trying to file through the cluttered mess of information in my head. Ghost-sickness is different. It's caused by residue left over after feeding. Most of the cures are nasty. They require the infected to drink potions to make them expel the poison."

James couldn't drink or eat. That wouldn't work. "But you said almost all. There's another cure?"

Kat tapped her finger against her chin. "Yeah, I'm fairly certain I remember something about a black hen drawing out the poison like a magnet."

CHAPTER 20

Lilith tromped down the street, her backpack slung over her shoulder with her mom's heavy Grimoire weighing it down and a box of chicken under her arm. Well, a live hen, to be specific. Turned out one of the easiest cures for ghost sickness involved rubbing said creature on the patient.

That should prove interesting.

Her phone rang and Lilith dug it out of her purse, swiping her thumb across the screen to answer. "Trina, you are never going to believe—"

"You're in trouble."

Trina's tone, more than her words, made Lilith freeze. Trina's senses were frighteningly accurate. "Now?"

"Yeah."

She scanned the deserted street. To her right, thick shrubs clung to the side of the steep foothills. To her left, a ten-foot drop led to the Tolt River and, of course, there were trees everywhere casting shadows from the streetlights. "Can you see how?" Was she looking for a rock slide, a runaway car, a mountain lion . . .?

"No. It's gonna be bad, though. I think . . . ."

"What?"

"Doesn't feel natural. There's so much darkness. Maybe a daemon."

Oh, gods. She pressed her hand to her stomach, trying to decide if she should run for home or flee back toward the neighborhood she'd just passed.

"You said your Magic returned."

"Yeah." She didn't have any practical usage under her belt, but she had Magic. She started for home at a quick clip. "What do I do?" Something moved in the forest. The rustle and snap of dead leaves made her jump. "What do I do, Trina?"

"Make a sword."

As kids they'd often play-acted daemon hunting and she'd use her Magic to make weapons for all the girls in the coven.

"Remember? You used to—"

"I don't think a toy sword made out of cottonwood is going to help—"

A new voice interrupted their conversation. "I think you're right."

Lilith stopped at the sound of the unfamiliar male voice, her heart stuttering in her chest. She turned. "Oh, gods, am I in trouble."

He must've been seven feet tall and thick as the baobab trees she'd seen in Africa. A scar ran down the side of his face, a deep groove that held his mouth in a perpetual sneer.

"What's going on?" Trina sounded frantic. "Talk to me."

"I gotta . . . I gotta go." Her gaze shot to the side of the road where another silver-eyed male emerged from the bushes. *Shit!*

"Mm. Pretty little thing, ain't she?" Though shorter and smaller than the other, something about the way he swaggered onto the street made her suspect he might be the more dangerous of the two. He oozed confidence and she had no intention of underestimating him.

"Leave the phone on. Gods, Lil, I wish I was there."

"I know." She slipped her thumb toward the photo button on the side of her phone, praying the flash was on. Her gaze stayed on the men. "What do you want?"

"You."

Lilith pressed the photo button. The flash lit up the

two males in a brilliant burst of white light. They reared back, cursing. She ran, stuffing her phone in her purse, Trina still shouting at her. The backpack slammed against her spine with every step. The chicken clucked from being jostled around. Too much noise. They'd be on her in seconds.

Magic. Use your damned Magic.

Footsteps pounded the asphalt behind her.

Lilith reached to her side, imagining gripping the air and jerking it behind her like a massive sheet. Leaves and branches burst from the side of the road as if a gust of wind blasted out of the woods. The sound of her pursuer's feet altered as they stumbled amid the onslaught. She repeated her action as she darted to the side of the road closest to the Tolt River, this time focusing on the water rushing along next to the road. When the water sloshed over the asphalt, the sound of pounding feet stopped with a shout of outrage. Only one set of footsteps pounded the ground behind her now.

Her lungs burned. She wasn't used to running, and the stitch growing in her side became unbearable. Her strides slowed for no other reason than she couldn't maintain her speed, but she refused to stop. The overgrown drive leading to Haven House came into view.

And then disappeared.

Lilith stumbled to a halt.

The darkened street, the foothills, the river—they'd all disappeared. Now she stood in a sun-drenched desert. Her feet sank into the sand under her feet.

What did they do?

Frantically, her gaze darted around the sandy dunes and sun-drenched sky, looking for a seam in the illusion, a portal, something. The heat from the sun felt real enough. Oh, gods, had he transported her? Could daemons do that? Gasping for breath, she set her belongings down and dragged off her jacket.

Trina. Lilith dove for her purse, picking out the

phone. Trina?

"Is it over? Are you okay?"

"I'm in a desert."

"What?"

"The sun is hot, there's sand everywhere. I'm in a desert."

"No. No, they can't do that. They can't. It's an illusion."

"I don't think so. I can't see anything to suggest it isn't real." Thirty yards out, the sand shifted. Started to slowly spin. "Wait. There's something under the sand."

"He's trapped you in an illusion, Lilith. It has to be. He's gonna wear you down before he comes at you and you need to be ready."

Sneak attack. Right.

"Conjure the swords. You were trained to use them. It's your best shot."

Lilith dropped the phone back into her purse and closed her eyes.

The ground trembled. Whatever her attacker had planned was big.

She focused on the minerals around her, the metals in the rock. Not in the Sahara, or whatever desert he'd created an illusion of, but in Washington, in the mineral rich earth near the Tolt River. She held her arms out, fingers outstretched, and called the weapons into being.

Nothing happened at first. The tug of Magic pulled at her aura as the spell tried to take shape. The ground beneath her feet trembled from the daemon's talent, but the small bits of rock jumping up through the sand did so for her.

She lifted her gaze just as a mass of sand erupted before her. She ducked, shielding her eyes with one hand. Dust filled every breath, making each more difficult and leaving a gritty taste in her mouth. She coughed as the dust began to settle, and looked up.

Oh, dear gods. Big had been an underestimation.

What the heck was that thing?

Some sort of devil, she supposed. Black wings sprang out from a curved, muscular back. Long, thick horns jutted from its face, and the body reminded her of churning lava—a thick, black outer armor floating in chunks over the bright-orange, liquid fire underneath.

Her weapons materialized. She gripped the hilts of the swords, both blades as long as her arm, curved and wickedly sharp, and a bolt of satisfaction ran through her. She could do this.

She assumed the stance her fighting instructor had taught her. Legs spread for balance, one arm behind her head for striking, the other arm braced low in front of her for blocking. Remembering her training helped her to calm and center her mind as she studied the impossible beast before her. No such creature existed.

She was indeed stuck within an illusion.

Just her alone with this thing.

Those two daemons waited out there in the real world, preparing to watch her fight for her life.

And when they grew bored, and decided to kill her, she might never see them coming.

CHAPTER 21

He'd kill her as soon as he found her.

When Lilith said she planned to visit a friend, he expected her to take her car. He expected her to be home long before him. The door slammed behind him and he strode down the drive, hesitating only briefly before deciding he didn't need his bike. She walked; she couldn't have gone far.

How the hell did he protect a woman who didn't realize she needed protection? They needed to sit down and talk about this, but how much could he say?

At what point would the Watchers decide he'd said too much and issue a kill order on him for breaking the Discovery Laws? When he'd left earlier that evening, he'd half expected to be called out by another Guardian, but it had just been another assassination job. Which meant he hadn't broken any laws. Yet.

Maybe he needed to quit worrying. She couldn't possibly be human. Not with all the knowledge she had about daemon-kind.

As he neared the end of the drive, he slowed, cocking his head to the side. That sounded like steel hitting rock.

And male laughter.

He broke into a run, keeping to the narrow dirt path to avoid the fall leaves crowding around him. The noise increased, the slick clash and slide of a blade against something hard, bringing to mind a sharpening stone.

He slowed his pace as he reached the main road, remaining hidden to assess the situation.

"He'll be pissed as hell if you let her die," a male said.

"I ain't gonna let it go that far. Just want to wear her down a bit," another answered. "Make her easier to handle."

James shifted his position and two daemon males came into view, their eyes glowing with liquid silver as they watched something off to the side.

"We should get more than what he said." The larger of the two folded his arms over his beefy chest. "He didn't warn us about what she could do."

"Mm." The smaller of the two thrust his chin out. "That chick can move, eh?"

James leaned farther to the side so he could see the object of their interest. Lilith stood in the middle of the road brandishing two swords, her movements almost balletic as she fought some unseen assailant. He'd almost think she was putting on an exhibition, except her blades kept clashing with something he couldn't see.

"Look at her arms." The short one pointed.

Her veins stood out black against the pale skin of her hands, the spidery lines climbing slowly up her arms.

"She's overreaching. You better stop the illusion before she burns herself out."

"A little longer. I don't want to have to worry about her using her Magic on us again."

Magic? Christ, she was a witch?

Which made her fully human.

And left him fucked six ways to Sunday.

James stepped out of the cover of the trees, pulling his blade. He intended to go for the smaller of the two, the one creating the illusion, but the larger daemon blocked him.

His gaze dropped to the silver pendant around James' neck. "So that's the way of things, is it?"

"This isn't going to happen. Drop the illusion and back away from the woman."

The vampire recognized him—or, at least his status as a Guardian. An array of emotion projected across his scarred face. Fear. Rage. Desperation.

"I'll let you live if you leave now." James strode forward, fully expecting them to run, but these vampires feared whoever sent them after Lilith more than him.

The larger vampire stepped to the side, leaving a copy of himself behind. Then again both stepped to the side, each leaving a copy behind. And again. Eight. The Splitter vampire and his copies blocked him from Lilith and the Illusionist, who kept all his attention on Lilith. The copies couldn't be destroyed, just recalled by the Splitter. They felt no pain, had no emotion—just static on the inside. They were, however, solid. And they could hurt him, destroy him.

He needed to destroy the Splitter. James grabbed his second blade, holding the knife handle backward in his left hand, the silver blade cool against his wrist.

The Splitter and his seven copies shuffled forward, switching places as they did, until even if he'd tried to keep track of the Splitter, he'd have lost visual contact. Jesus, he felt like the mark in a game of three-card Monte. They surrounded him. James pivoted a slow circle, keeping on the balls of his feet, knees slightly bent, ready to move. He'd mark off the copies. With a little luck he'd stab the Splitter in the process and he'd have to recall the copies to conserve energy for the healing process.

Damn it, he needed to get to Lilith.

Three attacked at once. He kicked the first, sending him flying back into another. He spun, sliced across another's neck. His blade cut deep. The copies remained. The third punched him in the back. He stumbled forward into another copy. He swung his arm, slicing deep across his stomach. The copies remained.

But he'd marked two.

Another grabbed him from behind, the copy's arms coming up under his, then locking behind his neck, immobilizing him. Another lurched forward, one with a deep slash marked his neck—a copy. He jabbed, slugging James in the face hard. Once. Twice.

James leaned back into his captor, kicking his feet out. His boot connected with the copy's chin. As his leg came back down, he used the momentum of his body weight to lean forward, sending his captor over his back and onto the street. James brought the knife down onto his chest, marking him. Another copy came at him, throwing his fist out. James sidestepped the punch and grabbed his arm, thrusting his blade down in an arc, stabbing his assailant in the neck. Still they remained. He kicked the copy away. James threw his arm out, clothes-lining another copy running toward him, followed him down to the ground, and stabbed him. Nothing.

But he'd marked five of the eight.

James backed away. All eight regained their feet. They showed no sign of slowing, paid no heed to their wounds. He scanned the small crowd for the Splitter, searching for a clue, a sign.

If smart, the Splitter would stay out of harm's way and let the tireless copies take the beating. Two hung back. Neither bore a mark from his blade.

His gaze slid to the side to check on Lilith. "Six o'clock, Lil."

She spun, lashing out with her sword, but the Illusionist leapt back.

"Three feet."

She ran forward, slashing with both arms.

The Illusionist dodged.

A copy rammed into James, throwing them both to the ground. James punched him, swung his arm out, and cut his face.

When he looked up, one of the copies stared at Lilith, watching her fight. "Gotcha." James flipped the knife in his hand, holding it lightly by the blade. He cocked his arm back for momentum and let it fly. The blade flew straight to the mark. The Splitter, and all his copies faded to ash.

He turned just in time to see Lilith thrown across the street by her unseen assailant. She landed not a foot from the Illusionist. "Hard right."

Her arm lashed out and her sword scored across his legs and the Illusionist shouted. She turned as she got to her feet, her second sword piercing through the Illusionist's chest.

As James walked over to them, Lilith stepped back and blinked, looking around. Then her gaze settled on the Illusionist. "Ha! I got you, you bastard." She pulled her swords out of his body.

James grabbed him by the shirt, and dragged him to where one of his Guardian blades had fallen. He picked it up, pressing it to the Illusionist's neck. "Who are you working for?"

The Illusionist was breathing hard, he wrapped both his hands around James' wrist, trying to push him away. "Go to hell."

"Who?"

"Fuck you." He tried to wrest out of James' grip.

"Wrong answer." James lifted his blade.

The Illusionist's eyes widened. "M-man named Crowley. He ain't paying me enough for this shit."

James nodded. That's what he suspected, but he liked having the confirmation. He brought the knife down, burying it to the hilt in the Illusionist's chest and his body fell in a shower of ash. James sheathed his weapons and turned to Lilith.

Her blackened hands tightened on the grips of her blades and she widened her stance.

James paused, unsure of whether or not she meant to skewer him, too. He cocked his brow. "We fighting?"

Her gaze shot to what was left of the Illusionist before coming to rest on him. An exhale shook free of her. "No."

Still, he edged closer this time, not wanting to startle her. She didn't look like she knew what to do with the excess of adrenaline that must be pumping through her veins. "Let them go, baby. You're hurting yourself."

Lilith looked down, lifting her blackened hands. Her whole body jerked. The blades disappeared as she bowed at the waist, cradling her hands to her chest.

Those hands worried him. He'd never seen anything like it. "How do I help you, Lil? Do you need a hospital? Medicine?"

She shook her head. "Time."

"Not good enough." He wanted to pick her up and carry her back home, but he wasn't sure if she had any other injuries. "Where else are you hurt?"

A gasp broke from her lips and she stood, nearly head-butting him in the face.

He stepped back.

"It's better now. It's going away." A string of curses passed her lips and she jumped up and down. "Gods, that hurts."

He felt helpless. "Talk to me, what can I do?"

She shook her arms out to her sides. "It's healing. I'll be fine in half an hour."

Sure enough, the blackness had faded from her upper arms, slowly receding down to her forearms.

"Good." He gripped her shoulders. "You okay?"

"Yeah." But her voice quavered and when she threw herself against him, her wounded hands trapped between them, he couldn't miss the shudder running though her.

"You're all right." He tightened his hold. "I got you."

"I kept expecting them to leap into the illusion and kill me. I kept waiting and when they didn't . . . ."

"I know. You must have been crawling out of your skin. You did good." He kissed the top of her head. "Let's get you home. We need to talk."

She nodded against his chest. "I suppose we do."

He guided her toward Haven House.

"Wait. My stuff."

He jogged over to the side of the road, slung her

backpack and purse over his shoulder and tucked the box under his arm. Something fluttered within, trying to escape.

"I need my phone."

The way she held her arms, he had to assume they still hurt like hell. He dug through the bag, and picked up the phone. A picture of a Latina woman showed on the screen. "You've got an open call."

"I was talking to Trina when they attacked." She held her hand out for the phone.

Instead, he put it to her ear. "Just talk. I got this." She needed to rest her hands, and he wanted to hear what they said.

Warily, she met his gaze. "Trina?"

"I'm coming home."

"No. I'm all right. I don't want you getting in trouble. Everything is fine." Her gaze slid away. "James happened to be nearby . . ."

"James?"

"Yeah, he helped me take care of the, uh, muggers."

"Muggers?" There was a pregnant pause. "Yeah, all right."

Lilith flinched, probably from the sarcasm infused in Trina's tone, and kept her gaze from meeting his. "We'll talk later. Love you."

"You, too."

James disconnected the call and dropped the phone back in her bag with a shake of his head. "You two are close."

"Like sisters." She bit her lip.

Which meant they shared all their secrets. Great. So he had two human women who knew about daemon-kind, at least one of whom possessed Magic.

He shook his head. He never realized any witches existed outside the Grigori coven and they'd all been dead for centuries. He tucked the box under one arm and put the other around her shoulders. "Whatever is in this box, wants out."

"It's a chicken."

Another flurry of activity came from inside the box. "Why do you have a live chicken?"

"Well, a black hen if you want to be specific." She cut him a sidelong glance. "A live one." She was hedging, her tone wary.

"What do you need a hen for?"

"Oh, it's not for me."

Why did that sound ominous? James held aside a branch and they entered Haven House's private property.

"All right, I'll bite. Who is the chicken for?"

"You."

"Me? Lilith, I don't eat." He realized his mistake. "Chicken."

"It's a hen."

"I don't eat those, either."

She sighed, stopping on the path. "It's not meant for you to eat."

"Then what am I supposed to do with it? I doubt George is going to play nice with a live bird."

"I'm going to"—she grimaced—"rub it on you."

She was certifiable.

There was no way in hell anybody was rubbing him with a chicken. He picked up his pace, leaving her behind. And what about the poor chicken? Didn't something like that constitute animal cruelty or some shit?

"James." She ran behind him, trying to catch up.

He didn't stop. "That's some sick shit."

"Will you be reasonable?"

"Reasonable?" He set her things down on the porch and swung around. "You want to rub a live chicken on me. What exactly is reasonable about that?"

"Oh, grow up. You have ghost-sickness. It's the only cure I could find that didn't involve making you drink something, which we both know you can't do, harming an animal, or burning down the house."

Ghost-sickness? He folded his arms over his chest. "Explain."

"You know how you're tired all the time? You don't remember things that happened the night before? The fresh scars you wake up with? Nan is feeding off you."

He waited for her to break into giggles. She didn't. "Bullshit."

"I saw her." She reached up and dragged the collar of his shirt down, pointing to two oval scars on either side of his chest. "You've got more on your back."

He hadn't noticed the scars. Rarely did he have a reason to look down at himself and he had no reflection. They must be old, though. "If I had fresh wounds that size last night, I'd still be in bed healing."

She held up her bandaged hand. "Not if someone bled into the open wound."

He stared at her hand as her words sank in. "You know what I am."

"You're changing the subject."

Hell, yeah. He walked over to the porch steps and sat. He'd suspected she knew he was a vampire, but until now, he hadn't been a hundred percent sure. And now, he discovered it bothered him. A lot.

And she'd used her own blood to help him? He wasn't sure how he felt about that, either.

He was supposed to protect her, damn it. Now he had one more thing to add to his list of failures. Hell, what was he supposed to protect her from? She seemed fully capable of dealing with her own shit.

If what she had said was true, that meant not only had he allowed someone to get the upper hand with him, but he'd allowed a woman to do so. A dead woman. And the woman he was supposed to be protecting, had protected him.

Someone ash me now.

"James, this will only take a minute."

"No."

"If I'm wrong, no harm"—she spread her arms and

grinned—"no foul."

He cut her a dry glare. He needed to remember that one for Lou. "What's the point? If what you say is true, I'll be in the same condition in the morning. Besides, I feel fine."

"Do you?"

No. "Yeah."

"No doubts crowding in on you? No depressing thoughts? You're not having blackouts?"

She damn well knew he'd had some blackouts. And he had felt horrible that morning. His gaze dropped to her hands. Her arms looked better, but her hands still appeared almost . . . scorched. "What about your hands? You'll hurt yourself."

"Nope. This is a natural remedy. No Magic needed." She smiled, but there were still lines of strain around her eyes.

"You look like you're still in pain."

"It's fading." She shrugged. "Maybe holding the hen will be beneficial to me, too."

He rolled his eyes. "Get your fucking chicken."

She grinned, and part of him was glad he agreed just to see her smile.

"Take off your jacket."

He removed his jacket while she got the chicken, cuddling the panicked bird to her chest. "Shh. You're okay, little one. Shh." She stroked her hand down the bird's black feathers, cooing until it settled in her arms. "Stand still."

He folded his arms over his chest, barely repressing the need to roll his eyes again. He felt stupid. Ridiculous. He scanned the surrounding area, hoping to hell no one lurked in the bushes.

The bird clucked in alarm as she rubbed the creature down his arm.

He cleared his throat. "You know I have no reflection, right?"

"Yeah." She walked around him, gently stroking the

bird up and down his shirt.

"I can't be recorded, either."

"So?"

"Just in case you've got somebody filming this for a YouTube post."

She giggled. "Lift your shirt."

He glared.

"Come on. The directions said to rub the hen all over the patient's body. I'll only do your back. I wouldn't want you to feel violated or anything."

"Christ." He pulled his shirt off. "I'm feeling ten kinds of stupid right now, just so you know."

"But you're starting to feel more like yourself, aren't you?"

Not really. But he did remember Nan, now. He remembered trying to fight her when he'd been injured and failing. He remembered those fucking hooks. Still, he'd be damned if he'd admit he let the ghost of an old woman get the better of him.

She stroked the bird down his back. "You're being very patient with us."

"Us?"

"Mm, Betty and I."

Who the hell is . . . ? He closed his eyes. "Is Betty the chicken?"

"Hen. Yes."

"I'm done. I'm taking a shower now."

Her laughter followed him into the house.

CHAPTER 22

Rowena walked to her door, swung it open and gave the young man standing there a quick once over. Blond hair oiled back into neat curls, suit, tie, clean-faced. She sighed. "I'm not Mormon and don't wish to hear the word of God." She started to swing the door closed but hesitated when he chuckled. There was something decidedly sinful about that sound.

"I'm not a huge fan of His, either."

Rowena arched her brow. He sounded familiar. Where had she heard that voice before? "Who are you?"

"Sometimes who is far less important than what." He stepped back out of the halo of her porch light and his eyes glowed as the light hit them in the darkness. "I'd like to make a deal, Madam High Priestess Rowena."

Him. Goddess help her, he was becoming brazen. He'd walked right up to her house! "You dare—?"

"Oh, yes, I dare." He leaned against the outside wall and shoved his hands into his pants' pockets. "You and I have a similar problem."

Rowena folded her arms over her chest. "The only problem I have, is you." She'd ash the son of a bitch if it wouldn't draw the Watchers' notice. But she didn't dare start that particular war, not until she had the rest of the coven backing her plans.

He grinned. "You're going to be out of a job soon, won't you? Someone more powerful is in town. A witch by the name of Lilith."

She laughed. Good gods, where *did* he get his information? "Lilith?" She shook her head. "I don't know what you *think* you know, but not only is Lilith not in town, she has no Magic. Isn't this all becoming a little tedious for you? It is for me."

"Oh? That must not have been her I saw setting up house over at Haven House. Maybe a clone of hers who visited your daughter, Katherine, today and retrieved her mother's Grimoire."

The blood drained from her face. Lilith couldn't be back. She couldn't possibly have Magic.

"You know, up until tonight I wasn't absolutely sure Lilith was the right woman. She still doesn't quite feel right. Nothing like when she was a child. But now, I've seen a little of what she can do. She's quite marvelous." He leaned closer. "Why don't you invite me in, Madam High Priestess? We can discuss things privately."

"I will never allow you in this house." She started to swing the door shut again.

"Be a shame if the coven ousted you."

A tremor ran through her. The girls wouldn't do that to her. They wouldn't. Would they? But then why hadn't Katherine told her Lilith was in town? "What do you know?" She feared he knew much more than she did.

He shrugged. "Those of us who lurk in shadows hear things."

"I think you're lying."

"And yet, you haven't shut the door. I can help you. We can help each other."

If he knew anything, he'd brag about it. He was reaching, trying to trick her into a partnership. She shook her head. "Never. Not ever. Do you hear me? Step onto my property again and you'll find yourself in a summoning jar so fast your head will still be spinning when I twist the lid shut." She slammed the door on his shout of laughter.

Bastard. That daemon would never leave her alone. Somehow, she needed to do something about him.

And Lilith. She needed to find out if Lilith was indeed in town.

She paced the confines of her living room. If Lilith was here. If she had gone to Kat's house to retrieve her family Grimoire. . . . "Gods give me strength." That would give credence to Crowley's speculation that the coven would oust her. Her daughter hadn't been acting like herself lately; she'd dared challenge her over her plans and Rowena had no choice but to put the silly girl back in her place.

But Lilith might not understand that.

Tomorrow she'd visit Kat and find out what was going on. And if Lilith was indeed back in town, she'd deal with her. The question would be, how? She needed to discover if Lilith could unlock the Legacy stone, but she'd be damned if she'd hand over the coven to the girl. Either she'd need to recruit Lilith to her way of thinking, or she'd need to get rid of her. Nothing could be done tonight. Not with that daemon out there. He was another she'd do well to get rid of.

Needing to set her mind to something else, she sat on the couch and flicked her wrist. The television turned on.

"Two more soldiers have died while RI struggles to find a serum. RI's director, Dr. Edwin Moss is petitioning the public and scientists around the world for aid."

Rowena snorted. The humans wouldn't find a cure in time. "Goddess bless them, all those boys are going to die. What they need is Magic."

Magic.

They needed Magic.

Maybe some . . . immortality.

And she needed to get rid of Crowley.

Mm. Preferably without the Watchers noticing.

Rowena tapped her fingernails on the end table, grinning as her idea hatched.

CHAPTER 23

Lilith took time to take a shower after her fight with the daemons. Her hands felt better, the blackness on her skin receding to the very tips of her fingers. But her reprieve from talking to James was short-lived. He waited for her at the bottom of the steps. Without a word, he led her into the kitchen and pulled out a chair for her before sitting. "Now, tell me why you're here."

He thought it was going to be like that, did he? "You first."

"To protect you."

Lilith sat back. That's the last thing she'd expected to hear. "A vampire protecting a human?"

His gaze narrowed. "Cut the bullshit. What are you?"

She tipped her chin up. "Human."

His jaw clenched.

Well, damn. She couldn't tell him about the coven, but she didn't like lying, either. "I may possess a bit of Magic."

"A bit?" His gaze stroked down her arms to where the tips of her fingers held traces of black now. "What happened?"

She pressed her thumbnail to the tip of her index finger, testing to see if the feeling had returned. "I'm not very good yet. I'm out of practice and I lost control of the currents."

He leaned forward. "Those daemons, they said you

overreached. How?"

"I can manipulate the elements by using the Earth's energy. I allow it to flow through me, but when I lose control it burns, just like an electrical current."

"Elements?" His brows drew together. "How does that translate into swords?"

"I pulled the ore from the ground to summon the blades." She'd answered enough questions for now. "Why are you protecting me?"

"Because I was sent to."

"By who?"

He kissed his teeth, looking away. "Why did you come back?"

Gods, it was like dancing with words. She sat back and crossed her legs. "I got a note."

"I forgot about that." His brows knitted. "You thought I sent it. Why?"

She shook her head and shrugged. "I just assumed. You were here and it seemed odd."

"What did it say?"

"There were two. The first said 'The future lies in the past,' but the last one said: 'The truth lies in the past. It is time. Come home.'"

"Christ." He dragged his hand over his head and sat back. "The Historian, maybe. Sure as hell sounds like her."

Lilith arched her brow in question.

"She's the"—he waved his hand in the air—"holder of all daemon knowledge. A living Akashic records."

"She sent you to protect me?"

His gaze cut to the side.

"Exactly who sent you?"

"The Watchers. They sent me."

That didn't sound like anything the Watchers would do. "Why?"

He shrugged. "You're welcome to ask."

Lilith scoffed. The Watchers damn well spoke when they felt like speaking. They didn't explain themselves to anyone. "So you've protected me. Now what?"

His expression turned wry.

"You scared the entity away long enough for my Magic to be restored. You took out one of those vampires, and guided me to the Illusionist."

His eyes narrowed. "What entity?" He stood. "Is that what happened in there the other night?" He pointed to the ritual room.

Good gods, he was getting all riled up again. She kept her voice calm. "I captured it in a summoning jar."

"So, again, you saved yourself." He looked up at the ceiling as if praying for patience.

She folded her arms over her chest. "This is the twenty-first century."

A bark of laughter erupted from his chest. "I'm not worried about that, sweetheart. I'm worried about why I'm here and what's still coming."

Her irritation fled. "Right." She tipped her head to the side. "Maybe Nan has the answer."

"To what?"

"The truth lies in the past. I've searched the house top to bottom. I haven't found anything else that might be the truth. Maybe she has it. Maybe the truth I'm searching for will tell us what's coming."

His gaze narrowed. "How is it you know what the Watchers are? You haven't even asked why I haven't demanded more information, as if you're aware the effort is futile."

Shit. She wet her lips. "The information was in my Mother's Grimoire." *And, after being raised as a Grigori witch, I know exactly what you're up against in trying to communicate with the Watchers. Most of them were half insane.* The Grigori coven's powers came from the Watchers. While vampires inherited the worst of a Watcher, the coven had been blessed with their gifts. Perhaps that was the reason the vampires had turned on the coven during the Clearances.

He looked away, his jaw flexing. "So, what? You're

going to believe whatever Nan says? She's a malicious—
"

Now why would he worry about that? "Did Nan say something to you?" He was hiding something, didn't want her to hear whatever Nan had to say.

"Nothing she didn't say the night I killed her."

The fact that he refused to look at her worried her. What could Nan have possible said? "Tell me."

"What do you think she said, Lil?" He sat, slumping back in his seat. "She said she saw our future. That what would come to pass was an abomination." He shrugged. "Your grandmother might have been a bitch, but she still tried to protect you from me."

Lilith shook her head. "She wouldn't have crossed the street to save my life. She always said I was nothing. Useless. That I'd never become anyone of note."

He reached across the table and stroked his finger down her arm. "What about the birthmark?"

She tipped her head to the side.

"The crescent moon on your shoulder, what's it mean?"

Gods, he bounced from one topic to another. What was he after? "Nothing. It's just an odd mark."

He tipped his head to the side. "Come on."

"Seriously. It's nothing." She had no idea what he wanted her to say. Lots of people had birthmarks. "Do birthmarks mean something to daemons?"

He sat back in his seat, staring. "Maybe we should ask Nan." The way he watched her, it was almost as if he were looking for some kind of reaction from her.

"Okay. But what does a birthmark have to do with anything?"

He shrugged, glancing away. "Just a hunch."

A hunch he didn't seem to want to share. "Yeah, well, I've got the beginning of a plan." She grabbed her bag off the table and dug inside for the potion Kat gave her. "Does Nan always manifest in the same place?"

"The closet in your room."

"Okay." She found the small bottle and held it up. "I'll spread this mixture over the threshold and along the walls of your room. Nan won't be able to cross."

His expression grew shuttered. "What about me?"

She lifted one brow.

"I'm daemon. Will I be able to cross?"

"Of course. Don't worry, I won't lock you out of your room and leave you to Nan's negligible mercy."

She intended to keep him inside with her. She got up and walked upstairs, James close behind. Once in his room, she sprinkled Kat's potion at the edges of the room. The whole while, James didn't say a word. She'd almost thought he'd left until she glanced up. He leaned against the doorjamb, his arms folded over his chest, relaxed. . . . No, he wasn't relaxed at all. Despite his casual stance, his muscles were bunched tight, coiled to strike.

Her breath hitched and she straightened. The hunger in his expression sent a jolt of warning through her. She remembered visiting an exhibition on big cats as a child. They'd lined up the animals in cages and she'd felt sorry for them. Before she'd realized what she'd done she'd approached one cage, reaching her hand up to the bars to pat one of the lions watching her so intently.

The cat's handler had pulled her back. *"Ya never tease such a beast, miss. They'll gobble you right up."*

She felt like she'd been caught doing just that again. Her breath shuddered out and she took a reflexive step back.

James' expression shifted, his lips pressing together. He dropped his gaze. And left.

Damn him. Lilith pressed her hand to her belly, trying to quiet the flutters. She couldn't take any more of this on again off again rubbish. Why wouldn't he just take her? Take over and make her his? She'd damned well made her wishes known.

She turned back to her work, finished sprinkling the last of the mixture of herbs and salt around the edges of the room. This afternoon, the way he'd kissed her, she'd thought . . . she'd expected to make love to him tonight. Her whole body remained primed for his touch.

Then pull it together and go get him. Her gaze shot to the mussed sheets on the bed. She squeezed her thighs together to ease the ache. *Change into something sexier. Take a risk.*

A tremor raced through her. But what if he rejected her again? Her self-confidence was growing, but was still fragile.

He won't. He's your mate. And if he does, it's his loss.

She nodded. Stroked her hands down her robe. "His loss." *Right.*

Lilith went into her room, stripped off her robe and slipped on the baby-doll she'd worn the other night. He liked this nighty. He hadn't been able to keep his eyes off her legs while he'd riled her up over the book she read. The soft white material hugged her breasts, before falling in pleats just below her bum.

Closing her eyes, gathering her nerves, she shimmied out of her panties. She was aroused. Wet. Just from that single smoldering look he'd given her. As a daemon, he'd smell her long before he saw her. One way or another, she intended to discover whether he didn't want her, or if some misguided attempt to protect her held him back.

Lilith took a deep breath, shook out her hair, swung open the door, and went in search of her mate.

James paced the living room, his gaze never still. He needed to get his body under control. Came here looking to escape Lilith, but she was everywhere he looked. In the oddly erotic pagan art she'd hung on the walls. In the hominess of the knickknacks and books and the blanket folded over the back of the couch.

Worse, he'd helped her unpack today in this room. He'd made her come for him the other night in this room. He'd go into the kitchen, but then he'd start thinking of kissing her, of how she'd taken care of him that first night. And the sense of peace she'd enveloped him in this afternoon.

She'd made this place his home, damn her. Given him memories he enjoyed, that he couldn't escape.

He paused, closed his eyes, and drew in a deep, calming breath.

Except it wasn't.

The scent of her arousal laced the air, heating him from the inside out and bringing another inch of steel to his partially aroused cock.

And when he opened his eyes, she stood there, as if conjured from his lustful imagination. She wore one of those frilly night shirts again. The kind that hugged her unbound breasts before dropping in lose folds around the rest of her torso. It came to her upper thighs and a stiff wind would have all the material right up around her ears.

The damn thing looked far too easy to remove.

Jesus, she scared the shit out of him. He didn't remember fearing much of anything since childhood, but this wisp of a woman did the trick.

He sat on the couch before he did something stupid, like haul her up against the wall, wrap her legs around his hips, and impale her on his cock. He closed his eyes, breathing shallow in a weak attempt to escape her scent.

Still, he sensed her approach, heard the faint creek of the ottoman as she sat across from him.

Damn her. "You've got no sense of self-preservation, do you?"

"I want you."

His mouth went dry. He swallowed. "You can't possibly." *Say you don't. I'll corrupt you. Ruin you.*

The flats of her palms slid up his thighs, making him twitch. Forcing his eyes open. He needed every ounce of restraint to keep from grabbing her. And still, he feared he'd lose the battle.

She held his gaze as she leaned back on her arms, just like he'd asked her to that first night. She spread her thighs, blushing, and he dared not look down. "I do. I want you."

"Jesus, I'm a daemon. Even if I wasn't, I've never been a nice man."

She shook her head. "I'm not looking for nice. Just you."

He leaned forward, ready to pounce. Caught himself and forced himself to sit back. For all her aggressive moves, she shook like a snow-covered kitten. "You should have someone sweet. Tender. Romantic."

"I'd rather have intense." She bit her full bottom lip and he felt it in his groin. "Erotic. Hedonistic."

Desire slammed through him.

Once again, he had no idea how to categorize Lilith Caldwell. She spoke like a hussy, had the body of a goddess, and behaved like a shy virgin determined to be deflowered.

Honest to God, he didn't know which turned him on more. To hell with his ethics. His self-imposed morals. He was tired of suffering alone.

He wanted her. He shouldn't. She was a witch. A goddamn human with a book that gave her the knowledge of a daemon. An innocent.

She shifted. Spread her thighs a little more.

An innocent offering herself to him like some pagan sacrifice. Just like she'd offered him her home.

"Inhale."

Her scent flooded through him—lavender and the sweet scent of arousal. She was wet. Must be, to be throwing off a scent like that. His gaze shifted, zeroed in on her damp thatch of curls nestled between her legs. Fuck it. He was going to hell anyway.

James snatched her off the ottoman, dragging her into his lap, her wet heat pressed tight to the bulge in his jeans and they both moaned. It wouldn't take much for him to spout off, as hard as she had him. Their mouths crashed together, and he pressed harder, seeking the heat of her mouth. She spread her lips for him with a little cry of urgency that made his fingers flex into the soft curves of her ass. Already she moved against him, demanding his attention, tightening her thighs around his legs. She petted his face, then her nails bit into his neck.

He fumbled between them, desperate to free his cock. Needing to come, to take the edge off so when he finally sank into her, he could linger all damn night. He got the fly down, pushed the rough material of his jeans down a bit and pressed her hand to his cock. "Make me come."

Lilith leaned back, her gaze dropping even as she wrapped her hand around him. Her eyes widened. "Gods." Her pink tongue darted out, touched her upper lip.

She was beautiful. He dragged her tease of a nightgown over her head and tossed it on the floor. Once her hands were free, both came down to circle him in their tight grip, to rub over the sensitive head and send a fierce wave of need through him. She shifted her weight, reaching lower with one hand, slipping it into his pants to fondle his balls while she worked his cock.

He moaned. Cupped the back of her head to drag her back to his mouth.

She resisted. "I want to watch."

His breath hitched.

"I want to see you come." Her hand worked him mercilessly, fucking him in her tight grasp. "Come on me."

Christ.

His whole body drew up tight. Shivers burst out from his groin as the first ropy jet landed on her belly. Her grip rode him through the throes of passion, milked him dry.

Breathing hard, he reached out and swiped his finger through his come. Christ, she'd let him come on her. And some primal part of him rejoiced in seeing his mark on her skin.

She grabbed his wrist and their gazes locked.

Slowly, she lowered her head and took his finger in her mouth, swirling her tongue around him as she tasted his seed. "Mm."

His sated cock twitched back to life. "Witch."

She grinned.

James stood and laid her back on the ottoman, the cushion just long enough to support her from head to lower back, leaving her ass hanging off the end. "My turn." He kneeled between her legs, drew off his shirt and wiped his come from her belly. Still, his scent remained on her skin, mingling with hers, and Christ, did he like that.

He kissed the bend in her knee. Licked up her inner thigh and then paused. Let her feel the heat of his breath on her pussy. She squirmed, trying to get closer. "James." His name, one long, needy moan.

Hell, yeah. He liked that. Wanted more. He stood, leaning over her but not touching her anywhere, his hands braced on the cushion on either side of her. "Again."

She arched, grabbing his arms, her gaze spearing into him. "James."

He lowered himself, only his lips touching her, grazing along her nipple.

She thrust up, pressing herself to his mouth and he let her have her way, sucking her deep, battering the hardened nub with his tongue.

Gasping, she cradled his head. Her thighs brushed his jean-clad legs, trying to tighten around him, trying to lift her pussy high enough to reach him.

He nipped her, ran the uneven edges of his teeth over her nipple. "Behave."

"I need more."

Changing course, he suckled her other breast until he drew a moan from her. Until she writhed and gasped, demanding release.

"What do you want?"

"You."

He nipped her again. "I'm right here."

Her teeth clenched and she tried arching up again. He kept himself just out of reach. "In me. I want you in me."

Ah, God, he wanted the same. But she already had him hard as forged steel again. And she was damned close to finding release. If he took her now, he'd come as soon as her body convulsed around him. He wanted tonight to last. "Not yet."

He pushed away from her and she cried out. Tried to follow him. He shook his head, staying her with a look.

Her gaze remained locked on him as he finished undressing, her body never still, searching, wanting.

How the hell had he gotten so lucky? It seemed unnatural to him, such a beautiful young woman wanting him. But he couldn't doubt what he saw. Couldn't ignore the scent of her need. She wanted him. *Him.*

He knelt between her legs again, and licked over her damp curls. She cried out.

Christ, that was good. Honey and musk. He parted her folds with his fingers, baring her pink flesh and set in to drive her wild.

Had she said erotic? Hedonistic?

She might have asked for more than was wise.

He feasted on her, leaving her an over-sensitized puddle of writhing nerve endings. Her nipples peaked straight and hard, her thighs trembled and her pussy, dear gods, her pussy threw sparks and shivers streaking over her flesh in an endless demand for more. She arched, trying to push herself deeper to his mouth. He hauled her legs over his shoulders without lifting his face from her. Ended her ability to have any sense of control over what he did to her. He held one of her thighs, but released the other.

His fingers slid into her.

"Ah." She squeezed her eyes shut. "James."

The slick glide of his tongue rolled over her clit. He pumped his fingers into her, curling them with each outward stroke.

Pleasure exploded, rippling over her body and making her twitch and writhe. "James."

As the waves of euphoria subsided, he stroked his lips over her thigh. Her belly. Paused to nuzzle and suckle her breast.

His weight pressed her into the cushion, his cock teased the upper rise of her slit, and her body reignited.

"Beautiful." He kissed her.

She tilted her hips up, shivering when the broad head of his cock slid over her clit again. She gripped the back of his head, wrapped her other arm around his neck.

James lifted her and stood. He turned, laying her down on the couch. As he came down on top of her, he hitched her leg over his hip, her other hung off the edge from the knee down, leaving him plenty of room. Leaving her spread wide open.

He lifted just enough to get his hand between their bodies. His thumb slid across her clit.

She was close. So close.

His hips flexed against hers and the head of his cock slid past her entrance. Just. Holding her open, but going no deeper. Teasing her.

She squeezed her eyes shut, gripping his shoulders and arching her back. There wasn't an ounce of give in him. "Please."

He rained kisses along her jaw, pausing to teethe her earlobe, to rake his teeth down her throat. Shivers exploded across her skin.

He sucked her nipple into his mouth, and her world shattered. Her whole body jerked and shuddered, the weight of his body the one thing keeping her grounded.

Still, she wanted more. She wrapped her body around

his, her legs circling his waist, her arms pulling him closer.

She opened her eyes and found him watching her.

"Now you're mine." He flexed his hips.

Lilith's lips parted on a gasp as he filled her. She arched, lifting her legs higher, spreading them wider, as if doing so would give his cock more space. The intimate invasion left her trembling, as her body struggled to accommodate him.

But, dear gods, yes.

He stroked his thumb over her cheek. "You okay?"

She shook her head. Nodded. Held onto him for dear life.

And he slid the rest of the way in.

Overwhelmed, Lilith bit his shoulder. A small retaliation for the way he had her pinned beneath his weight, spread wide, stretched open, vulnerable and possessed.

The beast chuckled.

And then he started to move and she forgave him. Wrapped him tight in a full body embrace and moved with him. Pressed her mouth to the thick cords of muscle in his neck. Nipped. Sucked. Gods, he was hard as hell everywhere. His muscles bunched under her hands.

He lifted partially off her, raking his gaze down her body, watching where they joined. Her gaze chased after his. Locked onto the sight of his sex-slicked length easing out of her body only to sink right back in. She stroked her hands down his chest, lightly pinching his nipple before lifting up to stroke her tongue over the hardened nub.

Holding her tight to his chest, he sat back on his heels, then back on his ass, reversing their positions. "Mm." He reached up to fondle her breasts. "I like this."

She rotated her hips, her lips parting as her clit rubbed against him. "Me, too." She leaned forward, arching her back so he could suckle her breasts while she rode him. Another orgasm slowly built, so sharp, so strong she almost feared it. She tried to slow her pace, to ease away, but he wouldn't let her. He held her tight, his strength adding force to each thrust, his hips rising to meet hers, sinking him deep, his cock touching just the right spot over and over. "James."

"Say it again."

"Can't." She couldn't catch her breath. "Gonna make me scream."

Harder. Faster. Each thrust bussing her clit.

"Good. I want the whole damn world to know you're mine."

His mouth fastened to her breast and stars burst behind her eyes. Her whole body convulsed and she did scream his name.

Still he kept after her. Their bodies slapping together. Their breathing harsh. The scent of their arousal thick around them.

He tensed beneath her. His whole body surrounding her as he shouted her name.

His grip eased and she rested, boneless, over his chest trying to catch her breath. "Hope . . . I'm not . . . too heavy. Can't move."

She bounced a bit with his laughter. His arms came around her and he kissed the top of her head.

"You move . . . I'll just drag you right back."

Gods, she loved this male.

Lilith rubbed her eyes, wanting nothing more than to curl back up in James' arms. They'd hardly slept. Sometime in the night, he'd carried her upstairs and made love to her again. She arched her back and stretched.

"Come on, baby. It's dawn. Nan's coming."

James had already pulled on his pants and handed Lilith's robe to her. With a grumble, she got out of bed and put it on, wrapping the garment closed and tying the belt.

"Not a morning person, eh?" He gave her a quick kiss. "Me, neither."

She pressed her weight toward him, wanting to linger.

"Twenty minutes. Then we can sleep."

She nodded, rubbing at her eyes.

"Here we go." He opened the bedroom door and stood back.

Lilith fixed her gaze on the darkened hallway.

Now that the moment had arrived, she didn't know what to ask. Not really. Should she tell Nan about the notes? Ask her what truths she knew about the past? Ask her why she felt she needed to beat children? She fisted her hands at her side, staring into the darkness.

James came and stood with her. He brushed his hand over her cheek. "She may not have any answers, Lil."

"I know."

"And you can't believe everything she says."

Her gaze shifted to his. He was worried.

Footsteps skittered up the hall.

One long, thin arm reached across the opening and braced on the door frame. Nan may have become solid, but her flesh was a sickly gray, too thin, too tight over her bones and tendons.

James arm came around her. "I've got you. We're safe."

She nodded, but still gripped his hand for support.

Nan came into view. She had no hair, her features so sunken as to be almost indistinguishable. And her mouth didn't look like a human mouth at all, the thin lines of her lips vertical instead of horizontal. She wore no clothes, but any features that might distinguish her as male or female were gone. He ribcage seemed to be split into two to support the second set of arms—the ones ending in feeding hooks. She appeared far more alien that paranormal, but then Lilith had often wondered if they were one in the same.

"Nan?"

"You." The one word came out as a long accusatory hiss. "I should have killed you when I had the chance." Her beady black eyes darted between Lilith and James.

Lilith swallowed past the lump in her throat. This was the only blood relation she had. This thing. This creature who even in life had hated her. "Why? Why have you always hated me?"

"You aren't like us."

"I am. I'm a witch. I follow the laws."

"No." Her denial echoed in the room, making Lilith jump. "You are not. You are different. An abomination."

James snorted. "And here all this time, I thought I was the abomination."

Nan's eyes narrowed. "You, too, must die."

Lilith squeezed his hand. "I don't understand why. Or how I'm different."

Nan used her hooks to motion her closer. "Come here, Granddaughter."

James' arms tightened around her.

"Answer my question, Nana."

"You think I'll help you?" Her raspy voice edged up. "You think I'll tell you how to complete the abomination?" Her gaze searched the room. "Where is the dybbuk?"

"The—?" The hair on Lilith's nape stood on end. Both she and James looked around the room. Had she put something in here? Had she summoned some—? "Aimee." Lilith swung around and took a step toward the door. "You're talking about Aimee."

"You named it?" She laughed, a dry rasp that brought to mind wind-swept leaves.

Lilith's lips parted. "Why?" Why had her own grandmother cursed her with that creature?

"To hide your bastardized Magic from the likes of him. From daemon-kind. They'll use you. They will turn you against your own kind, use you until nothing is left before they toss away your carcass."

"You lie." James took a step closer and Lilith stalled him by squeezing his hand.

"Do I? I told you before, and I'll tell you again, Daemon. You will never get what you truly want. I've seen what will come. I've seen you destroyed."

James kept his expression void of any reaction. He must have heard all this before. "What about her birthmark? What does it signify?"

Again with the birthmark. Why wouldn't he believe her that it meant nothing?

For several moments, Nan stared at him. Then she left, slinking into the shadows of the hallway.

Lilith turned to James. "Do you think—?"

He held his finger to her lips. "Not until she's gone. I don't want her to overhear." James coaxed her back to bed, curling his large frame around hers and held her tight. For the next quarter hour they listened to Nan tear the house apart, banging doors, and throwing objects. The house didn't grow silent until dawn arrived.

Lilith sighed. "I wonder how much of a mess she left."

"Sounded like she wrecked half the house." He used his fingers to pull her hair back from her face. "You okay?"

"She's my only family. I don't understand why she hates me so much."

"Why does she think you're different? You said your mom had a Grimoire, so I'm assuming she was a witch. Was Nan?"

Gods, this was getting too close to places she didn't want to go with him. "Nan lost whatever Magic she had after her first heart attack; it happened before my mom died."

"But she said she had visions and saw our fates."

"Maybe when she had Magic. But things change, James. You and I have both changed, even since our first meeting. Whatever she saw . . . it doesn't mean anything unless you allow it to." She lifted onto her elbow to look at him. "She's hoping you'll believe her.

She's hoping that because you believe her, you'll create that reality. You can't believe her."

He nodded. "I understand."

"You can't give her any power. Don't even let yourself think about what she said."

He pulled her down and hugged her. "I won't think about it. Now, how do you think you're different from them?"

Lilith's lips parted, she had no idea what to say and was saved from having to answer when James' phone rang.

He answered. He got out of bed and stepped away from her. "Hey, Lou."

The volume was high enough that she couldn't help but hear the woman on the other end. "I've got a lycan in my trailer. He'd wants to set up a meeting with you."

"Me? Why?"

"He says he wants to speak to whoever has highest rank."

James cursed. "Then send him to Crowley."

"He doesn't want to speak to Crowley."

"All right." James dragged his hand over his head. "I don't know what I can do for him, but I'll meet with him."

They set the time for that night and James hung up.

He'd grown tense during the short conversation. Would meeting with the lycan male be dangerous? "Are you friendly with the lycan?"

He shrugged. "We ignore each other for the most part. Occasionally, our paths cross if one of theirs goes moon crazy or one of ours goes rogue. Then we work together to sort out the problem."

Rogue. She'd heard the term before, but had no idea what it meant. "What's it mean to go rogue?"

He climbed back into bed with her. "It's a flexible term. For most vampires, it would mean they're overcome with blood lust."

She grinned. "I thought all vampires had that."

"It's common with neophytes—newly transformed vampires—but after a while, we can control our base urges." He grinned. "Unless of course we find a particularly tasty bit." He made like he would bite her, scrapping his whiskers on her throat and making her laugh.

She swatted him away. "You're trying to change the subject. What are other reasons a vampire could be termed rogue?"

He flopped onto his back and pulled her close. "Guardians have stricter rules. We're not allowed to transform anyone."

Her brows furrowed. "Even your soul mate?"

His teasing grin faded. "Lilith, we're vampires. We have no soul, no mate. And the Council doesn't want us too attached to anyone."

"Oh." Her chest tightened. She didn't like hearing him say those things. Vampires did have mates. She was his mate, damn it. She'd known she risked trouble with the coven by being with him, but never considered the possibility the Council had any influence on mating. "What's the punishment? Do they put you in jail or something?"

"Jail?" He laughed. "We have no jails." He pulled Lilith down, tucking her head beneath his chin.

Lilith stilled in his arms. What had she done? If anyone found out about them, the coven and the Council would both be out to ash James. And once the Council found out about her, they'd discover the coven. "I'll never tell anyone." She leaned up on her arm to look down at him.

His lips curved, and he stroked her face. "I'm content. Whatever comes, I'll keep you safe."

She sat up and frowned. "If neither of us says anything . . . ."

He shook his head. "We're never alone, Lil. There are no secrets, aside from those never spoken and never acted on."

She closed her eyes. *The Watchers.* "I didn't think—"

"I did." He pulled her back down, wrapping her tight in his embrace. "I knew and I'd do it all again if had the chance."

CHAPTER 24

James eased his bike down Haven House's drive and onto the main road. Just as he was about to gun it, he caught sight of someone familiar. And unwelcome.

Damn, he didn't like Julius Crowley this close to Lilith. He gave the bike enough gas to bring him to Crowley's side and flipped up the visor on his helmet.

"James."

"Jules." He made sure to keep his gaze well away from Crowley's. "What the hell are you doing here?"

He rocked back on his heels, stuffing his hands in his pockets. "You spend a lot of time in that old run-down house."

James shrugged.

"I haven't seen you out and about much."

"They've only been sending me one or two jobs a night."

"Oh?" One blond brow arched. "Isn't that interesting."

James clenched his jaw. "You got something to say, Crowley?"

"Just seems odd. The Council might think you've gone rogue."

Rogue. James scoffed. "Seriously? I go a few days with minimal assassination jobs and that means I'm rogue?"

"Look at me."

"Fuck off." He'd never look this male in the eyes.

Julius laughed.

The sound sent a shiver of unease up James' spine. "What do you want?"

"I want to know what's in that house."

"Dust. Cobwebs. The ghost of an old woman."

Crowley bent at the waist, trying to sidle into James' line of site. "There's a human in there."

James got off the bike, his hands fisting.

"I came to see how you were doing. Door shield blocked my entrance."

James grabbed Crowley by the shirt front and hauled him up until they were nose to nose. Still, he kept his eyes lowered, focusing on the son of a bitch's clean-shaven chin. "There's nothing in that house for you."

"Oh? Not a pretty brunette who likes to wrap her long legs around your waist and scream your name?"

James released him. What the fuck? He must be guessing. Jesus, he had to be. The windows were boarded up for Christ's sake.

Crowley tipped his head to the side, trying to get in James' line of vision. "You didn't happen to notice a crescent moon birthmark on her skin while you were fucking her, did you?"

James withdrew his blade. Pressed it to Crowley's throat. "She's innocent. She's not who you're looking for."

"Careful now, pleb. I disappear and the Council will come looking. Then what? They'll see you shacked up with that pretty, very human brunette. They might think you've broken the Discovery Laws. They might think you really have gone rogue."

Goddamn it to hell. He released Crowley. "She doesn't have a birthmark. Not a crescent moon, not anything."

"Liar. I can feel the power in that house. It's not as strong as years ago. . . . What happened to her?"

James focused on Crowley's shirt front. "Nothing. She's just a plain human woman."

"With a pentacle hanging from her rearview mirror?"

Shit. "She fancies herself pagan."

"A witch."

"A pagan. There are no witches left." Except his. And no one was touching her.

Julius smiled, straightening his shirt. "Just remember, when she destroys the rest of us, she'll ash you, too."

James shook his head. "You don't know what the fuck you're talking about. The Watchers would tell us if she were a threat. We're part of the balance they protect."

"You're sure? Why don't you go ask the Historian?"

James flinched.

"What? You thought I didn't know you allowed the bitch to live? You think I don't know about that little cabin you set her up in? You can't hide from me."

If he'd known all this time . . . . "Seems funny you haven't done anything about it."

Crowley smirked. "Perhaps I will. Are you going to warn her?"

He wished to hell he could look Crowley in the eye and see his expression. What the hell was he after? He was almost goading him to speak with the Historian . . . but how the hell would that benefit Crowley?

"Don't underestimate me. You're on notice, Pasquino."

He flinched a bit at hearing his last name. Jesus, how did he know that?

Julius smirked. "Yeah, I know your name, Samael James Pasquino. Don't fuck with me, boy. I'll give you forty-eight hours to bring Lilith to me. Believe me, you don't want me to take care of things myself."

James got on his bike. Two days. He had two days to pull together some kind of plan and run with Lilith. He needed to get to Lou's. See if she'd discovered any news.

He slapped the visor down on his helmet.

"Oh, and James."

He paused.

"If you run, I'll ash every last one of the daemons who work for you."

Lilith had just finished her meditation when she heard the sound of a car pulling up. Curious, she opened the front door. A little red Honda convertible drove up, a familiar ebony-haired woman behind the wheel.

She raced down the steps. "Trina!"

Trina cut the engine and leapt out, letting out a shriek of joy. A full head shorter than Lilith, she'd always made up for size in sheer volume and presence. The women hugged each other, rocking from side to side one minute and jumping up and down the next.

"I didn't expect you for ages yet." Last she'd heard Trina still had six weeks of her enlistment left.

"They let me off early for good behavior." Trina grinned.

"Look at you." Trina had grown her hair long again, and the dark locks framed her face in a becoming way. "I love the new style—it suits you."

Trina's slender body was a combination of curves and sleek muscles men never failed to notice. Where Lilith was slender, Trina was more voluptuous. She also had the advantage of a constant tan, with her Latina coloring.

"Let's get your stuff inside." They each struggled with the heavy bags. "What'd you do, pack the ship?"

"Hey, my whole life is in these bags." Trina dragged the heavier two up the stairs. "I thought I did pretty good, getting all my stuff in four bags."

"If you drove up ten minutes ago, James could have done this."

"James?" Trina quirked her brow. "What happened to only letting him stay a few days?"

Lilith's cheeks heated.

"Mm-hmm." A knowing gleam entered Trina's eyes. "Hussy."

Lilith sniffed. "Witch."

Trina rolled her eyes. "So where is he? Out for a bite?"

"Work . . . maybe."

"Let's get the bags upstairs. We'll have ourselves a drink and you can tell me about this James-who-might-be-at-work."

Ten minutes later they lounged around the kitchen table, a bottle of vodka and a two-liter of Sprite between them, courtesy of Trina. Neither drank often, but their first night together they always got sloppy and told all. Lilith poured half a shot of vodka in each shot glass. Trina followed with the Sprite, filling the glasses the rest of the way.

"No tattoos this time, right?" Lilith referred to the last time they'd done this. The next morning they woke outside a tattoo parlor in Portland amid the shouts of an irate taxi driver.

Trina laughed. "No more tattoos. All right, you ready?" Both women covered their shot glass with their hands, raising them above the table. "On three. One, two . . . three." They slammed the glasses down and rushed them to their lips, the carbonation from the Sprite foaming, making the shot easy to swallow.

The warm sensation of the alcohol spread through Lilith's joints.

"Wow, another one or two of those and I'm going to be under the table." Trina wiped her palm on a napkin.

"Yeah, right. I bet you're used to drinking with all those handsome sailors." Lilith laughed. "All right, you first, I want to hear how you got out early."

"No way, you can't give me teasers about your mate, and then leave me hanging. You're first." Trina leaned on the table. "What's he like?"

She grinned. "Big."

"Where?" Trina laughed.

"You're impossible."

"Come on, girl, details, please." Trina poured them another drink.

"He's tall, maybe six, six-one. He's . . ." She did her best body-builder pose. "Built, lots of muscle, your type of guy. Handsome, strong features, full lips." Lilith drifted off.

Trina rested her chin on her hand. "Mm, good kisser?"

"Wonderful."

"Good in bed?"

Lilith grinned, unable to restrain her smile.

Trina stared. "Oh, my gods, you're glowing."

Lilith covered her blazing cheeks with her hands. "Shut up."

"You never go to bed with anybody." Trina slammed back her shot, wincing. "I mean . . . holy shit, you got laid?"

Lilith glared. "When you say it like that you make me sound like some ugly, uptight spinster. It's not like I had an entity attached to me or anything. You try getting freaky with a guy with something staring over your shoulder all the time."

Trina held up a placating hand. "My bad. You are correct. I'm not keen on being the object of voyeurism, either. I get it." She settled back in the chair. "So, when did he get transformed?"

"I'm not sure. He doesn't talk about himself much."

"A guy exists who doesn't revolve entire conversations around himself?" Her hand flew to her mouth in mock surprise. "Call the press."

Lilith laughed. "I don't know a lot about him. He has no family."

"A fellow orphan." Trina bobbed her head. "Okay."

"He's from Italy, but doesn't have an accent."

"So he's been in the States a long time. Is he dark-skinned, then?"

"Darker than me, lighter than you."

"Nice." Trina nodded. "Have you met any of his friends? Where does he work? How long has he been here?"

Lilith took a deep breath. "So, we've kinda got this 'don't ask, don't tell' thing going on."

"Great. I've moved in with my best friend and her

boyfriend the ax-murdering vampire. But it's okay, 'cause we just don't discuss it."

Lilith's lips twitched. "Over-dramatic much?" She poured them another shot. "I like him. He's not like what Nan told us about vampires. He's controlled and intense and protective." She shrugged and reverted to speaking through their psychic link. *Had the Clearances not happened, we'd have been working closely with him—he's a Guardian.*

One of Trina's brows rose. "He told you that?"

Lilith shook her head. *I've seen his blades.*

Really?

Lilith nodded. "I like him."

"You're repeating yourself." Trina folded her arms over her chest. "Are you trying to convince me you like him, or are you trying to convince yourself you *just* like him?"

"You shouldn't read so much into everything." If she told anyone about her feelings it would be James, and she wasn't ready to do that yet. Not until she told him everything. But what if he didn't want her once he found out she was part of the Grigori coven? She regarded Trina. *He doesn't think vampires have mates. The Vampiric Council forbids Guardian from being attached to anyone.*

"And you haven't corrected his thinking."

I wanted to. They'll ash him if they find out about us.

So you'll do what you need to do to protect him.

It wasn't a question. Trina wanted to remind her of her duty. She need to protect him and protect the coven. The best way to do that, would be to walk away from him. The problem was, she really didn't think she could. Something happened last night and even though she had no way of knowing where James went tonight, she did. She *felt* him. It was like some psychic string linked them, drawing thinner, pulling tauter the farther he went. She had no doubt if she followed that feeling, that sense of his presence, it would lead her right to him.

That must be why the Council didn't want Guardians to mate. It put them at risk.

Trina's gaze narrowed. "What are you thinking, Lil? I don't like that look."

Lilith dropped her gaze. "I don't know if it'll be that easy."

"Easy? None of your options are easy." Trina cursed. *If you stay with him, he'll change you eventually. You'll lose your Magic and any place you might have within the coven. The two of you will be on the run for the rest of your lives, outcast from both the coven and the Council.*

Lilith looked away. *And the farther he goes from me, the more I can feel him.*

Trina cursed. She stood and another series of curses flew from her mouth.

Lilith waited, letting Trina's fury wash over her. Her friend wasn't mad at her. Nor James. Just the situation. And where Lilith always held things in, Trina vented enough for both of them.

Trina stopped and her lips parted. *You two didn't just have sex, you've mated. The two of you mated, and he doesn't have a fucking clue.*

"He's been fed lies for a very long time."

"And you *like* him."

Lilith pressed her lips together. She had no intention of voicing her feelings to anyone but James.

You're stuck with him now, does he care for you?

He took me, thinking he'd signed his own death warrant. What do you think?

That he's probably questioning his sanity and can't come up with a reasonable explanation for his behavior because he has no fucking idea how you two are linked. You have to tell him.

"I will." Lilith took a deep breath. "I have a plan."

"From what I remember, your plans never work out the way we intended them to."

A small smile tugged at Lilith's lips. "Yeah, well.

You're back. You'll help. Everything will be okay."

"Will I? I haven't decided yet if he's good enough." Her gaze narrowed into dangerous slits. *I might just ash him instead and save everyone else the trouble.*

Lilith shook her head. "You wouldn't upset me."

"Better upset than dead."

They stared at each other a long moment, a silent battle of wills.

Lilith frowned. "I forbid you to hurt him."

"If he hurts you, any vow I make now is void."

"Fine." James would never hurt her.

"Fine."

George sprang onto the table and meowed. "What? You want an introduction? George, this is Trina. Trina, George."

"When did you get a cat? Get lonely without Aimee around?" She reached over to pet him.

"Nice." She rolled her eyes. "Actually, he belongs to the ax-murdering vampire."

"Oh, well, there you go." Trina sat back, waving her arm out to the side. "He must be all right if the cat likes him."

"What about you?" Lilith rested her elbows on the table, pinning Trina with her gaze. "I want to hear about what happened to what's-his-name."

Trina groaned. "I knew you'd bring him up."

For years, every time they spoke, Trina had a new guy. Then for a while it was all about one guy in particular, Trevor. Then nothing. No Trevor. No more men. Period.

"It's been two years." Lilith shook her finger at her. "Two years ago, you said next time we got together you'd explain." And then Trina had avoided coming home. Avoided meeting Lilith when she was near ports where Trina's ship had docked. She'd been hiding from her for two years. And it hurt.

Trina gave a negligent shrug she didn't buy for a moment. "He proposed."

"So you dumped him."

Trina had never been one for long-term relationships. The six months or so she'd spent with Trevor was unheard of.

"No," Trina said quietly. "I accepted."

"You what?"

"I know, moment of insanity. Luckily, I caught him with his pants around his ankles, banging a third class petty officer." Trina's effort to sound flip failed miserably.

"I'm so sorry, Trina." Lilith placed her hand over her friend's. "I can't imagine." Trina never let her feelings get involved. She'd taken a risk with Trevor, and it'd been shoved back in her face.

Like I said, I got lucky. Who would want to spend the rest of their lives shackled to one guy? No one is that interesting. Trina pulled her hand away and did another shot, wincing.

There was more to the story, but she sensed Trina wasn't ready to share. Afraid her friend would shut down if she pried, she changed the subject. "We might as well get all your news out now—so how did you happen to get released from the Navy early?"

"Oh, no, it's your turn. Tell me about Aimee." Trina's eyes narrowed. "I've been waiting for you to tell me what happened."

"Wait here." Lilith left to retrieve Aimee's jar. She set it down in front of Trina, presenting it with a flourish. George hissed and leapt off the table. Lilith laughed. "Bad memories, maybe."

Trina picked up the amber jar, squinting. Shadows moved restlessly against the glass. "Aimee?"

Lilith nodded. She caught Trina up on everything that happened since she'd returned to Haven House.

Trina rolled the jar back and forth across the table while she digested the story. "I never considered a dybbuk. To be honest, I didn't think there were any left."

"I knew Nan hated me, but I never thought she'd

curse me."

Trina picked up the jar and shook it.

Lilith's phone rang. "Hello?"

"Lilith, dear."

She froze as she recognized the voice. Her gaze shot to Trina. "It's so good to hear from you, Rowena."

Trina winced.

"Lilith, I heard you were in town and I want you to come to dinner tonight. Just to catch up."

"Well, I . . . ."

"Now, I won't take no for an answer, dear. You've been away from home far too long. I need to see my girl."

Lilith pulled the phone from face to stare at it. Granted, she'd always considered Rowena sort of a surrogate mother, but she never considered Rowena felt the same. "Ah, sure. In that case, I'd love to come."

"Perfect. I'll see you at nine-thirty."

They said goodbye and hung up.

Lilith glanced at Trina. "I'm having dinner at Rowena's place tonight. Wanna come?"

Trina stared at her as if she'd lost her mind.

"Well, I wouldn't want you to feel left out. I'm sure she'll be ecstatic to know you're home."

Trina shook her head, paling. "Don't tell her. I'm not back. Not really. I came for a visit, that's all."

"What is going on with you?"

Trina leaned back in her chair, letting her head fall back.

Gods, she was worried about Trina. She wasn't acting quite herself. And she still hadn't told her how she'd come to be here weeks early. "Did you have leave you forgot about?" It worried her that Trina kept avoiding the subject. Trina going AWOL from the Navy was the last thing they needed.

Trina's eye's filled with sadness before she dropped her gaze to the thick tangle of plastic bracelets covering most of her left forearm. Lilith hadn't taken much notice, but they weren't something she'd ever seen her friend wear before.

"I promise no one is searching for me, Lil. I didn't break any—" Trina shook her head. "The Navy released me free and clear, okay?"

"Trina?" Lilith's gut clenched. She reached over and covered her hand with hers. "What happened?"

"I'm not ready to talk about it." *I just . . . I knew I couldn't keep hiding. And I had to come home because you're going to need me.* Trina met her gaze. *I didn't want you to go through this alone.*

Something had happened. Something bad. She hadn't seen Trina cry since Rowena had forced her to sign with the military at seventeen, but tonight, she looked like she might break into sobs at any moment.

"I'll just hang out here while—"

Dear gods, Nan! "Listen, Trina, we have a bit of a ghost problem right now. If you stay here tonight, you'll need to stay in James' room with us. Kat gave me a potion, but it was only enough to protect one room so I could question Nan."

Trina shook her head. "I think I'll pass. I've no desire to see that bitch, either."

She didn't like the idea of leaving Trina alone. "You're sure you don't want to come along to Rowena's?"

"Now you're just being ridiculous. We have enough problems without that." Trina shook her head. "A hotel will suit me just fine for a night or two." She reached over and put the cap back on the vodka. "You can't drive."

"I'll walk."

Trina pulled a face. "Eager to meet up with more daemons?"

Lilith glared.

"Go get ready. I'll clean up our mess and when you're ready to go, I'll use the Traveler's spell to send you there. When you're ready to come home, just call me."

"All right." Lilith sighed. "And when you're ready to talk, you'll call me. Right?"

Trina looked away, but she nodded.

CHAPTER 25

James stepped inside Lou's bloodmobile. The lycan sat back in the corner, his long legs stretched out, his hands stacked behind his head. A young guy, no more than twenty-five, with neat bundles of dreadlocks hanging around his face. He kept his goatee trimmed tight to his skin. His baggy clothes were expensive and a sliver ankh hung from a chain around his neck. "James, right?"

He nodded.

Lou motioned toward her guest. "This is Will Wear, James."

"Will." He glanced back and forth between the two, taking in their dower expressions. "What's going on?"

Lou shook her head. "Nothing. He just got here." She tucked herself in her chair, leaving the patient seat for James.

James sat and gave Will his attention. "What can I do for you?"

"We got people all over, you know that. Our packs rotate through areas, leaving our properties for the next pack and moving to the next. Seattle's been pretty quiet compared to the rest of the world. We try to stay in touch with you guys. We get to know those of you in our area." He leaned forward, bracing his elbows on his knees. "Shit's going down, man. And our holy man is worried that you'll all start blaming us."

James regarded Will. Lycans tended to keep to

themselves. They protected their family and faith viciously, and took great pains to keep their secret. Most could pass a physical as a human. Their kids attended public school, their men and women worked regular jobs. Nomadic, they moved every ten years or so, so humans didn't become too suspicious of how little they aged. Will and his pack had only been in the Seattle area about a year.

James had no idea where he got his information or how accurate it might be. "Okay. What are you seeing?"

"Guardians are disappearing. A lot of them."

"You're sure they're not being transferred. Not on down time?"

Will stared. "You're not acting surprised, but you don't know for sure, either, do you?"

James leaned back in his chair and looked up at the ceiling, hoping to hell Will caught the warning. The Watchers saw and heard everything. Insubordination wouldn't be tolerated.

Will cursed. "Our hem-it-netjer said we're beyond all that, man."

"What the hell is a hem-it-whatever-you-said?"

"The Watchers have no real connection to our world. For centuries, they'd choose a human to put into a temporary trance and speak through them to communicate with us, but the exercise is draining. Once done, they're useless for days."

That's how Guardians used to get their assignments, from humans in a trance-like state. "Right, so now they use technology—texts and emails."

"For you. We have a holy man, one who devotes his life to being their mouthpiece, he's completely surrendered to them. Using him to deliver their messages doesn't drain them. They asked my hem-it-netjer to look into the missing Guardian. *They* said the Guardian disappeared. And they wanted us to find out where they went."

James froze. How the hell did something disappear

from a Watcher's sight? They saw fucking *everything*. He glanced a Lou. "Is this place clean?"

She nodded, wiping her palms down her thighs. "Checked myself less than an hour ago. We're clean."

Will listened to the exchange. His lips parted. "You don't trust the Council."

This time James cursed. "Watch what you say, damn it." He glanced away and let out a sigh. "I have some concerns." He pinned Will with his stare. "*Concerns.* Right?"

Will dragged his hand down his chin. "My hem-it-netjer says something is very, very wrong. Something we haven't seen in eons is walking free."

The hair at James' nape stood on end. What had Crowley said the other night?

She's dangerous.

To who?

To us.

He shook his head. "What else do you know?"

This time, Will glanced up at the ceiling. "I know that this thing, it cannot lie. It uses its truths to hurt and manipulate, which makes it all the more dangerous."

James cocked his brow.

"When I was a kid, my hem-it-netjer often told us tales of Ra's second coming."

James leaned back in his chair. Lycans loved to tell stories.

"See, back in the day, our people worshiped Ra as The God. And when we discovered Ra was only one of the Grigori, tricking us, come to search for a bride among our women, we fought him. And we lost."

"He cursed you."

Will nodded. "Now we forever worship Ra—Ramiel—because we fear him. Though we know the truth, we do not often speak the words out loud."

Of course they wouldn't, the Watchers would hear them and might decide to punish them further. "Why tell me?"

Will remained silent, waiting.

James thought over the story. The Grigori had tricked the Lycan—letting them worship Ramiel as a god, when he was only a Watcher. And now they waited for his second coming. *Jesus, the Lycan thought they had a Watcher on the loose.* He nodded. "Got it."

"Do you?" Will stood. "I'm not so sure. My hem-it-netjer, he's old now. He won't last much longer and no new holy man has been named. The Watchers, they don't seem to see the need for a new mouthpiece."

The Lycan took their traditions seriously. So did the Watchers, for that matter. James glanced at Lou, then turned back to Will. "You think the End Times are coming?"

"For a while, we thought maybe someone new would arrive, maybe someone outside our pack, someone special who possesses Magic, a woman who could corral the growing darkness. We call this person the Beacon." He searched James' face. "You haven't met anyone like that, have you?"

Seen a woman of Magic who'd shone light on the darkness of his life? Just one. James shook his head.

"You sure? Because the Watchers seem to like you, man. We've been hearing your name a lot."

A pent-up breath shook loose from his lungs. Something was very wrong with this whole scenario. Will had just suggested the Lycan believed a Watcher was loose here on Earth, heralding the End Times. In the next breath, he said the Watchers had them looking for the Beacon to stop the Watcher. Meanwhile, Crowley said the Watchers wanted him to kill the woman with the crescent moon tattoo. Jesus, were the Watchers fighting among themselves, now? And how the hell did the Vampiric Council fit into this?

Who am I protecting her from?

Everyone.

Will leaned forward. "No one new in your life?"

"No." James reached into his backpack and pulled out

a business card, the small white rectangle blank except for his cell number, and handed it to Will. "Keep me in the loop."

Will took the card and stood. "Times are changing, man. Things are moving fast, coming to a head. You need to decide where you're going to stand."

"I'm a Guardian."

"The Guardians are dying." Will cursed and looked away. "Daemon-kind will be revealed to the masses soon. I don't know how and I don't know why, but I can only think of one reason for someone to be taking Guardians out. They're going to go public. And if we don't know who it is, we can't stop them. We can prepare, but we can't stop it. And once that's done . . . ."

There would be pandemonium. The humans would panic. Hell, daemons would panic. And his role would be gone. "I'm a relic."

Will nodded. "We all are—those of us who have kept the secret. You need to be flexible, man. Move with the times. We're gonna need big, strapping boys like you. You just gotta pick a side. Are you going to continue to protect the humans—?"

"I don't protect them." Did he? He protected one human. A human he might soon find himself fighting against in World War III.

"What about daemons, do you protect them? Think about what's going to happen, man. Think about our kids, our women." He glanced at Lou. "Not all daemons hide in the dark. Think about what the humans are going to do to us."

Jesus, he was right. The daemons would be the ones needing protection. They were the minority in this world these days. They were . . . domesticated.

Will shouldered past and let himself out of the trailer.

James turned to Lou. Her hand covered her mouth, her eyes damp. "We're in trouble, aren't we, big guy?"

"Nah." He took her hand in his, but when he met her eyes, he couldn't lie. "Maybe."

"What do you think the Council will do? They might see this as the perfect opportunity to erase the other daemon races."

"They might." The Council was comprised of a bunch of elitists. "Or they might see it as an opportunity to get the rest of daemon-kind to bow to their will."

Lou cursed. And it sounded so strange, he realized he never heard her cuss before.

"Look, I'm not sure where all the pieces are going to fall. Or how big the fallout will be." He squeezed her hand. "But I know I protect you."

Lou threw her arms around his shoulders. "Is it stupid that I'm scared?" She let out a watery laugh. "I've lived through two world wars, James, but this . . . this scares the hell out of me."

"It's just because nothing like this has happened before." It's because they didn't know what the hell *was* happening. "We can't predict the outcome." But he damned well knew who could. Maybe he needed to pay the Historian a visit. "Look, I don't want you spending all your time stressing over this."

She nodded against his shoulder.

"You bring the bloodmobile down to Carnation. There's a spot down near the Tolt River where the humans won't bother you. You'll be close to me. Close enough for me to protect you."

She looked up then. "Your . . . friend won't mind?"

He shook his head, though he wasn't sure at all. Trees hid the spot he had in mind from the house. Lilith might not realize Lou was even there. "Once you're situated, send a message, one the Council won't see, to the rest of our team to let them know."

"I'll send an IM through the HV site. I know you don't like us using those human vampire chat rooms, but it's the only place we're anonymous."

"That's good. That'll work. Tell the Guardians your place is our meet point from now on. Tell them, if they're in trouble, come to you."

"Got it." She sniffed.

He wiped away a tear from her cheek and smiled. "How long have we worked together?"

"Little over a hundred years now."

He nodded. "Have I ever let you down?"

She shook her head. "Never."

"Okay, then. Chin up. Make me believe you've got a bit of faith in me."

Lou sniffed and wiped her face. She twisted around in her seat and reached into one of the coolers. "I have that extra something for you. I think, all things considered, I'll keep extra on hand from now on. Just in case anyone else needs some."

He cocked his brow in question. "Are there other Guardians mixing with humans?"

She shrugged. "You know how it is during times of conflict. In some, it brings out the worst, and in others, the best."

CHAPTER 26

Blessed be! Look at you, Lilith. You're all grown up," Rowena said. "And into such a beauty. You remind me of your mother."

"Blessed be." Lilith pasted a smile to her face. She'd have rather spent the evening with Trina, but the last thing she needed was for Rowena to show up at Haven House. "It's good to see you again."

"What's this? Your Magic is back." She gave the impression of surprise, happiness even. "This is wonderful. Oh, do come in. We've got a lot to discuss."

She stepped inside, glanced around. It'd been years since she'd been in Rowena's house, but not much had changed. The little living room off the foyer still brimmed with books, plants, and various other Magical brick-a-brac. The house still smelled of dried herbs. "You have a lovely home. It's so peaceful, tucked away back here against the mountains."

"Thank you, it's sweet of you to say." Rowena poured on so much sugar, Lilith felt ill.

"I just set dinner on the table. Come on in and we'll eat."

She followed Rowena through an alcove to the dining room. A long, cherry wood table fully occupied with women filled the room.

Dear gods—the entire coven came for dinner.

Rowena took her place at the head of the table, but remained standing and indicated an empty seat to

Lilith, one seat removed from her left. Perfect. The "Judas seat."

She settled into her chair. Behind Rowena and just to the side stood a headless sewing mannequin dressed in Rowena's ceremonial robes, complete with what she assumed was the Legacy Necklace—a long silver chain holding a blood-red stone.

"Let me reintroduce you to everyone." Rowena drew Lilith's attention away from the necklace. Starting with those nearest, she made her way around the entire group. "This is Abby." Lilith smiled at the woman sitting between her and Rowena. Waif-thin, mousy brown hair surrounded her pale, skeletal face.

"On your other side is Zoe." Zoe appeared to have just stepped out of the salon. She'd applied her makeup perfectly and not a strand of her shiny blond hair strayed out of place.

"Next we have Fiona, Violet, and Gina." Lilith leaned forward to see them past Zoe, and all three women nodded in greeting.

"On the other side of the table we have Debbie and Claire." They both smiled warmly. The twins were beautiful enough to be runway models, from their long blond hair to their size four jeans.

"And finally we have Sheri, Meredith, Brenda, and, of course, you remember my daughter, Katherine."

Lilith smiled in greeting to each, and they all returned her gesture, though Katherine seemed uncomfortable.

"Ladies," Rowena said. "You all remember Lilith. She's to inherit her post, now she's regained her Magic." Rowena sat. "Let's eat."

"You've outdone yourself." Lilith glanced down at her plate. "This smells wonderful."

"Nonsense, I just ordered out and arranged the food on nice plates." She flashed a coy grin. "I've never ordered from this restaurant before, so let me know what you think."

Rowena waited for Lilith and the others to taste the food, so Lilith took a bite, almost surprised at the pleasant taste. "You picked a good place. It's delicious."

Several other women murmured their agreement.

Rowena preened under the praise. She slipped a laden fork between her lips and hummed with pleasure.

Fiona peeked around Zoe. She held her long, raven-black hair away from the table with crimson-tipped fingers and arched one sooty brow. "When did you get your Magic back?"

"Oh, yeah," Sheri said. She had flawless ebony skin and beautiful curly hair with so much body it fluffed itself around her face in a halo, her appearance a complete opposite from the awkward youth Lilith remembered. "How did it happen? We want all the details."

Lilith decided to stick as close to the truth as possible to avoid getting caught in a lie later. "A few days ago. When I got to Haven House. I started turning lights off and on before I even realized what I'd done."

"How fascinating." Rowena sipped her wine. "I wonder . . . . You know, I think Nan has forgiven you for using Magic against her. She must have decided you've been punished enough."

Several of the women stared at her, waiting to see what she would say.

"Oh, Nan is as unforgiving as ever." Lilith set her wine glass down. "I'm in the process of evicting her spirit from the house."

Rowena's penciled-in eyebrows rose so high on her forehead they all but disappeared under the curl of her bangs. "Really?"

She nodded. "Kat helped pick out the spells."

Her green eyes cut to Kat. "Did you?"

Kat set her fork down and lifted her napkin to her mouth. Her hands shook.

She shouldn't have said that. Now she'd gotten Kat into trouble. She sent her an apologetic look.

"How's Aimee?" Rowena tipped her head to the side. "Odd, but now your Magic has returned I don't feel her presence like I used to."

"I don't know. Once we got to Haven House, she vanished. I haven't seen her since."

Rowena's eyes went hard, but just as quickly her mask of friendliness returned.

"Thank the Spirits." Meredith slouched in her chair. She'd dyed her blond hair black, with only the tips remaining their original yellow. Her cupid doll lips pursed. "I can't imagine living with something like Aimee. It must have been horrible."

Zoe leaned toward Lilith. "You must be so relieved."

Lilith nodded. They had no idea.

Fiona shuddered. "Did you ever figure out what she was?"

Lilith shook her head.

Rowena raised her glass as if in a toast. "You must have forgiven yourself. That's why Aimee is gone."

Again, Lilith nodded. If she opened her mouth, she feared she'd ask Rowena if she knew about Aimee and how the entity had stolen her Magic. And that would upset all Kat's carefully laid plans.

"You know," Kat said, and sat back against her chair and folded her arms over her chest, "I never did understand what Lilith needed to be punished or forgiven for. Just because some stranger claiming to be a cop went upstairs and rescued her? And Nan died of a heart attack." She gave her mother a pointed stare. "You said so yourself."

Lilith covered her grin with her napkin.

"Well, dear,"—Rowena gave her a tight smile—"I can explain it in detail after dinner."

A fork rattled onto a plate somewhere farther down the table. A hush fell.

Goddess preserve her, she'd been in the coven's presence fifteen minutes and already she'd created trouble. "Kat meant no offense, Rowena." Lilith dabbed at her mouth with her napkin. "I'm sure explanations aren't necessary."

"Of course, I'm sure you're right." Her voice sounded pleasant enough, but the glare she fixed on Kat looked lethal.

"You know what this means, don't you?" Claire spoke from the far end of the table.

Everyone turned to her.

"We have all thirteen members," Claire said. Her bright blue eyes lit with excitement. "Katherine can keep filling in until Trina gets back."

"Lilith will be ready within a fortnight." Brenda's eyes were closed when she spoke, indicating she used her prognostic abilities. When her eyes opened, they fixed on Lilith. Brenda tipped her head to the side as she regarded her through black eyes. Or maybe they looked so dark because she dressed in black all the way down to her ebony-tipped nails.

Rowena leaned forward. "Did you see something of importance, Brenda?"

Lilith's stomach clenched and her breath hitched. What if she knew about James? Lilith held her breath as Brenda continued to watch her, and everyone else continued to watch Brenda.

Brenda's gaze shifted to Rowena. "Lilith will be ready in a fortnight. She'll be a positive addition to the coven." Brenda's gaze dropped down to her plate.

What did that mean? Had she seen James and been okay with it? Did she see them being successful in removing Rowena from the coven?

But the high priestess interpreted the portent a different way altogether. "At last we'll defeat the vampires." Rowena sounded ecstatic. "Your mother would be so proud, Lilith."

Her entire body went rigid. She hated when Rowena spoke of her mother. She forced herself to paste on another false smile. "Thank you. I hope she is."

"When will Trina return? Do you know?" Violet asked.

Her hair was cut close to her head, her ebony skin dark as pitch. She had light brown eyes that looked almost amber.

"She should be back in about seven weeks."

"How nice," Zoe said.

Abby smiled. "The two of you were always inseparable."

"Until Rowena enlisted her in the Navy." Lilith mentally cringed, she shouldn't have said that.

Again the table fell silent.

If Lilith had been a little wild as a child, Trina had been the devil incarnate, and neither Nan nor Rowena had much patience for either of them. As Trina's legal guardian, Rowena signed Trina up for the Navy when she turned seventeen to keep her and Lilith apart.

"I did it out of love, dear. We had her best interest in mind." Rowena eyed her over the top of her wine glass.

Lilith offered a small smile and nodded—more like Rowena's best interests. A magician of the highest talent, she had a knack for making trouble vanish. The joke was on Rowena, though. Trina, stubborn to the last, had re-signed for two additional tours, halting all Rowena's grand plans for the coven.

"Trina was always a firecracker." Abby chuckled, drawing Lilith back to the conversation. "I swear I always got so angry with her for her antics, but I think now we're older, we'd all get along great."

Lilith caught what appeared to be a silent message in Abby's expression . . . an apology?

Laughter bubbled up from Gina, gaining everyone's attention. She'd been so quiet until now, obviously still shy in group settings. She brushed her chin-length brown hair from her face. "Remember when Trina got into a fight with, oh, what's the name of the mean girl from fifth grade . . . Beth! And Lilith—"

Several of the women shook their heads or coughed into their napkins. Gina paled as she noted the not-so-subtle warnings. They were never supposed to use

Magic around humans. Not only had Lilith done so, but all the girls were present when she used Magic on Beth, and no one reported the offense to Rowena. She'd be furious to find out now that Lilith had used Magic around a human and the entire coven had covered for her.

"What?" Rowena's green eyes bounced from one guilty face to another. "It sounds like a great story. You must finish."

Lilith shrugged. "To be honest, I don't remember."

"But I'm so curious now, Gina? Fiona? Anyone?"

Kat's glass of wine tipped over. She, Rowena, and Brenda all scrambled to clean up the mess before the liquid spilled off the table and soaked into the carpet.

"Damn, you're clumsy," Rowena shouted.

Violet spoke into the commotion. "What I'm dying to know, Lilith, is if you've been practicing your Magic and meditation? You must be if Brenda thinks you'll be ready for induction in two weeks."

Lilith nodded. "I never gave up meditation. Since I've regained my Magic, I practice spell work every day, too."

"Good. That's the best way to increase your power," Debbie said.

"And it's the perfect time with the waxing moon," Gina added.

"Of course, now you're reunited with the coven," Abby said. "Being near others with Magic will also increase your power."

They ate in silence for a few moments. Finally, Rowena said, "We should fill you in on all the gossip."

Sheri grinned. "There have been eleven births in the last six years."

"And guess what?" Gina said. "They were all girls."

Rowena laughed. "Isn't that fabulous?"

No surprise there, not with artificial insemination and gender selection available. Rowena wouldn't have had it any other way.

The women went on and on about the children. Their

love for their little ones showed in their animated pride while discussing the monumental feats of potty-training, ballet class, and soccer games.

Abby was more reserved than she remembered. Lilith got the impression her daughter was sickly and wasn't around the others often. And Kat didn't brag about a child at all. She joined in talking about the other children, though, which made Lilith think she might be the only one there, aside from her, who wasn't a mother. That had to chaff Rowena.

The talk of children lasted through the meal. After a while, the subject changed to specialties in Magic.

"I think every member of the coven is strong in their powers," Rowena said, "but a few have developed a higher-than-normal proficiency in an area or two."

"Kat is our expert healer," Gina said. "You wouldn't believe how good she is. When my daughter fell off the monkey bars last year and dislocated her elbow, I brought her to Kat. She healed the break in two hours, and Kat hasn't even inherited yet. She's amazing."

Kat blushed. "You should see how accurate Brenda's portents are, and Claire's dream Magic. They're the amazing ones."

"I wonder if you'll develop an area of specialty now your Magic is back," Violet said to Lilith.

Lilith shrugged. She knew her specialty, she still needed to master manipulating the elements, though.

"What do you see, Brenda?" Rowena took a sip of wine.

Brenda's eyes shifted between Lilith and Rowena before closing again. The room grew quiet while the women waited for Brenda's prediction. "Elemental Magic."

Rowena appeared startled by the prediction. "Which element?"

"Once whole, she'll rule them all."

Whole? What did that mean?

"You mean be able to manipulate them all," Rowena

corrected.

Brenda stared at her for a moment before glancing away. "All right."

A chill swept up Lilith's spine at Brenda's flippant tone.

"You know," Kat said, "we're going to have to find a new purchaser now."

"Oh, true," Sheri agreed. "Lilith can't be traveling if she's going to be a part of the coven now."

"It shouldn't be too hard." Lilith smiled. "I enjoyed the job."

"And you were good at it." Fiona wiped her mouth with her napkin. "Once you took over, the quality of our products went up, and sales started shooting through the roof. The coven has never been so successful with our Magic supply sales."

Lilith smiled.

"Would you like more wine, dear?" Rowena topped off her own glass.

"No, thank you. I should get going soon." When Rowena's eyes shot up to hers, she felt the need to provide an excuse. "I just got a new cat and have never left him alone for so long. I'm hoping he hasn't destroyed the house already."

"Of course—it's getting late, and felines . . . they can be fickle creatures." Rowena smiled, seeming to accept her excuse. "We won't keep you much longer, but I do have a gift for you."

"You shouldn't have," Lilith said automatically as Rowena got up.

"We should send some of the leftovers home with you, Lilith." Fiona and Debbie both sprang from their seats. "We'll help you find everything, Rowena." The twins ushered Rowena out, closing the kitchen door in their wake.

Katherine stood, motioning Lilith to the mannequin holding the Legacy Necklace. Lilith got up and made her way around the table.

Katherine motioned to the necklace. "Try it on."

"What? Are you crazy? She could come back any minute."

"Fiona and Debbie will keep her busy. We've had this planned for ages." Kat held the necklace out to her.

Lilith bit her lip. "How will I know?"

"We'll all know. The legend doesn't say how, just that we'll know."

Lilith took the necklace and slid the silver chain over her head. As soon as the tear-shaped stone came to rest between her breasts, it jolted her to another time:

The others were with her as well. Not in physical bodies. They appeared more as apparitions, their bodies invisible but for a faint blue outline of their forms and features. She stood on a dirt street between rows of rustic cabins with the others. The area was devoid of life, or so she thought at first. When she saw the first signs of movement, she stood transfixed in horror.

She had no idea what the creatures were. There were two of them. At some point they'd been human, but not anymore. Their bodies appeared stretched, their forms twisted and bulging with unnatural muscle mass. They made animalistic sounds as they moved about, searching for something, sniffing the air as they wandered in and out of buildings, their eyes gleaming.

A flash of light lit up the area, and a group of women materialized.

Lilith's breath hitched. The old coven. These women were past-life versions of her and the others. Their features differed, but not enough to make each of the witches unrecognizable. The high priestess stared straight at her for a moment before she spoke to her coven. "Find him. And remember, none of the Nephilim can be allowed to leave this place. Should any of us be bitten, the rest must destroy the fallen."

Just then, one of the creatures let out a war cry. Nephilim, as she had called them, swarmed in from every direction.

The women spread out, away from one another. They generated round orbs between their hands. Some sizzled with electricity, others blazed with fire. The night sky lit up as they hurled the balls toward their attackers.

The Nephilim raced into the onslaught, unfazed by the coven's arsenal. Those struck, fell, their bodies engulfed in flame before their bodies crumbled into soot and ash. Electricity jolted and seized others before they, too, erupted into flame and burned into nothingness.

But the coven was outnumbered, and soon overwhelmed. Witches dashed in every direction, dodging the creatures' grasps as they fought.

One of the twins, either Debbie or Claire, fell first. A creature caught hold of her long blond hair, snapping her neck back so hard bone snapped. It dropped to the ground with her, sinking its shark-pointed teeth into her neck. It ripped flesh from the body, chewed, and swallowed before the creature began lapping at her blood. The other twin rose up behind the creature. She let out a scream of pure anguish and outrage. Bolts of energy crackled around her, her arms raised high overhead, swinging down and to the side. A nearby tree did the same, toppling down and crushing the Nephilia. Barren winter branches sank deep into the creature's flesh seconds before it burst into dust.

Lilith blanched at the violence.

In another area a young man, maybe in his twenties, stepped onto the street. She wanted to shout a warning to him. He seemed so young and innocent with his curly hair in a disarrayed tangle on his head as though he'd just woken. Then she noticed his eyes glowed silver.

The Nephilim ignored him, running around him to fight the women.

"I am Lilith, the Original."

Lilith swiveled her head to find the voice. Almost like gazing into a mirror, except this past-life version of her wore old-fashioned garb, a long, heavy skirt, and serviceable top. The past-life Lilith spoke to the young man.

"I banish you." Her eyes closed then, and her lips moved silently, furiously, as she cast her spell.

The man sauntered toward her, laughing. The strange, broken sound, gave the impression of insanity. "What are you up to, little witch?" He circled her with the interest of a hungry shark. "Ah, Psalm 91. So you're the woman Lady Augustina speaks of."

Past-life Lilith's words faltered. She sucked in a shaky breath and started again.

"Lilith, the Original? Maybe." He circled again, oblivious to the chaos surrounding them. "But you don't feel anywhere near as strong as you should."

Past-life Lilith continued her chant, but her body had begun to shake. Her voice wavered, not quite so confident.

He withdrew a dagger from beneath his coat and plunged it deep into Lilith's chest.

A scream ripped from her throat. At the same moment a scream erupted from another nearby. Lilith wheeled around, searching for the source. . . .

Someone shook her. She opened her eyes to see Fiona in front of her. "Rowena will be back soon."

Lilith sucked in a hard breath, clutching at her chest. She'd felt it, the burn and sting of the blade. "What was that?" She looked at Kat.

"The Clearances. I've had a similar dream since childhood. I've never seen that part of the events. My dreams focus on the end of the battle, when almost everyone is either dead or transformed into those creatures." Katherine rubbed her throat. Her spine straightened, and she met Lilith's gaze. "I've heard Mother call you that . . . the Original. Nan, too, when we were kids."

Claire spoke. "You're our high priestess."

"To hell with that," Sherri said. "You're the Original, whatever that is."

Lilith shifted positions. "Did any of you see who else fell when he stabbed . . . me?"

Everyone shook their heads.

"Did anyone recognize the man?" She glanced at each of them, but none knew him.

A cacophony of coughing came from behind the kitchen door.

Kat touched her arm. "Don't say anything. We'll elect you high priestess at your induction. We'll take care of everything. She can't challenge us all."

"Hurry." Fiona tugged the necklace over Lilith's head and got it back onto the mannequin just as the kitchen door opened.

Rowena took in the odd scene with a sweep of her eyes. "What's going on?"

Her face must be as white as the other women's after the horrors they had just seen. Those who weren't in the room when she put the necklace on seemed unaware of what had happened.

"Nothing, Mother." Kat's smile looked feral. "We were just admiring the Legacy—"

A sharp rap at the door interrupted her.

Rowena sighed, walking into the other room. "Who the devil is that?"

Lilith leaned toward Kat. "Are you going to be okay tonight?"

"Yeah."

Claire smiled. "Kat is leaving with me. I'll make sure."

Brenda grabbed her arm to gain her attention. "You can control all the elements, Lilith."

Lilith stared. "I'm learning to."

"Yes, but from what I saw in my vision you've forgotten about the fifth element, void. You could use that to trap your skin-walker."

"Void?"

"Mm." Brenda closed her eyes. "You need to picture absolute nothingness and then call it forth. But be careful, make sure to keep it contained, envision a bubble of void, or a box, not just void."

Lilith nodded. She had a thousand questions to ask about Brenda's instructions, but the deep rumble of a male voice rolled into the dining room. Lilith's face heated as she recognized James' voice and she gripped Kat's hand in hers. "Oh, gods."

She ran into the other room, drawing up short at the horrifying sight of James standing on the porch.

He pointed to her. "See. There she is."

Rowena's fierce green eyes locked on her.

"James and I had plans this evening. I-I pushed our date to a later time when I received your invitation."

"I see." Rowena turned her attention back to James. "My girls don't date."

Oh, gods. She'd forgotten. "I haven't been part of this . . . family for a long time."

"Indeed." She stepped back. "Come in."

Lilith squeezed Kat's hand, whispering. "He needs a formal invitation."

Kat's eyes widened.

"I think we'll be late for the movie if we stay." James looked her way. "You ready, Lilith?"

Rowena's gaze narrowed. "I'm afraid I must insist."

Kat darted forward and threw her arms around James. "It's so good to see you, for a moment I didn't recognize you."

James eyes widened, but he put his hand on her back, patting her.

Kat whispered something in his ear, too soft for the rest of them to hear.

He chuckled. "Well, all right, then."

She released him, and he stepped into the room.

"What did she say to you?" Rowena's gaze snapped to Kat. "What did you say?"

James grinned. "Oh, she just reminded me how protective mothers are. Said if I wanted to make a good impression, I should visit for a bit."

Rowena harrumphed.

Desperate to turn the high priestess's attention from James, Lilith spoke up. "Rowena, I'm dying of curiosity. What's the gift?"

Rowena handed her a crystal jar. The curved opaque glass shone a deep purple. The lid, solid silver. A summoning jar, one designed to hold larger creatures than Aimee.

Lilith swallowed past her suddenly tight throat. "Why, that's lovely."

"Perfect to hold the darkness of most any daemon." She glanced at James and made a waving motion with her hand. "But of course, I joke. We're all in the Halloween spirit."

His smile turned tight.

Gods, this wouldn't end well.

Did he remember them? The coven sure seemed to recognize him right away. The blond twins reached out to touch his arm, tentative smiles playing around their lips while Abby seemed to want to disappear into the wall plaster.

Rowena narrowed her gaze on him before scanning over the women. "Everyone seems to know our guest but me."

"He lives in town." Kat kept her eyes trained on the ground at her feet. "Carnation isn't very big, Mother. I'm surprised you haven't met him."

"Introduce me, Katherine."

Kat's gaze shot up, locking onto James'. "He's James, uh..."

Lilith's stomach bottomed out.

James cleared his throat. "James Pasquino, ma'am." He held out his hand.

Rowena slipped her hand into his. Her gaze widened and she tried to pull him closer.

He refused to budge.

"What are you?"

All at once, the room erupted into female voices

offering explanations and excuses.

James grinned. "I'm a friend to these women."

"Are you?"

He nodded once, but didn't expound.

Lilith pressed to his side, her hand sliding up his arm to take his hand from Rowena. "Thank you for a lovely evening. We need to go." She tugged at his arm, pulling him away.

They'd made it down the porch steps when Rowena's voice stopped them.

"Lilith, dear?"

She half-turned, glancing back over her shoulder. "Yes?"

"Don't forget about Samhain. We'll induct you back into the . . . family then."

A trembling smile played over her lips. "Of course."

"You'll need to bring your own."

Her brows furrowed. "My own what?"

"Daemon."

James froze, keeping his back toward the house. Lilith avoided his gaze; she'd fall apart if she saw his expression.

"That's what the jar is for, dear."

She nodded.

"We'll destroy them at midnight as offerings to the Grigori."

James closed his eyes, his mouth setting into a grim line.

"Not a problem, Rowena. I'll come prepared."

James walked toward his bike, pushing Lilith ahead of him. He grabbed his helmet off the handlebars and fit it over her head, pulling the strap tight under her chin. Once on the bike, he glanced at her over his shoulder. "Get on."

"It's not what you think."

"Get on the bike."

Lilith shook like an autumn leaf by the time they reached Haven House. James didn't speak, but she couldn't miss his hurt, his sense of betrayal in the tenseness of his muscles and the grim set of his mouth. She'd withheld information and now this must look horrible to him. What must he think of her? Did he plan to even give her a chance to explain?

She followed him up the steps to the house, pressing her palm to her roiling belly. This felt worse than when Nan had realized they'd used Magic against her. Worse than that day her mom caught her with her fingers in the cake she'd made for the school musicale. Worse than when she and Trina had fought over a boy in high school.

He unlocked the door, tossed his keys onto the entryway table and started up the stairs.

"James. Don't walk away."

He leaned his hip against the railing, staring at the wall, refusing to look at her.

"You don't understand what happened tonight. I haven't been part of the coven since I was a child."

"Well, congratulations. All you have to do is destroy me and you're in."

His soft monotone made her stomach bottom out. Why wouldn't he yell at her? "Stop it. No one is going to destroy anyone. I had to protect the coven."

Slowly, he nodded. "Yeah. You gotta do what you gotta do."

"Damn it, stop that." Trina would get like this and she hated it because they couldn't talk until Trina had vented her anger. That's what James needed to do. It'd make them both feel better.

"Stop what?"

"Acting like this doesn't matter." She tossed her hand out to the side. "Acting like you care less what the coven is planning. That you don't care if I'm part of it." She raised her voice. "Look at me."

He snapped his head to the side and the dim lighting lit his eyes as if from within, giving them the silver sheen of a nocturnal predator. "You withheld information from me."

"Yes."

"You've cast me into the role of the evil daemon, assuming I'd harm those women if I knew."

Her throat tightened. She nodded.

"And now, after I find out that you're going to need to summon a daemon into that"—he pointed at the jar she held—"fucking jar, now, you want me to look at you."

He stormed down the stairs and crossed the entry to where she stood. "I'm looking and all I see is a woman who doesn't trust me. A woman who's happy to use me for now, then later, use me as a sacrifice for her coven's betterment."

"No."

"I didn't hear you arguing with Rowena. You didn't tell her no."

"You don't understand. Let me explain."

"Do you expect me to stand aside while you hunt daemons?"

"No, but—"

"So what does that make us?" He cupped her throat, using his thumb to tip up her chin, forcing her to meet his wrath. "What's that make us?"

"You know—"

"I don't know whether I want to kiss you, or spank your ass and hope to knock some sense into you."

A little flame of hope ignited. He hadn't given up on her. "We're going to overthrow Rowena, but we can't do it until Samhain."

His jaw flexed. "When you'll be sacrificing thirteen daemons."

"No. That's why we're overthrowing her. The coven hasn't been able to until now because they need me and Trina."

CHAPTER 27

Jesus, he was falling in love with a woman who wanted to destroy his people.

And that, simply, couldn't happen.

Crowley had been right.

She was dangerous.

He closed his eyes. "Jesus. It's them."

"What?"

"Guardians have been going missing. Over a hundred in the last month." His eyes opened and speared her with his gaze. "Your coven has been ashing Guardians." He broke free from her grasp and started up the stairs. He made it up a couple steps before he turned, needing to vent some of his anger. "Goddamn it. We work for the fucking Watchers your coven worships. We're the ones who maintain balance between humans and daemons. Us. And you're coven is dropping us, one by one."

"That's impossible. They wouldn't. You're wrong. Rowena might, but the rest of the coven has purposely failed every mission they've been sent on. They've been telling her the coven needs to be whole before they can be successful."

She seemed to want to believe what she said, her heart remained steady, she oozed sincerity, but maybe she was deluding herself. "You sure about that?"

"When I went to visit Kat the other day, bruises covered her arms and neck from standing up against Rowena, and—"

"Standing up to Rowena or fighting Guardians?"

"They don't want this war, James. None of us do. We're going to stop Rowena."

Jesus, he wanted to believe her.

She edged closer to him until she stood on the same step. "Please look at me."

His gaze dropped to hers and when he saw the tears glistening in her eyes it damn near broke his heart all over again. She'd never been one to cry. She didn't do so the night Nan beat her, nor when those daemons had attacked her. That she did so now, made him relent.

He pulled her into his arms. "I'm furious with you."

"I messed up. I should've told you about the coven. That is my mistake and I can't tell you how sorry I am that I put you in the position you were in tonight. But I swear to you, none of those woman are killing daemons, save Rowena—I can't speak for her. The rest want out."

"All right." He kissed the top of her head, tightening his hold. "Okay."

"I just have to keep the charade up a few more days. Rowena can't suspect anything."

"Do you have any other secrets I should know?"

She shook her head, then sighed. "Well, yeah. Trina's home."

"Here?"

"No." She sniffed. "She stayed in a hotel tonight. You know, because of Nan, but her stuff is in the guest bedroom."

"What else?"

She shook her head, then huffed out another breath. "I saw what happened during the Clearances."

Christ, he needed to remember to ask her this kind of open-ended question often. At least once a week. "How?"

"We have this necklace with the Legacy Stone—the high priestess of the old coven locked the memory into the stone. I know who killed the coven."

That was one of daemon-kind's biggest mysteries. He pulled away to look at her. "Who?"

"Well, I don't have a name. But I saw him. He called me the Original."

"The what?"

"The Original. He killed me, the whole coven. And there were these creatures—Nephilim, they called them."

James shook his head. Whatever she thought she'd seen, it couldn't have been real. "There haven't been Nephilim since the Great Flood."

"I saw them. They were real and the vampire had control over them."

"A vampire? No. The memory must have been corrupted, or maybe it was a projection or an illusion. Only a Watcher can create Nephilim. Besides, a coven would make quick work of any vampire."

He didn't like her involved in this. If he had his way, she'd stay far away from the coven, because when the Vampiric Council discovered they were back, all hell would break loose. "Why does the coven need you and Trina?"

"When a high priestess is elected, each member of the coven gives her a token of her powers. In order to overthrow her, we all need to take back those powers at the same time. It has to be unanimous."

"She'll fight."

"I know."

James pulled away to look at her. "And I'm supposed to protect you. I can't let you go up against her alone."

She shook her head.

"The Watchers sent me to protect you. I can't—"

"Quit saying that." She backed up a step. "Why would the Watchers care? You came here that night because I summoned you."

"What?" James went cold. What the hell else had she lied about? "You said you didn't know my name."

She shook her head and tried to go around him. "I misspoke. Forget it."

"The hell I will." He blocked her path. "Did you lie?

Did you know my name?"

"No."

They weren't going anywhere until he figured out what the hell happened. "Come here." He took her hand and walked into the living room and pointed to the couch. "Sit."

"Are you gonna stop growling at me?"

"If you give me some straight answers for a change."

She rolled her eyes, but sat her butt on the couch.

He pulled up the ottoman and sat in front of her. "Now tell me what happened that night."

"You wouldn't understand—"

"Try me."

"James—"

"And I damn well know you need a link to the daemon you summon, something like a name, in order to do so, so don't lie to me."

"But, I—"

"Lilith, I swear to God you do not want to give me any excuses. Just tell me what happened."

Leaning forward, she stabbed him in the chest with her finger. "You need to quit interrupting me. I'm not a criminal to be interrogated."

He caught her hand in his, holding it to his chest. Christ, she was a brazen woman. Daemons bent on mischief gave him far less sass. "You've never been afraid of me, have you?"

Slowly, she shook her head.

"Why?"

"I was about to tell you when you interrupted."

He grimaced. "Fine. Talk."

"As I said, you wouldn't understand unless I gave you a bit of history and told you about what happened earlier that evening." She narrowed her eyes at him, as if waiting for him to send a barrage of questions at her, but he held up his hands in surrender. She sat back. "So, I came into my gifts early."

"How early?"

"Birth." He didn't make any comment, so she added, "It's not a common thing among witches. Most don't earn their Magic until puberty, but our generation has quite a few early bloomers."

"Such as?"

"Trina came into hers when she was just a few months old. Several of the other girls came into theirs right after their mothers passed away."

He nodded. "Go on."

"The girls in the coven didn't like me and Trina. We were the outcasts of the group."

"They were jealous."

"They were scared."

He cocked his brow in question.

"Of Nan. We all were, but Trina and . . . We always got into trouble, which caused problems for the other girls, too."

"That's what happened that night."

She nodded. "We were studying the creation and the goddess' hierarchy—it's a bunch of crap. I'm pretty sure Nan made it up. I've never seen her version anywhere else."

His gaze slid to the bookshelf, to all the religious tomes she had. That's what she was after, for whatever reason she wanted to prove them wrong. "Let me guess, daemons were somewhere under the scum on a worm's belly?"

"Pretty much. My mom used to tell me about the creation as a bedtime story. I had it memorized, and there was no way in hell I would accept what Nan taught us."

That piqued his interest. More than anything, he'd like to hear her version of the story, but he needed other answers first. "You argued with her about that?"

"Sort of. Specifically, she had focused on life mates that day. How men and women were created in twos and therefore all humans had life mates. So Trina wanted to know about our life mates. To which Nan said we didn't have any because even though we were human, we were also linked with daemon-kind through Magic."

She'd lost him now. He couldn't figure out why in the world such things would matter to a couple of human girls.

She scowled. "Are you following this?"

"Yeah, I just don't get why it's important."

"It's an important subject to girls." She took a deep breath. "Trina and I wouldn't drop it. We'd just watched *Raiders of the Lost Ark*. All of us watched it on the VCR. Me and Trina were sitting on that ottoman eating popcorn and when Indiana wrapped his whip around Marion and pulled her into his arms Trina elbowed me and said, 'My mate is gonna be just like him.'"

James chuckled. He could just about picture that. Trina had been precocious as hell when he'd met her twenty years ago. "And you? What did you want?"

"I didn't know what I wanted, really. Just that I wanted to be loved." She pressed her palm to her stomach and took a deep breath. "So while taking my punishment, I summoned my mate for protection to prove Nan wrong."

James stilled.

A tiny flame of hope flared up inside him. And he stomped it back out.

You have forty-eight hours to bring her to me.

Hope was a dangerous thing.

"I'm a daemon. A vampire. I don't even have a goddamn soul, Lilith. I can't be your soul mate, or life mate or whatever." He stood up, because he couldn't sit there staring into those damned eyes of hers for one more second. Hope stared back at him and that was a damned dangerous thing.

"You had a soul when human. That's what I told Nan that day. How I got her so mad. I told her all daemons had been human once, so if all humans had soul mates, then so, too, did daemons."

He closed his eyes. "And witches." That's why it had

been so important to her. Little girls wanted there happily-ever-after, their knight in shining armor.

Instead, she'd gotten him.

"Yes."

I curse you to destruction before you get what you truly want.

He looked up at the ceiling, half expecting lightning to slice through the plaster, striking him dead.

"It's nothing more than a coincidence, Lil. I was hunting down a baldander when it happened, a Historian. The fucking Watchers spoke through me. They told me to surrender, to save you, and when I did they brought me here."

"They might have spoken through you, but they're trapped on Machon, James. If they could make daemons do whatever they wanted, they wouldn't need Guardians to act out their wishes. They could stop the daemons who tip the balance by forcing them to their will."

He shook his head even though what she said made sense. "And that's why you weren't scared of me that night." That's why he zoned into her location tonight without any effort. "Why you've never been afraid of me."

She wound her arm around him, flattening her palm against his stomach, pressing her cheek to his back. "The goddess would never give me a mate who would hurt me."

"Bullshit."

He *had* hurt her.

He'd killed her.

If Lilith spoke the truth, her goddess had mated her to the worst sort of bastard.

I curse you to destruction . . .

Was that what this was, his punishment? He'd killed her in a previous life, now she'd get her revenge in this one?

"James?"

What else could it be? He held no delusions Lilith

might want anything more than sex from him.

He broke from her embrace and started to head for the door.

"Where are you going?"

Shit. He didn't dare leave her alone, he still needed to protect her. But, damn it, he didn't have to listen to this shit.

James strode toward the stairs.

"Aren't you going to say anything?"

"No." He hit the stairs two at a time.

"I'm your mate."

He whirled around. Came back down halfway. "I didn't ask for a mate. I asked for my fucking humanity. My goddamn reward."

"James." The disappointment infused in her tone twisted his gut.

"I'm a daemon."

"I know." She stepped closer.

"A vampire."

She didn't stop until she stood on the stair beneath him. "I know."

"Yeah, well, I'm not convinced you've taken any time to ponder the significance of that."

Lilith leaned back against the wall and turned her head to the side, baring her throat.

"You think I won't?"

"I have faith in you."

He sucked in a hard breath. She always did that. Gave him things he didn't even realize he wanted. She stood there, calmly watching him while inside he felt like he was breaking apart. "Stop it."

She shook her head. "I. Have. Faith. In. You."

His lip curled in a snarl, the desire to lash out brimming over.

"I'm your mate."

He took a threatening step toward her. "Says you."

"I love you."

He slammed his fists against the wall on either side

of her. The whole thing shook, but not Lilith. She smiled. Slid her hand up his chest to cup and pet his neck.

"Maybe you just need to have a little faith, too."

And just like that all the rage slipped right out of him.

She offered him everything he'd never risked wanting.

He'd be a fucking idiot not to take it.

For however long this lasted.

One night or two.

The memories would keep him warm in the Eidolon Wastes.

"Say it again."

"I love you."

He held her face in his hands. Pressed his forehead to hers while he absorbed those words. Never, not once in the millennium he'd walked the Earth had anyone spoke those words to him. He wanted to say them back, but the burning in his throat kept anything he might have said at bay. He gathered her deeper into his frame, tilted her face up and kissed her. Whispered his lips over hers, trying to be sweet, trying to give her romance.

She lightly sank teeth sank into his lower lip, making shivers gather at his lower back. "I won't break, James."

Not on his watch, she wouldn't. He lifted her, letting her wrap her legs around his waist. The short little skirt she wore rode up, giving him access to her soft thighs, the wisp of lace between her legs. He pressed her into the wall, rolling his hip so the bulge in his jeans hit her just right, just enough to make her gasp.

He stroked his hands up her thighs, pushing her dress up higher until it bunched around her hips.

She glanced up at him through her lashes. "So, we're good?"

He held her face in both hands. "You've teased me. Sassed me. Lied to me. Withheld information and failed to follow my order to stay put. If you were mine, I'd spank your ass."

Her breath hitched and he'd be damned if her eyes didn't flare with jade fire.

Christ, did she like that idea?

The air in the room seemed to grow thin, his breath sloughing in and out of his lungs like liquid fire. "My mate doesn't withhold information."

She shook her head. "No more secrets."

"She doesn't lie to me."

"No."

"My mate obeys me."

Her chin came up a notch. She didn't pull away, didn't get angry, just challenged him with her stare.

"Take off the dress." He didn't move an inch to make the job easy, keeping her pinned with her back against the wall, her legs around his waist.

Slowly, she lowered her hands to the clasp on her lower, right hip. With a flick of her fingers, it gave and she spread the first fold open to reveal a little string tied into a bow on her left hip. She tugged it free, shrugged her shoulders, and was free.

She hadn't worn a bra. Her small, firm breasts stood at full attention.

He pulled her away from the wall just long enough to let the dress to fall to the floor.

He slipped his fingers under the thin bits of elastic holding her panties up and gave them a sharp tug.

She jumped a little. Chuckled. "I liked those."

"I'll buy you more." He pulled her panties out from between them.

All she wore now, were those knee-high leather boots. The scent of lavender, leather, and aroused woman shot straight to his cock.

"It's my job to keep you safe and you've made it impossible. Going where I can't follow. Walking the streets at night. Keeping secrets."

One, single nod of acknowledgment.

He rubbed the flats of his hands on her ass. Slow, full

circles. "And you failed to obey a simple request." The tips of his fingers brushed her slit. Her bare slit. Holy Christ, she'd shaved bare. His breath seemed to get caught on the realization. *Focus.* "My mate obeys me."

She shivered. "You seem stuck on that point."

"Yeah." He smacked her ass.

She gasped, her nails bit into his neck. Shivers shot down his back.

"You will obey me." His hand covered more than one of those soft, round cheeks of hers. Damn, she was small. Gently, he rubbed the spot he'd smacked.

Her thighs flexed slightly, dragging her against the bulge in his pants. "Make me."

Fuck. Her dare rolled through him, sending another shot of desire through him. His fingers twitched. He landed a slap to her ass. His fingers burned, he damn well knew her ass did, too.

She moaned, arching her back and pressing into him. Lifting those sweet breasts.

James raised her higher on his hips, taking one rigid little point into his mouth, sucking hard while soothing her bum with his hand. Gently, he bit down on her nipple and tugged.

"James."

His hand glided over the warm, curved surface of her ass. So soft. So smooth. Smack.

"Gods, yes." She held him to her breast, rubbing against him, seeking what she needed.

"Yes, you'll obey?" He reached lower, letting his hand hover just below her slit.

"Yes."

Half pleased, half disappointed, he moved his hand. "No!"

He lifted his head, watching her expression. Moved his hand back to her pussy. "Here?"

She ground down on him. "Please."

He let his hand fly.

They both moaned.

Her legs tightened around his hips, she arched up, biting her lip, closing her eyes as if savoring the sting.

Now. He needed to be buried in that tight pussy before he came in his goddamn pants again. He turned, carrying her up the remaining stairs and into his room. He kicked the door shut.

Lilith wriggled out of his grasp and backed away. She held up her hand to stay him when he would've followed. "Get undressed."

He grinned. "Make me." He didn't know why he said it, she had no hope of forcing him to much of anything, maybe just to see what she'd do.

She flicked her wrist.

His clothes disappeared. He jumped a little, frowning. "Goddamnittohell." He took a step towards her. "No Magic."

Her lips spread in a devious smile. "Then I guess you'll have to do what I say."

All his muscles tensed, his eyes narrowed. He didn't like the sound of that. "Like what?"

"Put your hands behind your back."

"Lil—"

Her smile disappeared. "Now."

A prickle of unease slithered down his spine.

Maybe you need to have a little faith, too.

Jaw clenched, he did as she said, clasping the fingers of one hand over the wrist of the other. More than anything, because he wanted to see what she was up to. "Happy?"

Her gaze stroked over him, head to toes, as tangible as a caress. "Not yet." She came to him, ran her palm over his chest. "Don't move." She lifted up and kissed his jaw, trailed little bites down his chest.

"What are you doing?"

Light as a butterfly's wings, her fingers trailed over his nipples. Her mouth followed, her teeth testing his pectoral muscle. "Before you go all alpha again, I want my turn." She stroked her tongue over his nipple and his cock jumped.

She circled his dick in a light grip as she made her way down his body, until she knelt in front of him, naked except for those goddamn boots.

"Lil—"

She took him into her mouth, all that warm silken heat surrounding him, scattering his thoughts.

He reached for her, unsure if he wanted to pull her away or drag her closer. As soon as he touched her face, she pulled back her lips, holding him in her mouth with nothing but teeth.

Right, then. He put his hands behind his back.

With a chuckle, she tucked her lips back around him, dragging her mouth down his length, closing her lips and pinching his head slightly as she withdrew.

"Christ." He closed his eyes, searching for his control and finding none. "I'm not gonna last."

"Don't want you to."

"Lil—"

"You'll be rock hard ten minutes after." She cupped his nuts in her palm, weighing them. "So, give me this." She blew over his head and gooseflesh broke out over his skin. She met his gaze and lapped up the bead of pre-come that appeared. "Let me see what I do to you." Her lips stretched over his shaft as she took as much of him as she could, one of her hands following every stroke making up for what wouldn't fit into that luscious mouth.

Chills darted over his skin, gathering at the small of his back. His breath came harsh and fast. He couldn't contain the little jerks of his hips that sent him deeper into her mouth. She kept her hand on him, taking care of herself and making sure he didn't go too far while she pleasured him. He liked that, not having to worry, having permission to let go even if only in this.

With her free hand, she raked her nails down his stomach, drawing his attention back to her. Their gazes met while she worked him, while she fondled his balls.

The slick stroke of her mouth urging him to come. She hummed in the back of her throat and he jerked as the vibration washed over him. Helpless, he held her face, stroked her cheek while he came. Her mouth tightened around him, that soft tongue lapping at him, her throat closing around him as she swallowed.

Weak-kneed and overwhelmed, his whole body twitched as she let him fall from her lips. He dragged her up into his arms and she instinctively wrapped herself around him in a full body hug. Christ, he liked that.

He carried his mate to the end of the bed.

His mate.

His.

"On your knees, sweetheart."

She grinned. "Did we find your favorite position?" She lowered her knees to the bed and turned around, positioning herself on hands and knees, giving him a prime view of sweet ass and damp pussy. She crawled back a bit until her feet hung over the edge of the bed. "How about this?"

"That works." He'd just come so hard he'd seen stars and already he dick started to thicken again. He ran his hand over the red hand print on her ass cheek, reached down to cup her mound. He stroked down her scarred back with his other hand.

She tensed. "I forgot."

She started to get up and he pushed her back down. He'd forgotten, too. The scars from Nan's whip covered most of her back. Thick knotted lines and thin white streaks. Christ, he didn't deserve her. Didn't deserve any of this.

"Just go, then." Her voice trembled. Her body shook. She seemed to draw inside herself right there before his eyes. Gone was the temptress from a few seconds before.

Hell, she must have sensed his withdrawal and came to the wrong conclusion. He pulled her back against him, sensing sympathy wasn't what she needed. He fisted her long hair, twisting once until her head came back to rest on his shoulder, baring her throat. "You just fought like hell for this, and now you're telling me to leave?"

"You don't want me."

He pressed his erection against her ass. No way in hell could she hold that lie. "Try again."

"It's ugly."

"I'm ugly."

She shook her head. "No you're not."

He kissed her neck. "When I watch you looking at me, I feel like the sexiest male around." He trailed his lips down to her shoulder, nuzzling. "But when I see others look at me, all I see is fear and revulsion. So, am I reading you wrong?"

"No."

He eased away from her, letting his gaze trail over her body; her breasts, high and proud, the sleek muscles of her abs, that bald little slit he needed so desperately to get inside. "And when you watch me, looking at you, how do you feel?"

Her breath hitched. "Hot."

He grinned, releasing her hair, stroking his hand down her back. "Smoking hot." He met her gaze. "Are we done?"

"You were withdrawing. I felt it—like you'd left the room even though you stood right here."

"I failed you that night. Again." He shook his head. "It'll never happen again. Understand?" She nodded and he almost flinched at the absolute trust he found in her gaze.

Crowley would die.

They would run.

He'd keep her safe.

"Take me inside."

She lowered herself to her hands, reached between her legs and fitted his dick to her heat. He helped her spread her legs wider and watched as he disappeared into her. Watched as her muscles clung to him as he pulled out. "You're mine."

His to protect.

Breathless. "Yes."

"All of you. I want it all."

His to love.

"Yes."

And in return, she'd get him, for whatever that was worth. He leaned over her, covering her with his body, kissing the marks on her back.

She tightened around him, her inner muscles gripping, signaling her release. He reached around and gently pinched her clit, staying her orgasm. She cried out. "I was—"

He grinned. "Waiting for me. Right?"

Her low moan wrapped around him, drawing his balls up tight.

James stilled inside her. For a long moment, she hung there, suspended on the cusp of release, but the way he held her clit lessened the urge, diminishing it. "James." Her accusatory tone did nothing but make him chuckle. "You're killing me."

"I'm making this last."

Releasing her clit, he started to move, letting the need build again. She pressed back into every thrust, his balls slapping against her clit, his hips smacking her ass. Her breasts swayed and bounced with each thrust and even the kiss of the air made her tingle and arch. As if he'd heard her thoughts, his hands came around to cup her breasts, kneading, then lightly pinching. The tension wound tight in her belly, demanding release. Just as she began to tighten around him, he withdrew.

She gasped, her unfulfilled desire so sharp it almost hurt. She fisted her hands, ready to fight when he turned her over.

He easily caught her swing, pinning her hands over

her head as he came down on top of her. "Feisty tonight?"

She frowned. "You're a pain in the ass."

"But I'm your pain in the ass." He kissed her, slow and sweet, nudging his way back into her. "Together, then?"

She wrapped her body around him, nodded into his neck. He rocked against her, setting a steady pace and as she got caught again in desire, she couldn't stop petting him. Couldn't keep herself from kissing and nipping and biting. He did things to her, this male, her mate. Made her wild and uncontrolled and inconsolable in her desire for him. She arched and clung, her whole focus on the slick glide of him, the weight and strength of his body.

His mouth trailed along her exposed throat, kissing and licking. His lips parted against her throat, she felt the edges of his teeth and her breath caught and held.

They hung there, suspended, his mouth over her throat, his cock sliding in and out, their arousal heavy in the air. His muscles all locked tight around her, holding her close, protective and threatening at the same time.

And then he kissed her throat. No bite. No teeth. But she still felt marked, possessed. Claimed.

"Gods, I love you."

His mouth came down over hers, his thrusts grew faster, harder. Her pussy clenched tight around him, *she* clenched tight around him. Release hit like a flash fire, hot and fierce at first, lingering and smoldering after.

His hips jerked once, twice and pressed hard, as if trying to sink as deep as possible. His whole body shook with the force of his orgasm. His arms contracted around her as he shuddered, and when he relaxed, he pressed his forehead to hers. "Love you, too, sweetheart."

CHAPTER 28

There was no doubt in Rowena's mind after dinner tonight. The coven was uniting against her. They were keeping secrets. They were protecting Kat from her.

And it was all Lilith's fault.

She'd always been rebellious, her and Trina both, and she dare not take any risks. She needed Lilith to be cooperative, and after tonight, that seemed unlikely.

But she had a plan.

She placed blue-and-white scarves around the door of Haven House and placed a glass of water near the door. As she lit a blue candle, she called forth the goddess Yasmina—conductor of souls. "Great goddess, allow Nan to hear my voice, to be commanded and compelled by me."

The candle blue out. The water drained.

Rowena grinned.

She pressed her face to the front door. "Nan, you must possess Lilith."

I cannot reach her. She's protected her space.

She frowned. Hadn't Lilith said something about that at dinner? She'd said that Kat helped her. If that was the case, Lilith must have used the dried herb mixture she herself had taught Kat. She got down on her hands and knees and blew under the door. Closed her eyes and used her Magic to push the air across the floor. Up the stairs and through the bedrooms. It wasn't enough to alert anyone who might be awake, but it would scatter any dried herbs lying on the floors.

"Nan, you must possess Lilith."

Yes. Yes, I will stop the abomination before it starts. He will die. She will die.

"No. Don't kill Lilith. Possess her. I need her."

I will kill him.

"Yes. Kill him. Possess her. And wait for my instructions."

Rowena glanced up to see her nemesis standing behind her at the base of Haven House's porch steps, hiding in the shadows. Good gods, how long had he been standing there? She straightened.

"Bright blessings, Madam High Priestess."

Great. This was the last thing she needed. "What are you doing here?"

"Making sure you aren't seen." He glanced away, staring up at the darkened sky for a moment. "They've mated each other, you know."

Rowena froze. No wonder James hadn't left Lilith after the fiasco at her house.

He tsked. "Nothing good can come of this should he bite her. Not for either of us."

She stared. This male held the same beliefs that Nan had. Rowena shook her head. No witch, no matter how rebellious, would allow a vampire to transform her. It was an abomination because the witch would lose her Magic as her Vampiric talent took over.

"As always, my offer stands." He rocked back on his heels. "It would be in our best interests to unite forces. We'll destroy him and share her." A shudder wracked through him so hard, his head snapped to the side. His pleasant demeanor shifted to something fierce. His hands fisted.

She still couldn't quite figure him out. "You're jealous."

His body relaxed and he let out a soft chuckle. "No. I require her Magic but for a short time."

"I'm not a madam."

"And that's not the type of magic I want." He smirked. "I need her to work one spell. That's all. Then she's all yours."

One spell. His request seemed so innocent, yet much could be done with one spell. "I don't trust you. Go away. I've got everything under control."

"Of course, madam." A shudder ran though him again. "What did you do to Kat?" The accusatory question shot out of his mouth rapid-fire.

Rowena reared back.

He took out his blade and she prepared to cast against him.

But he sank it hilt deep into his own thigh. He pulled the blade out and sheathed it. His jaw clenched tight, but he smiled. "Just say my name if you change your mind. I'll hear you."

Two voices. She'd distinctly heard two separate voices. And both knew far more than she wanted them to know. So was he possessed, or crazy? "What's your name?"

"Julius. Julius Crowley." He made a little bow and turned, whistling as he limped down the drive.

The fool male was stupid enough to give her his name?

No. He'd been far too careful over the years to commit such a novice error now. So whose name had he given her? An enemy's? The weaker consciousness living in that body? Something was up with that male.

He was different . . . and not in a good way.

CHAPTER 29

Dawn came and went, but Nan didn't show. They stayed awake, waiting for her, but the house remained silent.

"Come on, let's get some rest." James stretched out on the bed and pulled Lilith to him. He couldn't seem to stop touching her. "Tell me the story your mom told you."

"The Creation story?"

He nodded, kissed the top of her head and tucked her closer to his frame.

"Once upon a time, the goddess walked the vastness of space, alone with her mate. They loved each other and expressed that love physically, creating life." She kissed his chest. "The Grigori were first, two hundred beings of great power. Eventually, we'd come to know these beings as gods—Zeus, Ra, Thor—and they'd give birth to daemon-kind. But before that time came, the goddess created other beings, creatures made of light with no free will. They were the keepers of time, of space, of peace. As powerful as the Grigori, as knowledgeable, but lacking their passion and emotion."

Ah, the angels.

"The goddess created homes for all the beings. Machon for the Grigori and their kin. Raquia for the Angels. And Earth for humans. The goddess could see all their futures, their struggles and their final redemptions. And she saw that it was good."

James smiled. She made it all sound so . . . divine. So planned and accepted.

"The daemons came last, but were no less favored."

He tightened his grip on her.

"The Grigori came to Earth, seeking to mate with the daughters of men. They wanted to create life, like the humans. They felt cheated thinking the goddess gave the humans something better than what they had. They set themselves up as gods, sharing their secrets with men. And men worshipped them, offering these gods their daughters. Some angered the Grigori and were cursed. Others pleased them and were blessed."

As far as he knew, only the Grigori coven had been blessed. All the other races had been cursed.

"But the Grigori could not impregnate their chosen mates. One of the Grigori grew frustrated and bit his mate. She changed, all his anger and spite turning her into a Nephilim. The other Grigori saw what he'd done and did the same. The Nephilim were a plague upon the Earth, destroying mankind."

That's what he was. Descendant of the Nephilim. Born of violence and anger.

She lifted her head to look at him. "My mom never explained how vampires were born of the Nephilim."

"We're the watered-down version."

"Okay, you gotta explain that statement. Nephilim aren't in my book of daemonology."

"So, Nephilim A bites someone and they become Nephilim B who bites Nephilim C, well, by the time you get to Nephilim E, the Watcher's DNA is so watered-down you end up with"—he shrugged—"me."

She laid her head on his chest. "Ah, my mom told me vampires carried the Grigori's talent, but none of the rage and anger of the Nephilim. Now that makes sense."

"Because of us, God destroyed everything."

She shook her head against him. "The goddess sent a flood to wipe the Nephilim from the Earth, but she saved mankind and she saved daemon-kind." Lilith sat up. "If she thought your kind evil, she'd have destroyed vampires with the Nephilim." She laid back down and settled against his chest, tracing his scars with her fingers. "Instead, she allowed the Nephilim to remain long enough to ensure the vampires' existence. You have purpose in this world, James. You may have lost your faith, but the goddess never loses faith in us."

Faith? No one had given him a reason to have faith in a long time. Who would've imagined he might find some in a pagan woman? He curled himself around her, wishing he could sink right into her skin. Wishing he could take on her faith as his own.

Eventually, he'd have to tell her the truth. He'd need to confess to killing her in her past life.

Then they'd both discover the truth about faith and forgiveness.

Nan appeared in the doorway later that afternoon, well before sunset.

Lilith bolted upright. James' alarm hadn't gone off yet. She glanced at him as she donned her nightgown.

James tugged on his pants. "She's early."

"How?"

Nan grinned, her teeth soiled, pointed. One of her long, thin legs flexed over Kat's potion, her foot landing solidly on their side of the protective line.

Tiny tendrils of smoke spouted off her skin. Nan sucked in a breath, hissing.

Lilith grabbed hold of James' hand. "It's working. I told you it would work. She won't be able to cross."

He backed away from Nan, pulling her with him. "It's not."

Nan placed her hands on either side of the doorjamb. Slowly, moaning and hissing, she pulled herself through. "Now, that's not so bad."

"It'll get worse. You're smoking. Any minute now, you'll erupt into flames and be sent back to your own realm."

Nan shook her head, stalking forward. "Oh, it hurts. It's pissing me the fuck off. But I'm not going anywhere. Not until I've got what I came for."

"What?"

"You."

Nan lunged forward, the second set of her arms, the ones ending in vicious hooks, lashing out. Lilith started to call forth a void, to trap Nan, but James grabbed her, pulling her behind him. He grabbed hold of Nan's hooked appendages.

Lilith staggered back. Nan was far stronger than she'd expected. She needed James out of the way, then she'd trap Nan in a void and exorcise her spirit from the house. "James, move out of the way on the count of three."

"No."

"I've got this. You need to move. One." Lilith gathered her resolve, grounding her energy by linking her spirit with the world around her.

"Two." She used that grounding to pull more energy toward her, to put as much energy as possible behind her spell.

"Three."

"Goddamn you." James shoved Nan back and leapt out of the way.

Lilith conjured the void, just like Brenda had instructed, a box of pure nothingness around Nan.

She straightened. Good gods, it worked. It worked!

James pulled himself up from the floor and dusted himself off. "She's gone?"

She shot him a cocky grin. "I told you I could handle this."

He had an overwhelming need to lecture her to within an inch of her life, but the brilliant smile she bestowed on him stayed his words. For now. He didn't have it in him to sour her success. But later, later he'd lecture her for putting herself at risk.

Lilith's smile faded and he realized he must be glaring at her.

He started toward her just as a blur passed from the void to Lilith and disappeared.

Her eyes widened and her mouth gaped. She held her hand to her throat as if choking.

"Lil?"

The void disappeared.

She lowered her head, holding up a hand for him to stay back, and her whole body shuddered. Something moved beneath her skin, slithered down her arm, making her wrist jerk.

What am I supposed to protect her from?

Everything.

Shit.

"Lilith?" He stepped closer, his hand closing around her outstretched arm. Her skin felt like ice. "Baby?" He didn't know why he kept trying to get her attention. He knew he wouldn't like what he saw. "Look at me." With a finger under her chin, he tried to coax her face up.

Her head snapped up with enough force to pop bone. Her eyes, her beautiful, ancient eyes weren't there. Above her slack features, two solid white orbs stared at him. The vitality he loved in her, gone. Her features had taken on an ashen quality, her veins black beneath her skin.

His chest tightened. He'd failed her. No. He'd pretty much condemned her. Never should he have allowed any of this. He'd had one job, damn it. "What can I do?"

The voice coming out of her wasn't Lilith's. "Watch her die, Vampire."

Jesus. For over a millennium he'd hunted and killed daemons. He had more experience in killing than he ever desired to have in anything. And yet, he was helpless in this. He'd never tried to save any of the possessed beings he'd met. "Lilith. Listen to me. I need help here. What do I do?"

Her body trembled and shook, her posture jerking this way and that as if two forces inside fought for control. "Stab her." Lilith's voice.

"No." For a moment, her skin seemed to clear, the midnight spider webbing of veins, fading. The only way to stab Nan, would be to stab Lilith, too. "Give me something else. Anything else."

"She's weak." She gripped his shirt in her fist; a shudder ran through her. "Get the information and stab her."

An outraged shriek erupted from her mouth, her body thrashing, lifting and levitating, as Nan fought for control.

"Tell me what to do." He muttered the words, desperate for any advice. Even from the Watchers. "Come on, you bastards, you wanted me to protect her, tell me what to do."

His phone came alive in his back pocket and he jumped. He wrested his phone out of his pocket. The screen announced he had a text from No Number Available. He clicked the message open.

Kill her.

One shaky hand scrubbed over his head. "No." Then, firmer. "No." He threw his phone on the bed.

In the corner, the clock radio flipped on. The dial rotating back and forth playing bits of songs, excerpts from commercials and talk shows. "Careful now . . . ." A male announcer's voice. The dial spun. "Watching you . . . ." A vocalist. "Closer now . . . ." A woman's vocals. "Seeing you . . . ." A child's voice.

The Watchers were warning him.

His gaze traveled back and forth from the radio to where Lilith thrashed against the ceiling. "I'm not killing her." There had to be another way.

The dial spun, and the volume leapt up. "Do as you're told."

The angry lyrics repeated, raising in volume. "Do as

you're told."

"No. She'll not die tonight, not by my hand."

The dial spun. "I'm coming for you."

The radio turned off.

Jesus. Would they send other Guardian? Would they come themselves?

No. The Watchers were trapped on Machon. They couldn't come here.

He looked up, but Lilith was gone.

Shit.

He grabbed his blades and strapped them on. If someone did show up, he'd be ready for them. He walked out into the hall and glanced both ways. Lilith still struggled with Nan, across the ceiling and down the entryway wall.

James raced down the stairs, grabbed hold of Lilith and pulled her back down, pressing her feet to the floor.

Lilith settled. He cupped her slack cheek. "Nan, why does Lilith need my protection?"

"She's dead."

His gut knotted. "She's not. You're lying. Tell me why. Why does she need my protection?"

"I'll not allow the abomination."

What the hell was she talking about? They'd already mated. "It's already happened."

She laughed, her cackle all the more eerie for the fact that Lilith's face didn't move. "You know nothing, Vampire. You think you do, but you don't."

"Stop talking in riddles." All this time he thought him mating Lilith was the abomination she'd spoken of. "What's the abomination? Why does she need my protection?"

"They're one and the same."

He shook her. "Explain."

A sound escaped through Lilith's parted lips. Then another. And another, until they blended into a tune. Like the slow winding of a Jack-in-the-Box by a nervous child. One afraid something other than a happy clown might jump out when the lid opened. A child's song. He recognized the tune: "Pop Goes the Weasel."

"I know you can hear me, you bitch. Answer my question."

Outside, the porch creaked.

They were coming. He needed to get Lilith out of here.

Upstairs, a door creaked open.

He gripped Lilith's clammy upper arms and he rotated a slow circle, forcing her to keep pace, the position allowing him to stay focused on her while checking their surroundings over her shoulder.

Someone was coming.

Her dead eyes stayed on him while his shifted to the shadows, their movement giving him the chance to make sure nothing snuck up on them from the dark rooms surrounding them.

The water turned on in the bathroom upstairs.

The lights flickered off.

Who was coming? The Watchers themselves? A Guardian? Something else?

He had no idea what to expect and he didn't dare let Lilith out of his sight, not while that bitch possessed her. The cabinets in the kitchen started to slam open and closed.

His body jerked as Lilith added lyrics to her tune. "All around the Guardian realm . . . ."

"Stop it." Around they went, the dark kitchen appeared empty. Nothing moved on the stairs. The living room remained still. And noise came from every corner of the house.

". . . the vampire stalks the humans. . . ."

Jesus. Where was the threat coming from? Or was this just Nan fucking with him?

"No one knows what he really is." Her slack features spread into a sickly smile. "'Til out pops the Watcher."

James froze. Watcher?

She lurched at him. Her eyes turned blood red, her

teeth jagged little spikes in her mouth.

He stepped back, tripped, and fell.

Lilith hovered over him and everything, the furniture, the books, the paintings rose up from their assigned spaces, hovering with her.

He scrambled back.

The boards covering the windows started to shake, the nails whining as the boards shook loose.

A stream of late evening sunlight blasted through the room, trapping him in the corner.

Fuck.

She flew toward him, arms outstretched, fingers arched into claws.

He grabbed hold of her, turned, and pressed her to the wall. She screamed, thrashing against him, clawing his face and gnashing her teeth.

"Come on, Lil, I know you're in there." He restrained her, trying not to add additional injuries to her body. "Help me."

Her struggles ceased, and for a moment, he thought her free, or at least in control.

He stepped back. Lilith stared up at him. Lilith. Those gorgeous eyes of hers almost glowing from the reflected sunlight. She gave him a jerky nod. "I got her. She's d-dead."

Dread filled him. He took another step back and looked down.

She'd stabbed herself with his Guardian blade. Must have taken it while they struggled.

"Oh, God." He dropped to his knees in front of her, ripping her nightgown to see the damage. She'd plunged the blade hilt deep into her stomach. "What did you do?"

Her knees buckled and he eased her fall, pulling her into his arms. "You stupid, stupid, woman, what did you do?"

"Saved us."

No. She'd saved him. And for what, to go back to his old existence? To wait for her to reincarnate again? "I'm not letting you go."

She smiled. Blasted woman. How dare she? "It's okay."

He shook his head. "No. I can't. I'm not letting you go."

"It's fine. I'll . . . ." A deep sigh escaped her lips and her eyes slid closed.

For a terrifying moment he thought she'd died. But her heart still beat. Barely.

She'd hate him for this. And he couldn't decide what was worse, having her alive and out of reach, or dead.

The radio flipped on, sparking off disconnected noise as the dial rolled, settling on Elton John's, "Someone Saved My Life Tonight."

Oh, so now the Watchers wanted her back.

Well, they were in luck, because so did he.

James laid her on the floor. The main artery in the neck would be the quickest, but the artery in her leg would be almost as good and be easier for her to hide the scar from his bite.

He held little resemblance to the vampires of Hollywood. He had no fangs to make neat, little twin holes in her flesh. His teeth were no different from hers, and his bite mark would be big and ugly.

He pulled up her nightgown, running his cheek down her inner thigh, scenting out where the vein lay closest to the surface.

Her pulse had slowed, thinned.

When he found his mark, he pressed his lips to her skin. "Sorry, Lil." He closed his eyes, opened his mouth wide and sank his teeth deep into her tender flesh, shuddering at the inaudible pop of her skin breaking. The warmest, sweetest of tastes filled his mouth, causing a raging battle between heart, mind, and instinct.

She came back to consciousness with a shriek, her heart lurching into a rapid tempo. Her body tensed, and then she tried to buck him away. Keeping his mouth on her leg, he shifted positions, throwing his leg over her torso to keep her still. He wrapped both arms around her leg, holding her tight, to keep from doing any additional damage.

Fighting him off was futile, but still she tried, struggling against him. Her screams tore at him. He tightened his arms around her, trying to keep from ripping her flesh any more than necessary. Within seconds, she faded, weakened from blood loss. He met her gaze, gutted by the tears leaking from her eyes. She'd hate him for this. She'd never forgive him. When her blood flow slowed to a trickle, he needed every ounce of discipline he possessed to fight the instinct to continue to feed and finish her off.

But he refused to let her go. James sat back and pulled her lifeless body into his arms. "It'll be over soon. I'm so sorry, baby. It's going to be all right. It'll all be over soon."

CHAPTER 30

"What the hell are you doing?"

James whirled around at the unfamiliar voice. A woman stood in the entryway, she'd left the door open behind her, allowing sunlight to pour in around her. It made her appear surrounded by a bright aura.

She was just a bit of a thing with dark hair and deep brown skin. Eyes dark as onyx drifted to Lilith before darting back to his. "What did you do?"

Christ, this must be Trina.

He laid Lilith down next to him and started to rise. "She'll be—"

"You're in the wrong house."

James blinked.

Slowly, he got to his feet, glancing around at his surroundings.

Where the hell was he?

A small Latina woman had spoken. She didn't look familiar. Her heart thudded, heavy in her chest.

How the hell had he ended up in a human's home?

He glanced around at the miss-matched furniture, his gaze lingering on the couch and wide ottoman. Something wasn't right.

He did recognize this place, but it didn't feel right. Everything seemed off kilter.

"I said, you're in the wrong house." She clenched her jaw tight, though her tone held no overt inflection, the way she fisted her small hands and the rigidness of her spine spoke volumes for her mood. "Easy mistake to make, I suppose. I won't call the cops if you leave now."

James eyed the sunlit entry and slowly, he shook his head. "This isn't right." He looked around the room again, this time his gaze falling to the brunette lying on the floor.

Lilith.

He edged closer to his woman, his gaze returning to Trina. *She's a witch. She's fucking with you.* "Whatever you're doing, stop it."

Her eyes widened a fraction, then narrowed.

"I'm trying to help her, damn you." He bent to pick Lilith up, but all around him, the house groaned.

"Don't touch her." Trina's long black hair whipped around her head as if caught in a stiff wind.

The house shuddered. The walls flexed and bowed.

"Jesus, Trina. I know what this must look like. Nan got to her. She got in her."

"You killed her." She stepped deeper into the room, closer. Behind her, the door slammed shut. Whatever control she might possess over her Magic, she didn't appear to be exercising any of it.

"I didn't. Nan was here. She—"

"Nan's dead."

"Her ghost." Chunks of plaster exploded from the walls, revealing the inner skeleton of the house, the wooden boards and beams. He ducked, shielding his face as glass shattered. Lilith's knickknacks exploded. Bits of drywall, glass, and pottery flew around like shrapnel. He shouted to be heard over the destruction. "Lil stabbed herself because Nan possessed her. She would've died. I bit her to keep her here."

That was the wrong thing to say.

Her expression darkened. Around them, the inner woodwork of the house imploded. Studs and struts broke, their splintered edges pointing into the room and the house seemed to fold in on itself, the room shrinking, thrusting those sharp bits of wood and steel closer to him.

The sheer force of the adrenaline flowing through him, made him lightheaded. "Don't do this. I'd never hurt her."

"You're a vampire."

He eyed his weapon on the ground next to Lilith. "I don't want to hurt you, Trina."

Her eyes widened.

"Yeah, I remember you. I helped you. Her. I'm trying to now, as well."

For a few seconds she seemed uncertain, her Magic waned, the house partially righting itself. He wasn't fool enough to think this was an illusion. It was more a sign of her strength that she had such control, distorting everything around them without permanently destroying it all. If she continued, he had no doubt, that after she'd ashed him, the house and everything in it would return to its original state. Everything but him.

He lifted his hand, pointing to Lilith. "She's going to need to feed. I have blood upstairs in my safe."

"You've ruined her." Again, energy whipped through the house, broken boards straining toward him. "She'll lose her Magic. Her friends. Everything."

James leapt, tackling her. He wrapped his body around hers, trying to prevent hurting her in the fall. It was enough to break her concentration.

The house resumed its former state. Everything snapped back to where it had originally been.

They rolled across the floor and he pinned her beneath him. "Stop it. We need to take care of Lilith right now."

She didn't answer. Her eyes seemed to look straight through him. She didn't fight. She didn't shout.

"Trina?"

She didn't respond. She almost looked as though she'd gone into some sort of fugue.

A pinpoint of pain erupted in his head. He winced,

sitting back on his haunches.

"I wish you dead." Trina spoke the whisper-soft words.

Christ. His vision blurred and he fell back on his ass, clutching his head. His erratic breath came hard, fast. That pinpoint of pain ruptured in his skull, sending shock waves rolling though his body. He tried to crawl away from her, every movement more strenuous than the last.

Then he realized he was going the wrong way.

Trina wouldn't stop.

Not until he was ash.

He needed every ounce of energy to turn himself around, dragging himself across the floor. Pain burst behind his eyes and the world flickered and then went dark. His vision disappeared. Blindly, he felt for Trina. Grasped hold of a foot and yanked her toward him.

A blast rocked thought the room, tearing him away from Trina. For a terrible second he thought that was it. That it was over for him.

But the pain in his head stopped. His sight returned. He blinked his eyes, breathing hard. For a minute, everything was too bright. Too blurred. Then the light faded and the world seemed to right itself.

Lilith crouched over him. "Are you all right?"

He nodded. Christ, had he died? Was he dreaming?

Her gaze went to her friend. "Trina?"

"Yeah."

He glanced at Trina to find her staring at Lilith with the same degree of confusion he felt.

Lilith appeared . . . the same as before. She definitely wasn't under the strain of a first blood-lust; if she had been, she'd be tearing Trina apart, not asking after her health. Lilith reached for him, cupping his cheek in her warm hand. "What happened?"

Warm. She was still warm. He circled her wrist with his palm. Christ, she had a pulse. Her heart still beat. He'd bitten her. She should be a fucking vampire. She should be in blood-lust. He got to his knees, pushing her back and lifting her torn nightgown to see the knife wound on her belly, his bite mark on her thigh. Both healed. Only pale scars remained.

"He bit you."

His head snapped to the side at Trina's accusatory tone. Then he looked up at his mate. "Nan possessed you. You stabbed yourself to destroy her."

Her eyebrows furrowed; she seemed to be trying to remember. Her eyes closed, her lips pressed into a thin line and when she opened her eyes, tears rimmed her lashes. "My gods, what did you do?" She looked down at herself, skimming her hand over the fresh scar on her belly, then her inner thigh.

His gut rolled.

"They'll considered you rogue now."

A breath shuddered out. She was worried about him? Not pissed at what he'd done? "You're my mate. That's more important."

"James." Her eyes welled with tears.

"Don't do that. Don't cry." His tone was far too rough in his ears, but he opened his arms, knowing Trina would start a fresh fight should he make a move for Lilith.

She threw herself into his arms. "I'm right, though? They'll be sending someone now."

Trina shifted her weight. "Who?"

He met Trina's gaze over Lilith's head. "The Vampiric Council."

"Why?"

Lilith lifted her head. "Guardian's aren't allowed to transform anyone." She glared at him with red-rimmed eyes. "He just signed his own death warrant."

Trina started to pace.

Lilith lifted the edge of his shirt, wiping at his chin.

Shit. He could imagine what he must look like with her blood drying on his face. Shame burned a pit in his gut.

She forced him to look at her. "Whatever you're thinking, stop it." She licked her thumb and scrubbed at the corner of his mouth.

"Jesus, Lil." He captured her hand in his. "I swear to God, if you ever do that again, I'll put you over my knee." His gaze shifted to Trina.

Her hand covered her mouth, her eyes twinkling with merriment. "Oh, gods, your face. That was priceless."

Lilith scowled, a pretty blush staining her cheeks. "I'm sorry. I—" She moaned. "What are we going to do now?"

"Nothing." He shook his head. "You didn't change. They won't touch you. There's no proof—"

"The Watchers saw." Trina propped her hand on her hip.

He shrugged. "I had their permission."

Both women stared.

"They spoke through the radio."

"You're sure that wasn't Nan?" Trina asked.

For a heartbeat, he wavered. "The Watchers."

Trina's gaze narrowed. "How do you know?"

Christ, she was an argumentative woman. "Because the last message, the one giving me permission came through after Lilith stabbed herself."

Trina's stance relaxed.

Lilith was frowning at her friend again.

He stroked the back of his fingers down Lilith's arm. "Are you sure you're okay?"

She continued to stare at Trina. "You can't hear me, can you?"

The corners of Trina's mouth turned down. Panic flashed across her features. Her gaze shifted to James. "What did you do to her?"

What the hell? He thought they were past this. "Nothing that I can see, except to give her the ability to self-heal."

Trina's lips trembled. "I can't hear her."

His gaze traveled between the two. "I don't

understand, you've been participating in the conversation."

She poked her finger at her head. "In here."

Lilith put her hand on his arm. "We used to be able to talk telepathically. I can't hear her anymore."

Trina took a threatening step forward. "You took her Magic."

Lilith shook her head. "I don't think so. When I came to, I used Magic to break the two of you apart." She held out her hand and a flame burst up from her palm.

They all jumped back.

"Shit." Lilith stared up at the scorched ceiling with wide-eyed awe. "I think it's stronger than before."

"Or maybe it's linked to your emotions," Trina said. "My Grimoire says a vampire's bite removes a witch's Magic."

James scrubbed his hand over his head. "Okay, look. Everyone needs to calm down."

Trina motioned to Lilith. "We don't know what the hell you did to her."

"I transformed her."

"Into what?"

James let out a string of curses. This was ridiculous. He pulled Lilith back into his arms. "As soon as the sun sets, I'll take you to the Historian. I'm sure she'll be able to tell us what the hell is going on." He'd been wanting to go see Augustina anyway. They only reason he'd put it off so long was because Crowley seemed eager for him to go.

"Twenty bucks says the Historian tells you, you did it wrong."

He released Lilith and took a step toward Trina, fisting his hand and poking one finger at her. "I'm gonna try to like you, because that'll make my mate happy, but you better simmer the fuck down, Sunshine."

Trina reared back. Her gaze slid to Lilith and she shrugged. "I like him. Keep him if you want."

As if she had any say. "You don't—"

"Okay." Lilith stepped in front of him, dragging his gaze to hers with her hand on his cheek. "Everything is fine." She glanced at Trina. "No more antagonizing my mate."

He took a breath, keeping his attention focused on Lilith. "I'm going to go clean up."

She lifted up on her toes to kiss him. "Thank you."

CHAPTER 31

Lilith waited until she heard the bathroom door close. "Do you have to be so argumentative?"

Trina swung around. "What the hell are you thinking?"

Lilith sighed. "We'll talk about this later." She headed upstairs to dress and Trina followed.

"He bit you."

"He saved my life." She opened her bedroom door and turned to glare at Trina. "At great personal risk, I might add. Why don't we talk about you? What were you doing to him?"

This time Trina looked away. "I don't want to talk about it."

"Right." Lilith pulled out a fresh pair of jeans and tugged them on. "Of course not."

"I meant what I said, I like him. Big as he is, he doesn't have much of a temper."

Ah, so that's why Trina kept pecking at him even after realizing they were safe. The question was, why did the state of his temper matter so much? Was this related to whatever had happened to her while they had been apart? "What is going on with you?" She gave Trina her back, pulled off her ruined nightgown and put on a bra. "You're hiding something."

The doorbell dinged. A fist banged on the door.

They both froze. It was too soon for other Guardian to come for James, wasn't it?

Trina thrust her chin toward the door. "You want me to get that?"

"No. I want you to stay out of it." Lilith pulled on a shirt and walked to the door, but Trina grabbed her arm.

"It's daemons. Three of them."

"They're probably here for James . . . because of what he did."

Her eyes narrowed. "How would they know so soon?"

"The Watchers."

Trina shook her head. "They'd still need time to contact the Guardians . . . and they'd need time to get here."

Lilith met Trina's gaze. "Please don't sell him out."

"They won't even know I'm here."

It was more than she'd expected. Lilith went downstairs and opened the door.

As Trina had said, three daemons stood on her porch. Two dressed in street clothes stood back from the door. The one on the drive, a handsome, dark-haired male, wouldn't meet her gaze. The other, a carrot-topped hulk, grinned smugly.

The third resembled a Mormon missionary. Everything about him begged his trustworthiness, from his youthful face down to his pressed suit. His curly blond hair had been moussed back tight against his scalp and his doe-like brown eyes exuded an innocence she didn't buy for a moment. He looked familiar. Why did he look familiar?

"Ma'am, I'm Julius Crowley." He flashed some kind of badge at her. "Can I come in, please?" He had an auctioneer's voice that seemed to fill the house. Fill her.

Let us in. Invite us.

She caught herself about to do as he asked, her hand tightened on the door, wanting to slam it shut, but unable to. She swallowed past her suddenly dry mouth. "Is there a problem, Mr. Crowley?"

His gaze narrowed. "Ma'am, we believe you're

harboring a wanted man in this house. It's a serious matter. If you'd invite me in, we can talk in private."

Trina stood off to the side, out of view. She ran a hand through her hair. "They're fishing."

"Is someone else in the house, ma'am?"

"My sister." Lilith forced herself to smile. "I assure you, she isn't dangerous in the least."

"I'd like to come in and have a look around."

Let us in. Trust us.

She tried to take a step back, to turn away, but her legs wouldn't listen. Her heart rate picked up speed.

"Ma'am, you must understand—if James Pasquino is here, your life is in danger."

She froze as soon as he spoke James' name. Hot color flooded her cheeks. Damn. She'd never been good at lying. But it was more than that. He was doing something to her. Influencing her. Pushing her. Had she been a regular human, she'd likely have already invited him in.

"There's no one here by that name." She massaged her temples.

Trina walked closer. "Are you okay?"

She waved her back, hoping she got the silent message. "Yeah, I've got a headache or . . . something. Get me some Ibuprofen from the medicine cabinet upstairs."

Trina stared at her for a long moment, likely trying to decipher her words. "Yeah. I'll bring what you need right down."

"Lilith."

Her gaze returned to Crowley.

"Pretty name. Pretty name for a pretty lady," Crowley said, his voice almost oily. "How about you let us in?"

Trust us, pretty lady. Invite us in.

Pain flared behind her eyes. She wanted to shut them, to look away from him, but couldn't. She struggled against saying the words he wanted to hear.

"He's here, I know he's here."

"Yes." *Oh, gods, why did I tell him that?*

"Lil?" Trina stopped at the top of the stairs.

Something slithered in his eyes.

The hair on Lilith's arms stood on end. "Ibuprofen." *James.* She needed James.

"Lilith, do you trust James?" Crowley asked.

She couldn't look away from those big doe-brown eyes, even as they changed, even as he tried to burrow like a parasite into her mind.

"Do you know who he is?"

Tiny golden snakes slithered in his eyes, winding over and around and through.

"What he is?" He sounded so reasonable. "Let us come in."

Such a little thing to ask. Let us in.

Lilith stepped toward the door. She needed to see in those eyes. Thousands of tiny snakes slipping and sliding around and over.

Viperous. Serpent-like, they glided faster.

"I can protect you. Invite us in, Lilith." Crowley's voice grew urgent.

Now. Invite us. Say the words. Invite us.

He'd never seen such a horrifying sight. Lilith feet from Julius Crowley, reaching her hand out.

"Shut up!" James descended the stairs two at a time, Trina hot on his heels. "You bastard, we were friends— what happened to you?" He pulled Lilith from the doorway, turning her so she couldn't see Crowley. "Lilith." Her gaze was far away, her body stiff. "Look at me." He gave her a little shake. Wiped his hands over her eyes and shook her again. "Wake up, damn it."

She blinked. Glanced around. "James." She pressed her hand to her eyes. "There was this guy—"

"He's still here." He eyed the men in the doorway from over her shoulder, careful to keep his gaze from Crowley's. Two others stood in the background past

Julius; their eyes glowed, reflecting the house lights. He pulled her into a fierce hug.

"I'm okay." Her words were muffled against his chest.

He leaned away a second later to cup her face in his hands. "Don't meet his eyes again."

"What he said is true, Lilith," Julius said. "We're friends. We've been friends for years."

James hugged her tighter. "Don't listen to him. It's okay. Everything's okay now."

"He helped me find you."

James shook his head, kept his gaze on Lilith. "Bullshit."

"I've been talking to him about you for a week now. Right, James? Did he tell you about me, Lilith? Why would he hide the information unless he planned to help me?"

"He's lying." James tightened his hold on her.

She nodded. "I know."

Crowley chuckled. "I can't lie, Lilith. James can, though. Did he tell you he's killed you before?"

Shit. How the fuck did Crowley know so much? He stared at Lilith, his gut twisting as her expression turned wary.

And of course Crowley kept going. "You tried to protect him, keep him safe, and for your troubles, he planted a sword in your chest while you were tied helplessly to a pyre."

James let his hands drop, refusing to lie to her. "That's not how it happened."

"That's exactly how it happened, Lilith. Trust me."

She shook her head, as if denying Crowley's accusation, but the pain of his betrayal, her hurt, shone bright in her eyes.

"Damn it." James looked away, his hand smoothing over the top of his head. "I was going to tell you."

"No, you weren't." She stepped back.

Julius seized the opportunity. "I told you the truth, Lilith. You can trust me." Then, to James, "Quite the woman you got there, James. Are you upset to know I was in her mind? If it makes you feel better, she's tough. I've never had to work so hard."

He turned to Julius. "Shut the fuck up!"

Lilith flinched. She feared him. She only saw the monster now. "You weren't going to tell me."

His chest tightened. James searched for something to say to allay her fears, to get her to understand. To keep her with him. Finally, he agreed. "No, I never wanted you to know." He took a step toward her, but Crowley's next taunt stopped him cold.

"The Council isn't going to like this, James. You, here with a human woman? You, doing nothing while Guardians are disappearing? They might think you have something to do with it."

His mind reeled. So the Council did know about the Guardians . . . or at least Crowley did. He'd known someone high up the ladder had to be involved. And Crowley fit the bill—the Council's right hand. "Jesus, it's you, isn't it? You're responsible for the Guardians disappearing."

Crowley offered a taunting smile in response.

He was going to ash the son of a bitch. "Stay inside, Lilith. He can't hurt you as long as you don't invite him in." Growling, he strode toward Julius. Fists clenched. His muscles tensed ready to fight.

"I'll follow you." Her quiet threat stopped him short of the threshold. "You step one foot outside and I'm coming, too. You know I will."

He eased a step closer to her. Did she still care? Maybe still want him?

But she backed away. "You'll draw the entire Council here."

Julius laughed at his predicament.

James paced, trying to come up with a solution. If he allowed Julius to hang around the property, he'd make a nuisance of himself. Eventually, he'd end up with one of the women outside.

As owner of the property, Lilith had rights. But he feared her knowing her power. He feared she'd use it against him. James threw his hands up in the air. What the hell. He didn't have any other options. "Tell him to go away."

"Go away?" It came out more of a question than a demand, and even then Crowley swayed on his feet.

"You're the Original, aren't you?" Julius watched Lilith intently. "I've been waiting a long, long time for you."

"Mean it, Lilith." James barked the order.

Julius started laughing. The eerie sound carrying a note of madness.

She shot James a mutinous glare. Then she braced her legs apart and closed her eyes. Her delicate hands balled into fists at her sides. When her eyes opened again he felt a palpable difference to her, a change that energized the air around them.

Her voice was strong, commanding. "Go. Away."

Julius's mirth died abruptly. His eyes widened as something impalpable grabbed him, plucking him off the porch. He twisted, raging impotently against the intangible foe as it whisked him away over the porch, beyond the lawn, and disappeared into the trees. His associates followed the same way.

A tempest blew through the room, slamming the door in its wake.

Stunned, James stared at her. "A bit more, uh, forceful than expected, but it works. They're gone now. You're both safe. They can't return here."

She watched him with a wary skittishness that tore at him. He needed to make her understand. "Listen—"

"How dare you."

"Lil, let me—"

"No." Her voice echoed in the entryway. "You don't get to explain. I felt like shit the other night because I withheld information and you, you milked it. You let me feel bad. You let me tell you I love you and you said it back."

"I wanted to protect you."

Her gaze narrowed. "Protect me or yourself?"

"You don't understand what he is, he—"

"I think I do. I think I understand far better than you." She pointed to the door. "He was the man I saw in the vision. He killed the coven. He controlled the Nephilim during the Clearances. And you . . . you're in league with him? Have you taken turns killing me off during each of my lives?"

He shook his head. "It's not like that. He's part of the Council, as soon as I dust him, they'll—"

"I want you out."

"—kill us all. I just needed a plan before I took him out. I wanted you safe—"

Her eyes became warning slits. "Go aw—"

"No!" He shouted the denial, wincing when she jumped. He stuck his hands up in surrender, walking around her, backing away toward the door. He released a sardonic laugh, shaking his head. "I'd rather walk." He opened the door, backed outside, and closed it behind him.

Christ, she'd almost banished him from the property.

Well, he'd let her have her way.

For now.

But they were mated. They had to work through this.

He glanced down at his bare feet and hesitated. He considered going back for his boots and shirt, his hand pausing mid-air, inches from the door knob. He sighed. He had a spare set of clothes in Lou's trailer. At least he had his keys, wallet, and blades. He didn't know where Julius and the others went, and he sure as hell didn't want to risk finding out through the same means.

Lilith sat on the bottom step before her knees gave out.

Trina flew down the stairs as the sound of James'

motorcycle faded. "What the hell was that?"

"I don't know." That pinpoint of awareness she had with James started to thin, not much, but enough to remind her he wasn't with her. "Weird, huh?"

"I'm not talking about you zapping creepy guy to goddess-knows-where." Trina scowled down at her. "We'll get to that later. I'm talking about James."

She shrugged, covering her face with her hands. "I panicked."

"You panicked?"

She gave Trina a good glare to let her know she treaded on thin ice. "You did tell me to do everything you would do."

A hurt look flashed over Trina's face. "I didn't tell you to adopt my psychosis."

"Look, you didn't see him last night. He made me feel so freaking guilty. I'm pissed as hell at him."

"He didn't *make* you feel anything. You felt guilty because you were. And now he feels guilty. But are you giving him a chance to ease his conscience? No."

"What he did was worse."

"You are so pig-headed!"

Lilith rubbed her hand against her chest. Damn it all, now she was starting to feel guilty *again*.

Trina stormed out of the room, but she returned seconds later. "Lilith, I've never seen you so . . . ." She searched for the right word. "I don't know . . . free. Happy." She pointed to the door. "And that big, bad-ass vampire turns to mush every time he looks at you. It's disgusting. I can't believe you kicked him out."

Lilith scowled. "You know, a quarter of an hour ago you were trying to ash him. What the hell do you want?"

"I told you if he hurt you any vow I made would be void. I saw you lying on the floor and his face covered in blood and I saw red."

"I understand that. But after. You kept pushing him. Antagonizing him. Why?"

Trina paled. "I wanted to see what would happen. I

needed to know if he was one of those guys who'd forbid you to see me. Or get mean."

The haunted look in her eyes damn near broke Lilith's heart. "What happened?"

Trina shook her head. "This isn't about me." She waved her hand toward the door. "I see something in your eyes when you look at each other, something I'll never have." Trina shrugged. "You just threw it away."

Lilith's eyes welled up with unshed tears. Trina was right. "What did I do?"

"He's perfect for you." Trina met her gaze. "You're lucky, Lil. You shouldn't have kicked him out."

"I needed time to think. Everything's moving so fast. I don't know what to do about the coven. Or the Council."

Trina sat next to her. "Every relationship has its issues."

Lilith snorted. Easy for her to say, she wasn't the one in the middle of such a mess. "Why didn't you ever go searching for your mate?"

She shrugged and looked away. "I got caught up with Trevor."

"But now." Lilith searched her friend's face. "Why don't you find him now?"

Trina plucked at the black plastic bracelets covering her forearm. "It's too late for any of that."

They sat in silence, each lost in their own thoughts, heads together. She shouldn't have kicked him out. They needed to talk. She needed to give him a chance to explain.

Lilith straightened. "I need to call James."

"You know"—Trina bumped her shoulder with her own—"since you are dating a vampire and all, does that mean we'll get to make you a corpse bride."

Lilith rolled her eyes. "Stop it."

"We'll go totally Goth. Black flowers, black dress. Play a bit of Manson. It'll be great."

"You're such an ass." Lilith chuckled.

"Yeah, well, you're laughing." Trina smiled. "You just

need to add a little irreverence to your life."

Lilith's humor faded. "You think he'll come back?"

"Eventually," Trina said with mock seriousness. "You kicked him out half-dressed. He'll probably at least come back for his boots."

CHAPTER 32

James had gotten spare clothing from Lou and then headed out for a drive to clear his head. Relationships were not his forte. He'd avoided all but the most necessary—his relationship with his teammates in the Seattle area.

He'd fucked up.

After taking Lilith to task for withholding information, he'd done the same. He understood why she'd gotten so pissed. Hell, he would've, too. But the rest . . . . He had to try to explain, but there would be no way to do so without putting himself even further out of her good graces.

He turned off the freeway and headed for home, for Lilith. He had to talk to her. Somehow he needed to make things right again.

As he turned on Highway 202, his phone rang. He activated the Bluetooth in his helmet. "This is James."

"Someone's trying to break into the bloodmobile."

"Lou?" She sounded panicked, breathless. He hit the gas, racing his way home. "Did you hit your alarm?"

"Yeah. But I caught a glimpse of the guys—one of them has a Sentry tattoo."

Christ. They were from the Council. This had to be Crowley's doing. Had the son of a bitch called in his whole team as rogues in revenge for what happened at Haven House tonight? "I'm coming. Did you lower the bar on the door and press the alarm?"

"Yeah, but—" Her hushed words turned into a scream.

"I'm almost there. The other Guardian will be coming, too." He hoped.

"I-I think Walker is gone. He didn't s-show for his appointment."

Goddamn it. Why the hell had he gone so far? Lou took care of their crew; she didn't fight. "You got the blade I gave you?"

She didn't answer. For a moment, he thought she'd hung up.

"Lou?"

"I got it."

He started breathing again, pressing as hard as he dared on the accelerator.

"They're almost in."

"Put me on speaker so you can use both hands to defend yourself."

The speedometer sat at one-hundred-twenty and he still needed to travel ten plus miles. "Five minutes. I'll be there in five minutes."

The sound of something shattering came through his earpiece. *Five minutes.* He had to slow as he entered Carnation, moseying past the fucking cop sitting just inside town limits, but two other bikes approached from the other direction.

That left two of his guys unaccounted for. Maybe they'd arrived already.

As soon as he hit the turn off, he gunned the bike again, racing through the residential streets.

He listened to the sounds of struggle, the occasional curse with a steadily building dread. He wasn't going to make it in time.

A muffled male voice said something. He couldn't make it out, but he heard Lou's response clear enough. "Fuck you. Fuck you."

It grew quiet then. He pulled up to the Tolt River, parked his bike and ran down the embankment as the sounds of other bikes approached. They had this. They'd get the son of a bitch. Lou would be fine. He promised her he'd protect her.

The bloodmobile came into view as he rounded the bend. Her attackers had shattered the aluminum door and left it in pieces on the ground. The siding around the opening bent inward from the forced entry.

"Lou!"

Footsteps pounded the ground behind him. He paused long enough to ensure they belonged to his team then ran into the bloodmobile: Empty. The Sentries had left the place a mess. All Lou's neat stacks of papers were scattered everywhere. One of the coolers hung open on busted hinges. They'd ripped her clothing from one of the overhead compartments, leaving them strewn around.

Ghost and Shadow crowded the doorway.

"They took her hostage; we can get her back." He gasped for breath, his gaze scanning over the mess they'd left behind, looking for a lead, a clue as to where they'd gone. "They took her host—" The knife he'd given her, the Guardian pendant she always wore, both lay in a small pile of sooty ash.

Ah, God. They'd killed her. He swore. Punched the coolers lining the wall to his left until his hand went numb.

"Shit." Ghost walked up the three steps and dropped onto the patient chair, his gaze locked onto the ash-coated floor.

Shadow came inside, too, his expression taut.

Walker came in last, out of breath. "I don't know where the hell they went, but there's no sign of them."

"They were Sentries."

Ghost snorted. "No way—"

James cut Ghost off. "She called me." He picked up the phone from where it still sat on the counter, still with the line open. He ended the call. "She said they had Sentry tattoos."

All the Council's Sentries had a web-like tattoo on their necks. Even if they'd worn a collared shirt, the tattoo would've been visible.

His gaze shot to Walker. "Where have you been? She said you missed your appointment yesterday."

Walker squared his shoulders. "I've had a couple guys following me. Didn't want to lead them here. I lost them about an hour ago."

"Do you know who?"

Walker shook his head, then jerked his chin at Lou's remains. "I'd wager it was probably the same guys. Maybe when they realized I wasn't going to be an easy target . . . ."

"It's not your fault. You didn't know." James motioned to the ash. "Maybe we should . . . ." His throat tightened and he looked away. *Damn it.* "I don't want to leave her here." No, she wouldn't want to be alone. "Any of you got something we can . . .?"

Shadow leaned down and began scraping up her ash with a piece of paper into an unused blood bag. "You know, Lou, I finally thought of a joke for you. Isn't it funny, I never did come up with one, and now, when you can't hear it, when I can't hear you laugh, now I think of a decent joke?" He scooped the ash into the bag. "I'll save it for you, for when we meet someday in the Eidolon Wastes."

Ghost cleared his throat. "I don't understand. We work for the Council. Why would they do this?"

James explained what had been going on with Crowley. "He's had the opportunity to snatch Lilith when she's gone out by herself. I don't understand why he's so bent on my bringing her to him."

Ghost folded his arms over his chest. "Almost sounds as if he's scared of her. Maybe he thinks she'll be more cooperative if you bring her to him."

He'd never considered that. Could be possible.

"Maybe we'd better stick together for a bit," Walker said. "You know, 'til we figure out what the fuck is going on."

James nodded. "I'm headed home. Why don't you guys come with me?" He pointed to the computer. "Grab the laptop, her phone, anything that might have information on us." He bent down and picked up Lou's blade and necklace.

Shadow blocked James' path. "You look guilty as hell. Why?"

"I told Lou I'd keep her safe; of course I look guilty."

Shadow backed away and let him pass. "So we're . . . what . . . rogue now?"

James shook his head. "We're not, but the Council will put out the word we are. We'll have to watch for Sentries and other Guardians."

Several curses flew from their mouths. Goddamn it, they were young. The oldest had only been on his team about fifty years. They'd never been through a daemon conflict. They didn't have the experience to deal with this shit. "Come on."

They trailed after him, up over the bank, through a dense stand of trees to Haven House's yard. All the lights in the house were on, Trina's car was parked out front. Jesus, he wasn't certain Lilith would take him back, much less allow his team into her house. He led the way up the steps.

"Uh, dude, there are humans in there. The door shield . . . ."

James nodded. "You're all to be on your best behavior. If they let us in, we'll be safe for the night. We'll have time to make plans. If not, I have a bolt hole in Seattle."

Instead of walking inside, he knocked.

Trina answered the door. "Oh, hey, James. She's—" She trailed off as her gaze found the other daemons sanding behind him. She turned and shouted, "Lilith!"

When Lilith arrived, she folded her arms over her chest, not even glancing at the other males. "Where have you been? I've been trying to—"

"You kicked me out."

Her gaze softened. "I needed time to think." She reached out to touch him and finally glanced at his team. "I take it they need sanctuary?"

He nodded, unable to look at her. What must she think? He hadn't even apologized yet and here he stood, needing a favor.

Her gaze shifted to his team. "What do I call you?"

"Walker, ma'am."

"Walker you are welcome into this house as long as you wish us no harm."

"Thank you, ma'am." Walker stepped past them and went inside.

"Call me Lilith, please."

James met her gaze. So she did know the appropriate way to invite a vampire into her home. And yet, she'd given him free reign over any home she lived in, no matter his intent.

She repeated the process with Ghost and Shadow, before turning to Trina. "Can you get them settled? It looks like they've had a long night."

Lilith turned to James. "Come with me."

"Lil, I wanted—"

"Not here." She reached for his hand. "Come on."

He took her hand, letting her lead him up the stairs, past the commiserating glances of his team, past Trina bringing blankets down to the guys.

Lilith led him into her room, her territory, and closed the door. "I can't sleep in there." She nodded toward his room. "Not until the memory of what happened with Nan wears off a bit."

"Thank you for letting my team in." It took everything he had to speak past the knot in his throat. He sucked in a deep breath and turned away, blinking hard to remove the burning in his eyes.

She put her arms around him.

"What are you doing?"

"You look wrecked." She rubbed her cheek against his back. "Like you need a hug."

Christ, she must still be furious with him, and yet she offered comfort? "I failed to keep a woman under my protection safe tonight." He expected her to push away from him, but she hugged him tighter. "Doesn't that worry you? It's not the first time. Maybe the Watchers picked me to protect you because they knew I'd fail."

Finally, her arms fell away. He deserved her scorn, but he still felt a pang at the loss of her warmth.

She walked around to face him, cupped his cheeks in her hands. "Or maybe they picked you because they knew you needed a success to bolster you."

Tears threatened, a weakness he'd never allowed himself and he'd be damned if he started now. He tried to turn away, but she wrapped her arms around him, clinging to him with the same seamlessness of starlight on night.

He hauled her up, burying his face in her hair to hide his shame.

"Who was she?"

"One of my team. We worked together for over a century." He sniffed and pulled away, a shudder running through him. "You would've liked Lou. She always called me these ridiculous nicknames and made me tell her a joke every time I saw her."

"Ah, so she kept you from becoming too serious."

He nodded.

"She sounds lovely."

"I told her I'd protect her."

Lilith searched his face, using a thumb to wipe away a tear. "From what?"

He swallowed. "Julius Crowley threatened to ash my team if I didn't hand you over to him."

"What?"

He shook his head. "I thought I still had time. He said forty-eight hours. I didn't expect an attack so soon. I didn't expect one from the Council. Jesus, I thought we were on the same side."

"What does Crowley want from me?"

He shook his head. "I don't know. He wants you. I'm sure it's because you're different." He opened his arms in a helpless gesture. "Everyone seems to want you—Crowley, the Watchers, the coven, Nan, the dybbuk, the lycan, those vampires who tried to nab you off the street, but no one's saying why. It's weird, though, with Crowley. He acted like he expected me to bring you to him. To get you to agree to whatever it is he wants. One of the guys thinks he's afraid of you and I'm starting to agree."

"Why didn't you tell me about him?"

"I never planned to help him." He paced the length of the room. "I didn't want to scare you. I wanted to figure everything out on my own so you'd never have to worry. Then, he threatened to come get you himself and I thought, no way. He could've done that before and he hasn't. I don't know what changed."

"So something prompted him. Maybe the fact that you bit me?"

"Maybe. You didn't exactly transform as expected and he knows things." He dragged his hand over his head. "He's a fucking mesmerist, but he acts like a seer. He knows things that have happened in this house, things he has no right to know."

"And the other thing he said?"

"That I killed you?"

She nodded.

He forced himself to hold her gaze. "I did. When I was a human, I killed you."

Lilith searched his face. "Why?"

"You were a witch." He shrugged. "I was a Templar. It was during the Crusades. I've always been a bit of a bastard. Take your pick."

He seemed to want her anger. The guilt from what happened tonight, from whatever he carried around from the past must be eating him alive. But she refused to accommodate him. "Tell me about your human life. All of it. From the beginning."

For the space of a breath, something crossed in his face. Fear? Anxiety? Then it passed, the emotion shuttered behind a stoic mask.

She became a little nervous herself, knowing her reaction to his past would be important. If he let her all the way in, she couldn't let him down. "I want to know you. All of you." She sat down and patted the bed next to her.

He closed his eyes and sighed, but he sat next to her. "My best guess is I was born in eleven forty-six. No one kept track back then, especially not for the bastard son of an Italian noble. My mother was a working woman, and, like I said, she died in childbirth. They told me, she called out the name Samael right before she died. They thought she wanted to name me after a demon."

She stroked his chest, hoping to soothe him with her touch. "He's the angel of death. Perhaps she called out in greeting to him."

"Maybe. My father hated it. He named me after the apostle, James the Elder. I lived with his soldiers and grew up learning to fight—swords, archery, hand-to-hand combat—whatever they'd teach me."

"Now that I can picture." She smiled. "You look like you belong in medieval times, wearing a sword nearly as big as you. What about the rest of your family?"

"Two half-brothers, one older, one younger." He leaned forward, bracing his elbows on his knees. "I never knew them. They lived with our father and, like I said, I lived in the barracks. Then, in my teens, an epidemic of cholera spread through Pisa. So many people died. Bodies lined the streets. You can't imagine death on that scale."

His gaze met hers, and she shook her head. "No, I don't think I could. The illness affected your family?"

He nodded. "My older half-brother died. Within days, my younger half-brother fell ill, and no one thought he'd survive, either. If he died there would be no heir for my father's title and lands. A religious man, he prayed for his youngest son's recovery, promising me to the church in exchange. Within twenty-four hours my brother recovered. I went to the seminary the next day."

"A son for a son?" She couldn't imagine being so cold.

"It was a matter of honor. He'd made a promise, and I saw it fulfilled. I liked to learn new things, and the priests in seminary taught everything, theology, writing, reading, arithmetic, and history. I devoured it all, though I preferred to fight. And in those days, the church needed fighters for the Crusades."

His eyes stared far away, lost to the past.

"A Templar came to Pisa seeking recruits. I petitioned the seminary and my father to let me go fight. I can still remember how proud he looked as I rode off. He must have spent half his fortune to gain my entrance to their ranks." He laughed ruefully. "I never saw him or my brother again and I sometimes wondered if he would've been so proud if he knew how many lives I ended in the name of God. I expected to see horrible things. Still, I wasn't prepared."

"I don't think anyone could be." She traced the outline of his jaw, trying not to think too hard about what he saw. The things he had done.

"I was a ruthless soldier. Had to be to survive. Still, others were far worse. And the Saracens didn't care who fought for them. You can't imagine the number of women and children I saw on the battlefields. I vowed to never kill either, and I stayed true to that until the day I lost my soul."

He stayed quiet a long time and she sensed this part of his story he'd rather forget. Mentally, she braced herself. "What happened?"

"Several witnesses accused a woman of trying to kill me by means of witchcraft."

Her gut twisted. *You can't change anything in the past. He's not the same man.* "You ordered her death."

Back then, they burned, drowned, or hung those suspected of witchcraft. She knew this, read about it, but it still left her chilled.

"I tried to save—" He sighed. "No, I won't lie. I didn't do a damned thing to save her, not until the end."

She smoothed her palm over his cheek. "Start at the beginning."

"They said she'd tried to shoot me off my horse with bolts of fire. By the time I found her, they'd already started the torture." He cursed. "I took off my fucking mantle because I didn't want to get her blood on it. She refused to confess or renounce her beliefs. But they claimed they found the mark of the devil on her right shoulder. A birthmark in the shape of a crescent moon."

He traced her birthmark with his finger, his gaze seeing straight through her into the past. A shiver raced down her spine. That's why he was so concerned with the mark.

"While I stood there trying to give her last rites she didn't want, she baited me. She changed me—made me actually think about all the things I did in God's name. I didn't want her to burn. I tried to plead her case to the commander, but he refused to listen. I felt so powerless."

"Did you know her before that day?"

"I didn't meet her until that evening and she was dead by nightfall." His eyes fell away again, and his voice became more hesitant as if he chose his words carefully or maybe tried to remember. "She claimed to be protecting me, and though I denied the need for a woman's protection, I could see she believed what she said. She told me I'd lose my soul that night. She predicted we'd meet again someday and she thought, maybe, if I learned to be more open-minded she might like me." His lips curved in a half smile. "She asked me to kill her before the flames reached her."

She could see the dilemma he'd faced. Vowing to never harm a woman, then having to break his own code of ethics or watch her suffer. "And you did."

He swallowed hard.

"That's not something to be ashamed of. You prevented a horrible death."

"She had those same beautiful, ancient eyes. She liked to spar on faith and philosophy." He caressed her face as he spoke. "Just like someone else I know. Twenty years ago, when I walked into the room across the hall, I thought for a moment I'd gone back in time. I could almost hear the sounds of armor and horses." His eyes filled with regret. "I never forgot. Not one day has passed that I didn't wish things ended differently. Maybe I—"

"James, don't." She pressed her mouth to his in a soft kiss, then let her forehead rest against his. She hated seeing him like this. "For whatever reason, it happened that way. It wasn't time for us to be together. We weren't ready and, since then, we've changed, we've grown. Now is our time. I don't want to waste it on regrets, and I wouldn't change a thing, because maybe it would change us, how we are together."

"How can you do that?" He trailed his fingers down her face. "How can you take an atrocity and turn it into something beautiful?"

"I believe everything we do, even the smallest action, affects everything else. It sounds like a horrible day." She smiled tentatively. "One I wouldn't like to live again, but if it hadn't happened, would you have been transformed? Would you be sitting here with me now? Everything has a purpose, and even when horrible things happen I think eventually those events bring about good. Sometimes we just can't see it until later."

"What about when we met twenty years ago? What good came of your grandmother's cruelty, of her death?"

"You found me again." She shrugged. "Nan never hurt another child." A small smile tugged at her lips. "And who knows, maybe those events altered future choices of the other people involved in some way."

He grew serious. "Could you ever forgive me?"

"If I thought you'd done something that needed forgiveness, I would." She brought her lips to his and kissed him. "So, was my past-life-me right? Did you become a vampire the same night?"

"I did." He tensed again, his expression darkening. "It was eleven seventy-seven. We'd secured a major victory over Saladin's forces in Montgisard. The battle, nothing short of a massacre. The dirt tinged red with Crusader and Saracen blood. I went out onto the battlefield to give the sacrament of extreme unction. Usually, several of us would go, but I wanted to be alone. I hadn't even retrieved my sword. I couldn't. There I stood, in the middle of the battlefield, amid the carnage unarmed and alone.

"I came upon two men feeding on the injured. When they noticed me . . . it happened so fast. I don't think they intended for me to survive. They almost ripped my throat out." His hand touched the scar at the base of his neck. "Someone must have found me because later that night, I woke beneath a shroud. If I'd slept much longer, they'd have buried me. When I sat up, the prayers changed from last rights to exorcism." He scrubbed his hand over his head. "They were my friends, the only family I knew.

"But I couldn't think past the sound of their hearts. I couldn't control the blood-lust. I couldn't stop. I killed them all." He met her gaze. "You know, there *are* times when you shouldn't fight. When the only way to survive is to lower your gaze, keep your mouth shut, and be still. But they were all fighters. And they all died." James rested his elbows on his knees, letting his head hang. "Saladin and his army took the blame for what I did."

Lilith shivered. She didn't want to hear this, but she knew he needed to tell her. To tell someone who loved him enough not to turn away in revulsion. She braced herself for the reality of his past.

"From what the history books say, the Saracens captured and killed two hundred-fifty soldiers. I think perhaps the Muslims suspected what had happened." He stood and paced the length of the room. "Maybe they'd seen similar destruction before, I don't know, but they beheaded the dead I left. Maybe to ensure none rose again. I returned to Pisa, to the seminary and told my mentor what happened. He asked me to come back the next night. To give him time to find a solution."

"What happened?"

He laughed humorlessly. "When I returned, I found proof of my excommunication nailed to the church door. I think he intended to distract me, which he did." He shook his head. "You see, he'd gathered the men from the village to destroy me. I wanted them to, but as a vampire, my survival instincts are much stronger. I fought, killed, and ran. I couldn't stand myself."

She'd never given it much thought, how vampires felt about transformation. Never considered that they might battle with themselves over instinct. She couldn't imagine what he'd been through. How he'd survived it all.

"Soon after, the Council offered me a position with the Guardians. I decided it sounded like good penance, so I accepted."

"You did what you needed to do to survive."

"I did." His voice toneless, he scrubbed a hand over his head and sat in the armchair. "And now I destroy those daemons who break the laws." His gaze landed on the full-length mirror across from him. In the reflection, he could only see the chair sitting in the darkened room. When he first went through transformation, his missing reflection gave the impression he no longer existed. Eventually, he admitted he didn't want to have to see into his own eyes anyway. The lack of reflection became a blessing of sorts.

He stood, needing to pace, to move, but Lilith blocked his path. She pushed him back into the armchair.

"What are you doing, Lil?"

"Starting over."

He stared, unsure what to say.

She knelt on the floor in front of him and started unlacing his boots.

"What does that mean?"

She tugged off a boot, pulled off a sock and sat back on her heels. "I'm not sure, but I feel like this is a turning point for us, don't you?" She stripped his other foot.

"I just told you I murdered you in your last life."

"Not my last life." She frowned, her brows drawing together. "Crowley got me that time. You got me in one of my lives before that."

"Flippancy doesn't suit you."

Finally, she met his gaze. "I don't know how to react. Is that what you want to hear? Because I don't. I feel bad. I wish you had done some things differently. It sounds like I should have done things differently. But it's a past I don't even remember and it bothers me that it's eating you alive. We're different people now and I don't think I particularly give a shit what happened back then except for the fact you're killing yourself over it."

He lifted his hips at her urging and she pulled his cargos and boxers off. "You don't care?"

"I don't know." She tossed the pants behind her and stood. "I mean, I hate that you kept it from me, since it involved me." She propped her hand on her hip. "Let me ask you this. If the same thing happened today. If someone told you I'd done something horrible, something that went against your current code of ethics, and wanted you to kill me, would you?"

"No. Crowley tried to tell me you'd be the end of daemon-kind, or at least that you'd destroy the vampire race. I didn't turn you over to him."

She crawled into his lap, tugging his shirt up and pulling it over his head. "So, you aren't the same person you were. Can we agree to that?"

He nodded.

"And neither am I."

"No. You're a hell of a lot more agreeable nowadays."

She laughed, a full-throated, husky sound that had him instantly hard.

"So can we bury the past and move on?"

"Yeah." As if he'd argue. He didn't know how much more time he'd have with her, but he'd be damned if he wanted to spend it fighting. Destiny had done everything in its power to ensure they found each other. The fates conspired to bring them together. "How the hell can you be so accepting?"

"My mother raised me believing in reincarnation. I believe that we each have a soul and that it's our job, in each life, to learn as much as possible." She sat back and removed her shoes and socks.

"Then how do you explain those who seem bent on not learning anything? Those whose sole purpose it is to ruin things for others?" *Like Crowley.*

"I think we all play the villain in at least one life." She shrugged. "Perhaps we make an agreement before we come. Decide what lessons we need to learn and choose someone to help us learn them. Or perhaps, at times, we as spirit become disillusioned with our process and have shitty lives."

"And daemons? How do you explain us?"

Her face lit up in a brilliant smile. "You've never considered the possibility that you chose your lot?"

"Never."

Her grin didn't waver as she stood and shimmied out of her jeans. "When I look at you, I see a very determined male."

"What are you doing?"

"Getting us ready for bed." She lifted her shirt and pulled it over her head.

Christ, she was a beautiful woman.

"I see a male, who takes his job of maintaining the

balance, of protecting me, seriously." She cocked her brow up. "Am I wrong?"

"You make me sound selfless, which I'm not. I do what I do in the hopes of regaining my humanity. I don't want to be one of the lost when the End Times come."

She rolled her eyes and huffed. She reached behind her and unclasped her bra. "There is a huge difference between being human with a soul and having humanity." The bit of lace dropped to the floor with the rest of their clothes.

"Humanity is having the qualities of humans, which includes having a soul."

Her panties joined the rest. "I'm not saying I have all the answers, or even that what my mother taught me is correct." She sat on his lap, curling into him. "But I'd much rather think that you chose to be here for me and to help others, than to think you're being randomly tossed about without a hope or a prayer."

"What if we are? Being tossed about?"

"Then I guess we need to hold tight to each other." She pulled his hand to her breast. "Touch me."

His hand shook when he cupped her. She couldn't possibly understand how her acceptance affected him. How much she calmed him. Her nipple hardened against his palm. She let her head fall back, her long hair brushing his leg.

The movement drew his attention to the mirror behind her and reality returned with brutal force. He stood with her, turned her so she faced the darkened mirror and sat back down. She needed to understand. In the reflection, she floated above the empty chair.

He dragged her back against his chest and drew his hands down her silken thighs, easing them apart until they rested on the outside of his, exposing her to his gaze. His cock throbbed at the visual feast she presented.

"I've never seen anything so beautiful."

"James?"

She created an erotic vision, so much so he found it difficult to draw in air. Her creamy skin reflected the moonlight, accentuating her dark nipples. And so soft— all satin and starlight to his touch. His hands played across her skin, grasping, kneading, caressing. And in the mirror, her eyes clouded with passion.

He entered her in one long thrust, clenching his jaw against the feel of her wet heat closing in around him. She arched, impaling herself farther onto his cock, and he shuddered with the excruciating desire she stirred.

"Look at us." He turned her face toward the darkened mirror, slowly flexing his hips. She needed to understand. His lot in life was a punishment. He waited for her look into the mirror.

"Do you see? That's my mark on this world: Nothing." He kept his hands gentle, skating them over her skin and pressed his lips to her throat. "You. You're beautiful. Look at you."

"Because of you." She wound her fingers with his, placing his hands over her breasts. "Look at my lips."

He nuzzled her ear. "Lush. Full."

Those lips spread in a sensual smile. "Only after you kiss me."

James froze, but her hands undulated over his, she squeezed her breasts with his hands.

"And see how flushed my skin is?"

He swallowed hard. "Like you've been kissed by the starlight."

"It's because I feel you at my back, I sense your gaze on me and feel your cock, your arousal thick inside me."

"Stop it."

She rotated her hips. "Watch us."

"I'm not there."

"I see you." Her hips rolled in a steady beat. Her gaze met his in the mirror. Not really, he had no reflection, but he felt as if she stared straight into his eyes. She pulled his right hand down her body, over her belly to the apex of her thighs. "I see you in the changes in me."

He touched her clit and she gasped, pressing onto his fingers, sinking him deeper into her body.

"A week ago, I'd have been too ashamed to watch myself being pleasured by you."

"Because I'm a vampire."

"Because I was ashamed of myself." Her hips flexed, her slick inner muscles dragging along his length, gripping him tight. "I thought I was too skinny. Too small-breasted. Too clumsy. Too scared."

"You're gorgeous. A goddess."

"Only to you." She reached back her arm, palming the back of his head and turned her face to his. "You make me feel beautiful. You make me brave. You might not have a reflection, but don't think you don't leave impressions."

His throat tight, he curled his arms around her. He held her tight, needing to be as close as possible, wishing he could climb inside her skin and discover whatever made her so fucking bright. He wanted her light. He wanted her. Needed her.

CHAPTER 33

As soon as the sun went down, James brought Lilith to a small cottage in Fall City. The home of Augustina Saar, the Historian.

Augustina allowed them entrance before turning to Lilith. "You'll give us a minute, please." She bowed to Lilith, pulling James away and speaking to him in hushed tones. "You should not have come here."

"I need to know what's going on, what's going to happen. The Watchers have given me an impossible task in protecting her. I can't even get a straight answer as to who I'm protecting her from."

"Everyone."

He snorted. "That's what the Watchers said."

"Then you know what you need to know. Go."

"No. Tell me what's coming." Lilith walked farther down the hall, gazing at the pictures lining the paisley walls. "Please. You know what it's like to be in love. I'd give my life to protect her, but I don't even know what I'm fighting. I can't keep her locked in Haven House forever."

Augustina shook her head. She threw up her arm. "I cannot see her future, Guardian, but only her here and now."

"But you knew she was important. You knew when she was a child."

"She bears the mark of the Original. Anyone who knows the early Histories would recognize that mark.

The vision I saw showed her in mortal danger. When I saw your struggles, I realized the Great Ones wanted you to help her."

"Why?"

"I am but a daemon. I do not try to understand the minds of angels. Not even fallen ones. Perhaps you should ask them yourselves."

Jesus, he hated this. "They're not talking."

"Then go to them."

He snorted. "Go and visit the most dangerous beings on Machon? Sure, as soon as the portals open to the daemon realm and I get over my uncontrollable preference for existing. You must have some idea why they sent me to her."

"No more than you." She sighed. "What do the Watchers do?"

"Keep the balance."

"Through the Guardians."

"Yes."

"And . . . .?" She motioned for him to keep going with her hands.

"So you're saying we need Lilith to maintain the balance between humans and daemons."

"It does seem so."

"They shouldn't have picked me. I don't even have a usable talent should it come down to needing to use it. I'm already on the Council's radar. I feel like I'm putting her in a more vulnerable spot than she'd be in if they picked someone else."

"Guardian, this I can tell you. You must do whatever it takes to protect that woman." She pointed to Lilith. "If that means you level a town because you need to use your talent, then you do so."

"I can't. Lilith is sweet. She's a caregiver. She'd never understand that kind of violence. I'd lose her and that would destroy me."

"Ah, and now we get to the heart of the matter."

He cocked his brow.

"What was the old woman's curse?"

"She cursed me to destruction before I got what I truly want."

"And what do you truly want."

"I want my mate safe."

She shook her head. "The old woman was fucking with you. Just so we're clear: If she did curse you to destruction, death curses die with the witch. So you're clear, even if the curse was legit and she wasn't playing with words, well, then you know that outcome as well, right?"

So it wasn't a death curse. Lilith might end up hating him, but she'd be safe. He nodded.

Her lips quirked. "Did you say she wouldn't understand violence? The Original?" Augustina held his gaze, then nodded toward Lilith. "Are you sure we're talking about the same woman?"

He glanced down the hall. Lilith turned, maybe sensing their stares and started strolling back toward them. "Yeah. That's her, right there. She had her first battle the other night. Shook her to her socks."

"Let me tell you a secret about your mate, one she may not yet realize." Augustina leaned closer. "She is daemon-kind's judge, jury, and executioner. She is our law. And soon, she will be the one all daemon-kind, including the Watchers, look to for guidance. Do not underestimate her. And do not think, because you are her mate, you'll be outside her law."

A chill spider walked up his spine.

"You'll use your talent if needed, because she won't think kindly on you for any show of weakness. They'll use you against her if they think they can, Guardian, so don't give them a reason."

"Who?"

"Like any monarch, she will have countless enemies over her reign. When you're told to protect her from everyone, you should take that advice to heart."

"Do you need more time?" Lilith asked.

James jumped slightly and pasted on a smile. "No."

"Thank you for being so patient." Again, the Historian gave her slight bow.

Lilith smiled. "We hoped you could answer some questions for us."

The Historian frowned, giving James a sidelong glance.

"We need help, Augustina."

Her gaze narrowed at his use of her name, his reminder that he could hurt her with the knowledge. The Historian's lips twisted in a semblance of a smile. "Of course, Samael."

James cursed under his breath.

"Come." She led the way down the hall and into a dimly lit room. Once she shut the door behind them, she asked, "What do you wish to know?"

Lilith opened her mouth to speak, but the Historian held up her hand. "I caution you to not say anything out loud that you would not wish your enemy to know."

Lilith snapped her mouth closed and looked at him. "Now I'm not sure what to ask." Her gaze returned to the Historian. "Are you my enemy?"

"Never."

"Did you send me the notes?"

Augustina nodded.

"Why?"

"Because things are changing, Lilith. There's much more going on here than either of you realize. In time, when you're ready to accept the challenge, those intrigues will present themselves. For now, let's say, I knew you were needed here. I knew it was time you met your mate as an adult and it was time for him to claim you."

"Why didn't my bite change her?" Lilith's gaze snapped to his and he shrugged. "It's not a weakness. I think our enemies already know the answer. We should, too."

She nodded. "Yeah, you're right."

The Historian shrugged. "She will not change." She looked at Lilith. "You cannot change, not until all of you has been transformed." Her gaze traveled back to James. "And even then she won't be quite like anything you've ever seen before."

He snorted. "Talking to you is like talking to the fucking Riddler."

Lilith smacked his arm. "Be nice."

But the Historian chuckled. "Sit. I can see you are in dire need of story, Guardian. Why don't I tell you a little about the Creation? You have a fondness for that one, right?"

He sat. "Yeah."

"Once upon a time, one man and one woman lived on Earth."

James rolled his eyes. "Adam and Eve."

"No, no. Before that." The Historian sat. "Adam and Lilith. Both possessed powers most humans have long since forgotten—mastery over the animals and elements—Magic. Unfortunately, they didn't suit. Adam wanted a submissive woman and Lilith needed a stronger mate. She fled Eden and shacked up with one of the Grigori, an Angel named Samael."

Lilith winked. "I guess it was fortuitous."

For the first time ever, he had a reason to like his name.

"Samael bit Lilith, giving her eternal life and for many years they lived happily together, until one day, Lilith saw that Adam's new wife grew fat with child. Lilith couldn't bear children and became jealous. For years she shadowed the humans, stealing the lives of their infants, until three angels came to tell her to leave. She refused and battled with them."

"That makes no sense. Angels are more powerful than all of us."

Augustina crossed her legs. "You forget, as both vampire and witch, her power rivaled the angels, and so, in the end, God intervened. He destroyed her immortality and struck Lilith's soul in two, forcing her two halves to reincarnate time and again until they learned humility, compassion, and love. Once the three lessons were learned, her immortality would return and she'd resume her place in the world."

"So there are two of us?"

The Historian nodded. "Two halves of the same coin. Night and day. One of you burns bright as a beacon, the other remains shrouded in starlight. She will not be known, her Magic will not be felt, until she has been transformed."

Lilith nodded.

"Who—"

The Historian shook her head. "Don't ask. Speaking her name would put her in danger and she is not ready." She looked at Lilith. "But you know. In your heart, you know who I speak of."

"I think so."

James sat back. If he had to take a guess, he'd assume the other half must be Trina. That woman was as dark as Lilith was bright. Then again, Crowley hadn't acknowledged Trina when he came to Haven House—so perhaps not. "You worked with the Council for centuries. Why did you leave?"

"Because Julius Crowley became a threat. Always lurking around, asking questions."

"About what?"

"Who. The question is, about who. I'll give you one guess."

"Lilith."

"Mm."

Lilith shivered. "He killed the old coven during the Clearances. Him and those monsters, the Nephilim."

The Historian tipped her head to the side. "Is that what happened?"

James' gaze sharpened. "I would've expected you'd know."

"Why? Because I'm a seer?" She shook her head.

"Visions get murky around that male same as they do around you, Lilith. The only things I can tell you about him is what I've seen for myself."

"And what's that?"

"He wants the Original."

"To what end?"

"I can't say with any certainty."

"Can you guess?"

"There have been signs for centuries now." She shook her head. "Signs of the End Times. Signs that the balance will be tipped."

"Like what?" Lilith asked.

"The portal to Machon closing. The Clearances. That's when it all began. After that—?" She opened her arms in a sweeping gesture. "Mankind has advanced more in the last three hundred years than at any other point in history."

James shrugged. "Humans have technology now. They've needed to worry less about survival in the last three hundred years."

"Yes, yes, but why? Why this sudden burst of inspiration? Mankind hasn't had such an explosion of knowledge since before the Great Deluge."

Holy Christ. Was she saying what he thought she was saying? The Watchers. They must have been giving humans information.

She held up her hand. "Don't answer that. We're done."

"What about Crowley?"

The Historian lifted her hand in a staying gesture. "I'd remind both of you this conversation—no conversation—is ever private."

James didn't want to let it go. If he could get the answers, perhaps he'd have a chance at defending himself and Lilith against the Council. "Crowley is helping them, the ones who have gone rogue." He must be in league with the Watchers, at least the Watchers who weren't helping him and Lilith.

"I cannot tell you more."

"Crowley suggested I come here."

She stared. Her lips parted. *"Why didn't you tell me that at the beginning?"*

He'd never seen this woman rattled. Not even the night he'd faced her in that back alley in Seattle. She showed fear then, but not like this. Her gaze darted around the room as if she might find someone lurking in the room, eavesdropping.

But then, maybe she would. "You fear the Watchers."

"Everyone with a lick of sense fears the Watchers." She stood. "You need to go."

"No. I'm not leaving until you finish answering our questions."

"I've said all I can say with certainty. The rest is for you to discover on your own, and, if you are wise, to never speak aloud."

"James," Lilith said, tugging at his arm, "we should go."

"No. Are they in on this? The Watchers? Whose side are they on?"

The change in the Historian was instantaneous and dramatic. Her skin split apart along heretofore unseen seams, a thick dark mass billowing out from within.

Lilith grasped at his arm, pulling him back.

"Damn it, she's hiding something."

"She'll be hiding our bodies if we don't get out of here."

The Historian loomed over them. "Leave, Guardian, or I'll make good on the old woman's curse."

"Fuck."

He let Lilith pull him out into the hall and closed the door behind them. "The Watchers—"

Lilith covered his mouth. "Don't say it out loud. There's a reason she didn't want us to speak of it."

"How the hell are we to come up with a plan?"

She grinned. "Everything will work out. Soon, the coven will be on our side. Your team is on our side. We'll figure this out."

He opened his mouth and she covered it again. "Without us tipping our hand to our enemy."

James sighed. "Let's get you home. Come on."

CHAPTER 34

Rowena grinned. Everything was set. Her spell had taken root and the Director of RI had his cure.

Almost.

He was sending men. Lots of them. They'd set up watch on her property and the next time Julius Crowley showed his face around here, those men would grab him. Dr. Edwin Moss of RI was sure the answer to his problem lay within Crowley's DNA.

She giggled. This would be hilarious.

The Watchers would not suspect her involvement. The spell had been cast silently. She'd sought out the director on the astral plane, inspiring him through his dreams. No, the Watcher's wouldn't suspect her involvement at all.

And truly, there was little risk. The good doctor could try to take Crowley's DNA until his dying breath, but it was impossible. As soon as he removed Crowley's tissue, it would fall to ash. There was no risk of Moss accidentally making more vampires.

The infected humans would die, yes, but they would die either way.

And Crowley, Crowley would be out of her way.

Her doorbell rang and her gaze narrowed. One guess who that might be.

Rowena answered the door but before she could say a thing, Crowley launched into speech. "It seems your meddling did little but draw the witch and her lover closer together. Congratulations on making everything more difficult for all of us."

She reared back. "Excuse you?"

"Oh, I have no need of excuses. But you may. He's turned her."

Rowena's breath caught. Dear goddess help them all. "To a vampire?"

"Oh, no. No, nothing so mundane. She's changing to something the world hasn't seen since the beginning of time. Now you do need me. I'm offering you a chance to get her back under your control. What will it be, Madam?"

She considered him for a long moment. Finally, she stepped back.

One corner of his lips rose in a mocking grin. "The words, if you please."

"Providing you wish me no harm, you're welcome in my house for the next ten minutes, Mr. Crowley."

Crowley strode inside. "I've always wondered what a witch's house looked like." He made a show of observing his surroundings as he circled her living room, stopping to fondle the jars and crystals that littered the space. "Actually, I guess it's like anyone else's. A bit disappointing." He made his way over to her sofa, passing a large wall mirror.

She sucked in a sharp breath. She expected to see nothing in the mirror—vampires didn't have reflections. But this one did. This vampire's reflection showed a massive, twisted skeleton. It's alabaster bones, blackened as if they'd been charred.

He sat before she could discern any other details, making himself at home with a comfortable sprawl.

Rowena remained standing near the door. What the hell had possessed him? "What's your proposition?"

"You don't sound very enthusiastic."

"I doubt you have anything to say I want to hear."

"I may surprise you." He shrugged. "Your coven is

fully staffed now, is it not?"

She maintained his gaze, her eyes narrowing. As if she'd tell him anything.

Crowley grinned. "Let's assume it is. It would be the first time since Roanoke you've had thirteen mature witches in the coven, hm?"

She gave a non-committal shrug.

"I find it interesting you haven't made a move yet. Having trouble with some members?" His eyebrows popped up. "Bit of mutiny, perhaps?"

Again she shrugged, choosing to say nothing.

"Still, it's quite an achievement." Then, in a more dramatic voice, sounding like a TV announcer, he said, "They are ready to seek revenge, to take their rightful place among the creatures of the night." He chuckled. For a few heartbeats he did nothing but wind and unwind one of the pillow tassels around his finger. He grew serious again, gazing at her thoughtfully. "I want Lilith."

"So you keep saying. Why?"

"She has something I want. Same as you. Why else would you have hid her Magic all these years?"

She gasped. "You know about the dybbuk?"

"I know about far more than the dybbuk." Crowley crossed his ankle over his knee. "What would the coven do if they found out who killed off all their mothers?"

Slowly, Rowena sat.

"We both know what Lilith is. What she can do. And I imagine she'll be pissed as hell once she figures everything out. She's not stupid."

Rowena looked away.

"My plan would aid us both." His expression turned sly. "You've planned an induction for her tonight?"

She nodded.

"My deal is this." He leaned forward. "I want you to induct her, and then I want to speak to her. She'll be yours again by dawn—think of the havoc you can wreak among the vampire race with her special brand of

Magic."

"What spell?"

He smiled. "A simple exorcism."

She should've known. Now that she'd gotten a glimpse of what possessed him, she could understand all the risks he'd taken in an effort to get to Lilith. Still . . . . "You've waited all these years for her? I could've worked that spell."

"No, madam. What I need will require a bit of extra finesse. Give me three minutes with your coven before Lilith arrives. I'll have them all on your side."

She laughed. "You think you can convince my coven in three minutes to help you?"

"I'm a mesmerist. They'll do what I say. As a bonus, I'll make sure Lilith doesn't remember anything about the dybbuk or your role in her curse."

Hm. A mesmerist. That would be helpful. It also explained his frustration with her throughout the years. She'd spell-cast her mind when Trina was young to keep the little troublemaker from seeing her thoughts. Apparently, the spell worked against mesmerism, too.

If he could mesmerize her girls into obedience . . . but, damn. She'd already cast the spell on Dr. Moss.

Timing would be everything. Perhaps she could have an obedient coven *and* have him removed before he used Lilith's talents. She'd have to be cunning, Crowley couldn't be allowed access to Lilith. She grinned.

"You have yourself a deal Mr. Crowley." Rowena stood. "I'll call the coven together. But—"

Crowley cocked his brow.

"My daughter, Katherine, she'll be as immune to your talent as I am."

A shudder jerked his head to the side. He clenched his jaw. "Then bind her. Keep her silent and out of my way."

CHAPTER 35

Trina walked in from the kitchen as soon as they returned to Haven House. "You're going to be late if you don't hurry."

"For what?" Lilith asked.

"The coven takes back their powers tonight, right?"

Lilith closed her eyes. "With everything else, I'd forgotten."

"We can't bail on them."

James shook his head. "Have you forgotten about Crowley? He could ambush her anywhere between here and there."

Lilith held up a hand. "How about this, Trina can use the Transportation spell to send me. I'll go from being under your protection to the midst of the coven."

"You can't argue that, James." Trina folded her arms over her chest. "Not even your Mr. Crowley would be brazen enough to face a full coven."

James relented. Not that he had a whole lot of choice. He knew how important it would be to have a high priestess in place who supported daemon-kind. He leveled his gaze on Trina. "You're going to be there, too?"

She nodded. "I'm going to show up at midnight, after Rowena casts the circle and starts the rite."

Lilith wet her lips. "Once the circle is cast, coven members can enter, but no one else."

"And no harm can be done to anyone within the circle." Trina shrugged. "Unless one of the witches leaves the sacred space . . . then all bets are off."

Lilith snorted. "Like Rowena would do that. She may have a bit of all our powers, but together, we're still stronger."

He relaxed a little. While Lilith was still learning to use her Magic, Trina was scary as hell with hers and it sounded like they had a plan.

Trina nodded. "Come on, let's get ready."

Even knowing Trina with her scary Magic would be close at hand, he couldn't shake the feeling something bad might happen. "Maybe I should go. I'll stay out of—"

Both women shook their heads.

"You wouldn't be able to enter the circle to get to Lilith anyway," Trina said.

"And if you get too close, she'll sense your presence, which will cause even more havoc." Lilith tipped her head back to regard him. "Besides, didn't you say Will is on his way?"

He nodded. The Lycan had called. He had some news.

"You'll be so busy planning, you won't even miss me."

James scoffed. "Don't count on it, sweetheart." He bent down and gave her a quick kiss. "Go on."

The two of them went into the room under the stairs and James retreated to the living room.

Ghost looked up from his book. "What did you learn from the Historian?"

If you're wise, you won't speak it out loud. "Nothing." James glanced at the title of Ghost's book and groaned. "What are you doing with my mate's book?"

A slow grin spread on his face. "This is you're mate's book?"

He frowned. "She likes the plot."

"Yeah, me too, man." Ghost chuckled. "It's all about the plot."

Walker harrumphed. "Nah, I prefer those character-driven stories."

"Oh, this one has that, too." He glanced up from the pages, grinning from ear to ear. "They're very driven, just thrusting the story forward, they are."

"She's with the coven." Trina walked into the living room as someone knocked. "I'll get it." She turned on her heel and headed for the door.

A moment later she walked in with Will.

James made the introductions. "This is Ghost, Shadow, and Walker."

Will looked at James. "And plain old James. You really are a relic, aren't you? How old are you?"

"Old enough to correct the accounting of the battle of Montisgard in the history books."

Ghost folded his arms over his chest. "You're as old as Crowley?"

"Older." James had to resist the urge to squirm under their questioning gaze. "I trained him."

Shadow let out a low whistle. "Damn. You should've ashed his ass, instead."

"He wasn't always a bastard." James shrugged. "Back when I worked him, he was . . . funny. Laid back. Everybody liked him."

Walker snorted. "That's what happens when you get too chummy with the Council."

"Maybe." He looked at Will. "I'm assuming you have news?"

"Yeah, some good, some bad, some worse." He took his phone out and pulled up a map app. "So the Watchers gave our hem-it-netjer a location. We're not sure what's going down there tonight, but we think it has to do with the missing Guardians."

Shadow pulled off his baseball cap and put it on backward so he could lean forward and see the map. "That's not far from here."

James kept his attention on Will. "I'm assuming that's the good news?"

Will nodded. "The bad news is, there're lots of vehicles not far from this house. Military-style vehicles. Whatever's going down, it's some serious shit."

Great. "So, we'll have humans to deal with."

"Yeah."

"Military vehicles." Walker shrugged. "What are we talking here, two? Six?"

"I'd estimate about fifteen. Maybe sixty men."

They all swore. "For what?" Ghost asked.

Will shook his head. "Don't know. They want something, though. Bad."

James nodded and looked down at the map. Then he looked again. "Shit."

"What?"

"I know that place. I've been there. It's down the street."

Trina edged closer and looked over his shoulder. "Our high priestess, Rowena, lives there. The coven will be performing their Samhain ritual and she's not going to want anyone around—not daemon or human."

James pulled a face. "All evidence to the contrary."

Trina scoffed. "Rowena's a bitch, don't get me wrong, but she's spent her life plotting revenge against daemon-kind in retaliation for the Clearances and hiding the coven from the cowen."

Ghost's brows furrowed. "What's cowen?"

"Non-Magical humans." She turned back to James. "You won't have to worry about the humans. The coven will take care of them and any daemons who wander into their territory won't be wandering back out."

"I need in there."

Trina shook her head. "The coven will decimate you. You can't be thinking to go over there."

CHAPTER 36

Blessed be. It's good to have you back."

Lilith pasted on a smile. "Blessed be."

"We're already outside." Rowena led her through the house and out into the back yard where the coven had erected a stone circle.

A beautiful night, the full moon highlighted everything in silvery hues. Quiet, too. The only sounds that of the Snoqualmie River sprawling behind the property and the snapping of a bonfire.

Her coven sisters had already prepared for the ritual and taken their spots in front of each of the stone pillars. The same spots they'd been assigned as children.

She took a deep breath and waved to the coven.

No one returned her greeting. In fact, none of the women even glanced her way. Had something changed?

"Now that you've regained your Magic, it's the utmost privilege we bestow upon you tonight. Your ancestors will be proud to see you join their ranks as one of the greatest, most powerful witches in history. Did you bring your gift for the Watchers?"

She handed Rowena Aimee's summoning jar, but her attention remained on the scene before her. For a heartbeat, everything looked as she expected it to, but a shiver still raised the hair at her nape. All the women from the coven wore their Sabbath robes and the altar had been prepared for the ritual. A bonfire burned off to the side, lighting up enough of the area for her to see the flames reflected in the Snoqualmie River and shadows dance on the base of the Cascade foothills just beyond.

Rowena's *athame* lay on the stone altar at the head of the ceremonial grounds, along with several summoning jars meant as offerings. Candles decorated the base of the altar and incense infused the air.

"Is something amiss, dear?"

She couldn't quite drag her gaze from the scene. Everything seemed as it should, nothing appeared to be out of place. She saw no sign of danger, but her gut had gone queasy and heat flushed her face.

Something wasn't right.

She scanned the faces of each of her coven sisters. Everyone seemed sedate. Happy. Calm. When her gaze reached Kat, she froze. Kat didn't move, but she wore an expression of warning. Her wide eyes stared back and after a second or two, Lilith realized she was screaming, trying to shout out, but couldn't.

Dear gods, they had her Magically bound.

Her gaze snapped to Rowena. "What have you done?"

Rowena shrugged. "What I needed to do to protect my coven."

Lilith backed away a step. Then another. And came up against an immovable obstacle. She turned, half expecting to discover James had followed her.

The silvery eyes staring back at her belonged to Julius Crowley.

Lilith took another step back, her gaze sought Rowena's, and the malevolent intent held her immobile for several heart beats.

Crowley chuckled. "I think she's on to you, Madam High Priestess."

Lilith fisted her hands. "Go. Away."

He laughed. "You don't live here."

Why wasn't the coven doing anything about his presence? She ran.

"Bring her back," Crowley shouted.

Lilith stopped as the women in the coven started

toward her. Oh, gods, he had them all under his control. "Don't touch me!" The heel of her boot caught on the uneven ground, and she fell.

Claire, Gina, and Meredith raced toward her.

Lilith held her hands out, palms facing them. Pulling energy from the Earth, she allowed it to flow through her body and out of her palms. The burst of energy forced the women back.

"Lilith," Rowena said. "Stop before you get hurt. This is for your own good. You're special."

Lilith backed away. "You're crazy." She tried to raise her arms to cast a shield, but couldn't move her arms, as if heavy, weighted rope encircled her. She glanced down, but there was nothing to see, no physical tethers to attempt to unfurl. "No!" A binding spell. She thrashed against her invisible restraints.

Crowley waved the other witches away and came to stand next to her. "Don't fight me, little witch." He spoke low enough no one else could hear, his breath brushing her ear. "We wouldn't want anyone to get hurt."

Out of the darkness surrounding the circle, four male daemons strode closer. Each put a blade to the throat of one of the witches.

Lilith stilled. "What do you want?"

"You'll see soon enough." Crowley strode closer to the altar. "First things first, Madam High Priestess, induct Miss Caldwell into your ranks, if you will."

Rowena's green eyes narrowed. "This wasn't part of the deal. I never said I'd allow you within our circle while we worked Magic. You never said any other daemons would be here."

"And yet, that is exactly what's going to happen." He pointed toward Kat. "Or your daughter will be tonight's first sacrifice."

Rowena's gaze bounced from hostage to hostage and when she came to Kat something crossed her features, something like fear. Casting the circle would protect Kat. No harm could come to those within the circle's confines.

Rowena's lips trembled and she pressed them into a thin line. "Fine." She took her place before a small altar, tucking Aimee's jar into the pocket of her Sabbath robe before starting the rite.

"Great Watchers all, you are welcome. Join us." Rowena picked up her *athame*, a long, wicked dagger, and lifted it over her head. "I cast this circle for our protection. Let no harm come to us within its boundaries." She pointed her *athame* out as she rotated, the razor-sharp point of the knife marking the circle in the air.

Violet called the first corner, inviting the Watchers to join their ceremony. "Hail to the watchtower of the East, Watcher of Air. I command thee, join us in this rite; grant us knowledge over the elements. Hail and welcome."

Meredith, Fiona, and Debbie called the remaining corners.

The protective shield closed around them, but each of the candles remained unlit. Odd, the candles usually lit as the Watchers sent their powers to the coven for their ritual.

Rowena didn't seem to notice. She focused her attention on Crowley. "Now the circle has been cast and Lilith's presence during our rite makes her one of us." She came around the altar and faced Crowley. "You may as well have your men step away. You can't harm us in this circle."

Crowley smiled, nodding to the male who had his knife at Kat's throat. The red-headed male lifted his blade toward Kat's neck. Crowley shouted, "No!"

Lilith stared at him. What the hell?

His face contorted and a shudder ran though him. Crowley's gaze narrowed. Then, he stilled. "Do it."

The male holding Kat drew the blade closer, but when a finger's width from Kat's skin, his hand began to shake. His lips pressed into a thin line as he struggled.

Finally, he looked up and shook his head at Crowley.

Crowley's smile faded. His attention jerked toward Rowena. "If we can't harm you, then the opposite must also be true." He stepped closer to Rowena. "You can't harm us."

She shrugged. "It seems we are at an impasse, Mr. Crowley."

"Are we?"

Rowena's lips curved.

"Eventually, you'll need to leave this space." He walked a tight circle around Rowena. "You'll need to eat. Drink. Rest." When he stood behind her, he leaned over her shoulder. "How angry do you want me to be when that time comes? I can wait for all eternity, madam, and I'll be as strong as I am in this moment."

Rowena's gaze locked with Lilith's. She seemed to be pleading with her, but for what she didn't know. She couldn't do anything while bound.

"Summon him." Julius leaned forward and handed Rowena a slip of paper. "Here's the name."

"Why?" Rowena opened the paper, her glance shooting up to meet Lilith's. "Why is this necessary?"

"I need her cooperation tonight. You're going to ensure I get it."

Rowena spread out the slip of paper Crowley gave her on the altar. For a heartbeat or two, her gaze met Lilith's, her expression one of regret. Then she spoke. "Samael James Pasquino—"

Lilith's stomach bottomed out. "No." This wouldn't be the gentle summons of a child calling her future mate. This summons would leach his power and make him slave to his summoner.

"—I summon thee. To obey all commands made by me. For this we ask or something more, so mote it be, we do implore."

"Don't do this." Lilith struggled against her restraints. How did Crowley know his name? Had he been watching that night as James stood out on the porch begging entrance? Is that how he knew his full name?

Oh, gods, this was all her fault.

The coven joined in, chanting. "Samael James Pasquino, I summon thee. To obey all commands made by me. For this we ask or something more, so mote it be, we do implore."

Crowley approached her. "What's wrong, little witch?"

"Don't do this." Lilith struggled against her invisible bonds. "You don't need him. I'll do what you want."

He closed his eyes and inhaled deeply. "Your mate, he has no faith. He'll blame you for this, I think. How much do you want to bet that when he arrives all you'll see in his eyes is hatred?"

Lilith lifted her chin. "Then I guess it's a good thing I have faith enough for both of us."

Her words sounded strong and true, but inside she feared Crowley was right.

CHAPTER 37

James checked his watch. Still fifteen minutes to go before Trina would head to Rowena's. She'd finally agreed to allow them to come.

Trina folded her arms over her chest. "You boys need to stay away from the coven. Concentrate on the humans."

Ghost scoffed. "Come on, how tough can a few witches be?"

For a moment, James stared. Then he realized that none of these guys had ever seen a witch in action. He glanced at Trina. "Show them."

Her eyes narrowed. "I'm not a parlor trick."

"And I don't want them freaked out in the middle of a fight."

"Fine." Trina propped her hand on her hip and regarded the others. "What do you want me to show them?"

"Whatever you did with the house the other night." That should earn the coven some healthy respect. "You know, minus actually trying to kill us."

Trina motioned them closer. "Keep away from the walls."

They all gathered around the table.

Trina closed her eyes and the hair on James' arms stood at attention.

All at once, the house folded inward. Studs and pipes pierced through the plaster, their jagged edges coming within a hair's breadth of the vampires.

Ghost jumped. "Fuck me."

Samael. . . .

James shook his head. She didn't leave them any space to move around, the shards and spikes of Haven House's infrastructure mere inches from the vampires. His team looked ready to start climbing on the table . . . until they looked up and realized the ceiling was in the same condition.

"Make it stop," Walker said. "We get the goddamn point."

James chuckled, putting a hand to his head to alleviate a growing pain behind his eyes.

Samael James Pasquino. . . .

Trina let out a little laugh and the house returned to how it had been.

"How do you do that?" Shadow motioned to the wall. "Holy shit, that was intense."

"I work chaos Magic. I can manipulate things at the atomic level." She shrugged. "Most of us have niches. Lilith has elemental Magic. Brenda, precognition; Kat, healing Magic; Abby; ice."

"And Rowena?" James stretched his neck to the side.

Samael James Pasquino. . . .

Trina propped her fist on her hip. "Rowena is the high priestess. As long as she remains such, she has a bit of everyone's Magic—she can do it all. My advice would be to stay the hell out of her way and focus on the daemon. Let the coven deal with Rowena."

James nodded. Christ, he felt like shit all of the sudden. He turned his attention back to the map app on Will's phone, blinking hard to clear his vision, and made the picture larger. "The Snoqualmie River runs behind the property and next to it is a campground. I doubt anybody will be using it this time of year. Across the street and down a ways is a farm." He slid his finger to the right. "This here is an access road on the other side of the campground."

"What about the other side of the river?" Ghost asked.

"Foothills," Trina said. "Steep ones. Don't get yourselves cornered on that side of the river, you'll have nowhere to go."

"All right." James shook his head, blinking hard. "Let's head out."

Will stopped him. "You all right?"

Samael James Pasquino . . .

"Yeah." The whole room spun.

Will grabbed him before he fell on his ass, lowering him into a chair. "What the hell is wrong with you?"

"I don't . . . ." Will's image wavered in front of him, blending with a vision of trees and a bonfire. James rubbed his eyes.

Samael James Pasquino, we summon thee.

The words thrummed through his mind. "They're summoning—!" He shouted as his whole body seized up and he fell to the floor. "They're . . . ." He couldn't get the words out. He stared up at the concerned faces of Trina, Will, and his team, and he couldn't tell them what was happening. His vision flickered again, and for a split-second he saw Lilith. Saw a bunch of women in dark, hooded robes. The bonfire made their shadows stretch into unnatural shapes across the pentacle carved into the ground.

Then Trina came back into focus. "Don't fight, James. It'll make it worse."

He didn't think it could get a whole lot worse. All his muscles locked tight, his teeth clenched so hard his jaw felt ready to snap.

"We're coming. Do you hear me? We're on our way." She pushed at the males. "We gotta move. They're summoning him. Something must've gone wrong."

Her voice grew distant. The room around him faded and then he was there, trapped within the pentacle, staring at Lilith.

James' mind spun.

This couldn't be right.

It couldn't.

Before you get what you truly want, I curse you to destruction.

He shook his head. He refused to give Nan's memory any power over him. He never believed in her curse, he'd be damned if he started now. But was it possible he'd finally found absolution, discovered paradise—his paradise—only for the person who embodied those things to also be his downfall? He'd known Lilith had the capabilities, the powers to destroy them all, but it never occurred to him she might do just that.

After everything he'd risked for her . . . .

James lifted his head and met her gaze. She stared back at him through puffy eyes, and though she didn't speak, he could see the truth written in her expression. She hadn't done this.

Crowley.

James scanned the area, searching for the son of a bitch. He felt like he was encased in Jell-O and it took every ounce of energy to move his head. There. The smug bastard grinned.

Come a little closer, Crowley. It didn't matter that he was stuck in this pentacle. If he got half a chance, he had every intention of ashing the fucker.

Crowley strode over to Rowena. "Now make your offerings to the Great Ones."

James' breath stalled in his lungs. Offerings. Christ, they meant to kill him.

"No." Lilith struggled, making him realize they'd bound her. "Rowena, don't do this. Don't listen to him."

"Fight me fair." James tried to shout the demand, but it came out soft as a whisper.

Still, Crowley heard. The corner of his mouth kicked up and he shook his head. "You know too much." He looked at Rowena. "Perform the offerings."

Lilith shouted a denial.

James swallowed hard. This was not how he intended to go out of this world. He was stuck. Lilith was trapped within a binding spell, the rest of the coven appeared to be either in league with Rowena or mesmerized by Crowley.

Trina was on her way.

But how long would she take to get here?

Everything was spinning out of control.

Rowena performed the offering ceremony, but nothing happened. The glass jars should have shattered as they went up in flames. Lilith's mate should have burned alive. But nothing happened. This was just like the night she'd made the offering to Hekate. And just like that night, Julius Crowley was here. He was doing something. Preventing the Watchers from hearing her. Maybe from seeing her.

But how?

"The Watchers are displeased," Lilith shouted. "They're refusing your offerings."

Rowena shook her head. "No, I've displeased the Watchers before. They let me know; they didn't ignore me. This is almost as if they can't see us." Her gaze narrowed on Crowley. "What have you done?"

He shrugged. "I suppose I cast a larger shadow than I realized."

A shadow? Vampires didn't cast shadows.

Watchers did.

Dear gods. Was he possessed by a Watcher? He couldn't be, the Great Ones were invisible, stripped of their flesh. Her gaze shot to the side, searching the shadows for the RI men who'd be coming for him. This wasn't good. Not at all.

Crowley shuddered, his neck popping as he walked toward James and withdrew his blade. "I'll take care of the sacrifice myself."

Rowena swallowed. Could Watchers cause harm within a protective circle? If so, they were all in trouble. Warily, she watched him approach James. He lifted his arm and swung his blade toward James.

The tip of the knife stopped centimeters from James' skin.

A breath shook from her lungs. Thank the gods, he could do no more harm within this circle than anyone else. Thank the gods. She wiped her palms on her robes.

Crowley's gaze shot to hers.

Rowena wet her lips. "What's the problem, Mr. Crowley? Did you think yourself above the laws of the Watchers?"

"Crossing me is not wise, Madam."

"Oh? What are you going to do about it?" Nothing. He could hurt her no more than she could hurt him.

He turned to Lilith. "She conjured the dybbuk, Lilith."

Lilith's accusing gaze shot to hers.

Rowena gasped, glancing between Lilith and Crowley. "I did it for you, dear. To protect you from males like them."

"You cursed me?" Lilith shook her head. "I trusted you. All these years, I trusted you."

She'd never gain Lilith's cooperation now. Not without Crowley's help. Damn him. "I was protecting you, dear girl."

"How did cursing me, protect me?"

Gods, she needed to make Lilith understand. "Look what happened without Aimee." Rowena jutted her chin toward James and Crowley. "They started crawling out of the woodwork. You've always attracted their attention, like honey to bees. You used one to kill Nan." She motioned to James. "You think she was the first they killed? Do you? It was only a matter of time before they killed the rest of us."

Lilith's mouth twisted, her gaze darted to James, to Crowley. "What are you saying? They killed the last coven? Our mothers?"

Rowena shrugged. "What would you have preferred I say? That they died trying to keep you from harm?"

Lilith recoiled.

Crowley tsked. "She's lying."

"Shut up." Rowena took a threatening step closer to him. "You've said enough."

"Not about their deaths being your fault, Lilith. That part is true." He grinned. "But about who did the dirty deed."

Rowena tried to cast against Crowley, but the protective circle wouldn't allow the spell. "Shut up!"

"See, she wanted you and your power all to herself, so she killed everyone who might oppose her."

Lilith shut her eyes. "Dear gods, you killed our mothers. All this time I thought their deaths accidents, but you're responsible for it all."

"She wanted you all to herself, Lil." Crowley walked closer to Lilith.

What was he doing, trying to mesmerize her? She couldn't allow that. "Stay away from her."

Crowley ignored her. "I've never lied to you. I can't lie. I'm the one you can trust."

Rowena turned to Kat, and released her binding spell just enough for her daughter to speak. "Tell them. Tell them I did what I had to do. You know how much I care for this coven."

Kat shook her head. "How could you?"

Rowena looked at Lilith. "I did what I needed to do to protect this coven." Why couldn't they understand that? "You'll never understand everything I sacrificed for this coven."

"By killing the last?" Lilith shook her head.

Crowley spoke up, his grin showing how much he enjoyed stirring the pot. "Your mothers wanted to reunite the coven with daemon-kind. They wanted to rejoin the Council, but Rowena refused to allow that."

Rowena shook her head. "You don't understand." She set her focus on Lilith. "But you do. You know all about how important sacrifice is. You'd do whatever you had to do to keep your coven safe, wouldn't you?"

Lilith's jaw clenched tight and she blinked rapidly. She stared past Rowena. "Kat? How do you want to handle this?"

Rowena shook her head. "Handle this? You can't handle a damned thing. You'll do nothing."

Lilith ignored her and continued to stare at her daughter. "Kat?"

Kat's lips trembled. She pressed them into a straight line. "She's yours."

Crowley grinned. "Seems your days are numbered, madam."

"Shut up." Rowena came around the altar and rushed Crowley, her fingers curled into claws. She stopped as if frozen inches from him, the circle protecting those within, even Crowley. "You said you'd fix this, instead you've ruined everything."

He grinned. "So, now we seem to be at a bit of an impasse. We all want to kill each other and the Watchers can't see us, so they can't intercede. Perhaps I'll take Lilith and go."

Rowena laughed. "Only witches can walk in or out of the circle."

"She's right."

As if to prove her point, Trina walked into the middle of the tension, striding into the circle. Oh, dear gods, as if they didn't have enough to contend with. "*You.*"

"Who are you?" Crowley took a step back. "I've never seen you before." With each word, his voice grew louder. "Who the hell are you?"

Rowena stepped back. She'd never seen Crowley lose his composure before. The way he stared at Trina . . . . Interesting that as much information as Crowley had about everyone else, he'd never seen Trina. Was he a Watcher or not?

With a flick of Trina's wrist and a few mumbled words, she cast away the invisible bonds restraining Lilith and Kat.

"Thank gods." Lilith gave Trina a quick hug and

hurried to the closest witch.

Trina and Lilith. The two of them were walking disasters. Already, Lilith was waking her coven sisters from Crowley's spell. Trina headed for Kat. "Trina." Rowena held her arms open. "I'm so very glad you're back."

Trina's glare settled on her as she walked past, leaving her chilled. "Don't talk to me."

"You understand everything I did was with your best interest at heart."

Lilith turned away from having woken Abby. She scoffed. "Always with our best interest at heart. I think we're all sick of hearing that."

Trina took a threatening step forward. "You will never understand the pain you caused me. *Never.* You don't have the capacity to understand the hell you put me through. But understand this: by sending me away, you taught me that I need no one. By abandoning me to my fate, you taught me that I create my own destiny. By withholding any love, you taught me hate. And now you will reap what you've sown."

Rowena backed away. Trina wouldn't listen, she saw that now, but not all was lost. She could salvage this. Maybe she'd made a few bad decisions, maybe there had been a better way, but she'd done what she'd done to help the coven.

Trina held up her hand, backing toward the edge of the circle. "If either of you move, I'll step out of here."

"You'll break the protective spell." Rowena shook her head. "It'll be a blood bath."

Trina shrugged. "Do I look like I give a fuck?"

Rowena glanced around. One by one, the witches returned to their senses. Their hard eyes staring at her. Their faces masks of anger.

How could she salvage this?

CHAPTER 38

Lilith released him from the summoning. "Samael James Pasquino, I release thee from all summons to use your free will as you see fit, for this I ask or something more, with respect and love I do implore."

The summoning spell released him and James dropped to his knees, breathing hard.

"Come on, get up." Crowley circled him, withdrawing his blades. "Get up."

He sensed more than saw Lilith start toward him and he waved her back. He didn't want her anywhere near Crowley when that shield came down.

"Don't do this, Trina," Rowena shouted. "They'll kill us all."

He didn't hear Trina's reply, focusing instead on Julius. James got to his feet, swaying with another wave of dizziness. He leaned forward, bracing the heels of his hands on his thighs.

This was a raw deal if he'd ever had one. He blinked hard to clear his vision. Rowena's summoning had fucked him up good. He needed time to recover, but there was none.

Steeling himself, he stood, arming himself, the weight of his blades reassuring in his grip.

The coven was awake, alert. Walker and Ghost stood outside of the protective circle, eyeing up Crowley's men, waiting for the shield to come down. Shadow stood by the bonfire. Even as James watched, Shadow engaged his talent and his shadow spilled out of his mouth, pooling on the ground before shaping into *its* own being. The shadow stood, regarding them all for a heartbeat before taking flight.

Everyone was ready.

And somewhere nearby, humans surrounded them. He didn't see Will, so he must be dealing with the humans.

He glanced at Lilith. She looked scared as hell but even as their gazes met, her chin rose a notch. "I got this, babe."

Christ, he sure as hell hoped so. He nodded and Lilith stepped back across the ring of stones.

The shield went down.

Crowley attacked.

James dodged to the side, turned and backed away. His vision started to clear as adrenaline spiked through his system. He needed a few more minutes.

Crowley lunged, his arm sweeping down in a long slash James narrowly avoided. His breath kicked up a notch.

Come on, focus.

Unable to look his opponent in the eyes, he watched Crowley's feet, looking for the tell-tale shifts in weight to signal his next move.

Slowly, they circled. Crowley thrust his arm out, slashing the air, testing him. The others fought around them. His conscience nagged him to check on Lilith, to make sure she didn't need his help, but he didn't dare let his guard down.

James flipped the dagger in his right hand so the blade lay against his wrist, and inhaled deep. Smoke, incense, and sweat rode in each breath. Heat warmed his back.

"Look out!" Trina's voice.

Shit. The bonfire. He changed course with a shake of his head. Crowley had almost backed him straight into the flames.

Kill the fucker. Focus, damn you.

He needed one good jab. Just one.

Crowley struck. With each step forward he slashed out. One arm, then the other.

James went on the defensive. Dodging. Blocking

Fuck.

Crowley's blade slid down the back of his hand, slicing open the skin over his knuckles.

James shifted his weight, kicked Crowley in the knee. Made him stumble back with a curse. James advanced, keeping Crowley from retaking the offensive. Three strikes and at last he hit flesh. Just a graze, a slash down Crowley's chest, but it was something.

Crowley's back came up against one of the stone pillars surrounding the coven's ritual space.

James grinned.

He had him.

He had the fucker.

James lifted his blade. . . .

And Crowley disappeared.

What the fuck?

He couldn't do that. He was a goddamn mesmerist, how the hell had Crowley—?

His nape prickled. James whirled around, barely fending off Crowley's strike from behind. Their blades locked together, both their bodies straining for dominance. James outweighed him and slowly, bit by bit their locked blades pointed toward Crowley's face.

"Look." Crowley's voice shook, his words broken over his breath. "Look at me."

James gave him a quick shake of the head. No way in hell. He pressed harder.

With a shout, Crowley bucked, throwing James off balance and breaking the stalemate.

James wiped the back of his wrist over his mouth, breathing hard. Almost.

He felt stronger now. Focused.

Crowley attacked. Slashed in a downward arc. James stepped back, let his arm pass and grabbed his wrist, lashing out with his other blade. Crowley lifted his trapped arm, locked his second blade with James' again.

They pushed away from each other.

"You trained him better than you thought." Crowley grinned.

Him? "Who?"

Crowley's smile faded.

James narrowed his gaze. "You mean, Jules?"

A war cry broke from Crowley's lips and he ran at James.

Gunfire erupted. Both Crowley and James reacted, ducking at the low, staccato pops. James glanced past Crowley. Men surrounded the coven and daemons. Shit, where was Lil?

His moment of inattention cost him. Crowley rammed into him, driving him back several feet.

Pain seared through his gut as Crowley's knife sank hilt-deep.

For a split-second panic gripped him and he expected oblivion. But no, this was a plain steel blade. *Goddamn, that hurt.*

"You son of a bitch," a woman screamed.

They both turned to see Rowena stalking toward them, her gaze locked tight on Crowley. Fire blazed from each of her hands as if she held burning coals in the palms of her bare hands.

"You will rue the day you fucked with me." She raised her arms and long streaks of flame shot out from her hands toward Crowley.

Crowley vanished.

And reappeared behind Rowena.

How the hell did he do that? Was he using Magic?

The two of them struggled, disappeared behind one of the standing stones.

Jesus, he had to move. No matter which one of them won their battle, the victor would return to finish him off.

Even as James' gaze hardened and his determination deepened, his knees gave out. He fell on his ass. He released his grip on one of his blades and grabbed the hilt of Crowley's. Steeling himself, he yanked it out of his stomach. Black checkered his vision and he closed his eyes.

You gotta get up. You can't let Crowley get hold of Lilith. You can't let the humans leave here.

He needed to get up.

Where's your faith?

James opened his eyes, half expecting to see Lilith's curious gaze staring down at him.

A soldier of some kind stood there. A young one. The damn fool didn't even have the sense to keep his weapon trained on him.

The kid spoke into a walkie-talkie. "I got one here. He's wounded. No, it's not Crowley, do you want him?"

Christ. What did they want with Crowley? How did they even know about him?

A static-filled voice fired back instructions: "Hold him. We'll take him, too."

Not tonight, they wouldn't. James waved the kid closer.

The soldier lifted his gun, but took a step. Leaned down. "What?"

James lashed out. Gripped the kid by the collar and dragged him down. Before the human so much as grunted in protest, James sank his teeth into his jugular. He pinned the soldier, using his weight to subdue his death throes. Blood spurted into his mouth with each terrified thump of the kid's dying heart. Warm, salty, and metallic, nothing had ever tasted so good.

Still, his gut rolled, repelled by the thought of killing for blood again even as his wounds healed and he grew stronger. After all this time, the words for Extreme Unction came back to him and, in his mind, he recited the last rights for the soul he stole.

James opened his eyes, watching the area around them as he finished the kid off. He didn't see Crowley, but couldn't miss Lilith with her silver swords. He wiped his face on the soldier's uniform, sheathed his blades, and grabbed the soldier's gun as he got to his feet.

Yeah, Crowley should've ashed him while he had the chance.

As he strode toward Lilith, he took out the soldiers taking potshots at the daemons and witches. Lining up shot after shot, he evened their odds a bit. The coven seemed to rally, closing ranks, fighting more aggressively. They formed a loose circle around the daemons. Kat allowed him to pass with a nod of acknowledgment. Ghost, Will, and Shadow still fought Crowley's crew. Walker wasn't there.

Damn.

He brushed away the pang of another loss.

As he approached, Lilith and Trina both stilled, their attention arrested on a blond male, one of Crowley's crew.

Will ran past, transforming as he went. His large, muscular body grew bulkier, his shoulders broadening. Biceps and chest strained against the fabric of his once baggy T-shirt. The leather belt holding up his over-sized jeans burst at the buckle as he filled in the pants. Formidable thighs stretched at the fabric. His neck thickened until the necklace he wore became a choker, the silver ankh riding high against the thickened tendons at his throat. Both nose and jaw elongated into a snout. Amid the sickening sounds of snapping bones, teeth reshaped and rearranged to fit the muzzle. The shape of his head altered, his ears melted away and new longer, pointier buds sprouted from of the top of his elegantly shaped head. Short, coarse, black fur covered every visible skin surface. When the transformation finished, he resembled Anubis.

James pulled the women back.

The blond sprang up, shifting form mid-air. A new body enveloped his completely. And when he landed, he stood on all fours.

The son of a bitch shifted into El Chupacabra. A large, hairless, unnatural-looking canine with the thick, scaly, tail of a crocodile. Razor claws adorned its great paws, and rows of wicked teeth burst from its wide muzzle below piercing red eyes.

James hadn't seen one of them in decades.

El Chupacabra lunged for Will's throat. Will swung out his arms, knocking El Chupacabra to the side. It sprawled in the dirt, rolling, clawing at the ground before it righted itself. The creature didn't have time to do anything else. Will leapt onto its back, sinking his teeth into El Chupacabra's neck.

The two became a blur of claws and teeth.

"Go." James pointed, urging the women away from the two creatures, before they became collateral damage. "The soldiers are here for Crowley."

Both women turned to stare. "What?" Lilith asked at the same time Trina asked, "Why?"

"I don't know, but we can't let them leave with him." He glanced at Lilith. "Rowena's dead?"

Lilith shook her head. "She disappeared. I don't know where she went."

Trina's eyes widened. "I think I found her. And twenty bucks says she's somehow responsible for these mercs."

James turned around. Flames engulfed the trees near the river. Crowley stumbled out of the inferno with Rowena emerging right on his heels.

James lifted his weapon and strode toward the pair. Trina stayed him. "Leave Rowena to us, focus on Crowley."

"No problem." He knew better than to engage the high priestess. He wouldn't stand a chance against her Magic. He lined up Crowley in his sights and squeezed the trigger.

The bastard moved and the shot barely grazed him. Still, Crowley hadn't seemed to notice him yet, so he lined up another. His curly blond hair sat right in the notch of his sight. James squeezed the trigger.

Nothing.

With a curse, he threw down the gun and drew his blades. He crept closer.

Lilith and Trina had gotten to Rowena, they had her arguing about something.

Crowley still had his back to him.

James lifted his blade.

Rowena swung around and lifted her hand. "No."

James froze. Not because he wanted to. The bitch had done something to him. He couldn't move. He tried to speak and couldn't.

That's why Crowley hadn't turned around. He couldn't.

Rowena took a step closer. "There's something wrong with that one. I intended for the humans to finish him off, but . . . ." She waved her hand to Crowley. "You can kill him later. After we clean up this mess and get rid of the mercs." She shook her head. "If the Watchers see this, if the Vampiric Council finds out, there will be war."

There was no stopping that now.

Lilith spoke his thought out loud. "You ensured a war when you joined up with Crowley and lured the humans here."

"But the Watchers. They can't see us." Rowena pointed to Crowley again. "Not when he's here. We can pretend none of this happened." Her gaze narrowed. "The way he casts a shadow over us, I'd almost think he's a—"

"Don't!" Lilith's shout drowned out anything Rowena might have said. "Do not speak another word." She glanced at Trina. "Can you release them?"

Trina nodded. With a flick of her wrist, the invisible bonds loosened.

Everyone moved at once.

Julius dashed away even as James brought his blade down.

Lilith summoned her swords, stepping toward Rowena.

Fire burst from Rowena's hands, missing Crowley and setting more shrubs on fire, before Lilith forced her to turn and fight.

James went after Crowley. "Trina, keep the soldiers away and put out that damn fire." He lunged, nicking Crowley. "You love causing trouble."

Crowley winced. Down to one blade and wounded, his odds weren't so good now. "And you never did die easy." He lashed out with his blade.

James knocked his arm to the side with one arm, jabbed up with his other.

Crowley blocked him. Reared back and head-butted him.

Shit.

James stumbled back a step, tightening his hands on his blades.

Crowley attacked again. Punched James in the jaw, bringing his blade around the side.

It was a good move. One James didn't expect. He should have landed the blow, but at the last second, he dropped his blade.

James couldn't stop his momentum and stumbled past, barely catching himself before going headfirst into the blazing shrubs.

Crowley picked up his blade, mumbling to himself. "Fucking prick, stay out of this."

James' gaze narrowed. Again he had the sense that Julius might still be in there.

A cry escaped Crowley and for a split second he seemed different. "Listen." His head jerked to the side. "Listen to me."

James circled, watching his opponent.

"No." Crowley shuddered so hard his neck cracked as

his head jerked to the side again. James glanced down as Crowley pulled his blade out of his own thigh.

Christ. He wasn't just in league with a rogue Watcher, it had possessed him. "Jules?"

"Az—"Crowley shook his head violently. "No." The denial burst from Crowley's lips and he went on the attack, slashing his blade from side to side as he advanced. It wasn't a good ploy. The wild maneuvers put him off balance. Jules knew better, damn it. He'd taught the son of a bitch to fight. Was his old friend even in there?

James stepped back for every wild slash Crowley made, watching for his opening. On Crowley's next downswing, James rushed him, catching his arm and knocking away the blade.

The two of them tumbled to the ground. He could make the killing blow. He could ash him. But, Christ, if Jules was in there. If the dumb shit was still alive and trapped . . . . "Jules?"

"His name—" Crowley thrashed beneath him, seeming to struggle against himself, the same as Lilith had done with Nan. His jaw clamped tight and he arched off the ground. "His name—"

Come on, yes. Say his goddamned name. Lilith could exorcize the Watcher with that information. She could banish it.

An ice cold wave slammed over them. The world went topsy-turvy as the biting liquid ripped James away from Crowley. One instant, he had nothing to grab hold of. In the next, the tide pulled him down to the ground. Raked him over stone and earth. He slammed his blade into the dirt. Held on.

The heavy weight of the water receded with the same startling speed as it arrived.

James gasped. Sucked in a deep breath and coughed.

Trina. That had to have been Trina putting out the fire. Smart ass.

He pulled his blade from the ground and stood.

Crowley was nowhere in sight.

Rowena staggered to her feet a couple of yards from him, glass tinkling within her sodden robes. She glanced up and her eyes grew wide. She screamed.

Something the size of a toddler emerged from her robes. Skinless, with hair standing in wet tufts around its reptilian head, the creature scurried up her body. Its three-fingered hands anchored on the sides of her mouth. It squeezed inside.

Holy mother of God.

James stepped back.

Aimee.

That's the creature Rowena had cursed Lilith with?

Rowena reached her hands out to him. *To him.* She wanted help from him.

He shook his head. "That's your karma. Not mine." He turned away, searching for Lilith. Only a handful of the coven still stood. Will. Ghost. And soldiers. Christ, soldiers were coming out of the fucking woodwork.

A handful of them carried a hooded figure. Crowley. "Goddamn it."

Crowley or Lilith?

Will bounded after the soldiers in Lycan form.

Lilith, then. Will would get Crowley back. He turned back in time to see Rowena make a suicide run into the midst of a group of soldiers. They all opened fire. Her body jerked and wrenched in the hailstorm they unloaded on her.

Just then, Lilith walked out into the open.

Christ. "No!" He waved her back.

Her gaze snapped to his.

She jerked.

Once.

Twice.

The shots meant for Rowena hit her square in the chest.

Her brows furrowed and she looked down at herself, then crumpled to the ground.

"Lilith." Trina ran to her friend, skidding to a stop on her knees at her side. "Lilith."

The gunfire stopped.

James held his breath as Trina turned Lilith's limp body over.

Trina's shout of denial confirmed the worst. A sob broke from her and she pulled Lilith into her arms.

A horrible sound filled the battlefield, a howl more animal than human. Lamenting. Anguished. James gasped, out of breath. He tried to suck in air, but couldn't.

He dropped to his knees. The sounds of the fight around him faded as his world narrowed, pinpointed. He could feel the wind on his face, the damp earth under his knees soaking through his jeans.

He doubled over from a searing pain in his chest. A physical pain, unlike anything he'd known, spreading out from where his heart should be. He glanced down, expecting to find he'd been shot, too. There was nothing. No physical wound. Just a cavernous, empty agony.

He'd failed. Again.

Someday . . . . Your destruction.

When the old woman cursed him with destruction, he expected his own oblivion. He expected the end of his existence. He'd accepted that. Not this. Not like this.

Nothing could have destroyed him more.

The hot steel of a gun pressed against his neck. "Stay down. I'm not messing with you."

He didn't care. Welcomed the numbness. If they were indeed life mates, two halves of a whole, then she was everything bright and loving and good about him. She reintroduced him to life, to love.

And what did he do? Took her soul. Her life.

"Lilith?" Trina leaned back, staring at Lilith, shaking her.

Slowly, James rose. Was she alive?

"Stay down." The muzzle pressed harder to his head.

No. She didn't move.

The corners of his mouth drew down, trembling. He drew his lips together in a thin line. He needed to say goodbye. To touch her again, one last time.

"Get down, buddy. Don't make this any worse."

James took a step closer.

The soldier pistol-whipped him across the back of his head. Pain streaked through his skull and he fell to his knees as darkness checkered across his vision. He battled it, determination commanding him. He struggled up, shaking off the darkness.

James stood and for a split second he thought he saw Lilith move. Trina looked up, her eyes widening, then shook Lilith again, her lips moving rapid-fire.

The soldier behind him pressed the muzzle of his weapon to James' head. "You don't give up, do you?"

Was she alive? He took another step.

"I swear I'm going to shoot."

Lilith looked up, her gaze coming straight to him.

She was alive.

Relief surged through his veins, making him dizzy with joy.

Her mouth opened on a single word. He couldn't hear her, not from this distance, but he read his name on her lips. "James.

A sense of deja vu assailed him, bringing him back to his last day as a human. To the evening when she'd done the same thing as her executioners lit a pyre beneath her feet.

In that moment, he knew she'd been right—everything had happened for a reason. Even though he'd failed her then, she still had faith in him. An unshakable faith that he'd save her. That he was good. That he deserved her love.

Humbled, he could give no less in return.

He had faith.

In her.

And in whatever deity had brought her into his life. Whether God or goddess or whatever, he could give a shit. Whatever deity was out there, had given him his own miracle, his own paradise in her.

And he'd be damned if he let anyone take that from him.

He closed his eyes, allowing himself to descend into the darkness of his Vampiric talent. Let his consciousness sink into the old familiar agony.

Have faith. She'll survive. She'll keep our allies alive.

His veins turned to ice as he called on that old pain, drawing it to him.

Have faith. She'll keep you from going too far. She won't let you get lost.

James put all his faith in her.

And let go.

CHAPTER 39

"Can you move?" Trina asked.

Lilith nodded. She hurt everywhere, but she could move now. James' bite may not have changed her fully to a vampire, but she'd acquired the ability to self-heal.

Trina tugged at her. "We should go." The soldiers all focused on James and no longer paid any attention to them. She regained her feet with Trina's help, her whole body protesting the movement, but her gaze remained on her mate.

A strange purplish-black light surrounded him. His eyes were open, but they were the eyes of a cadaver, with milky cataracts obstructing his pupils. His skin had turned translucent, leaving the thin layer of veins and muscle beneath his skin visible.

His words from the day before came back to her. *I couldn't stop. I killed them all.*

Lilith swallowed. She didn't know if she should be more concerned about the guns or James. She had no idea what talent he possessed, but if he feared using it, she knew he had his reasons.

A new sound filled the air around them. At first, nothing more than the howl of wind, but as it grew louder, the sound changed to unearthly voices screaming in rage. The hair on her skin stood at attention.

Louder, it came closer. From the east, a shrieking, growling, wailing chorus.

Everyone, now united in fear of the unknown, turned to find the source of the screams. They no longer fought among themselves.

A new enemy came.

The clearing, and those there, stood silent. No one moved, fear reducing them all to their base instincts, and they waited on that basic level, like animals sensing a predator nearby. Watched. Listened.

Danger was coming.

Death was coming.

Through the darkened forest, the first signs of a purplish-black emanation grew. The light approached from the southeast. The caterwauling becoming more ear-piercing as the strange light drew near.

A chill crept up Lilith's spine making her shiver, raising gooseflesh on her skin.

Instinct urged her to run.

Reason told her there was no point.

An arm reached around and encircled her from behind. She started, sucking in a quick burst of air.

"Sh. It's me." Will spoke close to her ear.

His head popped between hers and Trina's, his arm yanked her closer to Trina and back against him. "All right, ladies, you stick with me, and if you've got a god, I'd start praying."

Trina glanced back. "What is it?"

"James." Lilith whispered his name like a benediction, hoping to invoke his mercy on them. "It's his Vampiric talent. I'm not sure what it is."

Will tightened his grip on them. "He's a necromancer. I've heard stories of this in my pack. He's making the dead walk tonight." He stared into the forest.

The cemetery sat to the east, at the edge of town. Dear gods, that must be where they came from.

The light reached the clearing, and through the crowd she made out the shapes of humanoid silhouettes racing toward them.

Guns fired, sounding the war drum. Men fled in all

directions as the misty light surrounded the soldiers on the front line of this new war. The shouts of the men's terror blended with the snarling and shrieking already filling the air. Amid the nightmare the humans begged for their god's intervention with desperate prayers.

"It's James, though, right?" Trina's voice shook. "So we're safe."

"I'm not sure he has any control," Will whispered.

They were all fighters. And they all died. Lilith repeated what James said yesterday. She looked at Will and Trina. "James told me there are times you shouldn't fight. When the only way to survive is to lower your gaze, keep your mouth shut and be still."

Lilith glanced around, searching for anyone from the coven. Kat stood not too far away, staring into the forest. Lilith called out to her and repeated the instructions. Katherine raced to tell the others.

Will regarded her. "All right, ladies, turn around, heads to my chest, eyes closed tight."

Neither had ever been much for the damsel in distress thing, but they didn't argue. Her gaze met Trina's for the briefest of seconds before she pressed her face to Will's shoulder. He leaned on them even as his strong arms wound protectively around them.

"Will?" Trina whispered. "Are you okay?"

"No more talking." The urgent strain in his voice, more than his words, had the desired effect.

A body rammed into them. They stumbled. Will righted himself, pulling them tighter in his embrace, standing straighter.

A burst of frigid air passed by.

The sounds were horrendous. The grim music of annihilation—sickeningly wet chords and bone-crunching acoustics harmonizing the macabre melody of death. Never in her life had she heard grown men scream in such a way. The shouts conjured disturbing images mind-wrenchingly offensive in their gruesomeness. A glacial chill chased urgent footsteps passing by.

Then, an unholy scream.

Her stomach churned. Burning bile caught in her throat, and she fought to choke it back down.

She dared to open her eyes and found Trina staring back, wide-eyed. Her breathing came in short little pants much like her own. Lilith tightened her hold on Will, overwhelmed with gratitude for his solid presence.

Trina's gaze shot to the left, over Lilith's shoulder. Her lids fluttered rapidly over her flat, dead stare. Her lips parted as if she would speak. Will gave them both a squeeze, and naught but a squeak escaped Trina's lips.

Lilith couldn't decide if she wanted to see what frightened Trina. Then she had no choice.

It was there, behind and between them, challenging Will with its empty gaze. She couldn't imagine how Will could stand so strong in the face of something so vile. The creature wasn't even paying her any attention, and she already shook.

She wanted to turn away, but its ghoulish visage seized her attention.

The creature had been human at some point, but no longer. Now, something dark had touched it. A purplish glow enveloped its emaciated form. The empty eye sockets radiated it. Its sallow skin, rotten and decayed, left one whole side of its corrupt face exposed, the alabaster of its skull visible underneath the ragged edges of putrid flesh. Its teeth were jagged and needle-pointed, as if it spent its afterlife filing away at them for such an occasion.

The creature's attention shifted to her. It inspected her with the same morbid curiosity she'd given it. It jerked its face closer and, opening its mouth, let out an ominous shriek designed to petrify.

Both Trina and Will jumped with the same terrified enthusiasm she did.

The creature's head jerked to the side, as if it saw someone more to its liking. It bounded off in search of other casualties, and as she let out the breath she'd been holding, Will and Trina did the same.

The creatures swarmed around the campsite, the yard, then off into the shadowy forest.

The night returned to its natural inky hue, leaving her a clear view of the holocaust, the devastation even more terrifying in its permanence.

No soldiers lived. Their weapons lay discarded on the ground, some still held by severed hands or arms.

The coven appeared shaken, but alive, scattered around the bloody remains of the dead.

James was one of the few still standing. She extracted herself from Will.

"No, don't." He reached out to pull her back.

She shook him off and kept going, stepping over limbs and walking around bodies. She breathed through her mouth, to avoid the stench and calm the nausea. She'd never witnessed death before, let alone in such a brutal way.

The same purplish luminosity shrouding the creatures surrounded James. The thin layer of his veins and muscle showed beneath his skin, his eyes a murky, pearl-white behind his ashen skin. For the first time, he fit her childhood image of a vampire.

She'd done this. In coming here tonight, she'd forced him to use his talent. He'd tried everything else to get them out of here. He'd used deadly force his last resort. A choice that must have been a difficult one for him to make.

His story about his transformation in Montgisard, came back to her. *I couldn't stop. I killed them all.*

She thought he'd referred to blood-lust, not his Vampiric talent. At the time, she didn't process it, two thousand dead. It wasn't something one man, no matter how good a soldier, could do. But a necromancer with a dead army could.

He'd been so ashamed. He would never forgive himself if innocent people were killed and she didn't know where the creatures escaped to.

She was afraid to touch him. Afraid the light radiating from him might harm her, but she needed to try. Holding out a trembling hand, she placed it on his chest. The air around him felt frigid—he was freezing to the touch.

"James, you have to stop now."

He was unresponsive, lost to the trance he'd placed himself in.

She wrapped her arms around him, pressing her body to his. He always warmed with her heat. "James." She spoke louder this time, giving him a hard squeeze. "Come on, I know you're in there. We're safe now. Call them off." She cupped his face. "Please." She pressed her lips to his. "I love you." Again, she pressed her mouth to his, and after a moment, she felt him kiss her back. Lilith's eyes shot open as his arms wound around her and held her close.

The roughness of his voice whispered in her ear. "I thought I lost you. You were so still."

"Everything is fine." She could hardly breathe, his embrace was so tight, but she didn't care. She pressed her face against his chest, happy to let him squeeze her to his heart's content.

James finished his shower, dressed and went downstairs. Lilith sat on the floor in the living room alone, surrounded by candles.

Trina must have gone to bed.

He sat on the couch while she finished, unable to hear any of her whispered words. One by one, she blew out the candles, until she reached the last, a thick red ball of wax. That one, she set in the empty fireplace and allowed to continue burning.

She turned to him and smiled.

"What's all that?"

She glanced toward the stairs. "You heard the

Historian, I won't have my full powers until my other half is transformed." She bit her lip, twisting the hem of her nightgown in her hands. "I petitioned the Goddess to bring my other half's mate to us."

James gaped. He couldn't imagine that Trina—if she was indeed the other half of the Original—would be thrilled with Lilith's plan. "Are you sure you know what you're doing?"

She let a sigh. "It's not like I can ask permission without giving everything away to our enemy, now is it?"

He motioned her closer.

Lilith joined him on the couch, curling up beside him. "I know it might not be a good idea, I know she's hurting right now, but how bad could her reaction be?"

James let loose a bark of laughter. He couldn't help it. Whoever showed up here would have a hell of a battle with Trina.

Lilith swatted him. "Be nice. I want her to have what I have."

"I know you do, but maybe you need to let it happen in its own time." He kissed the tip of her nose. "You've entered my life three times now. Each time at just the right moment—a moment when I was open to different ideas, a moment when I needed you, and a moment that changed my existence forever. I thought I was forgotten, but it was only that I was blind to seeing the angel right in front of me. What we have." He gave her a little squeeze. "Is a miracle in its own right."

She leaned up and kissed him, slow and sweet. And pressed her forehead to his. "And we owe this, us finding each other, to the Historian. I'm just helping move things along."

"I know." James tugged her back against him. Held her close.

"We can't hide what happened tonight. The Council knows we're back. Will wasn't able to prevent the humans from capturing Crowley. We have to get him back."

"I know."

"And we need the other half of the Original."

James sighed. "I know." War was coming, he just wasn't sure from which corner. This was the quiet before the storm, but they had to live for today. And today they would laugh and talk. He would retreat upstairs with Lilith and make love to her.

Tonight was hours away yet. They could worry about all the rest when it arrived. It was the only way to survive an uncertain existence.

Somehow they would find a way. They would recover and destroy Julius Crowley. They would survive whatever the Council threw their way.

They were together, and that's all that mattered. He had everything he ever wanted, and so much more.

OTHER BOOKS BY CARA CRESCENT

The Last Marine

ABOUT THE AUTHOR

Cara Crescent currently lives in the Pacific Northwest with her children and three overly dramatic ferrets. When not writing, you can usually find her curled up with a book, engrossed in a movie or playing video games with her best friend.

Please visit her on the web at www.caracrescent.com

www.ingramcontent.com/pod-product-compliance
Lightning Source LLC
Chambersburg PA
CBHW060931120726
47910CB00002B/284